THE BOOGIEMAN

Clive Atwater

ISBN 978-1-957220-68-0 (paperback)
ISBN 978-1-957220-69-7 (hardcover)
ISBN 978-1-957220-70-3 (digital)

This is a work of fiction. All of the characters, names, incidents, organizations, and dialogue in this novel are either the products of the author's imagination or are used fictitiously.

Rushmore Press LLC
1 800 460 9188
www.rushmorepress.com

Printed in the United States of America

CONTENTS

PREFACE

I HAD FOR SOME TIME, PAST TENSE, BEEN INORDINATELY CONFINED to an eerie cryptic and oblique remnant context of a pseudo iconic period silently indicative of a distant and long ago, pragmatic Victorian age. Yet however, I began to find myself progressively remanded to the morosely dismal realm of a shadowy twilight existence subliminally cast in the bizarre confines of a sallow and imminent sense of ambiguity. Yet even though at such an early age I had subliminally come to atmospherically inherit a jaded and cynical life's perspective. In that such that over a lengthy and enigmatic period from then onward, had abjectly eroded a marginal sense of warm inward complacency I may have been in possession of, prior to my induction, into that stately, historic, and creepy old house which carried themselves onward well on into later adulthood to a more ill-defined and prominent degree. I had thus forth initially found myself mortally stricken with a stark sense of ill recompense in that on frequent occasions were spent in sole contemplation of a subtly perceived hidden and stately presence so unspeakably horrific, yet wholly unseen, and innately sensed that played out it's ghastly connotations in a shadowy sequential aura.

Thus consisting of vague and subtle inferences to a soon to be mortal retribution and rampant damnation, emanating from that pale blue dusky third floor hallway alcove subtly inferring a heinous darkened presence incepted in a cynical and jaded sense of introspect. Thus of which had impishly crept it's way into the lofty eaves of my lurid subconscious in their vague, obscure and shadowy content.

This became eerily more apparent as time progressed and our family having got more settled into that big creepy old house. And as yet had remained readily pervasive factors as well as mentally harrowing aspects thus of which seemed to more be in lying prevalent and innate qualities to the old house itself. Thusly I was figuratively remanded to a stark isolated realm, solely imprisoned to the dismal confines of a dimly lit shadowy twilight world by the potential resurgent manifestation of a stark goonish and ogre-ish horror which imminently resonated from within third floor walls which struck me with an unspeakable sensation of abject dread, terror,…subliminally pervasive in it's all inclusive ill designs and threatening to materialize at any given moment without warning,…

I was thusly shrouded behind an impenetrable barrier of paralyzing fear and feigned silence of which I had arduously maintained an ongoing and inward struggle to ultimately reconcile within myself the stark mental images of a dark sinister enigmatic force that heinously manifested it's pitch blackened evil silhouette within me by now harried and traumatized psyche. And upon much inward contemplation, at furthered time intervals, I found myself mortally stricken with an intense reverberating terror that resonated an unspeakable and indescribable horrific droning sensation from within that heinously rendered my central nervous system. Frozen, shuddering it to it's very core, whereby my blood ran alarmingly cold, especially in my face and eyeballs and I began to shake in an uncontrollable vibration.

Moreover in previously having been insidiously deluged by a steady succession of faint, and partialized mental images of a gnarled blackish ash grey gourde like mutation that wretchedly inhabited either the attic or the basement. Thusly incepted at the subliminal level, such morbid conceptions that lowly manifested themselves in a ghastly convergence upon my acute mental perception. Prior to this though, however, I did not possess any inward curiosity nor the inclination to expound upon any preconceived notions regarding the possibility of a said "Boogieman" wholly realized or the potential existence of a dark shadowy underworld of the elusively macabre. But I did later on, however, become morbidly enamored by such ominous connotations emanating from within clandestine regions of that historic old house. Thus of which were subtly indicative of something so vile and abhorrently evil yet impishly vague and in descript in it's elusive form. This factor alone, in and of itself, lent to a grossly heightened level of morose apprehension resonating from within.

These goonish images had surreptitiously seeped from deep within the vast regions of my inward psychological retention ultimately paralyzing me to such a grave state of ongoing ghastly fear, in that of something so dreadfully ominous possibly inhabiting either the basement or the attic. But the attic was the primary focus of my heavy laden dread. And although these images were seemingly and insidiously inlaying and ignominiously implanted by a despicable, veiled and aloof source referencing that of a dark enigma wholly unseen and morosely indicative of a self subsisting insurrection that inherently embraced the total embodiment of a vile and reprehensible omnipresence. A dark cryptic silhouetted figure surrealistically highlighted in a bleak outline of a grayish blue haze thus of which abhorrently presented itself to my subconscious and insidiously inhabited a clandestine third floor region of a decaying old house in Cuyahoga Falls Ohio set in the late 60's. In that had such a dark knotted gourdish abomination were to lowly manifest itself openly in the raw. That to the naked eye would've been so starkly horrific and visually repugnant to the constrictive bounds set by the conscious mind it would've beggared outward and definitive description, yet it remained wholly elusive and concealed from sight. And in all my despondent hopes to rationalize the ill conceived sense of a dreary moroseness and looming imminence which resonated from within that I was chronically stricken with a pensive illconceived sense of isolation, Yet I fervently held to the self aspiring notion to seek out in all diligence the elusive source of just what was solely responsible.

I had thus inwardly sensed from the onset that of a gross level of sinister energy emanating itself from that third floor region of a once stately old turn of the century house. Thus of which had been silently inferred through macabre and indiscriminate inferences symbolic of a stark and reticent horror that remained outwardly hidden from sight, perpetually undulating in it's catastrophic intent and confined within attic walls.

Yet I had on several occasions stood there in a post state of abject terror as creepy images of widened goonish eyes were gawking back at me, yet as I stood there quaking in mortal terror amid that small, musty, dismal and clammy third floor hallway. A ghastly ogreish visage slowly began to materialize,…eerily manifesting itself through an imaged porthole that had cylindrically dissolved itself and melted open to momentarily reveal the stark bug-eyed gawk of a soiled indigent looking, drooling, pale bumpy and pock marked skinned goonish entity with it's vile mutated form crouched down and crumpled up and readily poised in an undersized compartment on the side of that pale blue wall in the dreaded third floor alcove. Ghastly images such as these presented themselves to my mind in a subtle sequence of inferred ominous doom. and were subliminally reinforced to me at periodic intervals. And then outright mostly by my father, and then by my grandmother, aunt and uncle as well; thus of whom had maintained ongoing moderate levels of contact and interaction with us as at the time as well as a sufficient levels of sadism within their personas. I had apprehensively maintained a nagging inward feeling to go forth and sound the alarm despite a pervasive variable of inner conflict, and heightened level of self intuitiveness.

In further remittance of my fears, I was thusly however grossly remanded behind a feigned and impenetrable wall of isolation and silence. In that for over an extended period I was duly bound by the persistent and disturbing notion that something so grievous and morally abscessed lay festering behind that attic door and was so surrealistically horrific that it steadily remained inconceivable, emotionally and psychologically traumatizing without due reproach. Wholly, I came to fear with such a morbid sense of grave aberration regarding what became an ill perceived and dreaded location in the house, was now only to be outwardly negotiated through a wary form of subterfuge. And just at the mere thought of an unspeakable resonating terror which was gravely accelerated by those faint and obscure partialized images that bore with them such ghastly implications.

And the mere fact that they had never completely manifested themselves wholly intact as fully realized mental composites had only served to further intensify my fears. And this factor alone, lent to among other things, a shocking sense to the harrowing prospect of a stark revelation, to manifest itself in a leveling retribution and impending doom. And yet even at the tender age of about five or six was I able to comprehend the pent up sense of the grave level of imminent danger that to others was outwardly unapparent. Yet they had remained elusive from my mental conceptions in their subtle configurations. Yet in their hazy incompleteness they had remained eerily haunting yet pervasive and elusively unattainable in much if any concrete sense accompanying with them their cryptic connotations. Nonetheless I was left with an ongoing agitated sense of fear and frustration at having been circumvented and denied more finalized mental composites. And for the most part the mere fact in that in many instances they had only partially availed themselves unto me in their stark, goonish and unnerving content that usually left me with anxious feelings of frustrated, anticipation. Yet they, over an extended period, insidiously proceeded to undermine, threaten and torment all sedentary aspects of my otherwise inward sense of quiet resolve and contentment, well being and security. And the total summation of such a dark elusive being that had foisted it's sinister aura amidst such a dismal enigmatic figure.

Shrouded in the silent connotations of historical remnant of a distant bygone era. Subtly indicative of harboring something so grossly mutated and horrific that fervently wanted to get out of either a basement or attic enclosure but was nonetheless forcibly contained there behind such massive, solid and sturdily constructed dead bolted oak doors that, at the time, seemed as though they were ten feet tall. And although these profound and garish visages had remained prevalent and unsettling factors even for many years after. Those visually faint and obscure off whitish images representative of such somber and ghastly partialized mental composites seethed deep from within the dim foggy mist at the depths of my lurid premonition. They held out for me such a heightened sense of graven fear in that they where almost as fervidly heinous as what was potentially restrained and concealed behind the locked attic door itself remanding me to such an extreme sense of isolation coupled with a non-conveyant state of solitary despondency.

And in all their innate secretiveness brimmed over in a bleak and sallow impish haze that indiscriminately superimposed it's darkened ominous shroud amidst the more mundane aspects of my early childhood that lowly transpired into such a psychologically inhibiting and harrowing period. Those dismal and sallow images that lent themselves to a ghastly surrealism that lowly resurfaced themselves insidiously within my psyche were pervasive and enigmatic. Wholly iconic of that period they encompassed such peculiar and perturbing aspects of a distant past which proved to be nothing more than sparse and fading mental residue. Yet, these subtly implied vagrant visages were held over from that lengthy and unsettling period. And one's that somehow survived from their initial point of conception although subtly alluring and morbidly enticing, at the time, sparked an underlying terror from within.

And although these unsettling factors seemed to be somehow inherent, they silently linked one to a remnant sense of profound historical connotations, amidst the intense gravity of a veil of prophetic significance. This was a prevalent and underlying factor for more sinister energy, which profusely emanated itself deep from within those ominous attic walls shrouded in their sallow configurations, that I had thusly inwardly perceived. And in all the strangeness held out by the overall setting itself only lent themselves as post secondary enabling factors, an indiscriminate backdrop, such that they were subliminally characteristic to the house and neighboring settings themselves in lending to it a certain underlying aspect that these events were seemingly somehow preordained to transpire.

And although they were unsettling factors to that grandiose old house, and to that I can personally attest!, were ones that surely did not arise merely from pure happenstance, nor were they allegedly one's of my own manufacture. Those mentally oblique objects that have long since faded from the realm of my conceptual intuitiveness in all the ghastly and horrific splendor of their grim, sallow parchment moroseness. These images lay morbidly festering and taunting to the very depths of my inward perception, starkly intensifying in the level of goonish horror they once held out so very long ago.

They were innately sequestered there as preliminary objects that initially sparked an underlying dread, ones that laid heavy on my chest like a fifty pound block of ice. At once, I slowly and apprehensively trudged up a ponderous and dismal flight of stairs on one of those occasions. And had only thus far had eluded themselves from the more defined aspects of a more pristine and unobstructed view, and stirring to the more pronounced aspects of the imagination in their visual clarity. And although resurfacing periodically and presenting themselves, in the more altruistic and surreal format to my mind's receptive eye, I was furthermore bound in a sort of psychological prison to their grim underlying connotations of imminent doom. And although they were those of which were predominantly responsible for my ongoing mental and emotional anguish in that they had festered and proliferated themselves far beyond the crude baser objects that had initially manifested themselves within the grim pretext of their nightmarish realm. And yet I have somehow temporarily managed to dismiss, suppress or banish their dark insidious and impish intrusion from the innermost depths of my mind's long term retention as unshakable and disturbing visages for an ongoing extended period of decades now. Thus only to have them recently and indiscriminately come to pass in the bleak and sullen moroseness of their innate ambiguity, they initially held out in the subtle restrictiveness of their vague sallow and visually opaque realm. In that they have only recently cajoled, prodded and made ill references to those faint subtle and washed out mental images of that strange period but only presently availed themselves in more pronounced clarity. Yet in all their ghostly and impish representations they still remain eerily faithful to those faint washed out remnants of an impervious setting. Thus of which, highlighted the ominous and foreboding presence of a towering and seemingly indestructible withered grayish or cream colored basement or attic door.

Denoting the attributes of a formidable barricade that intuitively restrained a dark, self contained vile insurrection, an unseen force due soon in it's blustering and volatile attempts to unleash itself and go on a heinous and monstrous rampage, only to have to be reckoned with from the illuminated world on the other side. And from the wary point of dreaded and fearful anticipated subterfuge, I had thusly maintained a longstanding and feigned silence at an inward nagging predisposition to convey these unsettling aspects but on a much grander scale than I had earlier intended, either by written dispensation or verbal conveyance only recently though to at least immediate family members or friends. And although I'm no longer a quivering quaking six year old boy standing there before drab and darkened foyer of the old house, I can only tell you that for years now the faint partialized remnants of those hazy off white images amidst a gray misty fog that I held fast to in a feigned anguished wall of silence, have stayed.

And in all it's like mindedness, I was morosely plagued with a much dreaded apparition I had thus earlier perceived that musty, dismal enclosure to have had the appearance of. Yet over time, those dreadful implications and ghastly images have steadfastly remained,... although significantly diminishing over the years. But nonetheless, residual ones that have seared an indelible retentive imprint upon my long term psyche. Lest, these dismal notions were the grim result of a morbid predilection to a mortally ghastly connotation that surreptitiously abounded in the bleak and dismal alcove of an old house. And were ones that were subtly indicative of a bleak and malignant presence gravely restrained that loomed from within. These stark and mentally unsavory implications were pervasive and ongoing and were also responsible for a long held fearful and silent inhibition with no recompense. They dramatically magnified a despondent sense of a graven surrealistic horror amidst a very peculiar and socially enigmatic suburban setting of the late 1960's.

These vague residual images were morosely iconic and representative of something insidiously in lying to a harkened disquiet that bespoke an impending doom. Those inward fears of which manifested themselves unto me at the time plagued and haunted my primal intuitiveness for an extended period of time and ones for which I held to with grave anticipation would eventually come full circle as the grim culmination of some stark and profoundly horrific revelation. And although the house and the overall neighboring settings themselves were but secondary aspects that sorely lacked any significant degree of clarification, they served only as a dull and pale dreary backdrop to a grave sense of profound and looming uncertainty that held with it an impending wrath and retribution based on dismally eerie atmospheric conditions greatly lending themselves to that possibility.

And although I think most of us as children believed in, or were perhaps moreover acquiesce with such like minded notions that just eluded the conscious bounds of our limited or constrained imaginations and may have pervaded the misty darkened realm of our subconscious minds. It may have prompted us to believe in a said given moment with the impromptu suggestion thereof in a veiled and contrived formatted effort to manipulate or influence behavior in a given circumstance. Or in other instances may have been inadvertently relayed to us by an immediate parental or guardian figure but with a significantly milder degrees of interpretation who by over the years acquired moderate levels of cynical distain for life in general. This may have proliferated itself in caustic ways in a jaded life's perspective but not to such a significant or pronounced degree. And to those of us who may have been told that such wispy fictitious beings existed lay there in bed at night gazing out at looming distorted or exaggerated shadows cast from objects in our rooms from dim or reflective hall or night lights emanating from a partially closed bedroom door may have been met with a profound uneasiness in finding it very difficult to fall asleep. We may have also been told in such bold, colorful and overtly descriptive terms that the boogie-man was hiding beneath our beds or in a bedroom closet at night so better leave the light on and sleep with one eye open. Then there was the ever infamous warning I think I can safely say for most of us was one that was aghastly heeded. Don't leave your bedroom window open at night just because it's hot, the boogie-man might climb through it. But to most of us I think this was a warning that was ill noted with an overwhelming sense of ominous dread and rarely dismissed or taken on with a contentious degree of admonishment from an immediate guardian type overseer. Thus was literally taken out of it's initial point of context and permanently remanded to the figurative sense of the word, but nonetheless heeded with a wary form of subterfuge.

But what of our dreams? Or for that matter our nightmares... Are they merely the random culmination of some type of particled residual mental energy indirectly stemming from the subconscious mind? Flowing outwardly from the cognitive reservoirs in our brains throughout our mental receptors perhaps as an indirect result of life's experiences or mental conditioning be it positive or negative? Those that are peaceful and pleasant are nonetheless categorized as desirable, and may play out in lofty, misty, mind wandering daydreams for instance. In direct contrast to that however is stark goonish imagery that of which transcends themselves from within the dark cataclysms of a shadowy underworld. Frustratingly elusive and tormenting to the sub-conscious they present their surreal and garish imagery to us in dreadful nightmarish dreamscapes that constitute little more than garish images of stark reticent horror... And although I think I can safely say that for most of us are repugnant or undesired,...they emerge from buried and suppressed regions that inhabit our innermost fears,...fear of the dark,... fear of what may potentially be concealed there,...and fear of the unknown,... the shadowy manifestations of physically mutated and contorted monsters that fill most of us with utter revulsion for instance, would only play out in resonating nightmares. Accumulated particled secondary translucent mental residue that seemingly comes into play when displaying such ghastly images in our mental receptors as we lay sleeping at night? One might also argue that dreams are the intangible secondary result of one's life's experiences be it present day or over an extended period stemming from a subtle point of origin indirectly influencing our chosen path, based on a life that may have been generally copasetic or that of strained contention. Given the circumstance though fear, fear of what darkened evil presence may be pent up and looming within a bleak indiscriminate realm and could potentially and without warning lash out, or just what may be lurking within a large abandoned boarded up dilapidated old house at night if one should chose to enter it alone. Or for that matter what may be on the other side of a securely locked basement or attic door that apparently hasn't been breached in years. And any garish notions along the lines of proposed green slimy ogre-is monsters possibly existing in dark dismal and clammy basements or attics would nonetheless be a very distressing and alarming pill to swallow.

It is my personal contention in writing this book for it not to in anyway give off the indication in that it's sole intent is to be a casual lighthearted written source of amusement for it's readers, It is drafted in all avid seriousness and marked assuredness to the reader that any personal written dispensation is of my own volition and makes documented references to earlier true life events and in and of itself will stand on it's own accord in that regard. And from here on out I will strive, in fervid attempts, to nullify any long held contention or skepticism as they may arise that may be held by the reader. And it is purely from a personal observational standpoint to accurately document profoundly significant true past life occurrences that have transcended the bounds of mental constraint. This book is not only an attempt to bring into the full light of accounting, nefarious designs of a dark sinister force, but serves to duly provide a hardened and jaded introspection in part by the author. What could conceivably be lying in wait in those unexplored darkened hollows and the garish vestiges of horror that still remain buried and unseen within the dark regions of our subconscious? The goonish ogres that once occupied them that seeped from such a dismal indistinct realm that permeate our nightmares? Those dissipating images from that odd and peculiar period have long since transgressed themselves upon a once lowly and tormented psyche and have been remanded to the distant annals of residual obscurity. They once bore with them an architecturally inherent and historically based significance. These subtle inferences may be recounted and still be called upon to be brought into the full light of accounting and bear with them the grim testament of a horrific revelation bearing with it such cataclysmic designs.

CHAPTER ONE

Something in the Attic

As a small boy of about six or seven, incepted in a semi-rural type setting of Cuyahoga Falls, Ohio in the late sixties, I have in recent years found myself inadvertently drawn to recount at least two separate and inexplicable past occurrences, that have permanently etched a profound surreal images to the very pinnacle of my psyche stemming from what was only to have served eerie testament to a subtly odd and peculiar time period. That by which I also believed were somehow at the time predestined to transpire in having subtly transcended themselves down from early childhood mental images. That of something which I feared with grave aberration and had subsequently come to implant it's dark, sinister and elusive image at a lowly and subliminal degree to the inner most regions of my cognitive retention paying silent homage to a stark and resonating terror within. And for that harrowing and unsettling period remained unto me wholly unseen and elusive from the path of my naked eye's perception. Something so enigmatically reprehensible, a vile and insidious abomination a hooked nosed Grinchnode, if you will, that took up residence in my sequestered attic. Something so visually inconceivable and repulsive it beggars description in that it remained as an ambiguous, hidden self contained insurrection. Lowly festering in an obscure concave of putrefying malevolence, that of which remained completely isolated, aloof and resonantly evil, beseeching in it's insidious trepidation. Thusly sustaining itself in some type of solitary and perverse reservoir in the darkened hallows of my lurid subconciousness. That of a diabolical and sinister goonish surrealistic bug-eyed ogre if you will, malignantly havening itself up like some type of vile and fastidious hermit behind a securely locked attic or cellar door. Surreptitiously bound up in some bleak and ominous secluded haven on the 3rd floor hall passageway of a once grand and stately Provincial style turn of the century house that had been in an ongoing state of decay. These historical landmarks subtly reminiscent of a once thriving and lucrative socially enigmatic past in that they from all casual observations exhibited historically ambiguous connotations of a distant past. The brashness of temperament in their outward facetiousness. The haughtiness of frivolity in their external motif which was far more prominent some 40 or 50 years hence. And even in their withered and sallow state of decay the flamboyant levels of opulence they once exuded in their abounding spender resonated through. And although that in decades prior they had once boasted such gaudy and ostentatious levels of short term abundance, they stylized such socially endowed pragmatists of the period. And ones by which my family lowly came to reside in so very long ago and in their ghostly, decaying and hallowed shells they paid silent homage to a socially enigmatic turn of the century past.

Yet my heightened level of morbid fixation was further intensified by a nagging sense of allure to it's mystique and in the ongoing inherent crypticism it emanated.. And at the behest of my father's sadistically gleeful and maniacal warnings to duly exercise a wary form of caution, at least when negotiating that region of the house. Nonetheless I was invariably drawn to it, and was stricken with elusive images of the shadowy figure. That of something which was far too horrid to have actually appeared to me in the raw physical form. And as well as having been a disturbing visage of my own construct, in that I initially attempted to, unsuccessfully I might add, bury at the innermost depths of my subconscious.. Yet despite my futile efforts in doing so, they tenaciously adhered to that hazy outline, which underscored a perverse inner presence. That for which I much later on attempted to bring into the light of full accounting by way of more constrained and futile efforts at visual clarification but with little or no success. It was my long held contention to adhere to those earlier pre-conceptions that had subliminally implanted themselves to any distinguishable degree of edification.

I was, later on, able to compose a much clearer mental image. This innate horror I envisioned, which lead to a veil of silence and state of isolation, Usually that of some overtly ghastly and hideous fiend cramped and crouched in a small confined dark alcove, I can also recall that on many an occasion, standing there alone in the dismally faint and musty settings of locked basement or attic door foyers and entranceways of eighty or ninety year old houses. And with the pulsating whoosh of my heart in my ears, anticipating the sudden frantic and frenzied turn of a black cast iron or green corroded brass door knob from something stark, grim and ogre-ish that had vehemently stormed it's way to the top of a lengthy flight of stairs from the grayish darkened base of a dismal clammy old cellar.

Then in that terrifying instance this scenario finally played itself out in a nerve riveting scenario. As I mentally envisioned this big thick, massive oak door; that seemed to be about ten feet high with withered gray, red or olive green colored layers of deteriorating lead based paint which were etched and peeling away, fixed with an old iron deadbolt lock began to be forcibly battered from the other side by some grunting, sputtering, overgrown, and drooling goon. Then for what seemed to be an eternity, waiting through that terrifying instance as that black, rusty or corroded door. As it began it's violent frenzied outward jiggle it slowly spun back and forth. I would be standing there trembling and aghast in frantic anticipation and despondent hopes that this massive door would not only somehow be strong enough to contain such a volatile beast but also be able to withstand such a powerful barrage of blows by some heinous abomination from the other side and not be smashed asunder. Yet despite my faint and fervent hopes in that regard, what ultimately emerged was this putrid, pale skinned bald headed mutant covered with brown warts, a short stocky drooling ogre-ish troll, with three fingers and a thumb. And it's long revolting tongue protruding out of it's mouth, with boney rheumatic, gnarled looking knuckles dragging it's twisted limbs across the floor, partially clad in middle ages garb and wearing a spiked leather dog collar chained in arm and leg shackles. An unspeakable hideous two legged fiend that had been long since banished to the dismal confines of a cold musty cellar maybe decades prior as some harshly imposed sentence it had committed against a distant and previous owner. In one final and violent thrust amid the heaps of splinters and wood planks, the only remaining remnants of a smashed door and frame, for the sole purpose of fulfilling it's vile and malignant intent….the pointless unfounded retribution against little children. These particular types of preliminary visages surfaced at the very onslaught of my dark inferences regarding that ominous region of the house. They laid the very foundation for more prolific and wholly formed image's of indiscriminate horror. They were haunting and reoccurring, representative at least to me of a very real presence and a foreshadowing of things to come. These preemptive warnings were indicative of something that was far more monstrous than what I had originally perceived to be lying in wait for us within the walls of that old house. They seemed to emanate a bleak and oppressive aura of ensuing evil in that of itself was an element that at least to me was markedly present. It was not just a lame derivative from the raw construct of one's taut or bedeviled mind or the bogus byproduct of an over active imagination, but something bleakly stark, undulating, and clearly imminent. That of a morosely grim, looming and shadowy presence that sparked a heightened sense of something gravely imminent at the very depths of my fretful intuitiveness, that of which I inwardly held fast to and concealed from immediate family members. Resonated waves of bone chilling terror and paralyzing fear to the very core and essence of my central nervous system prompting a lengthy ongoing sense of dread and ensuing doom.. I was enveloped by a pervasive ill sense of an omnipresence which abounded and which was soon due to manifest it's twisted and mutated form and ultimately fulfill it's vile and putrid intent to commit heinous and abominable acts. I was mortally stricken with an innate paralyzing sense of doom just at the mere thought of incurring that dismal cold and musty powder blue shrouded in a grayish haze of the 3rd floor hall passageway. A dreaded and bleak prospect and one which relegated me to a subjugated state of grave terror. This ominous and inescapable fact I can personally attest, became more apparent to me as we further got settled into that old house and the longer that we remained there. It was just something I alone felt in a veiled sense from behind a dense and impenetrable partition of silence and walled isolation. That of something droningly ominous was soon to become a visually forthcoming and oppressive force that had come to plague my central nervous system as well as my psyche. This served to become an ongoing and besieging scourge elevating high levelsof mental and psychological anguish which besieged me for an extended period of at least two years. It pawned a gross undercurrent of imminent fear and dread in a vast cesspool of disparagement emanating from the house itself (especially at night) in going from one lighted room fixed with a brass or copper chandelier positioned high overhead and adorned with eerie little chubby winged cherubs

Such as the dinning room that sat adjacent to a darkened kitchen foyer and was partially illuminated by that light I was struck with a grave sense of impending doom besieging in it's grim connotations that seemed to resonate from the very objects in that room as well as from within the walls. I strongly sensed these types of things especially when I stood there alone…in that of a looming indestructible presence that resided within a shadowy underworld consisting of a vast maze behind the walls of that long since gone…house

"The Boogie-Man." Or perhaps the atmospheric tone itself was one that was predicated on the pretext of such dismal and gloomy presiding elements that would seem to promote such a harried mental state especially on the part of a taut childhood imagination. From that perceptual standpoint alone one could easily see how such eerie and larger than life enigmatic stigmas would seem to emanate from such darkened hallows.

These pervasive elements underscored or even exaggerated the innate peculiarities already present in the architectural guise that categorized the splendor and motif of the period. Such prevalent factors were outwardly visible unlike that of today were historically iconic in that they lent their designs to a modest level of ornamentation. Thus ingratiating one to a strong sense of a Provincial Victorian turn of the century past, in their acquiescence at varying levels of distinction and predication to stately prominence. Such structural oddities bore such imperfections that were not only questionable but impractical as they incorporated such features as slanted floors or concaved ceilings and alcoves. Disproportionate small and narrow doorways, for instance, that lead to massive oversized rooms, or passageways leading nowhere, or lengthy flights of stairs that would seem to go on forever would be inconceivable and implausible features to the draftsperson of today. But were among the peculiar eccentricities that bore such eccentricities yet leant a sense of character and longstanding-ness to a house or an old building of the period. By current architectural standard, for instance, are far more precise uniform and clinical in their stringent designs and implementation leaving nothing to spawn or stir the imagination and lack a solid sense of permanence. Only in thereby utilizing pre-fabricated building materials and foregoing many of the amenities of construct bearing with them the intricacy of fancy ornate designs the past incorporated in those same outlying features. Although if much of these intricacies of design were present today they would invariably seem to be among the many contributing factors which prompted any ill-conceived notions maintained regarding the alleged presence of a dark, elusive and silhouetted enigma that over a period of about two or three years persisted in reeking utter havoc with my fragile psyche and central nervous system through the daunted weeks and months ahead. It insidiously dwelt in underlying ambiguity in some far removed and physically inaccessible place in that most of us just refer to as the Boogie-Man, yet in the more odious sense of the word in that in this case is out of a postsecondary point of context.

I was stricken with vague and indiscriminate images of a remotely ghastly and garish form appearing to me late at night. I'd perhaps inadvertently catch in my peripheral vision in waiting up for one of my parents to come home from work or some late night errand while sitting in a spare drawing room. That of a momentary but fleeting image of a grayish brown colored, statuesque pasty or rubbery matted, floppy tufts of gloppy flesh from head to toe almost resembling the thing from the Adam's family. Much later on as we further resided in that old house I was haunted by these stark and chilling proposed images that would suddenly manifest themselves in a subtle format of fleeting visual context that would be incongruently standing by in a dimly lit room late at night.

And as I'd be sitting there, I'd abruptly turn my head to look straight on in the direction of the image as it disappeared…One of two inferences can be drawn here from this…one in that how visually pronounced dark and elongated shadows or faint and sallow illumination amidst big dismal and drafty old houses at night can distort, offset and embellish sensual perceptions especially from a distance. They can gravely lend themselves to the real possibility of a looming threat is ensuing, in that they can significantly diminish one's sense of security amidst the lone solitude of a dark old house.

But from all casual and outward appearances one could surmise that the houses in this neighborhood had once celebrated more vibrant and lucrative times in decades past but now had given way to the onslaught of time, the elements and a post-war era. These presiding factors were enabling to this sallow and dismal setting and enhanced a lurid childhood imagination. The withered and gnarled physical characteristics these old houses exuded. These features accentuated the odd peculiarities and eccentricities in what they exuded by what was mostly older inhabitants. Leftover remnants of a distant time period whom staunchly maintained a 19th century mode of conventionalism. The overall setting itself was surrealistic, a socially iconic metaphor leftover from a dwindling Provincial style past that at the time was beginning to dissipate from the American landscape. Years ago I remember my mother relating to friends and relatives that she had seen what appeared to her to be a ghost that was that of an old woman who lived alone in that house for years and had died in there while cooking a piece of liver on the stove.

My longstanding belief was that she had observed this from the vantage point of a next door window, and it was dusk. Anyway, I thought she saw the old woman pass by a window holding a lit candle in one of those brass holders with the handle that curled around at the end. But though just recently through personal inquiry I had learned that this had occurred while she sat in the living room of this house, which frantically prompted her to single-handedly move us kids and our belongings to the house next door while my father was at work. Her account of this was that the old woman passed right by her, I said did it look like a person? "No", she said, "A specter…"

I maintained sparse recollections of massive stately rooms throughout a sprawling provincial style turn of the century house exteriorly in a partialized state of decay. I'm haunted, to this day, by hazy images peculiar in nature furnished with little more than huge red, off white and yellow ocher ornately patterned throw rugs with long rustic gold tassels, that almost covered the entire length of the floor. I also have more vivid and prominent recollections of a large harp which lent itself to an enhanced degree of significance in the overall setting. It was a classic element of provincial style quality of aesthetics. This piece was eerily prominent throughout the house among all else considering the overall sparseness throughout the interior in the way of furnishings because I still have no recollection of what it looked like after we moved in our belongings. The old harp was positioned adjacent to the downstairs living room foyer and as I remember the rooms were fairly well lit by the outdoor sunlight in the day. And as far as I know it was one of the few remaining items that was auctioned off, yet I was still overcome by ominous feelings of dread as I ventured through it with a grave sense of inhibition. The upstairs rooms were massive as well, and were adorned with majestic box window units constructed in a thick redwood mahogany trim.

Elegantly constructed by old world Victorian era craftsman with a painstaking attention to elaborate and ornate detail, in that the high ceilings as I remember had brass chandeliers in the center and the corrosive elements of time, moisture and condensation had turned them a blackish green color. Each lighting fixture at the end bore a creepy little figurine with the wide eyed goonish expression of either a little cherub or a gargoyle contorting their bodies around each individual stem as they embraced the base of an individual lighting fixture integrated into a flourished ornate design. Or those drab black or brown turn of the century door knob housing units that denoted such an eeriness to each of these spacious rooms. And more often than not, the tumblers that once received a skeleton key to secure them closed were long since broken or frozen shut. Aside from the fact that all the rooms were almost empty, just about every one of them had those elaborately patterned Victorian style throw rugs in them.

The stairway banister was cherry red thick and wide and curled around at the end. I later on as an adult asked my mother why all these rooms were almost empty and where did the harp come from? She stated that the house was almost empty because we were just moving into it and anything remaining was at the time like the harp part of a city held auction that was held to raise funds to pay for some outstanding debts incurred by the former occupants. This news though enlightening, made me feel somewhat ridiculous, after questioning it within myself for years after. But in those times the region of the house when even mentioned by family members paralyzed me in the grip of unspeakable horror, was that small third floor powder-blue passageway and alcove. And that old three by three foot barn red wooden makeshift door mounted on the side of the wall and latched closed. Any inclination I had to further explore this region of the house was dashed after a harrowed discussion I had with my father and a more descriptive and colorful one with my grandmother, any perceived curiosity as to the possibility existing that of concealed valuables or extracting them from the other side of that locked door was superseded by an air of ominous foreshadowing. I remember as he sat in a chair in the living room rebuffing my requests to pry open the old makeshift door and excavate any contents thereof my ongoing persistence failed to wear down what was an immovable position on his part and was to me totally unreasonable.

Yet after an exasperating discussion on the subject my father paused for a moment, sat back in his chair and said. "Cameron I have very good reasons for why I tell you to do things. "Do you know why I don't want you to go up there or to unlock that door? "No" I said, and just then this medium built man in his early 30's with an already receding hairline leered over at me through those old 1960's horn rimmed styled glasses he lowered down with one hand Gleaned over at me like a Cheshire cat, his skin at first flushed white then red and with a deep throated voice that made my blood run cold throughout my slight six year old body and left me totally aghast. And through a fixated bug eyed leer and sardonic grin bellowed this ominous warning…. There's something up there behind that door. I can't even begin to describe the level of terrifying shock waves that ominous statement sent through my body… And after a long pause with my heart in my throat I timidly asked what? And over and over while jabbing me in the side of my ribs bellowed repeatedly. "The Boogie-Man", "The Boogie-Man". heh, heh, heh, heh, heh, he cackled in a maniacal and sadistic laugh which magnified my sense of ominous dread. I then attempted to form a mental image of what such a mutated ogre that lurked in that dark musty attic crawlspace would look like. And from that point on my now infrequent excursions to that region of the house were curtailed and one's made out of quiet necessity. I was no longer inclined to interpose that location of the house out of my fixed curiosity. In the weeks and months that lay ahead the mere thought of that dismal powder blue musty passageway resonated a sense of something set apart and insidiously evil behind that little door. And my attempts to avoid it whenever possible were duly exercised on a regular basis. Any half baked excuse was given to either my mom or grandmother as to why I couldn't go to the third floor and any reason was given at the time to a relative guardian. Just the thought of some mutated slime sputtering goon just waiting to get out to reek havoc on unsuspecting persons outlying is totally out of the question. And furthermore the possibility of the existence of a real Boogie-man would be ghastly. With the dreadful thought of this ominous region of the house relegated to the back of my mind it become possible to focus on basic functioning. Out of sight out of mind so they say. In the weeks and months that followed my daily routine consisted that of an uninhibited six year old boy attending kindergarten playing with other neighborhood kids outside in the yard or vacant lot next door after the city tore down an old house that sat there.

Yet with the passage of a significant amount of time my sense of abject terror at the thought of going back to that dark location of the house had marginally subsided. And a resurgence of my curiosity culminated with my diminished sense of danger. I began to feel more comfortable at the possibility of interposing that region of the house and perhaps pry open that old door which in months previous I regarded as the total embodiment of evil. My rationale at the time was that if there was really something on the other side of that door it would have by now made a volatile and frenzied attempt to bust out and have reeked outlying utter mayhem. This and the fact I got a little older and my sisters as well as others ventured up there freely and nothing ever happened to them. At that point I was no longer petrified, nor was the total summation of my fears,.. frozen aghast in mortal terror as I mentally visualized a grim ghastly dark abomination that inhabited this region of the house lying in wait. Needless to say I at this time was far more comfortable with returning to this area but with a wary sense of caution. So one day when my father was at work and my mother was busy with something I took a flashlight a screwdriver and a small pry bar upstairs to that cold, dismal, dimly lit musty corridor with the sole intent to unlatch the small disproportionately crafted makeshift door that was forged there so long ago, and finally dispel the mystery. Once there, I stood looking down on that peculiarly built, resembling that of a miniature barn door that was so out of place in such a semi-elaborate provincial style house steeped in subliminal historic connotations, and to say the very least it stuck out like a sore thumb. At this point my sense of quiet resolve was momentarily superseded by an overwhelming sense of morbid apprehension. If there was such a thing as a real boogieman it would be heinous and immoral for a person to open a locked trap door and free such a fiend onto the rest of the world. This thought momentarily sparked in me a sense of inward moral contention. Yet my strong overriding sense of curiosity prevailed.

And with in mind I knelt down and proceeded to remove the makeshift hardware that was so poorly installed and secured the door closed which temporarily granted me a false sense of security. And as I lifted up the heavy orange-ish red wooden door I could feel my heart pounding with a morbidly intense and a reverberating whoosh within my ears, my face was hot and tingly and I felt a sudden surge of adrenalin as I breached open the dark passageway to peer in, and was met with a sudden waft of cold clammy musty air that blew past my face. Then as I proceeded to lean the heavy old door against the wall of this small dismal corridor I sat back ambiguously waiting for some physically wretched and unspeakable mutated ogre to emerge from the darkness, but none did… the opening was pitch black and as I stood there poised for a few moments before I managed to summon up enough gumption to finally turn on the flashlight and shed some light on the whole enigma. So I aimed that big bulky1960's red flashlight at the dark opening and clicked it on. What was in there? Nothing just a cold, dismal and musty smelling six by nine foot cubby hole with a dirty dark brown wooden floor. Big snowflake like speckles of what appeared to be rotted insulation or large flakes of dust circulating about in some peculiar form of self propelled suspended animation. This I later on learned was a crude form of material used in construction in the early part of the twentieth century for insulation that consisted of ground and shredded up paper among other things thus of which, proceeded to cascade downward like a light snowfall and were illuminated by the light beam of the flashlight. It had almost a similar effect as one of those old holiday decoration glass paperweights with a snowman or Santa that you had to shake, to see the simulated snowflakes fall creating some type of corny winter scene. But an empty crawlspace, made for light storage was all there was. And not even what I had hoped for to be in there, containers of possibly some type of rare coins or semi valuable relics. Just some thick filthy dust and some crumpled up newspapers amidst some sparsely scattered debris. At that instant my heart as well as my stomach sank in utter disappointment. I almost felt like a puffed up balloon that just had all the air let out of it. Not only was there no wooden crates bearing a treasure trove of any significance, but there was also no monster in there either. Needless to say that not only had my sense of the imagination been greatly diminished but also my faith in those of whom handed down the elder legacy of thought provoking lore had also suffered the slings and arrows of indignation. Just then the fretful notion of being indiscriminately discovered against orders by either my mother or father having pried open this door what I believed at the time to be my parents instructions of grave significance to bypass that part of the house. I hastily slid that door back over the opening and re-secured the door with the bent nails and screws as best I could before being discovered.

CHAPTER TWO

A Dark Silhouette in the Night

THIS IS THE SECOND NOTABLE YET BIZARRE OCCURRENCE AS A CHILD THAT is still fairly visually resonant in my mind and makes me shudder each time I call it into account. It was at night and I am pretty sure it was a big white cab me and my mother took to the house of someone she knew or had some sort of dealings with at the time. It was a cool crisp Ohio autumn night the kind that exhilarates your external senses and resonates a heightened sense of exuberance of life at your inner core. Once we arrived at this woman's house the cab stopped at the end of the driveway and opened the rear passenger door of one of those fifties or early sixties tanks they liberally referred to as cars, now this is the image that has seared itself into my memory and will probably remain with me the rest of my life. I was seated in back with my mother, me behind the driver and her on the passenger side.

I remember the interior light was on and the driver a big stocky man shabbily attired turned and reached back over the front seat bench rests with his big meaty arm to either unlock the door for my mother to exit assisting her in some fashion. I recall seeing her out of my peripheral vision wearing a tacky dark green or brown ladies winter coat with a fur collar somewhat worn a little shabby and unbuttoned due to the fact it wasn't cold enough outside backing out the passenger side door. My eyes were focused toward the house across the street which sat vertically off to the right which sat back maybe thirty yards from the sidewalk and the faint luminescence emanated from the front porch doorway. And as

I randomly peered in the direction of the front window of the car a very ominous looking dark silhouette either hunched or partially crouched over with broad shoulders slanting one side up the other down. Arms a little to short for its body eerily dangling down to it's side with the fingertips lining up at waist level appearing to be well over six feet tall visually a little hazy looking a little like fur, creature-ish in nature float up the house's driveway embankment almost toward the garage side of the house and once it reached the top which was the darker garage end of the house, the only way I can describe it, it seemed to roll downward head first and then disappear. Just then I felt flushed with a dreaded sense of overwhelming terror coupled with what could be described as waves of cold chills that reverberated through my body and then I began to shake, but not uncontrollably and not for long I didn't want to draw attention to myself from either my mother or the cab driver so I managed to gain some semblance of composure. I have no memory of what occurred after that, getting out of the cab going in the peoples house or for what. This incident unsettled me in such a way because I know I really saw something it wasn't just a figment of my imagination yet I kept it to myself. I didn't want to see my father leering down at me with that Cheshire cat like grin, nor did not want to be on the business end of his unrelentless taunts or the belittling way he would carry them out. I inwardly knew at that point that if I outwardly divulged anything in that regard I would not only be mercilessly taunted I'd just never hear the end of it.

These however were my innate perceptions that I garishly maintained within for over an extended period, of the next two years or so in regards to that dreary and peculiar time, subliminally representative of a dark sinister presence potentially lurking about a shadowy bizarre maze within the walls of that old house. They became a permanent fixture of my mental persona that were subtly initiated at the point of atmospheric context. And although I think I can safely assume that we all as children may have been oriented to or indoctrinated with significantly milder versions of such a dark shadowy elusive fiend, by immediate parental or guardian overseers in our charge this was my initial conception. But there were other outlying events that took place in that they were far more pronounced in their composite. There was an unmistakable element of peculiarity to their nature however, yet they maintained a post secondary significance that was markedly inherent. They were indirectly linked as integral components of my dark underlying hidden intuitiveness and the stark level of internal anguish I harbored in just silently contemplating that terrifying third floor region of the house. They bore a far more pronounced degree of mental and visual clarity. And although they consisted of the more mundane events that transpired they served themselves only as a post secondary backdrop that surreptitiously encompassed a dark ominous aura emanating from hidden regions of the house.

And to far more unsettling connotations, nonetheless others remained more vivid and pronounced in lieu of the oddities inherent to their nature. I remember once having stayed up late one night waiting for my mother to come home from a waitressing job at a local manners big boy and her coming into a dimly lit living room as the front door of that darkened room opened and the sent of a hard day's work on her combined with a waft of cold crisp autumn night air and a bag of leftover restaurant surplus, consisting of fries and hot sandwiches filled the living room. And how the pungent scent of a carefully articulated blend of menthol cigarette smoke, spearmint pain relieving rub and codeine based cough syrup was synonyms with a visit from my knar led and withered life's jaded, cynical grandmother. Or in how she referred to a sofa in predepression era terms as a davenport. Or those sun lit mornings on tree lined Front street where I lived and my mother outside overseeing me and my portable battery powered lemon yellow with red trim replica of a 1930's roadster I tooled up and down the sidewalk on.

And how she had won it for me in a promotional type grocery store raffle. I remember being fixated with those varied colored transparent plastic water guns in my backyard under the shade of a massive tree, or those little plastic and balsa wood airplane kits they sold in the grocery or Rexall drug stores back then, the ones with the Styrofoam wings and were powered by a wind up propeller and a rubber band. And then there was my attendance at Crawford elementary school and the remnant distant and obscure impressions of it I am still haunted by faint residual images of dismal, clammy sallow colored hallways and those yellow fallout shelter signs posted at the base of stairways indicative of a cold war era. And how typical classroom protocol demanded strict unwavering adherence to the petty insignificant, trifling aspects and nonessential components of it's busied lesson plans.

They were things that were not only irrelevant as far as any practical or life success plan that pertained to the real world but were really straight out of the book of who gives a damn. And in all encompassing of the non-essentialness of their banality in that they were invariably foisted upon us poor unfortunate elementary schoolers who had no choice but to sit there and comply. They enveloped the total embodiment of trifling insignificance, wielded in an iron fist like reign of stern enforcement by an unappetizing array of quirky, frumpy and more than likely sexually deprived old maid teachers. Thus of who invariably had two foot long wooden paddles hanging up by leather straps in marked proximity of their desks for all to see as a constant reminder of who was in charge. These glorified psychological malcontents typically bore a whole host of inexplicable and unsavory idiosyncrasies, coupled with an over inflated sense of importance of useful purpose their self concocted and contrived curriculum actually served. Or how the chalky pale sallow appearance of those little classrooms that readily displayed cardboard cut out decorations like Washington and Lincoln year round. Or those velvet red ones of cupid and fancied hearts of different sizes fixed to classroom walls on Valentines day. And how at the behest of the teacher, boys and girls awkwardly exchanged cards and candy amongst each other. And those big old American flags. with the yellow tassels at the end that really looked as though they belonged in a post office or some type of annexed building we had to stand before at the beginning of each school day with our hands over our hearts to recite the pledge of allegiance to, yet another faded icon leftover from that era like that of itself, mass patriotism. Or the televised news footage of astronauts orbiting the earth our first grade teacher had our whole class watch. I'm pretty sure we were only there a hand full of years when we had to move as did every other resident for several city blocks because the city was tearing down all the houses to install a new highway through the neighborhood area. By 1969 were on Delia avenue Akron Ohio, and me and my sisters began attending Portage Path Elementary

The Little Town Behind
The Railroad Tracks

AVONDALE WAS A RURAL HOUSING PORTION OF THE MIDWEST IN THE 1980's it consisted mainly of early seventies style ranch homes set on somewhat hilly ground the residents where upper middle class that had a boat a two car garage a couple of kids and a dog. The neighborhood also had some longstanding retirees whom typically could be found out mowing their lawns on Sunday, to periodically break and sit down on a lawn chair with a glass of lemonade, a cigar and a newspaper.

On a sunny day the street would be dotted with children playing ball skateboarding or riding their bicycles. Or one might casually observe the woman hanging wash out on a line to dry. The teenagers girls mostly, hung out in groups of two or three or more. They were clad in black tees with the logos of eighties hair band rock groups on the front like, Autobahn, Sojourn, Black snake or White Scallion on them. They also wore slightly faded jeans and high top soft leather boots. Girls like this usually belonged to cliques like this as they all dressed similarly and listened to the same types of music. They typically drove around in late model firebirds, trans-ams or ameros, sometimes customized. As the parents had secure white collar careers, but not what one would classify as pseudo rich but well off enough to able to afford some of the nicer amenities for their children. Then there were the punk rockers with their black leather jackets, and those Samones, Motels or the clash patches all over them. Sometimes these jackets had big holes or slits ripped in them, Punk or New Wave music, that was just the style then. They wore long tasseled earrings and strange hairstyles but if a girl was kind of tall, slender and dark complected a raving beauty, this only served to accentuate that rare quality. And set back about a mile from the allotment was a set of railroad tracks that stretched for miles and sat up atop a linear mound of dirt and gravel that rose about twelve feet high snaking it's alongside the neighborhood and stretching for several miles running past the distant woods. The kids sometimes took this route as a shortcut to the country store about three miles away from this section of houses, for a pack of cigarettes a pizza or a bottle of soda. This was accessible via a long dirt and gravel road known as Racine way. This road was laden with thick black petroleum to prevent craters forming from displaced mud in the road when it rained. Or dry dirt from billowing up from the wheels of passing cars or trucks, especially on hot summer days. This oil had a strong pungent odor that was almost pleasant and distinctive and one knew when they were within close proximity of the road if they got a waft of that petroleum smell. This road began at the corner of the neighborhood ran up over the railroad tracks and went for about five miles through a scenic rural landscape until it ended at a paved and moreover traveled road. The postal carrier used this road to access the neighborhood for more ease in deliveries. Avondale was divided into three basic parts with two main housing sections and a sparse downtown area.. Adjacent to the aforementioned section of houses was a somewhat more impoverished area, known as the Washburn district. And yes it was on the other side of the tracks. It comprised mainly of small dilapidated semi-crude structures that were forged sometime during the post war era, and would appear to have been built for those working during the industrial age. This area was accessed through tree lined open fields with scraggly brush, patchy knee high weeds infested with, dragon flies, locusts and tobacco spitting grasshoppers. This field was partitioned from the railroad tracks by an old crab apple orchard that was about one hundred yards wide and three miles long. It stretched along side the tracks and was on the rundown side. And one Always knew if they were in close proximity of it because the air resonated with the scent of rotting apples lying at the base of the trees. This area was marked by the proverbial large barking cross bred junkyard type dog restrained by a huge chain to a tree or make shift dog house, out in all kinds of weather with it's annoying ear piercing bellows one could distinguish a mile or so away. This section mainly comprised of old trailer type homes which usually sat up on cinder blocks as well as did old 60's and 70's style muscle cars that seemed like they were always being worked on by long haired shirtless teenage, or mid-twenties guys to the sound of hard rock music blaring from old sixties or seventies portable radios. Their hands and jean fronts covered in grease and these cars, despite the fact that they were partially restored and customized they seemed to be in a constant state of disrepair. The yards were small and mainly consisting of foot and half high weeds that were typically unkempt and littered with old wash basins, beer cans, car parts or some other type of debris. Clothes hung from lines outside to dry in the warm summer breeze, and shabbily partially clad youngsters whom sometimes shoeless played on dirt roads running through the allotment. At various times of the day you could hear the distant car horn like wail of an approaching train. Portly old men from along since disbanded industrial age sat dirty unshaven and in sleeveless t-shirts on dilapidated old porches. They read their newspapers, drank coffee or smoked a pipe waiting for their monthly pensions.

Then there were the teenage girls and their ostentatious persona, the garish way they dressed and wore their makeup or the loud brash manner with which they carried themselves, the smoking, the drinking and the promiscuity were almost a monument to unrefinement, yet only served to reinforce longstanding stereotypes. But the most difficult task that lay before them was to try and figure out what do with themselves. This I suppose is more than likely due to the lack of restraints or boundaries set on them in their formative years by subsequently apathetic parents, or the deficiency in their education. Areas such as these were not commonplace, yet they did sporadically mark the landscape. They harbored those leftover from a long since departed industrial age, and forgotten by the rest of society, were trapped socioeconomically in these shabby conditions. And furthermore compounding their dilemma was the crude and limited level of education allotted them, was compounded with levels of opportunity locally available. There for insuring that the clutching grasping hands of these chronic and pervasive conditions to reach out over the generations to imprison them in it's cruel impregnable, and invisible capitalistic bars.

Myrna Langley lived in a trailer and resided in this area. She was a slight woman of about five one or two, in her early thirties, but a hard life consisting of drinking, smoking and a rough childhood lent themselves to a much older appearance like someone in their late forties or early fifties. She maintained an overall withered appearance and had dishwater blond hair streaked with dark brown and gray. She was a short circuit fuse that stood about five foot three and weighed about one hundred and seventeen pounds of spit and vinegar. She had an ornery streak a mile wide and spoke in a raspy exacerbated tone, she often felt more than obliging when it came to the aggravating prospect of just getting under someone's skin especially that of her significant other. She stereotypically always had a pack of Marlboros or a beer can in one hand, and always had something to say usually unfavorable about something or someone whether or not she was actually knowledgeable about it. During the hot summer months she went about in a halter top, a bandanna, shorts and dirty worn tennis shoes with no socks. Her house was an old yellow wooden trailer type hitch which sat up on cinder blocks and was a dark pine green color. Rickety aluminum framed lawn chairs with damaged webbing adorned the front porch, Pots of artificial plants and flowers sat on little tables and a porcelain cat with a wide grin holding a welcome sign in both paws sat guarding the front door. And wind chimes clanged with each passing breeze.

The house sat back about thirty feet from the gravel and cinder laden dirt road that ran past it. She lived there with her two young daughters ages four and seven. She had a boyfriend, named Smokey whom didn't live with her but stopped over every couple of days to sit up till all hours of the night drinking beer and watching television, or whatever. He was the stereotypical ruffian type who had long hair drank beer and wore his muscle shirts over a toned wiry build with tattoos on his arms. He was not a big man but posed a menacing and intimidating figure, for whom frequently spent time in and out of jail for bar-room brawls and the sale and distribution of pot. The inside of her house consisted of old rummage sale quality furniture manufactured sometime in the 1960's or 70's scuffed or dinged up, mismatched and somewhat tacky. Her little abode was somewhat dirty and unkempt but to not such a degree it was unlivable. The living room floor was littered with corn chips beer cans and cigarette butts. In the front of the room sat a large aquarium with large orange goldfish. The television was an old portable black and white from the nineteen seventies. The carpet in the living room was a soiled old green shag rug but throughout the rest of the house were several other shabby throw rugs. Smokey would show up many times unexpected, on either his vintage nineteen seventy three Honda, or his metallic green nineteen sixty eight Dodge Charger. Their relationship was the stereotypical dysfunctional one of a combined crude baser element and which the police had to be summoned to the residence on more than one occasion to intervene during one of those late night shouting matches which sometimes turned physical. These occurrences did not however typify their ongoing dealings with each other mind you, nor did they ever rise to a level significant enough to warrant either ones lengthy incarceration. But it did lay the foundation for an on again off again relationship, which was based more on similar lifestyles and harsh upbringings. And which was based more overly on ill based co-dependency rather than one forged in healthy interaction by two mature adults with a decent level of self esteem. As one could observe this was not the case. Yet these episodes were usually marked by her two daughters wandering around outside the following morning looking for some type of breakfast or their mother, and drawing the attention of inquiring and concerned neighbors, by taking them in feeding them and returning them home at the first signs of the mothers return from an overnight stay at a local holding cell. Yet despite harboring a deep sense of resentment for the selfish and reckless manner in which they conducted themselves. Upon returning her children after one of these episodes, neighbors maintained a semblance of restraint in regards as to what they said to the mother in the situation surrounding the children or the events that transpired the previous night.

Autumn in daylight served unto itself for it's residents as well as visitors alike to enhance the warm and cozy sereneness of a communal countryside setting, but with the encroachment of nightfall it took on more cryptic and eerie connotations, with the glowing incandescent light of the moon accentuating leafless knotted trees with their massive, gnarled and outstretched limbs seemed to emanate a creepy and surreal omnipresence. This combination of a partially obscured the moon, with it's smoky, swirling clouds superimposing it, which frequently stood majestically alone in open fields or alongside abandoned dilapidating structures like farmhouses or barns with faded chewing tobacco ads painted on the sides of them. These vacant landmarks once served as work havens for individuals and their families of long ago, and they sparsely dotted the vast landscape. Empty cow pastures with patchy, scraggly overgrown vegetation and partially intact barbed wire fences stood partially intact trounced yet erect illuminated under ghostly bluish-green light. There would sometimes be a piece of broken down farm equipment or machinery that sat positioned out in an open field reduced to only a rusty shell of it's former self which stood silent testament to it's long since bygone work inhabitants, a tractor, a thresher or an old disker. These objects sat visually opaque in the foreground and the combination of these factors gave way to the surreal illusion of an eerie crypticism that almost seemingly became self animated. This was accentuated by far more obscure imagery against an illuminated, translucent backdrop. Low lying sections of open ground with tall ratty grass, or meadows with dandelions and various types of field flowers emitting a sweet aromatic scent ran for several hundred yards, and led into distant woods that echoed the cry of the whip-poor-will or the hoot of a barn owl. In the thick of deep dark underbrush reverberated the chirps of crickets or locusts, concealed in the high underlying vegetation, yet from an elevated vantage-point one could immediately surmise that the prospect of a lone nighttime excursion through such uninviting terrain towards, and into those dark distant woods alone and unarmed would take a supreme act of unbridled nerve and by the utmost rare type of individual. As well as being an unsettling prospect to even the biggest toughest man one could find, and if one stood on the railroad tracks at night at the point were the road intersected and looked in either direction they might see the faint emanation from a distant light or two, or that of flashing yellow caution lights a mile or more away throwing its sallow yellow light in close proximity onto the tracks silently bespeaking a looming omnipresence in the distance. Or perhaps one might visually note that of some type of a small rickety wooden structure that once served as a checkpoint at a long since gone time interval highlighted against a pale bluish-green background. In lieu of such surroundings I suppose one might inwardly be stricken with the unsettling notion of the possible existence of a real boogieman looming in the distance, mental regions that maybe reserved in our sub consciousness completely devoid of light or knowledge, a dark haven for the unknown something with an insidious alluring mystique.

The disparaging prospect of this alone would be enough to discourage even the mere thought of interposing with an uncertain night time landscape alone. Yet one did not venture far from neighborhood proximity for a stroll at dusk unaccompanied and was not something undertaken by many. Most people adhered to that old adage there's safety in numbers. And in the town of Analomink you did not usually see a lone person walking down a secluded dirt road or through an open field on the outskirts of town at night for any reason, and if you did it was usually in a groups of three or more, usually teenagers mostly girls and those in their early to late twenties, but then again somebody usually had either a small handgun like a derringer or a snub nosed twenty two or a knife or some kind of mace or pepper spray. And then there were the stereotypical tough punk wanna-be guys who's mainline of activity consisted of habitually getting high, engaging in needless fighting and whom prided themselves on their expertise in the fine art of badassery and intimidation. They were typically shabbily clad in soiled ripped and worn out jeans black T-Shirts with hard rock or heavy metal bands colorfully illustrated on the front of them. With racial undertones they usually featured the grim reaper in some mock surrealistic tribute to death in a scene depicting a shrieking skeleton clutching a guitar and the emphasis not being focused on innate talent. This element usually had long hair and in their grave lack of attention to personal hygiene and infrequent clothing changes reeked of pot. But in reality their modest level of street fighting skills were tipped off with either a set of Chinese throwing stars or a set of numb-chucks. But even these guys wouldn't go out alone at night amid the alarming circumstances yet when they did, they were usually seen in groups of three or more.

It's just common sense, you minimized your chances of something occurring if you were in a group at night rather than by yourself. As the years elapsed and I got to be about thirteen years old I went to live with my father and grandmother in Akron Ohio in the mid-nineteen-seventies after my parents divorced. My fears of that old house in Cuyahoga Falls and it's bleak and ominous undertones by then had marginally subsided by then and I no longer was preoccupied by them. At night my grandmother would constantly reinforce the issue of keeping all the doors locked and the visually fresh image of her in my mind of the leering, and foreboding way she emphasized it. Not only were all the doors in the house locked but what I found most disturbing and unsettling was the fact that the bedroom door was locked as well. I often times slept in a separate bed in her room and we listened to police calls on an old bearcat scanner she prided herself on possessing at the time. Often times we sat there in our beds under the dull illumination of a night light sometimes until one or two in the morning listening to those frightful and disturbing calls heightened by sputtering staticky reception coming in over the receiver.

Sometimes you'd hear the sounds of glass shattering and people screaming as you were hearing the terrifying sounds of a breached home invasion that was taking place somewhere in the city. We sat there sometimes literally quaking in fear and the fact that a big cavernous gorge ran along for miles in the back of the houses on the street didn't help matters either. It was monstrous deep and wooded and one that had a tiered level dirt path carved out midway up for people to hike along sometimes with their dog. It separated Akron from Cuyahoga Falls and the swift rolling waves of the Cuyahoga river ran the length of it's base. There was a huge steel girder bridge that linked Akron to Cuyahoga Falls over the gorge. It was a massive lime green with real high safety railings along it's side similar to other bridges of it's kind. It was a gargantuan creepy old thing and it had an iron steel see through grid you could look down hundreds of feet into the gorge as you drove over it. I always hated having to cross it because even though you tried to close your eyes one couldn't help but peek and look down below. I vaguely recall my father telling a buddy of his how a man once committed suicide by jumping off of it. And that a crowd of gawking onlookers gathered round as police and ambulance crews were hoisting the body up on a litter and a woman became hysterical and passed out when the sheet covering the body blew off. He just had that kind of mindset leerily morbid. I also remember one time as my father late one night attempted to enter the side door from the garage into a dimly lit kitchen my grandmother had chain locked making his entry difficult as he fumbled around for his keys in that dark garage began to holler over and over Goddamit it's me will you let me in for Christ sake!!. And once she slowly poked her way over to open the chain lock and stood there clutching that old one shot horse pistol in her frail and gnarled hand he then began mercilessly ridiculing and belittling her as a total neurotic with ludicrous and unfounded fears. It didn't dawn on me at the time as a kid that this level of callas and cynical castigation directed at his own mother was not the status quo nor for all intents and purposes acceptable. I just thought this is how adults from stunted and crude upbringings that bore with them harsh unrefined old world-ishness behaved in that they remained stagnant in their level of inner growth and enlightenment were dysfunction ally all encompassing. But in fact his behavior was extreme excessive and bordered on abuse. She was a frail old woman in her mid 70's addicted to codeine from having undergone some crude type of surgery of the time for intestinal cancer of the time she had done in her thirties I think. Yet in maintaining a rare form of neurosis it typically set the tone for a night of partial insomnia and pervasive uneasiness as her paranoid delusions methodically played out harrying scenarios that in all the years I visited never transpired. And although she kept my fathers Ruger twenty-two caliber revolver under her bed for protection against a harrying home invasion she always perceived was somehow imminent. Nonetheless I frequently stayed with her on those prescribed visitations many times alone, my sisters didn't accompany me. To this day I'll never forget that old thing, it was a big bulky old cowboy style single shot thing that was manufactured sometime in the nineteen-fifties with white pearl handles moreover resembling something of a much larger caliber. I vaguely remember my father and a friend of his early on went target shooting in an open field or woods or something at empty paint or garbage cans with it. It was kept in a leather holster and stashed in various hidden locations only he and my grandmother were privy to. It was also clear at this point he had no interest in it anymore and hadn't touched it in years. He just didn't want me to touch it and made it emphatically clear for me not to go near it or mess with it.

One night this fearfully ill premonition did however manage to resurface and manifest itself in an unnerving and peculiar way. I was there alone as my grandmother had moved back across the street with my uncle. I was going from the hall to the kitchen when I heard what sounded like leaves rustling in what sounded like swift approaching footfalls in the front yard as they abruptly ceased and in a terrifying instance there was an eerie pause capped off with a sudden burst of loud knocks at the front door. Then the frantic, frenzied turning and jiggling of our front doorknob began it lasted only about ten or fifteen seconds but seemed like an eternity. I just stood there on looking paralyzed in fear. After it ceased, I heard the rustling of fall leaves being trounced under foot and the sounds of footsteps dissipating. With that I gained my lost sense of composure and breathed a sigh of relief. The daunting prospect alone in that my nocturnal visitor would have been able to breach that big oak doorway and gain entrance that solemn windy autumn night was totally unnerving in itself. Although this harrowing nocturnal experience was marked by a paralyzing rush of heart throbbing adrenalin in that I was totally immobilized by an old familiar fear. I always wondered since then if I could've gotten to that bedroom closet in my grandmothers bedroom closet in time to not only find but to retrieve the strongbox hidden by my grandmother that contained that old one shot horse pistol before a starkly crazed intruder somehow managed to gain entrance.

And then a sudden sense of calming reason swept over me as I came to the realization that it was probably just some dorky neighborhood teenager with a stale sense of humor that had nothing else better to do than to roam around outside on a windy night causing minor disturbances. And aside from the prevalent notion of an all encompassing evil residing within, or in how the door itself framed in decades old style peculiarly ornate wood trim bore a cracked faded ivory or cream colored forty year old deteriorating paint job, was the only thing standing between me and some grisly drooling volatile mutation. I would an occasion be plagued with the disturbing mental visage of a type of giant ogre with pale gray or a cream colored skin complexion a bald head beady eyes and spaces between rounded at the end fangs, barefoot, dressed in middle ages garb wearing leg shackles, that emitted a screaming type roar, waiting up there for a chance to burst out only to rip me to pieces. The stuff of garish nightmares… And the reoccurring flashbacks of my fathers colorful warnings of impending doom in that old house in Cuyahoga Falls Ohio years prior. "Don't go into the Attic" heh-heh-heh' it's locked for a good reason and the colorful, descriptive manner with which he drove it home. He used to go down in the basement when we lived on Delia avenue in Akron when me and my sister were upstairs in the living room he would take a big piece of sheet metal and rattle it. It simulated the rolling sound of thunder, and while he was doing it, he would cackle in a maniacal form of laughter. At the time it petrified me and my sister. I look back on some of this now in a moderate level of amusement rather than from a bitter and contemptuous standpoint. But at the time it was to me and my sisters serious business. Yet this was exemplary of his somewhat disturbed and sadistic sense of humor. But aside from anything any of us were conditioned to believe about an alleged being as children. The more logical and rational side of us dictates that upon any moderate degree of consideration toward the possibility of the existence of such an insidious and malevolent being, is that the only conclusion one could arrive at, would be such a concept could only otherwise be utterly dismissed as preposterous and absurd. It's garish notions and enigmatically embellished lore is rooted in the same dark realm of superstition and ignorance as The Hunch-back of Notre Dame, leprechauns or gargoyles. These archaic beliefs were reinforced among others by bands of roaming gypsies and snake oil peddlers who lived in crudely fashioned covered wagons in the deep woods whom passed down a dark enigmatic legacy of superstition in their lore. Such darkened notions were spawned by like minded old world sectarians who in all to many instances maintained crude backward and credibly indistinct beliefs based on questionable second hand accounts. Were by darkened dungeon like cellars harbored malignant, atrocious, goonish ogres and Provincial countryside's that were prowled by leering stone-faced trolls that would suddenly emerge from beneath cobblestone bridges to threaten the occasional passerby. And those of whom collectively bore a mob mentality whereby a few choice words shouted by even one instigator only served to fan the flames of blind rage in a lynch infused wave of ignorance pumped up a vicious mob to boil over rallying to a hasty rush to judgment completely null and void of the basic elements of due process bearing torches for the sole purpose of gathering suspected witches to be burned at the stake in colonial U.S.A. of the sixteen hundreds. It's dismal connotations were imaginatively embellished by it's long ago authors and intensified by the sallow withered parchment pages of those corny old story books that were laden with characteristic illustrations depicting lanky exaggerated physical proportions and goonish leering expressions drafted in pen and ink.

I still recall those nightly bedside sessions with my grandmother in that dreary old house reciting this 19th century pulp to me out of at that time, thirty and forty year old children's readers before I went to sleep. And those pictorially embellished representations only served to incite my already lurid sense of imagination. Yet now as a grown man forty plus years later in solemn reflection of memories such as these in their periodic visitations. I am able to take some solace in these in momentary diversion from present stress's and adversity. They afford me a subtle and pervasive source of comfort and ease. Like that of a warm blanket and brimming cup of hot chocolate, fireside on a cold, blustery winters night their ghostly remnants to this day still haunt me like a familiar old friend in a sort of diversionary form of refuge and haven from the blustering winds of the often trying times of the present. And even though those that were initially involved then are now long since gone and all that remain are my mother and one sister.

Sherri Dunn, Crystal Parsons and Julie Schaffer were close friends and lived in relative proximity to each other in the neighborhood they were in the tenth and eleventh grades at Pentagast high school and belonged to an exclusive type of clique. They only socialized with other kids that had similar composites as themselves in being exceedingly good looking and having come from families that were well off financially. They were not exemplary in school activities like cheerleading, Decca or other various group organizations yet within their immediate circle maintained a relatively low profile. After school or on weekends they spent time hanging out together in Sherri or Crystal's backyard. On a nice cool spring or fall day into late afternoon they sat on cushioned lawn furniture under the shade of a garage patio awning drinking cold sodas out of cans and listening to Eighties hair band rock music on a boom box. Sometimes on a sunny afternoon they'd collectively stroll down along a desolate dirt road and over railroad tracks to the general store for some type of food stuffs or a wanted item. Sherri was kind of on the tall side slender long jet black hair, brown eyes and dark complexioned skin tone, and like her counterparts was exceedingly beautiful, raving almost to the point of being surreal. She was kind of soft spoken and more articulate than the others, yet had an almost a habitual tendency to admonish the other two at even the most minimal of infractions. This would occasionally cause somewhat of a riff in their friendship. She dressed in dark clothing her jeans mildly worn, unfaded and favored dark crimson red or blue but brightly colored blouses. She also wore black tee shirts displaying the logo of some hard rock band on the front. And in cooler weather sometimes dawned a jean or a light brown leather Indian style suede jacket that had been hand fashioned with leather tassels hanging from the outer arms and bottom. She wore modest jewelry small earrings or rings and a very small ladies watch, She was also outfitted in knee high black or brown suede leather boots with flat shoe like soles. Hypnotically intimidating in their profound beauty and perfumed presence, she as well as her counterparts cast imposing flawless features that put the typical guy into a trance or simply reduced him into a quivering, tongue tied, befuddled, and jellied mass of insecurities.. Crystal was of medium stature had auburn hair, hazel eyes, and a slight build, her attire was on that of the more semi dress side or what was commonly referred to at the time as preppie style attire, a nineteen eighties slang term used to describe those whom attended exclusionary or private type schools and had to wear a school uniform. She prided herself on a more elaborate and extensive wardrobe than the other two and maintained a polished and meticulous appearance. Her extraordinary beauty was further enhanced by her stock in the area of refined social graces such as a non-flirtatious, and wistful persona furthermore maintaining a marginal degree of social retentiveness. Crystal had a slight but elongated face a wry seductive smile and would occasionally throw her head to one side and with one hand push her bangs out of her face or twirl her hair, smiling and mildly gesturing while conversing with someone. She was more prone to interaction with others outside her immediate circle than that of her counterparts yet maintained a more somewhat reserved demeanor. And those peers of whom deemed as relegated to a lower social station and typically rebuffed in this regard, referred to them as stuck up bitches, at least that was the terminology when I was in high school. This kind of social labeling among others, more often than not served as an instrument to reinforce longstanding stereotypes furthermore widening the gap between the classes and in many cases was totally unfounded. Crystal drove a refurbished candy apple red nineteen sixtynine GTO given to her by her brother who moved out of town and went away to college. It was customized and had a small hood scoop, aluminum wheels, wide tires, brown leather upholstery seat covers, and a torn down four fifty seven type engine her brother installed prior to his moving out. As well as having a pair of black foam rubber dice with white dots hanging from the rear view mirror. This car was her brother Troy's baby until he made it a gift to her upon graduating from high school and leaving home for college. He was always buying a new part for it and upgrading it wherever possible. On weekends he would wash and wax it in the driveway of their home on a nice day. But because he was unable to take it with him he made a gift of it to his sister with the understanding that she take extra good care of it in her stead. She and the other two would occasionally go places in it together, if it was out of walking distance or in cases of inclement weather. Sherri had a car as well a nineteen eighty corral blue trans- am, with one of those big eagle decals on the hood and a black vinyl interior. She did not like to drive and only did when it was necessary. She usually got rides from friends or family, if the girls went somewhere that was not too far away they walked and preferred the outdoors if the weather was nice. They preferred walking down a secluded country route usually old cordite road to somewhere on a cool spring or fall day. Only in the extreme oppressive heat of a summer day or the bitter cold of a winter one did they drive a car. For reasons being that you could roll down the windows and catch a breeze or turn on the conditioner. And in the winter they did not really want to trudge out through big snow drifts or skate on ice covered roads and one could always turn on the interior car heater to melt away the ice and warm up. And finally you saved money on gas foregoing automotive travel to destinations in close proximity.

Julie Schaffer was of medium height, stocky build and physically speaking, well endowed with well above average looks to where it was almost intimidating. She was more of an extravert than the other two and more lax in her choice of attire. She was a dishwater blonde, but with darker roots this became very apparent when either she washed her hair in the shower or went for a swim in a pool or at a lake and upon getting out sat there dripping wet forcefully and vigorously rubbing a towel in a back and forth manner into the side of her head in a drying fashion while chewing gum, and gearing up for the next phase of leisure activity whatever that was. She was of fair skin complexion, with a long wide face corral blue eyes and a slight overbite. In the looks department she could stop a truck, or cause a guy riding a bicycle to crash into a tree or a telephone poll upon seeing her walking down the street. She smiled a lot and had the annoying habit of while chewing her gum, roll it around in her mouth, continuously snap, crackle and popping it in her teeth. Her friends and family found it mildly disconcerting and when they periodically brought it to her attention as to what an annoying habit they found it to be, she simply smiled and said it's just something I've' always done, it's a part of my makeup. She was more extraverted than the other two, had other friends outside of their immediate circle and was less inclined to adhere to the limited constraints set by social classism. She favored contemporary pop, new wave and hair band rock. She listened to bands like Yes, Black snake, Sojourn, and Scallion to name a few. Music was an integral part of her life more so than social interactions or maintaining a steady boyfriend. She unlike too many others of that time was open to and listened to some dance and RandB music as a refreshing change when she tired of the other.

In any case Julie maintained a more racially unbiased and well rounded position on music selection than that of most of her peers and was more open and receptive in that aspect. She lived on Crandall Street, and her friends resided only a few blocks away on Sycamore and Tillman. This among others was an enabling factor in their close knit relationships. Crandall street was lined with old knotted birch trees standing only several feet high at full maturity, and were punctuated by the occasional spruce. The homes for the most part were meticulously manicured, well maintained and lent themselves to a significant degree to their aesthetic value. What with brightly colored rose bushes entwined on wooden framed supports fanning out and painted white adorned backyards or the sides of garages. The typical summer day was met with the proverbial roar of a lawnmower or the rotary chirping-clack of hedge clippers audibly intermeshed with the sounds of children immersed in some level of play activity in the streets. The pleasant aroma of someone cooking an evening meal transverse screen doors and kitchen windows resonating it's scent and wafting it's way through the warm evening breeze inadvertently summoning some to the dinner table. Yet unbeknownst to this quiet unassuming community loomed an insidious and hidden danger, that loomed in the shadows, awaiting to reign down terror and reek utter mayhem.

CHAPTER FOUR

The Telltale Signs of Forewarning

It was a warm breezy summer afternoon about five o'clock and Julie was standing in the driveway of her dark yellow ranch style house the garage door was up and an old seventies style leather bound radio sitting on a shelf inside was turned to a contemporary pop-rock station bleating out the song, and we danced by the Hooters in a tinny baseless audible reverberation with semi staticky reception and a partially bent antenna. She was washing down a supped up metallic gold nineteen seventy three Plymouth Roadrunner, customized with pin stripped Mag wheels in the back and a four fifty four engine dropped in it with a hood scoop and a decal of the infamous bird emerging from a puff of dust on the lower portion of the rear fender. The car was raised up in the back with a set of traction bars and a pair of fuzzy dice hanging from the rear view mirror and a bumper sticker of the famous rolling stones symbol of the lips and protruding tongue pictured on the trunk. Julie was wearing a pair of black spandex shorts and a blue halter top. She was standing there holding a garden hose dripping wet as she'd been in the process of rinsing the car with the spray nozzle portion of the hose. Over by the garage in the grass sat a big plastic wash basin with a shammy and hot soapy water in which some of the soap had spilled out onto the driveway and was running down the incline into the street. And inside the garage you could see some bent utility shelves with old cigar boxes and coffee cans with either nails, screws or small rusty old hand tools in them sitting there with various other objects like spent fuses or a beat-up flashlight with the light part that screws on at the end missing. The dull glow of the garage light overhead faintly illuminated the inside and one could see that it was inundated with boxes of busied clutter that had accumulated there over the years. The acquired state of disarray was in desperate need of a good going over in the way of a thorough spring cleaning, consolidation, reorganization, and the discarding of worthless junk. But such an undertaking was put on the back burner of procrastination for some time. And as the perennial rays of the setting sun cascaded their way down from high atop trees and the backs of houses, partially obstructing the view of approaching friends from across the street coming up the driveway to make casual inquiry as to the possibility of going for an evening stroll to the country store later on for a pizza or some other type of foodstuffs. Sharon Dunn and Todd Peterson came sashaying up the driveway as usual as Julie was partially knelt down to begin a shammy dry of this brutally rad muscle car before waxing it. Then Todd sauntered up the driveway and out of the blue made yet another thoughtless and inappropriate statement with the combined bumbling social graces of Gomer Pyle in it's articulation and the tact and articulation of Fred Flintstone he suddenly blurted out,… You know that is such a boss ride, what does somebody like you need with it anyway, when are ya just gonna give it to me!.

Todd Peterson was a tall lanky guy with long red hair and skin blemishes on his pock marked face and arms to a mild degree yet noticeable enough as a more severe case of acne which is common among adolescents. He was on the lean side and liked loose fitting clothing and in the summer he wore thongs cutoff jeans and ratty old T-shirts that really belonged in the trash bin that had various rock logos on them. He had the predictable habit of chiming serendipity to his friends as he greeted them or in parting it became one of his identifying trademarks. Julie was completely incensed and mortified at the total spontaneity of such a brash and unconscionable statement and was caught totally off guard. The brash and thoughtless disregard for her personal space and having invaded it by such an inappropriate display and embarrassing way in a comment like that and in front of everybody!!...It left her so stunned and taken back by it she was momentary at a total loss for words. He was definitely what was referred to as a head banger. Bands like the Scallions, Pocahontas, Blacksnake and VanGuard were prized items in his musical repertoire. He didn't buy a whole lot if vinyl or cassettes he mainly tuned into local hard rock stations instead. She just contemptuously glared up at him and said ya know dork-meister just when I think you've said the stupidest thing you could ever possibly say you surprise me yet again!!...And say something even stupider that the time before!!...like that for instance,...uh, were you dropped on your head as a child!...And in a leering gleeful response loudly retorted in answer to your question...when jackasses sprout gossamer wings and fly!! So jackass I guess your sort of permanently earth bound eh? "Todd, funee ...but seriously, Julie, flattery will get you nowhere, especially with the town stud..."Julie, Oh Gawd...Yet among other things he maintained a great admiration and appreciation for well restored and customized mid to late sixties and early to mid seventies muscle cars with medium sized box frames which in raw form had a lot of potential in the right hands. And he as well, had a deep and abounding admiration for those whom possessed the high levels of skill and dedication it took to see such an extensive and time consuming project through to it's meticulous completion. He had a lemon yellow nineteen seventy three El Camino with lightly rusted and corroded inch wide chrome trim that he continuously labored over with some sections of the body that were sprayed with gray primer. And even though he put hours of painstaking work effort into it, it still fell short of local customized standards. He really resented some of his friends for possessing such skillfully refined specimens of motorized mastery. Take his friend Julie for instance, I mean what cosmic and divine power had exclusively bestowed upon her the special privilege above all others especially him to be in the sole possession of such a bitch'in ride!! Nonetheless however what he lacked in time and money or in skill in getting it the way he wanted it, he made up for in enthusiasm. It was subsequently run anyway despite the partiality and unfinished quality of it's overall appearance. They periodically held auto shows in the downtown area during fair weather periods of the year which commanded the attention of local car enthusiasts. They would all come together almost religiously in a cult like order in a centralized downtown Mecca for a haughty display of their finished automotive wares in a classic muscle car Menagerie that featured a diverse range of customized and restorative mastery. It was a local event annually extended to the public for a showing, classic vintage, stock or customized muscle cars were featured there and they would be parked off to the side or paraded down the center of town, the muscle car portion highlighted a wide array of sixties and seventies muscle cars like the mustang or barracuda among others similar to it took their places in this automotive fashion show. Some of theses cars were in original stock condition but others were custom tailored to the owners individual preferences. Todd had a saying in this regard, there are many who choose to take on such a project, but few do it well, and fewer see it through, to completion, And even fewer yet, that do it right.

Although he was not as dedicated or skillful in these aspects as the aforementioned auto enthusiasts yet he did attend local car shows to swap ideas with and rub elbows with local buffs. Yet with the onslaught of each new show there was always some nuance that was brought to the automotive dinner table bringing with it a certain allure that captivated even the non enthusiast. And with the sudden and swift approach of autumn, with it's cool crisp and breezy air brought a much needed reprieve from months long oppressive summer heat. Thereby allowing it's residents to venture outdoors for quiet evening strolls around the block or letting their children play in yards, vacant lots or in the streets outside the restricted confines of an air conditioner. The neighborhoods of Avondale during fair weather conditions always bustled with some sort of mundane activity like that of someone pulling plastic trash bins down to the side of the curb, or out mowing their lawn or raking up leaves and bagging them. You'd also see small groups of people milling about the in middle of the street, engaged in some foisted level of interaction. And the nights were often cold and windy, you really couldn't leave your windows open at night because temperatures really dipped down to uncomfortable levels sometimes into the forties. And you had to start wearing either a light jacket or a hoodie. One night Mr. Barnett a sixty seven year old retired milk truck delivery driver from a dairy plant in Iowa was in the menial process of pulling his garbage pales down the front of his yard to position them in close proximity to the edge of the street for pickup;.

There was a half moon out and the sky was dotted with distant stars it was very cold breezy and dark. After placing the bins at the side of the curb he turned around to walk back up towards his house and a slow approaching car was turning off Primrose street to proceed up Crandall. The light from the oncoming headlights momentarily beamed onto the side of the adjacent house of neighbor Harriet Cromwell, about forty yards away from his. Amid the center of the light flash from the car headlights was a darkened shadow of a creature like form hunched over arms extended and claw like hands at the end. The head had some type of horns that were markedly visible yet somewhat hazy but distinguishable, and as the flashing car head light beam swiftly rolled along the side of the house but the silhouette seemed to remained almost stationary giving with it the illusion of an almost old movie like projector image moving only fractions until the car bypassed the house leaving the area dark again. At that moment Mr. Barnett stood frozen in abject terror amid the blackness at the end of his yard, he thought to himself, did I just see what I think I did? Should I try to make it to the house? Should I run in the other direction? No one else on the street was outside they were all either asleep in their beds or not at home at all, and aside from the faint illumination of a street light or two at the end of the block the immediate area was pitch black and whatever in was he saw was amidst. At first he just stood there momentarily frozen in unspeakable terror and then in an instant he made a frantic split decision to bolt for his front door. His wife Eloise was home but she was upstairs asleep. Whatever it was he saw there was a pretty good chance it didn't see him and had made it's way around to the back of the house by now and was oblivious to him. With that he sprinted with the full vigor of an eighteen year old kid on the high school track team, width and breadth he hurdled the three front stairs onto his porch and within moments he was hysterically unscrewing the door knob while frantically thrusting open the font door.

Once inside he slammed the door shut and threw the deadbolt swiftly into the locked position while panting in exasperation he whirled his body around to collapse and rest his back against the door emitting a loud sigh of relief. Just then he heard his wife calling to him from the upstairs bedroom, Emmett what's going on? Nothing dear I just had to chase away a raccoon that was tearing through our trash bags. Go back to bed everything is under control down here ok? He had to think of something quick to tell his wife as he did not want to arouse undue alarm in her as there was already a pervading and unsettling element of town suspicion regarding something gravely imminent was in the midst. And conveying much if any of the details of such an incident at this point may prompt her to think he was now ready to be committed to padded room at the state cracker box. In any case he did not want to divulge anything about what had just taken place until he was completely sure of the frightful and surrealistic image he thought he saw illuminated against the side of his neighbors old garage. Just then he frantically proceeded to the back porch enclosure off of the kitchen foyer that visually panned out into the backyard, he had a couple of high beam security lights installed there a few years ago as he had, had some trouble with a group of unruly teen age boys that roamed throughout the neighborhood vandalizing property and needlessly causing trouble at dusk. The police were summoned by various residents on numerous occasions because of their ongoing and menacing behavior until it culminated to such a level they were apprehended by local authorities and remanded to lengthy stays in juvenile hall.

Once he got to the back door he turned on the flood lights illuminating the back yard and peered out the window, but saw nothing out of the ordinary. He visually peered out over at the old wooden dilapidated one car garage with half of the peeling red paint eroded away. He also looked out over he and his wife's ratty little tomato patch fenced in with chicken coup wire, nothing…At that moment he neither saw anything nor heard anything. After an eerie pause of dead silence a few minutes had elapsed as he went to shut off the lights and call it a night and go upstairs, a low whining type of moan sounding something like that of a frail anguished old man almost distant, and tormented, over and over again in a low pathetic pitch, alone…alone… alone… alone…pierced the silence. As he stood there in the dark kitchen foyer listening he was overcome by an unspeakable paralyzing sensation of droning and reverberating terror…The kind were the skin on your face twitches with cold chills running through it. With this he abruptly switched back on the high beam security lights and the waning cry ceased. At this point he in his flustered and frenzied state of mind put that together with what he saw in the yard earlier and came to the stark realization that an unspeakable horror covertly lurked in the shadows. Yet the most perplexing question at hand was in what immediate and decisive course of action to undertake in instituting safeguards against such an insidious monster. Even the slightest miscalculation could have grave and disastrous ramifications. If he went to the authorities right away without obtaining further proof to substantiate such harrowing claims, he'd run the risk of being labeled the town nutcase, suffering an unceasing barrage of scoff and public ridicule. But what would the potential repercussions be if he just sat on this and did not sound the alarm, alerting the community to danger as grave as this?

This however posed itself as a moral dilemma and mental quagmire, it was one that needed sound and decisive action to reach a definitive resolution and soon. And also one needed in order to effectively eradicate the impending, and malignant threat that existed. After about an hour long attempt in self contemplation as to a possible solution he left all the security lights on until mourning as they were energy efficient anyway enabling him to do so as he and his wife were on a fixed income. He then warily went through the rest of the house insuring all the windows and doors were locked before he went to bed. Prior to going upstairs he switched on the front porch lights and peered out the front window to see if he could visually note any more bizarre abnormalities. Deeply unsettled and burdened psychologically with such pressing and disturbing facts. He went into the front hallway closet to retrieve a locked strong box which sat on the shelf over the cloths bar. The box contained his service colt nineteen eleven A 1 A forty five he brought back from Korea when he was in the army during the war. It also contained a partial box of shells and like the gun needed cleaned and oiled because they were old and corroded, but would fire nonetheless.

Upon retrieval of the old pistol from the hall closet. He stood there nervously shaking and holding it in one hand, pulling back the slide and releasing it to see if there was a round in the chamber and then in a frantic and befuddled manner began pressing cartridges one by one into the magazine. He hadn't fired a gun in years and really wasn't gauged to any kind of aggression or confrontation. He was only a medic during the war and hadn't really killed anybody. The gun itself did not grant him even a small sense of safety or security because whatever that was, he saw was not human or even animal and stood well over six feet tall and more than likely had the strength of about ten good sized men. Perhaps it could even turn a car over with it's bare hands, or bare claws case being. Or perhaps it was easily capable of uprooting a small or moderate size tree from the ground. It just puts me in mind of some unnerving footage I'd seen on television years ago, that of about ten cops attempting to subdue a man high on pcp in his drug infused condition he tossed them off himself one by one like rag dolls it was really creepy to watch. Just what would it take to debilitate such a creature? A bullet or even several potentially fired into such a being may have little or no affect and may just enrage it. Would it require heavier armaments like maybe an RPG or some type of anti tank weapon to have any affect on it? Upon contemplating that he was hoping this was maybe just a bad dream and he would wake from it soon. So he positioned the magazine at the base of the hand grip and with a vigorous thrust plunged it in, and tucked it in his waist band and returned the empty strong box to the hallway closet shut the door and made his way upstairs to dreadfully engage in what was to become his latest newfound activity, ... sleeping with one eye open.

Mourning subsequently arrived and Crandall street found itself amid a cool breezy sunlit Indian summer day, that was ushered in by the resonating chirps of birds and crickets. Aside from the dawning of yet another seemingly typical day, it was one marked by small bands of people milling about and discussing the strange and eerie noises and the few disturbances resulting in disheveled property spilling over from the previous night. This was the urgent and pressing topic among the few neighborhood busy bodies and locals organizing their own instigations and of whom couldn't resist starting trouble when and where ever possible. And also seemed to know everyone else's business and knew it even before they did. That particular mourning was a hub of activity encompassing various organized groups of residents or individuals probing into and conducting their own personal investigations, and questioning that which otherwise seemed out of place.

The conversation among some of the investigating locals was that of hearing strange distant bellowing type moans and then some unsettling noises followed by a loud crash as if a large heavy object like a large wooden basin had toppled over into a plate glass window or something. They made inquiries as to what each other or what if anything they themselves observed or heard throughout the night. There were also reports of the discovery of oversized claw like footprints throughout trounced on gardens of various residents. These sections of ground contained much richer, fertile and cultivated soil, than the usual type of ground and were more receptive to foot impressions. Someone or something had torn up the chicken coup wire fences surrounding these little individual gardens, leaving them twisted and tossed to one side. The discovery of some type of creature-ish footprints through and about served as a grim and disturbing find. And at this stage of the game local authorities were not yet notified or implemented, and a couple groups of locals were systematically probing the neighborhood looking for objects that would potentially link any further physical evidence to these strange and inexplicable occurrences of the night before.

Some garage and basement windows had been smashed out, garbage cans had been overturned and the contents had been strewn about. Reports of big loud dogs barking late into the night and then abruptly ceasing were noted by those conducting this ongoing investigation. It was very windy last night and either the loud gusts drowned out much of these sounds from whatever was causing such a fracas and yet residents did not find anything out of the ordinary because of that underlying factor. Well in taking into account the events that have just recently transpired Mr. Barnett no was longer going to have to worry about the possibility of appearing foolish or ridiculous to his fellow community members. Whatever it was he saw in that illuminated backdrop last night made it's presence known to others by going on some type of rampage unnerving residents and causing disturbances. And it directly instilled in him a palpable sense of terror. Now there was physical evidence to substantiate any theory or conjecture one might interject into any communal discussions pertaining to these events which are more than likely a dark and immanent omen of things to come.

I've lived sixty seven years, survived action in two separate Asiatic theaters of conflict and have resided here for going on twenty-five years now and nothing even remotely resembling this has ever happened to me or any one else I've ever known. I quit believing in monsters when I was maybe about ten and the boogie-man I think much sooner than that. There must be some rational and logical explanation for what I saw last night things like that are just not physically possible or probable in the real world. Yet in lieu of any self doubts he may have had in effectively alerting others to what he personally witnessed can now be carried off subtly and safely. And without the fear of a blind rush to judgment made in a moment of haste by those whom collectively would stand guilty of serious oversights while operating from the hastened standpoint of a mob-mentality. It's just a shame that people have to actually see something for themselves before they believe it. And the sad fact of the matter is more often then not it's too late at that point. Upon taking into account what he saw the other night it may require summoning the Army National Guard as a desperate measure. The door of an old garage had also been pushed in and sat crumpled up in the middle of the floor. And by that I mean the door where the car drives in. And amid all the chaos was the most startling and baffling finds of all. It was that of a very large German Sheppard which had been reputed to have been trained as a vicious attack dog chained to it's doghouse lying there on the ground on it's side dead with the chain pulled very tight and extended out as far as it would go. What was so innately freakish and unnerving about this discovery was that the animal was encased in some type of semi-transparent greenish blue ooze like substance that had dried overnight and at that point had the consistency of solidified, rubber.

And upon further examination one could visually note that of an open jawed, bug-eyed expression on the dogs face signifying that it had died of fright during an episode of extreme trauma. It must have seen something so utterly horrific that it caused not only its heart to stop but it's central nervous system to shut down as well…case being it just died of fright. And within the immediate proximity as well as outlying areas was a thick white milky glue like substance resembling pus or partially solidified latex house paint in streams or congealed in pooled up mounds all over the ground and emitted a strange foul odor. There were also globs of some type of other olive green blob like substance piled up and comingled with the other bizarre material found in the area as well it's just freaky and moreover it gives me the willies. Yet as local residents came together in their mutual and disorganized attempts to make some kind of sense of what ran amok late into the night leaving these freakish discoveries, and the mysterious circumstances surrounding them. Yet upon this latest, baffling and ghastly find the special unit of the police were subsequently summoned for further investigation.

Tuesday afternoon Julie called Crystal to ask her if she wanted to go out later for a walk to the general store to pick up a few things and maybe watch a late night movie after that on television. Crystal said yeah I'm not doing anything this evening anyway, let me call Sherri and Todd, and see if his brother Aaron wants to come to. Julie said ok, should I call you back to see what's going on or wait to hear? Crystal said no we'll just come over there it's about four o'clock now I'll round up who else wants to go and meet you there. Julie said ok and they both hung up. About a half hour later Crystal showed up in her car with Todd and Sherri, Aaron said he had something else he had to do. Her red GTO pulled up in the driveway and the loud blub-blub-blub of a supped up four fifty seven signaled others well in advance to it's arrival. She put the car in park and turned the ignition key to the off position pulled it out and threw the jingling keys into her small black handbag. With that she flung open the driver side door extending a long slender leg and placing a dark brown leather high heeled boot seductively onto the driveway concrete. A tall very beautiful girl with shoulder length auburn hair stepped out the driver's side door. As she stood up she tossed her head to one side and smoothing her hair out of her face with one hand her thin and slight bracelets and earrings made a clinking sound. She was wearing a light brown leisure suit with a brightly colored blouse just warm enough for a cold fall evening. Her friends Todd and Sherri exited the back seat and got out of the car to accompany her up to the top of the driveway to meet Julie. Julie had come out the front door and was standing on the porch and she shouted hey guy's what's up? Todd said oh the same old stuff. Crystal said what do you want to pick up for tonight? Julie said oh only a few things for this evening some popping corn some candy maybe a pizza. Crystal asked do you wanna walk or drive there? Oh I don't know I guess I kinda feel like walking what do you two wanna do? Crystal said sounds ok to me and she turned to look at Todd and asked what do you wanna do? He said I don't care it doesn't matter to me either way. Ok let's get going now I want to get back before dark Sherri said.

With that their little group proceeded to walk toward the end of the allotment to come upon a three mile long dirt road known as Racine way. They were on their way to a little country store called Fedders market, it was just at the end of this stretch of dirt road and up past the railroad tracks. It was a combination convenience and, grocery type store with bins of various non-food household items. Along the way they engaged in an array of meaningless small talk and sporadic horseplay as they walked this scenic country side route to the store. As they were walking Sherri asked the other two girls if they were going to the Sojourn concert that was being held at the arena in the neighboring town of Davenport near Atwater. Crystal said she didn't know as she had made other prior commitments but would see if she could postpone them because Sojourn was one of her favorite bands and she'd love to see lead singer Steve Donnelly and guitarist Chris Atkins and their light rock band perform live and in person. Her and Julie went to see Armageddon and the Scallions three years ago and they had a really great time. They bought black t-shirts with the bands logo on the front as well as other band memorabilia. Julie said she'd go if she could get tickets in time as it was only two weeks off and the local ticket holder was almost out, he had to submit a requisition order form to the main distributor for re-supply, and on such short notice too, and besides all the good front row seats were gone. This posed as a real hassle in the way of meeting ticket sales deadlines and any preparation thereof. But if they really wanted to go as a group they would have to make certain personal sacrifices. And as they drew nearer to their destination the evening sun began to set superimposing a sallow orange light through a dull blue and somewhat clouded sky. The air reeked with the strong pungent odor of thick black petroleum that this dirt and gravel road was laden with. Great big huge telephone poles a foot and half wide and a hundred feet high, protruded from low lying ditch or culvert areas which ran alongside the road and embankments covered with high grass that lead to elevated vantage points which usually on looked either a cow or horse pasture or some type of cultivated farmland containing either cabbage, corn, beans, wheat or whatever. Sparse tree lines and more densely wooded areas sat back a few hundred yards from the roadside amid this crop laden acreage. And big black cawing crows circled high above seeking that next lush patch of vegetation to plunder.

The route to the general store was a scenic and picturesque one at that, a landscape artist with a canvas laden with an easel, a case of oil paints and brushes would find an over abundance of potential subject matter that would occupy his talents for a long time. As they were walking further the conversation slacked off a little bit and Todd started fooling around shoving Sherri in a playful and bumbling attempts to trip her up and knock her off balance as she was wearing knee high boots with three inch heels. He wanted to see if she could maintain her stance or if she would stumble and fall spilling the contents of her handbag onto the ground in some sort of playful bedevilment. He was one of those friends you had as kid that every so often felt an overriding need to reinforce his position as the stronger one by pushing your buttons. And would proceed to do something he knew incensed you to the point would get a rise out of you. When I was about ten I had such a friend who was bigger and stronger than I was and would on occasion wrestle me to the ground putting me in some type of submission hold whereas I couldn't move. Then he'd proceed to grab and twist various fleshy parts of my lower torso to the point at first I began laughing and then in tickling me to the cruel point of exasperating pain, expelling just about all the oxygen from my lungs until I almost passed out. One thing was for certain though is that this type of juvenile sadist isn't going to let up until they work your last nerve or you knock them out cold first. And he was doing his best at it as he was belittling and teasing her. Walk much? He taunted laughing at her all the while she stumbled around trying to maintain her balance and almost falling down in the dirty oil laden road in the process. But with his third attempt she unexpectedly grabbed his wrist and reversibly swung him around in about a half circle causing him to very much deservedly go ass over teakettle onto the dirty oil laden road himself. Sherri a little miffed, mussed and disheveled slowly regained her composure to stand upright there in the middle of the road just laughing at Todd as he sat there dumped on his keister right there in the filthy black tar for a moment his face red and flushed with an exacerbated smile on it. Just then Julie shouted will you two just knock it off before somebody really does get hurt!…Now I think you've both more than amply succeeded in wasting enough time already!! "Sherri" But he's the one who started it!!…"Julie" I don't care who started it!!…. it's getting on my last nerve and it's already starting to get dark and I want to get back in time before the movie I want to tape starts, comprenda!?… Todd just sat there with his forearms crossed over his knees with a red and white flushed expression on his face turned to look up at Julie. And then sarcastically asked, Oh yeah!,…whatta they playing tonight on late night snore bore feature eh?…Oh yeah I can only guess, is it Frankenstein the crashing bore, or maybe Wolfman the crazed insomniac, or is it that old Boris Karloff black-n-white from about a thousand years ago,…nod off in the mummy's tomb?…ha, ha, ha, ha…Hey Julie, I think their even going to run a special bonus feature tonight on your behalf!!….Count Broke-ula lurks amid the vast darkened corridors of his eerie castle because he was unable to pay his electric bill!!…..Ha, ha, ha, ha,….Julie was moderately incensed not only by his lack of openness and appreciation for the old world classics but his incessant crass comments retorted well Todd, or is it Toad? I can see you just sitting there on the edge of your bed wiling away the hours late into the night burning the midnight oil in forging those clever little gems. But I still think your full of donkey-doo just the same!!... Mine are clearly a marked improvement over that crap you waste so much time in watching on what is it? oh yeah, barf bag theatre on Saturday afternoons that you for some unknown and dull witted reason insist on being almost religiously faithful to!!...You know you outta find better ways to invest your time like maybe doing some studying to bring up some of your shitty grades!!...And as for the ponderous pulp turned out by those big third rate money-grubbing production houses that have no sense of moral fiber or obligation to their large movie patronage. And like a steady unwavering stream of hurriedly slopped together Big Mac's shoved down the figurative shoot towards end consumption into the eagerly awaiting jaws of a spoon-fed dependant movie going consumer. And then Julie wide eyed intently leered over at Todd in a cynical and lowly condescending tone stated. A hastily prepared fast food diet that specially caters to a junk food mind. Then Todd just grinned and replied as only a teenage guy would know how in a seeded parable of wisdom and insight could,...that's BortheWicke theatre for your information deary, and the fright movies they play simply kick ass!!...Julie' Oh I give up you, you're hopelessly lost to a stubbornly ignorant cause!...And with one hand he slowly thrust himself up staggering to a standing position made the vast number of keys that were attached to a large chain at the end threaded trough his belt loops made a clinking jingling sound as he composed himself. He dusted himself off as best he could with a padding slapping motion all over but the seat of his shabby jeans that were now permanently blackened from the filthy oil covered road. He jerked his head of long tufted red hair in a vigorous swift motion from one side to the other in shaking the dirt off his second hand rummage sale clothes from the little tussle with Sherri and made some sort of incensing smartass comment at the girls in rebuttal, and the group then proceeded further on their way down to the old country store.

In the time remaining it took them to finally arrive at the old country store mainly consisted of random trivial small talk and the occasional squaring off in horseplay usually between Todd and one of the girls or against two of them. He was far more comfortable in their company and interacting with them as he'd known them since grade school and they'd all been friends ever since. As yet, other guys who were unacquainted with them found themselves an insecure bundle of nerves around them and very intimidated by their imposing well above average looks, and in their company they usually found themselves fumbling and bumbling just for words. Todd asked Julie what movie she was going to watch later when they got back. And she replied it's a late night double feature on channel thirty four. The house of wax and House on haunted hill with Vincent Price. These are two classics I just love and can never see to many times. and I want to get back in time to record them on my VCR. And tomorrow night they are showing Return of the fly and The curse of the mummy's tomb with Christopher Lee and Peter Cushing. Todd exclaimed well I see I won't have to bring any pop corn along with me this evening! It's already being furnished not with those old cornball movies being the main attraction!! Julie tensed and just what is that suppose to mean you insufferable gasbag!?.. It just means that those dreary and dusty old relics of bygone centuries are more cornball then they are scary, do you have the wolf man with Lon Chaney Jr. and the mummy with Bore-us- Karloff too?, get it!… Bore-us-Karloff, in that vast movie repertoire of yours to? Ha, ha, ha, ha,…Julie' Funnee!!…well as a matter of fact I do! It just so happens that they have an intrinsic and redeeming quality that, that Freddie and Jason crap you favor doesn't!!… And besides the movies of that era held out an inward imaginative demure that catered to an inner substance that's no longer present and you just don't see in very many people anymore, and with that subtly implying statement she just stared at Todd. They held to significantly higher standards of ethics and integrity that in the end produced a finished product of impeccable quality and entertainment value, the actors of that time unlike today had class, integrity and substance. And back then they knew how to draft a great movie as they didn't have to keep making numerous sequels to reinforce or solidify their image in the publics eye. And they also didn't have to resort to such cheap tactics as gory and graphic special effects to hold and captivate their audiences either in some lame effort to fuse together a weak or poorly written movie plot or storyline. But instead they were able to draw from well written and well structured content, dialogue, and pool of actors. Todd replied; Well I can see that this argument is a stalemate that's going nowhere with no winner, well if that's how you feel honey more power to ya!!…and thanks for the long dissertation just the same, but I think I'm going stick to my leather face and Mike Myers anyway, that corny stuff you watch puts me to sleep. I think when we get back I'm just gonna go over to the bowling alley or something and play some video games. Julie replied; and those ones you favor cause my stomach to do incessant flipflops and make me wanna hurl. And I hope you get eaten up by Pac-Man!!…Todd just looked over at her and mockingly commented Ooooh, that's harsh!!…And just then a slowly approaching car proceeded to pass by them emitting a loud resonating sound burst of gravel crunching underneath it's car tires. And as it passed by Todd threw up his arm waving them on in some cynical form of mocking dissent at life and the human condition in general as if they were longstanding friends of his that he knew. And simultaneously signifying his moderate level of distain and disparagement. And upon taking momentary stock of his own inventory of personal inadequacies, with one augmented display of contention, he rendered a rhetorical salutation, as he stood there amid his small group of unmoved and somewhat fortified counterparts in figuratively thumbing his nose at the whole world. And as the car slowly passed by with it's few occupants on- looking this blatant and satirical public display of minimal distain at life, the corners of their mouths turned up while they simultaneously shook their heads back and forth signifying their mild sense of distaste at his flagrant actions.

After it had passed by the little group Todd whirled around in a half circle facing the girls took off his cap and took a bow almost expecting them to applaud his somewhat embarrassing and juvenile antics. Crystal jokingly said, we just can't take you any where can we? Sharon said why do you always gotta do stuff like that all the time? Julie said oh he's not happy unless he's pushing somebody's buttons and getting an angered screwed up reaction from someone or embarrassing us in some way when were out in public. Sharon said why didn't you just whiz around bend over and moon them while you were at it? it would've been like the proverbial cherry on the sundae. Crystal was the only one of the girls laughing said I think it's funny. Julie replied, yeah you would, well you're the only one of us who does, and will you please stop encouraging him to keep it up!!… Todd laughing and red faced exclaimed c'mon gimme a break! Ya know you guys need to loosen up a little bit why do you gotta be so stuck up and serious all the time for? They carried on aggravating tripe discussions and mild arguments over things like this for a few more miles until they approached the little country store as the sun went down and dusk set in. Externally the store itself was a somewhat shabby and uninviting sight for passersby, the small parking lot was covered by white gravel and a dimly lighted wooden sign that read Fielders Market like the rest of the building sported a grayish white twenty five year old peeling paint job, and the other outdoor lights barely provided enough light for customers at night coming into the store. The sign had a hand painted illustration of various types of vegetables like corn cobs and carrot sticks by an artist that bore a minimal degree of talent in color usage or in their somewhat feeble, amateurish attempts at depicting realistic looking produce. The stores partitioned picture window had several signs highlighting store specials and prices on the usual items it carried. A scuffed and marred up phone booth with cracked sections of glass was positioned in close proximity of the store front. And Todd would always step inside it when he and his friends were there and jiggle the coin release to see if he could inadvertently cause any coins to roll down the shoot.

The dimly lit parking lot was a dismal gloomy sight were a couple of shabby cars were sitting, one was a metallic green nineteen seventy one AMC Hornet in rough condition with rust along the edges and a dirty unkempt interior laden with beer and soda cans food wrappers and ripped vinyl upholstery, with small sections of the body with holes rusted through it. No doubt it was an employees car that worked maybe part time and made minimum wage. The car had a tacky little decal of a hornet in flight on the lower portion of both front fenders. The chrome trim the hubcaps and a big obtrusive looking gas cap located towards the back of the rear fender were all covered with pitted rust and corrosion. The dashboard was cracked and soiled and had rosary beads hanging from the rear view mirror a little plastic statue of the virgin Mary and a pink troll with green hair sticking straight up mounted to the dashboard. On the back window and trunk latch combinations were various bumper stickers a local pop station being among them. Not by any means the idea of any ones dream machine but it ran and was mechanically sound enough to get it's owner to work and back. Cars like this were typical of the working class poor and ran up until the late nineteen eighties as well as the proverbial backyard mechanic that you just don't see anymore. Like those early seventies, Ford Pinto's, Dodge Darts, Plymouth Valliant's or AMC Pacer's these cars typified the working maintained 'em themselves by way of the longhaired greasy backyard mechanic guy who had his car up on blocks pulling out the engine so he could strip it down and rebuild it's transmission. I always remember seeing guys like this next door or down the block as a kid and then as a teenager bending down with their upper body submerged in the engine compartment, the hood up and loud rock music blaring from a portable radio. I remember as the nineties approached when I was in my late twenties like the rock culture itself, just seemed to slowly dissipate from the overall landscape. The look the style the dress and the attitude itself was gone I found it somewhat sad and disheartening to see it finally go. I thought the Rock cultural icon of the time would last forever, but it didn't I don't think anyone under thirty-five even knows who Peter Frampton was. I was later on told by a friend years later that the biggest reason you didn't see that any more is that auto manufacturers started producing cars incorporating parts that backyard dick's could not work on without special and expensive tools and were positioned so that no-one other than a certified technician could access them successfully thus ushering in a new age. The other car was an eighty five corral blue trans-am in just about mint condition with a pair of blue foam rubber dice hanging from the rear view mirror. And the third car a brown seventy four Olds Cutlass and not in much better condition than the Hornet had balding tires. And as the kids entered the store they were talking and bustling about in a mild commotion as they reached the front door and whipped it open, causing a corroded old string of bells hanging from the door to make a loud clanging noise as they entered. Todd was the first one who bolted in and the girls stumbled in behind him stepping up onto the stores dusty unfinished wooden floor. The inside was dimly lit with overhead fluorescent lighting and mildly reeked of the smell of rancid meat juices that air fresheners failed to mask for very long. This was something not entirely uncommon for farmers country type markets or meat sections in large grocery stores at various times. Almost instantly Todd went over to one of three wooden bins in the frontal portion of the store that contained an array of household non food items that were on sale or at a discount. It was full of various items like potholders playing cards, multi colored candles, car fresheners pet toys like a rubber squeaky cheeseburger and fries, kitchen witch wall hangings and little knick knack type items among a vast array of other things.

Julie was over at the snack isle picking up pre-packaged bags of popping corn, jumbo sized boxes of juju fruits and you know those caramel chewy things, now what is it that they call them oh yeah, milk duds. She went through picking up as much as she could carry as she had brought her backpack with her for this purpose. As for her late night movie watching session her and the other girls were going to have, was going to require a vast array of snacking supplies.

All Todd Picked up was a package containing two bungie cords, a pine tree car air freshener and a dashboard figurine of King Kong atop the empire state building. The base location was where you peeled and stuck it to your cars dashboard or could mount on the rear dash section instead. He was going to mount it on the dash of his El Camino. Crystal and Sherri were over at the isle that had stocked a minimal quantity of light cosmetics bath soaps and lotions. Sherri said to Crystal I want to get some suntan lotion and some bath oil beads I am almost out, what do you wanna get? Crystal said I would like to look at cassette tapes but I don't think they have any thing like that here. Just then the nightshift clerk passed by and was going to do some stocking and straightening up and then Crystal asked him, do you carry either blank audio cassettes or ones that are recorded on by various artists? The clerk a slender lanky guy in his late twenties with short reddish wavy hair and glasses with acne type blemishes on his face replied, yeah I think we have some aftermarket stuff against that back wall over there. And he pointed to the back corner of the store. Sherri exclaimed my God! Don't you already have enough of that crap, how many records and cassettes do you got? Crystal said no! you can never have enough music until you ultimately have everything that's worth getting. And in answer to your shrill question I have just under three hundred. And besides I need some new stuff for the tape deck I have in my car. Then Sherri looked off to one side rolled her eyes and in a kind of sighing exhale murmured oh gees... Then they quietly proceeded in the direction the cassettes were in and after several minutes Todd said are you guys just about finished over there? I want to get back in time to play some video games before the bowling alley closes.

Crystal yelled almost!.. just gimme a few more minutes to pour over these cassettes and we'll meet ya' up front as soon as were done. Ok I'm gonna go get Julie and were going to start checkin' out I think she should be just about finished with her candy and popcorn binge excursion. As they stood there Crystal slowly turned the circular wire rack the cassettes were on surveying the various types of music it facilitated to see if she could find any contemporary rock, pop or New Wave groups or solo artists. These cassettes were known as cut outs meaning that the manufacturer had inadvertently produced a surplus amount and had to sell them at a greatly reduced price, typically three or four dollars, records too. The corner of either the album jacket or the cassette cover had a notch cut out of it by some type of punch tool and a big sticker on it that said the nice price or bargain buys.

There was some classical and country music items which didn't interest her at all and they had a lot of odds and ends which appealed to only a small segment of the music buying public like Tony Bennet, Perry Como, Jim Nabobs or Burl Ives Christmas albums. Ah yes now here we go the Pet shop boy's the Semantics and the Hotels now were talkin'...Sherri said isn't there any like New Wave in there? Crystal said I haven't seen any so far just a lot of old fogy stuff that nobody under the age of a hundred and fifty would want. Well we'd better hurry up Todd is getting antsy. Crystal well Todd is just gonna have to deal with it, I want to stay here and look just a little while longer. Suddenly Todd and Julie came over bags in hand with the stuff they had bought saying what's the holdup? Crystal said I'm just about done here the Pickens' are mighty slim, oh here we go two more Guess, and Johnny hates Jazz,... And only three dollars a piece too... Can anyone lend me a couple of dollars I have four cassettes here and have only a ten on me. Julie said yeh no problem let's just check out and get a move on I don't want to be out too long after dark and game boy over here wants to get busy with Mario and Pac-Man. As they approached the checkout station there was old man Fielder in his soiled white apron with dried brown stains from the days meat and produce juices all down the front of it. His face had an outwardly withered and tired look to it. with the tell tale signs from a life's long sentence to hard physical labor written all over it. At that point having been in his early seventies, by all intents and purposes should have retired years before. With pencil in ear and notepad in shirt pocket uttered in an exhausted wheezy voice is this everything? before he started ringing up the order on a cash register the store had used since the early nineteen fifties. The kids fumbled around gathering up what little money they had while dropping lose change and small bills onto the counter and clumsily bagging their articles in a noisy commotion to pay for them before finally exiting the store for the night.

Once outside Todd staggered a little ways ahead of the rest of the group losing his footing and tripping on the gravel and almost falling down dropping his bag on the ground and spilling out the contents. Sharon grinned and said walk much? And the girls chuckled as they walked out of the little parking lot. It was a cold creepy night under the watchful eye of a quarter moon and a black sky that was dotted with the dull illumination of distant stars. As they proceeded further on their way back home they were under the street light the occasional telephone pole had mounted to it granting them some sense of safety and security. A couple of the girls carried a stun gun or mace in their purses and Todd was known to carry a hunting knife with a five inch blade, although some of the other boys have even been known to carry small handguns in their back pockets for just such an occasion. You never can be to careful when walking along country roads at night even in the daytime in a group. As they got midway home they started walking up the little hill type mound that rose about fifteen or twenty feet up. And positioned at the top was a very high telephone poll with a street lantern fixated and mounted to it's side shedding light onto a set of railroad tracks below in a about thirty five foot circumference. Once there the kids decided to stop and take a momentary break and go through their bags surveying what they bought. Several minutes had passed when through the rustling sound of plastic bags a distant waning moan like that of an old man echoed in the distance….alone…alone… alone…alone….Just then Todd pulled his face out of his bag and looked up at the girls with a startled frantic expression on his face and said will somebody please tell me what the hell that was? Crystal her face flushed white and her eyes bugged out almost beginning to cry, I don't know? Julie said what in the name of almighty creation was that God awful sound? Sharon was standing only a few feet away from the others and was looking in the direction of the distant woods and pointing toward it saying what ever it was it seemed to be coming from that location. Whatever that ghastly droning was, it was about a mile or so away in those distant woods and if we had to, we could make a break for it in a mad dash towards our neighborhood. Several more minutes elapsed as they all stood their in a harried, frenzied state and again that ungodly blood curdling distant wane that could've easily rattled Hercules or Paul Bunyan to the shear point of utter terror leaving them quaking in their boots. …..alone…..alone…..alone……alone then something sounding almost like the cackling of a turkey buzzard at hunting season…. ballada, ballada, ballada, ballada, ballada…..Todd whirled over at the girls white faced harried, bewildered and bug eyed, exclaimed,. What in the name of god was that!! Quick, follow me we'd better make tracks!! And in a brisk and steady jog they ran the remaining distance home which was about a mile, until they came to were they were on looking the street lights of their neighborhood and as they stopped, bending over and gasping for air after what had been an exuberant dispensation of physical stamina. They breathed a collective sigh of relief, turned to each other, hugged and knew then they were at least for the time being… within the safe bounds of home.

CHAPTER FIVE

A Gruesome Discovery

THE FOLLOWING DAY THE GROUND WAS PARTIALLY OBSCURED BY SWIRLING patches of light fog close to the ground and the dusting of frost on meadows, barns and houses, the kind were by when the mourning sun came up, steam rose from it as the warm rays hit it and began thawing it out. Detective Nate Chaffee had arrived early that mourning in his office, going over to his desk to begin pouring over the previous days progress reports when just as he sat down the phone rang. After picking it up on the third ring he heard a pressing voice that resonated in an unsettling tone of urgency…Detective Chaffee! There was a short silent pause on the other end and then a deep burly male voice bellowed. Hello!?…. detective Chaffee? Speaking…is this lieutenant Hodgkin's? No this is sergeant Lotus Tillman from the Moncreef county sheriffs department. What are you doing right now? I'm having my usual cup of coffee and trying to keep from losing what little marbles I have left….Well I think you'll wanna come down here right away I'm afraid there's something you need to see…and in a terse sarcastic tone, Chaffee replied…what sound so serious for? Is it froggy the gremlin sitting on a lily pad? How about the lucky charms leprechaun waiting in a clover patch to bestow upon us a pot of gold so we can all retire early? Or maybe the flying Wallenda's are back in town for the annual circus side show. Heh, heh, heh, heh. Boy you know I've always told you, you needed to get some kind of therapy this only proves it!!…ha..ha, ha, ha…Lotus…Yeah well I think you've been spending to much time in the sauna at that health club you belong to and the steam has shriveled your brain even smaller than it already is!…Now will you kindly put a sock in it for one single solitary minute!! I'm not screwin' around here!! you intellectual turnip patch!!! This is no joke I'm deadly serious!… now you get your paunchy, gin guzzling, cigar chewing carcass over here ASAP!! and move like you gotta purpose! meet us on the edge of the ol' crabapple grove, we've got jumbo econo-sized trouble, click!! And as this large imposing man of thirty plus years with the department, first as a patrolman and then a detective just sat there in his office chair marginally dejected at Tillman's hostile unreceptive response to his jokes, listening to the phones dial tone as the color in his face slowly began to drain and he started nervously shaking with the chills. He knew something was definitely amiss as he was not usually summoned by law enforcement agencies in neighboring jurisdictions for conferment or assistance unless it was under grave circumstances requiring a conjoined effort, like investigating a homicide or capturing an inmate who'd escaped from the state hospital for the criminally insane. Whatever it was he'd surely find out soon enough, Lotus never took that tone with me unless the situation was grave. On that note, detective Nate Chaffee lifted his Five foot eleven inch two hundred and seventy five pound body from his reclining office chair put his coat on shoved a note pad in his front pocket and stuck an unlit cigar in his mouth as he headed for the door.

As detective Chaffee made his way to the detectives parking garage across the street a deluge of unsettling thought prospects flooded through his head as to what disparaging situation lay ahead requiring such immediate attention from this outlying law enforcement agency. Once he came upon his big brown nineteen seventy eight Buick Le Saber in the deck he pushed the key in the door unlocked it and flung it open plopping his stocky and imposing frame into the drivers compartment. He set the spinning flashing colored police light on the dashboard of his unmarked car, lit the Churchill sized cigar he had in his mouth, and hastily turned the key in the ignition and starting it with the third turn of the key, putting the car in drive and sped towards the scene. The way there was a nervously anticipated rush to judgment with passing cars swerving out of his way and attempting to pull off to the side of the road before his unmarked unit picked them off as he blew by with his lights flashing and no siren. This had better be good or he was going to blast Tillman for his earlier bipolar rants on the phone. Sheriff Tillman and he had been friends for years as they had gone through the academy together, but in recent years that friendship had become somewhat strained due in part by a whole host of adverse factors that existed that led to departmental instability such as cutbacks in personnel or state funding, and those of seniority languished in their positions as they were passed over for promotions or advancement by younger more aggressive and less qualified or experienced applicants with far less time in the field than their mentors. The department as a whole found itself in the midst of an unruly transition as young rookies to the academy served as subtle haughty, crass and arrogant elements of upheaval. This was not outwardly forthright but indirectly toward their superiors but whose blatant deviation from instituted rules on discipline. They demanded strict adherence to it's guidelines on the part of applicants to departmental rules and regulations as duly specified articles outlined in the police manual. Thus bringing full circle a range of ongoing investigations to those pending regarding standard protocol in maintaining professional conduct displayed in interrogations of alleged suspects should be nothing short of just seeking the truth excluding the use of entrapment or coercive techniques. A belief still held by many old timers.

Any level of noncompliance on the part of prospective applicants should be met with swift and decisive action. I already know of several others guilty of similar infractions by those not only my own departmental unit, but those of deputy sheriff Harthgrove's branch as well. They were brought up on the proverbial carpet and held under the intense light beam of scrutiny and formally reprimanded, by the office of internal affairs. Others were even demoted or discharged from their respective ranks. Deviations from departmental guidelines were not only commonplace but were regarded as intolerable by it's overseers and they set in motion a detrimental chain of effects such as erosions in self discipline that also led to nonuniformity and order to what should otherwise have been a finely tuned and well oiled machine. Thusly displacing it's respective members of the rank and file of the department, and impeding it's overall performance as a whole at basic efficiency levels. And as an indirect result set in motion a downward spiral of events having a detrimental effect to these local law enforcement agencies as a whole, reducing the effectiveness at it's sole primary purpose of function, that of insuring the public's safety and security in subduing and apprehending those whom engage themselves in criminal activity and pose a menace to society. Thus fourth diminishing in a larger sense, confidence and trust in the publics mind. Aside from the departments desperate need for realignment and total overhaul. He found himself preoccupied with impending family and personal problems that had only served to drive a wedge into their longstanding friendship.

As he was exiting interstate thirty three and coming off the highway onto Eldenwile road for about a mile then onto the dirt and gravel road known as Racine way he traveled adjacent for a short distance along the apple grove. He didn't have to drive very far before he'd come upon a scene of mass pandemonium he saw hoards of plainclothesed and uniformed officers pouring over a small area not visibly clear from a distance as there were men standing around obscuring what it was that was the center of all the attention. But from what he could make out it was a somewhat confused and panicked one. He could also discern the dazed and bewildered expressions on some of their contorted faces frantically milling about like some type of flustered bee-hive conferring with each other. The object that held every ones attention was something that was so horrifically evident and baffling in nature. As he pulled off to the side of the oil laden cinder road he was suddenly overwhelmed by a feeling of dread that he couldn't suppress within himself as he immediately sensed something of a serious nature was immanent. It was also very apparent that the scene was emotionally charged. The open ground was littered by marked and unmarked units with flashing lights going, and the multiple mixed sounds of radio dispatchers from police units filled the air. And that upon further observation one could tell were haphazardly positioned when officers exited them in haste to diverge on the scene. The closer he got to the focus of all the chaotic attention he began to see at first small bands of news reporters hovering around the detectives and asking them questions. They aimed their cameras downward as the intense light of flashbulbs going off slightly illuminated the immediate vicinity.

Men many of them seasoned investigators, large and physically imposing emerged from a group of detectives patterned in a semi circle around something that was laying in the field. Apparently they had just seen something so ghastly that they were coming away with flushed and mortified expressions on their faces. Suddenly he began to feel within himself a sickening uneasiness coupled with confusion and an elevated level of awareness he acutely sensed from fellow law enforcement personnel frantically canvassing the scene. And one were time itself had almost stopped, he felt as if a cold tightening band chilling and terrifying wrap itself around his forehead and his stomach began to wrench itself up into unnerving knots. The muffled voices of fellow law enforcement officers audibly loud but not deafening rang in his ears. He was experiencing similar physical symptoms as one would who had just been in a serious car accident and was in a traumatized state of shock. He made no initial inquiry to fellow officers as to what was going on as he nervously just went over to observe it

As he apprehensively proceeded to walk through the little gathering of note taking officers to examine first hand for himself the source of what it was that had rattled every ones cages, he gently pushed by them to get a close look at what all the commotion was over. His eyes cast themselves down in a stupefying gaze at the body of what seemed to be an older man in his early to mid sixties dirty unshaven, tattered and shabbily dressed homeless transient with empty bottles of cheap liquor strewn about. This was not the first time he had, had to arrive on the scene to investigate a dead body that was discovered. But what had held these collective investigative units totally aghast was the fact that the body was encased in a semi transparent bluish green like material that solidified itself into what could only be described as rubbery. It would appear through this gel like substance that his face was flushed white with a bug eyed expression on it and contorted up in abject horror, as if he'd seen something so abominable it caused his heart to stop and he died of fright. It was almost like a giant oozy cocoon of goop had somehow been poured on this poor devil totally immersing his entire body in a some freakish bluish green rubberized coffin. There was also some black tar like substance in blobs varying in size and density around the body and outlying vicinity. And out a little distance further the discovery of a thick white pasty material resembling bird doo was made. It was in streams or in pools, it hung from trees in and around in the apple orchard and surrounding fields. Upon digesting this ghastly find and contemplating the possibilities of it's full potential, detective Nate Chaffee was suddenly overcome by his own perceptions surrounding the grisly circumstances by which that poor man met his demise. His eyes then bulged out of his head and his face exhibited the colors of the American flag one at a time as his cheeks and tongue protruded outwardly in a sickening fashion. He slightly bent over grabbing his stomach with one of his burly hands and with the other pushed fellow officers out of his way as he swiftly walked a comfortable distance away bending over to hurl repeatedly into the high weeds at the edge of the apple orchard.

Just then Sheriff Tillman went over to him as Chaffee was slowly attempting to regain his composure and stand upright. Lotus put his hand on one of his shoulders and with a concerned worried expression on his face said, Are you alright? What in the name of God was!!... …..I don't know…. we've all been trying to figure that out all day. Tillman a big statuesque man of six four with short black wavy hair slowly escorted Chaffee from the weed covered embankment back into the vicinity of the apple grove for further discussion. Chaffee almost crying and visibly shaken asked was there anybody else? No…he's the only one we've found so far these hobo's tend to inhabit in these remote outlying areas after panhandling in town, building makeshift camps and hopping freight trains that inadvertently pass by. They live pretty much come see come sigh lives and nobody misses them when they're gone. Then Nate asked what in the hell did that? Again I don't know I've already had that question put to me a hundred times already, by reporters and fellow officers alike. I've never seen anything remotely like this in all my Twenty plus years in law enforcement. I've already received frantic calls the past three nights in a row from a number of unnerved residents in that run down housing section past the rail road tracks. Calls came into my office late one evening reporting strange waning like moans coming from distant wooded areas punctuated by what sounded like the loud cackling heckle of a turkey buzzard, it's inexplicable and totally bizarre. I went out there a couple of times at night to investigate it for myself and found nothing. Chaffee…I heard they found a big German Sheppard in a similar state about a month ago but I didn't believe it and I didn't go into any particulars regarding it. I basically blew it off as a load of bilge water. Tillman…well now you know the particulars and can see for your self it's not. Chaffee.. By the way who's leading this investigation? Tillman, lieutenant Ross Dunbar from the Moncreef county investigative unit followed up by captain Bruce Furman directly under him. He's not from around here is he? I've never heard of him. No… he's from Chicago he's a good man with an impeccable record, he served on the violent crimes task force there for several years. Just then a tall, lanky and nerdy looking reporter wearing a long trench coat and thick black rimmed glasses, pen and notepad at the ready to start journalizing any details he could potentially exact from those law enforcement surveying this frantic and chaotic scene asked Sheriff Lotus? Any comment as to what you think that green ooze encasing the body of that man or what that other God awful looking goop was that was found strewn everywhere else? Lotus…at this point no, your guess is as good as mine, we are now in the process of taking samples for lab testing and analysis and will keep you posted as to any significant findings. With that the reporter shoved his pen and notepad in his upper coat pocket and abruptly turned away. He made his way in the other direction in a feigned and contrived attempt to randomly illicit facts from other unsuspecting officials. Chaffee… So what are we gonna do now? Lotus…at this point, exercise undue caution and do whatever it takes to insure against the prospect of a sharp rise in the mortality rate among the local residents. Take the initial steps it's gonna require to safeguard ourselves as well as the community at large against whatever this is without sparking a mass panic. We'll slowly bring people into a communal sense of awareness of their surroundings without causing undue alarm. We'll send out subtle little signs for warning those to keep their doors and windows locked at night, and we'll place an emphasis on crime prevention, instructing them not to venture out after dark for any reason. Kind of like slowly lifting a veil off of a persons face so they don't have a total meltdown before they actually see the monsters face. Chaffee on looking Tillman with a dull gaze in his eyes and his bottom lip pursed slowly nodded his head as he was taking this all in. Even if it's to the general store for a late night snack, any and all such activity will be strictly prohibited. And until we as members of this combined task force can get a line on just what's going on, this will be the law. We'll implement a nine o'clock curfew so that no one will be allowed out after dark for any reason. Furthermore any one who is deemed in violation thereof will be apprehended, and subject to arrest and incarceration. And in the for seemingly unlikely event this thing whatever it is, does somehow manifest itself to us in the physical sense. We would be able to deal with it on a moreover one on one basis in an open type forum. Don't divulge to much of anything to a probing and inquisitive public at this point, we still have to obtain more physical and concrete proof to the grim possibility there exists an ever present and viable threat to the local population. For the time being regular uniformed officers will assist us in our efforts in making intelligent assessments supporting any further findings down the line. Chaffee…is that all for now? Lotus… for the time being we've got to as much and wherever possible maintain the status quo. I also want to establish a direct line of communication in and among all surrounding agencies to be on full alert. With this Chaffee put his arm around his long time friend and gave him a parting handshake before getting back in his car.

Then as all the investigating teams some placing their note pads back into the upper pockets of their suit coats or lighting up big fat cigars got back in their police units and at varying intervals and proceeded to slowly extricate from the scene. In the midst of all this a big cream colored early nineteen seventies wagon like van pulled up to the location of where the body was and there where two officers were standing by to meet them. There was a red police like rotary light mounted on the roof and it was marked Moncreef county coroner on the rear upper portion of the cab on both sides. When it finally reached the scene in question it came to a stop and the doors flung open. Just then the two occupants in white hospital garb jumped out went over to the body for the grim and unwavering task of dispatching it. Together both orderlies picked it up and placed it in a rubber bag, zipping it closed placing it on a collapsible metal gurney conjointly raising it up and wheeling the stretcher into the back of the wagon. As they slammed the back doors closed, symbolic to what had by now become only a routine exercise. And one that had been done numerous times prior at the scenes of bad car accidents, suicides, accidental deaths and the like. Yet one could surmise that these practitioners of death were not only of a morose demeanor but detached to such a degree that they themselves had become almost as dead as the corpses they retrieved. And at this point in time, the sight of the graphic and grisly conditions they frequently found the human body in, have rendered them innately desensitized and undaunted. The cadaver retrieving paddy wagon were among the few remaining vehicles left at the scene and which were still caught up in the finalization end of processing the scene. There were still a few plainclothes officers milling about attempting to tie up any loose ends to conclude their obligations here to dissemble and disperse for the day. And as the evening sun started to set casting out it's sallow yellow orange-ish light against the motley shaped low lying clouds. All that one could say for this particular day is that it yielded many unsettling possibilities but few answers

CHAPTER SIX

A Hideous Face In The Window

THE NEXT MOURNING IN THE INDIGENT SECTION OF HOUSES LOCATED on the other side of the railroad tracks known as Washburn Haven, was a seventy two year old retiree leftover from one of the long since disbanded textile mills named Homer Griswold whom sat on his dilapidated old porch somewhat dirty, unshaven in a sleeveless t-shirt, to began his daily ritual of sipping a mourning cup of coffee, reading his newspaper, lighting up a cigar and loitering there well into the evening. Yet while opening it up to glance at the front page heading of the Wednesday's edition of the Moncreef County Examiner. He sat the paper down next to his coffee and ash tray sitting on the small shabby old wooden table next to him. The front page heading jumped out and grabbed his attention, Body of local homeless man found in apple grove yesterday afternoon encased in solidified green ooze. Upon reading this startling and unnerving headline he immediately began calling out to neighbors who were outside standing close by or the few others who may have been out on their porches as well. Hey did you see the front page of today's paper?!! One older lady in her sixties named Gertrude Hawks, said no and I haven't been able to see or hear at any news broadcasts yet on television or the radio either. I've been busy all mourning washing clothes. He then picked up the newspaper turned it around so she could see the headline. And as she stood on her front porch her face became flushed turning white and with a bug eyed expression she exclaimed, What in the name of Mary Anne Sikes is going on here?!! Just then a number of other residents adults and children alike came over and stood congregating and discussing it amongst themselves after citing the disturbing front page headline of the days paper. Did anyone else see the news last night? One guy yelled out. said they found something in a field but didn't divulge many details as to what it was. No... I had to work last night this is the first I've heard of it another resident chimed in. What could've been responsible for that green boogerish ooze they found, another lady resounded. Maybe it's just a group of local teenage pranksters another man said. A prank!!involving a dead hobo? another man loudly said....well maybe they found him like that and decided to pull some sort of sick and twisted joke on the rest of us by encasing him in that rubbery stuff and leaving him there in the apple orchard where someone would find it? C'mon I didn't just fall off a turnip truck!..that's pretty far fetched if you ask me. Then where would somebody get the substance that they found that hobo or the big German Sheppard encased in a month before then? You can get liquid latex in many hardware and arts and crafts stores as well as a number of mail order warehouses it's not that hard. So what your trying to say is that this is just some type of sick joke perpetrated on us by a local group of misguided youths? And Dusty Moors a tall lanky girl in her late teens who lived in a run down trailer house nearby...We'll what else would you say it was? Some sort of monster? Cameron Dillard a large stocky guy in his mid thirties with thick black wavy hair paused momentarily leering over at Dusty and murmured, well maybe...Don't tell me you believe in little green monsters now...And after a brief pause. he intently rolled his eye's her way and with a fixed glare nonverbally answered her question. Awwww God you've gotta be kidding!! This is just great!! Hey listen everybody!! Cameron here says it's the boogie man what do you all think? Ha-ha-ha-ha-ha-ha-heh-heh-heh ohhh boy. Hey if were gonna be stalked by a monster couldn't you come up with something a little more original like the creature from beyond or the crawling eye? I feel like I'm in one of those low budget sixties B rated monster movies Super host played on his Saturday afternoon double feature in the seventies!!.. Hey everybody better grab what essentials you can and head for the hills!!, Cameron here say's were about to be attacked by giant tomato people or maybe a giant one eyed Cyclops!! Ha, ha, ha, ha,…as the little group looked on….hey!…am I on candid camera or something? Just then her face turned red as a beat when she bent over grabbing her mid section laughing figuratively thumbing her nose at Cameron. Then he tersely exclaimed ok that'll be quite enough! I… that's right it will be quite enough!!… And I for one am not in the least bit amused!!… enough time wasted standing around here even remotely considering the outlandish possibility of some type of night stalking creature that doesn't exist!!.. lurking in the shadows waiting for it's next victim. I quit believing in the boogie man I think when I was about eight and the tooth fairy even sooner than that. And unless your really just yankin' our chains put a lid on it!! OK!!…it's completely and utterly preposterous for me as well as a group of supposedly full grown adults to stand around here entertaining such foolish and outlandish notions. Ok that's it!! If you don't want to be part of the solution, and not the problem in weighing all the possibilities in a free and open forum. You are more than welcome to excuse yourself from the rest of the group, nobody's stopping you!! but this is not going to turn into a heated debate over the present issues just because you don't like some of the proposals. And furthermore don't just stand there ridiculing and belittling those of us whom are serious about this. If you can't find it in within your self to put forth a concerted effort to arrive at an accurate conclusion based on the physical evidence as it presents itself, then quit wasting our time!…your input is no longer needed here COMPRENDE'. And needn't I remind anybody here in this group this is no laughing matter… we could in all seriousness be in grave danger!! I can't emphasize that enough!! We need to come together to safeguard ourselves from whatever did that to that man they found in the field and form a united front. Dusty, And just who appointed you lord and master? Cameron said… I did.. Are there any objections? Then he panned out at the sullen and bewildered expressions on their faces and was not rallied by any opposition. Good, I thought, as much as you can see your out voted I hate to be downright rude in all but…. take a hike. And on that note, the tall slender nineteen year old girl with long flowing auburn hair stood back in quiet recompense shaking her head back and forth, and contemptuously replied fine… but until you come up with a more sensible, mature and realistic possibility for me to consider, This is gonna have to be it for me, but I won't be party to any speculative nonsense based on some false pretense or half-assed hunch that will probably lead up to some hair brained witch hunt. And with that contentious speech she turned and walked away from the rest of the group. Then at that moment Cameron sort of appointed himself head spokesman of this newly found yet amateurish task force heading discussions in, and organizing as to what possible courses of action could be taken in safeguarding the immediate. His disheartening gaze fell out among this almost pathetic and disproportioned group of his peers that stood before him and he said if there's anyone else that feels the same way Dusty did now's your chance to back out.

There was a brief pause and then Cameron stood there with a wry look of anticipation on his face as if he almost expected to see one or more of them break ranks and answer with a resounding yes. And follow in the footsteps of their fellow neighbor Dusty. But he was only met by the blank and bewildered stares on many of their faces, almost as though they were looking to him for the next boldly stated directive. And as he sat on a set of rickety dilapidated old porch steps awaiting a response from this ill formed volunteer posse 'of misfits and malcontents which mainly comprised of prepubescent boys old men and middle aged women. He was determined to undertake a no nonsense approach in his newfound leadership of this pathetic little group. It was beginning to look more apparent that this was going to be a prelude to something that was going to culminate into some sort of fiasco. Ok then nobody else thinks I'm some kind of half baked jack-ass then…don't all jump at once.

I can see right now I've got my work cut out for me. Alright everybody the first item on the agenda is going to be in getting more competent and physically capable members. Does anybody here have access to a firearm!?…He waited for a response from the group but none came…then he muttered wonderful I guess I am the only one who does so far. Well we've dropped the deadweight anyway I guess that's a start. You kids need to talk to some of your dads… we need to get more men in the group that have a strong sense of keen insight.

We need to first and foremost form a neighborhood watch. Be aware of your surroundings especially at night as well as in seeing anything suspicious or hearing any strange noises. After somewhat fuddled and disorganized discussion amongst themselves. Initially it became almost a small and random misdirected lynch mob that at first, it's members weren't sure as to who or what they should seek out. But with the stern guise of a distinguished presiding judge Cameron figuratively lowered the gavel in any misdirected energy from the group in this outdoor venue bringing a semblance of order. Upon the abrupt departure by one of it's disgruntled former members the small order continued to struggle with proposed resolutions to resolve the disturbing and perplexing events that transpired in previous days.

Later that night a sullen tone was set to the run down and deteriorating stretch of houses. The greenish blue light of the moon highlighted the characteristics of the unkempt tattered and debris strewn landscape of the properties in and around the immediate vicinity of the old dilapidated structures in the area. This seemed to make appear that the presence of this yard clutter was even more pronounced at night than in the day. The twinkle of distant overhead security lights and shadows out lining dilapidated pastoral fences and barns lent themselves to a cryptic and somber mode to the casual observer as one also gazed upward to patchy swirling smoky clouds against a night sky partially obscuring the moon accentuating the mood with dull light of distant stars. The setting was much like that it was in the day you heard the loud resounding nuisance bark from a chained up or fenced in dog. Or that of a paunchy middle aged guy loitering around on his back porch smoking a cigarette or slowly nursing a can of beer while taking out a bag of household trash silhouetted against the dim overhead light of an old back porch fixture. This sort of mild bustling activity was typically carried on by residents until ten or eleven o'clock or until they went to bed. Myrna Langley and her boyfriend like clockwork kept their usual scheduled biweekly meetings of watching old movies on UHF's late night feature in the days before cable television.

This was accompanied by unprecedented sessions of mass junk food consumption, beer drinking, and smoking. This usually culminated in contrived, and pointless petty bickering and sniping. These pervasive and ongoing factors of their dysfunctional and unhealthy to most, relationship typified longstanding interactions between these two crude and abrasive people for the past several years. It was not only an arrangement of convenience but one of co-dependence and one that came to be relied upon basically because nobody else would have either one them. These outlying characteristics seemed to reinforce some of those leftover stereotypes from the nineteen seventies of rough and surly type people who worked in factory jobs or were on welfare that commonly resided among others like themselves, and relegated to living in trailer type housing parks, that for recreation frequented, bowling alleys, pool halls, and habitually getting into brawls in truck stops or in seedy bars in low ends of towns.

That night in the back of her house the yard clutter was accentuated by the dull glow of incandescent moon light almost giving off the impression there was more present in the poorly fenced in yard than there actually was. In the back of her old wooden trailer was a row of three garbage cans lined up under a rear kitchen window amid other scattered debris. Then suddenly a looming shadow slowly crept along the ratty, scraggly and patchy yard up toward the row of trash cans and stopping when the upper torso portion of the figure overlapped the top of the cans. The outline of the shadow had the appearance of a large bull or a Chinese Dragon but stood upright on two limbs it had a stocky body and notably big thick Billy-goat like horns protruding from the top of it's head that extended upwardly and curled around in a backward fashion. The shadow stood there fixated against the upper portion of the trash cans and against the side of the house for several minutes before subsiding in the same visually creepy reverberating manner as it did when it encroached.

The foyer section of Myrna's trailer home was dirty adorned with shabby tan, red and brown multi-colored low cut carpeting with a cracked, sallow colored, deteriorating, plastic transparent runner for wiping one's feet in the entrance way, a small umbrella stand sat by the front door. And a poorly installed light fixture mounted to the wall between a bathroom and the kids room off to the side was all there was and when it was on gave off a minimal amount of light in the small hallway adjacent to the living room. Smokey's arrivals were more often than not, loud, boisterous, uncouth and unannounced as he frequently as in many times past staggered onto the porch beer can and lit cigarette in hand banging on the front door repeatedly demanding entrance or sometimes inadvertently bursting in. And frequently driving home his point by a steady stream of barely audible broken obscenities. This particular night was no exception, he stood on the front porch of this modest little house pounding on the front door in yet another drunken, disoriented stupor fumbling around in his pockets for keys and inadvertently dropping loose change and a pocket knife onto the porch deck. Aggravated, and worried he may disturb the two girls sleeping in bed or in one of the back bedrooms she went over to the front door and flung it open. Smokey had his arm raised about to pound again on the door but there was nothing there prompting him to almost topple over with that last swing. Will you pipe down!! Myrna exclaimed… they can hear your big mouth all the way at the other end of the allotment!! what do you have your balls in an uproar over this time.

Smokey stood there swaying back and forth in the doorway wearing a black sleeveless muscle shirt, arms covered with various tattoos and a pair of old faded ripped jeans. He had a beer can and a lit cigarette in one hand and a stupid, dorky, grimaced expression on his face. Myrna abruptly grabbed his wrist and forcefully yanked this wiry little man forthright. Get your ass inside before the neighbors call the cops. As he stood there on the verge of collapsing he slurred the words you know if I wasn't so wasted I'd kick your ass. The immediate air was resonated with the smell of previously smoked pot coupled with alcohol breath and a body that was in need of a hot shower and a perfumed bar of soap. Ya!! you and what army?

Myrna sharply replied…Go sit your ass down over there on the sofa while I go check on the kids, do you think you can manage to keep quiet long enough for me to do that? He slowly stumbled his way through the poorly lit living room to collapse down on the couch and prop his dirty cowboy boots on a coffee table strewn with displaced pages from newspapers, cigarette butts, candy wrappers and other debris. The living room walls of this shabby little abode were outfitted with those old black out posters sometimes featuring a woman's head or maybe a unicorn superimposed by some type of surreal celestial imagery like a moon with a face and stars. And when you turned off the light portions of them glowed in the dark. These tacky home furnishings were further enhanced by a cheap nineteen seventies simulated wood grained paneling that was usually warped in places and a gaudy bronze colored aluminum wall clock from the nineteen sixties that hung on the wall that supposedly simulated the sun and it's rays.

After seeing to the girls and getting them settled in Myrna stood in the lit entrance way portion of the living room. To cast an angered gaze down at Smokey lying half passed out on the couch with his feet propped up on her drab beat up coffee table and barked git yer friggin' gunboats off of there this isn't a barn!…that's why all my stuff looks like shit!! And with one arm across his right calf in a brisk sweeping motion flung his legs off to one side onto the floor. This action prompted his upper body to rise up momentarily to a sitting position but due to his highly intoxicated state he just fell back against the sofa half asleep. If she had done something like this to him in a more sober condition she would have born the brunt of a more physical response from him and it would've more than likely hurt. She grabbed the T.V. remote and turned it to the all night movie channel and told him sit here I'm going to the kitchen for some popcorn and sodas. The T.V. sat on a small entertainment center with a stereo system on the shelf underneath it at the far end of the room in front of a big picture window divided into three individual sections of aluminum framed window housing. The sofa sat at the other end of this long room and was the only thing other than two other chairs to sit on.

The room was dark and the only other source of light aside from the glow from the T.V. being on was that of a lamp which sat in the corner of the room adjacent to the picture window which was off. As Myrna re-entered the room bearing a substandard quality of makeshift refreshments including popcorn candy and off brand sodas for the evenings set viewing activities. When she approached the sofa to place the foodstuffs down on an end table she was aggravated to see Smokey lying there passed out and asleep on her sofa. Well I can see your not going to be much company for me tonight, I guess I'll get all these goodies for myself then. She held up the remote to that old early nineteen seventies Zenith color T.V. with it's dull, sallow and crude picture quality and one which weighed a good two hundred pounds or so to the one who had to lift it. There were two movies that they played late into the night in succession of one another On the waterfront with George Raft and Marlin Brando, and The Maltese Falcon with Humphrey Bogart, Peter Lorrie and Mary Astor. This station ran a variety of these old films usually on Saturday nights of each week starting at ten pm: and going on until three or four in the mourning until the station went off the air and there was a test pattern. Myrna sat there alone as her counterpart soundly slept there on the sofa beside her. She sat there with a dazed glare in the semi darkened room under the bluish glow of illumination emitted by the television screen greedily consuming a miss matched variety of junk food snacks as Bogey portrayed a crude rough around the edges private investigator in this peculiar old movie having a somewhat absurd theme and nonsensical plot. That of which centered around a carved wooden statue of a bird that purportedly had the basis for great monetary value attached to it.

After about an hour or so she not only began to feel a little drowsy but totally bored with the movie. She'd stuffed herself with all the chocolate Twinkies, stale chips and popcorn she could cram into her Five foot two inch one hundred and five pound frame and was just about ready to crash right there beside Smokey on the sofa as her eyelids began to feel heavy and she wasn't sure just how much longer she was going to be able to keep them open. That's when she noticed a dark silhouette in the corner of the picture window at the far end of the room in back of the T.V. She didn't see it at first but now just took notice of it. It had the outline of a bull or a Chinese dragon or something and you could just barely make out the faint image of eye whites in the region of the head area. She was startled at first and her heart began to palpitate as she sat there trying desperately to come up with a rational explanation for what she was looking at. It's got to be that old rose bush that is located there as who or what could possibly be leering at me through my window at this time of night. She sat there for several moments contemplating with great apprehension as to whether or not she should get up go over there and turn on the lamp and see just what it is. Her curiosity took over as she came to the logical conclusion that there were no such things as monsters and that, Where the wild things are was just a children's pictorial story book fraught with creative and imaginative renderings. As she got to where the lamp was located in the darkened room she fumbled around for the switch and turned on the light to look at what was peering in the window from the outside. She was immediately met with a surreal image of abject horror. It was the face of a creature which resembled that of a Chinese dragon with thick huge protruding horns like that of a ram or a Billy goat located on the top of it's head just behind a set of large mottled mutated ears. It almost had the appearance of a gremlin with dark gray, wrinkled and leathery skin with warts and abrasions all over it. It's nose was like a gnome nose almost human like warted and curled around at the end. The mouth was wide long and toothy and gave off the impression of the front end grill of a late forties or early fifties car. It had broken rib like bones protruding from the top of it's head and on it's back. And finally two what looked like big seashells on the top portion and sides of it's head. As Myrna stood there in mortal terror unable to move and frozen in her tracks. She looked into the fixated gaze of this thing that was peering into her window from outside. What added to her heightened level of terror was that all else was dark with the exception of the monsters face in the window illuminated by the lamp. And to further compound this was she suddenly realized that if this thing could peer into this particular window from outside it had to stand in excess of Six and a half feet tall.

Just then she let out a blood curdling scream that reverberated throughout the house. She immediately screamed Smokey,!! Smokey!! Go into the closet and get the shotgun. It was an old moss burg four ten her father gave her for protection. As she ran over to the closet to retrieve the scatter gun from the closet in the hall area next to the kid's bedrooms, Smokey suddenly awoke from a dead sleep to the panicked and frenzied state of his chosen life's partner as she ran screaming through the house. He sat up in a semi disoriented state rolling the knuckles of his balled up fists in his eye's and chimed up what the F's going on? Just then she came back into the room with the barrel of the old scattergun pointed toward the window and she yelled,.. look there bonehead!! He visually panned over toward the direction of the picture window and noted the horror leering in at them like some mutated peeping Tom. The whites of this things eyes intensified as it's gaze became more fixated and it's his head began to slowly sway from side to side. It's Cheshire cat like grinning, with mouth pursed as it's vile little tongue jutted in and out. Holy shit!! Smokey exclaimed… what the hell is that!! She took steady aim as she was only going to have two shots from this old breach gun. With her body surging with massive adrenalin flow she cut loose with one load of buckshot in the vicinity of the creature. The picture window shattered and the glass flew everywhere, this was coupled with the sound of loud barking dogs and lights from neighboring houses suddenly being turned on. This thing let out a blood curdling scream as a thousand bb's tore through it's body. Ballada!! Ballada!! Ballada!! Ballada!! It screamed bloody murder as it reeled from the shotgun blast. Then it just stood there momentarily idle with the sound of hissing and mild smoke billowing out from all the entrance wounds on it's gnarled and grotesque body. Then something resembling a milky substance like white paste or bird doo-doo oozed out trickling downward and then a thick black tar like material superseded it slowly rising upward and bubbling over giving off the illusion of closing off and healing all visible entrance wounds. Holy shit it healed itself!! Shoot it in the head, See if it can heal itself from that!! blow it's friggin head off!! Here gimme the shotgun I'll do it!! You might miss!!

But just as Smokey rose up off of the sofa to relieve Myrna of the old scatter gun this thing began emitting an olive green gooey blob like substance from various orifices on it's vile form in heaping piles all around it.

Then it's stark eye's took on a light greenish intense glow as it opened it's grisly mouth real wide and emitting a lion like roar as a bluish green ooze gushed out like a river from it's wide open mouth into the room in some freakish boogerized meltdown. Initially it had an incandescent glow but the light subsided after it finally covered the two unfortunate victims as it streamed out in massive amounts. This bizarre material totally enveloped the two victims and flooded the entire living room as you saw their bodies enmeshed in and struggling to get free from this grotesque and freakish substance that totally enveloped the two of them, until it had finally solidified itself and encasing them in a rubberized tomb when all movement on both of their parts finally ceased.

CHAPTER SEVEN

Horrific Scene The Following Morning

THE NEXT MORNING WAS CHILLY. THE GROUND WAS COVERED WITH A moist wet dew and the surrounding air was permeated with a patchy swirling light fog as the sun was rising. A couple of heavy set men in their forties stood milling about the immediate area of the smashed out picture window dawned in sallow yellow trench coats, intently gazing up at the damaged area and making periodic entries in small hand held note pads while surveying the damage and assessing the scene. What do you suppose happened here? One of the men said to the other. I don't know I've never seen anything like this before in my Eighteen years of criminal investigative work. Who would want to break into one of these old rat traps? These people don't own anything worth stealing. Yeah you'd have to be pretty desperate to do that huh? Yeah that's for sure... what do you make of all this? An unsuccessful Band E maybe I dunno. Hello, I'm detective Cornwall from the Clover leaf region. And I'm lieutenant Applegate from the Pontiff county regions investigative unit. Holy gees what are you doing in this neck of the woods? I don't know there's a current man power shortage and all available personnel were collectively pooled from surrounding regions to look into the nature of these strange occurrences. Has anyone filled you in on any of the strange details yet? No all I was told was that there were several bizarre and unexplainable events in this area that warranted investigative attention, and that additional manpower was to be summoned due to this areas lack of inadequate resources. At this point, a crowd of onlookers began coming out of their houses to stand there in the tar laden cinder road to gawk at these law enforcement officials and fixated in some warped sense of morbid anticipation as they began to evaluate and assess the scene in an unwavering diligence in hopes of catching sight of something horrible or gruesome. Dusty Moors was among the crowd of onlookers but her outward demeanor was not the stern, sarcastic and boisterous skeptic she was in the little gathering of just a week or two prior. She had a scared and worried expression on her face as she watched the scene from the back of the damaged rickety old trailer house unfold. Even Cameron Dillard came walking up the inclined road to see what was going on in the possible hopes of having some of his suspicions confirmed.

Just then as more and more police arrived clamoring about the scene. It began to gain a busy noise type momentum as a uniformed officer came out of the house and told the two detectives, your both wanted inside. The crowds audible tone intensified as various onlookers began pointing fingers in the direction of the busted out window in the back of the old house while innately placing one hand over the side of their mouths and secretively buzzing hushed conversation amongst themselves. As the two members of this auxiliary task force entered the living room Cornwall was totally aghast at what he saw as he walked in, and exclaimed my God!! what in the hell did this!! Applegate didn't bear up as well, his face flushed white and his eyes bugged out as he staggered backwards out the front door and putting one hand over his mouth as if he were trying to keep from hurling. The living room floor was a sea of solidified bluish green transparent ooze. It began at the point of the television stand and ran it's way to reach the sofa and coffee table on the other side of the room. In the center of the floor were the twisted bug eyed writhing bodies of Myrna and Smokey captured and immortalized in a green rubberized death mask. Smokey had an expression of abject horror with his tensely contorted body, twisted limbs and his gnarled hands clutching the stock of that old shotgun. Me and five other uniforms have been here since six o'clock this mourning and we don't know what to make of it either. What in God's name could have done that to those two people and what is that God awful green gook? And why are there the bodies of people encased in it? We've all been trying to come to some kind of conclusion to that for the past five hours, your guess is as good as mine in this instance. I've sent a sample to the police lab to have it analyzed but haven't gotten back any results yet. Have you touched it? No..no..way I don't want to go any where near it!! I will… it's hard and rubbery, superficially it feels a little greasy… Bizarre is what it is!!! How's Lieutenant Applegate holding out he didn't look so good last time I saw em'…He felt a little queasy and I think he's past out momentarily in the front there is also a couple of members tending to him now. I think he'll be alright though. Hey what's a guy gotta do to get a cup of coffee around here? Keel over!! I'll have one of my men bring you one detective…I'll say one thing your sure gonna have your work cut out for you here. Sergeant can we get some of those people out side to disperse? how am I suppose to get any real investigative work done if I can't even hear myself think. As the uniformed cop was exiting the doorway he barked over at the crowd of onlookers alright everybody shows over. Ya can all go home now there's nothin' more ta see!! His voice fading as he got further and further away. And just as the door was swinging closed lieutenant Applegate pushed his way through the door extending a large Styrofoam cup of hot brew in one hand to give his newfound comrade.

Cornwall's back was to the front door and his friend entering as he stood there pensively looking downward and scratching the back of his head and a pencil pursed between two curled fingers. I don't get it, I just don't get it. The intruder if there was one was outside this big picture window or how else would you explain all the shattered glass in the yard? When I was outside I overheard some of these locals telling uniformed officers that very late last night about one or two in the mourning, they heard strange cackling noises like a chicken or a turkey buzzard, and a woman screaming followed by a thundering boom and shattering glass,… which would explain the shotgun here. That's freaky…There's more….some of the others closer by said that after the loud boom they heard a creepy high pitched scream but not like that of a frightened woman but like that of someone getting stabbed or in intense pain followed by a man yelling obscenities and then a lions roar. The plot sickens eh? This is gonna keep me up all night with creepy and freakish nightmares ya know... What do you suppose this green shit is? I've never seen anything like it before in all my life. It had to have been in a pasty or liquefied form before being somehow drizzled onto these two victims and then solidifying as it dried. These two look more like they died of shock or extreme fright so much so they could hardly move thusly affording whatever this crap is a chance to dry.

Excellent deduction Holmes said Applegate wittingly, Thank you my dear Watson Cornwall retorted back with a hearty chuckle. Come over here...Cornwall finger motioned Applegate over to the smashed out window, look down there in the yard. Yeh...broken glass so what, I've already seen all that everybody has big deal Ya know I think were pretty much finis- no look down and examine the ground below the window a little closer and tell me what you see? Applegate stuck his head out the window once more for a closer examination of the ground below the window. He paused for a while and said oh yeh it's bird shit I am really sorry I missed that thanks for pointing that out I....that's not bird stuff ... What are you talking about I've been walking around on this earth for forty five years and I think I know bird shit when I see it and that's bird s- It's not bird droppings, You know how I can tell Bird droppings when I see 'em? No but I can hardly wait to hear. They take on the appearance of dried white paint or cheap window caulk when it dries and has a black outline circling a pool of it. Great we have a bird doo expert here what else are you going to tell me that this is also another unidentifiable foreign substance of a freakish nature like this green gook in here? Yes that's exactly what I am saying, I think we should cover all the bases and send a sample of this too and have the boys in the lab analyze it. If what your saying is true then there's a possibility were dealing with...with.. Some kind of monst...Say it go ahead and say it. A monster? That's freakish and I don't want to talk about this anymore today. I am going home It's already three o'clock in the afternoon and if I stay here another minute I'm gonna put in for time and half. Your just scared ...YOUR DAMN RIGHT IM SCARED....The very thought of the possibility of some thing like that existing terrifies the hell outtalk me. Now when

I go to bed tonight I'm going to try to calmly rationalize some of these bizarre events of the past several months and come back down to earth and set my two feet firmly in place and tune into the faint little voice of reason everyone else seems to have forgotten about. Then Cornwall leered over to Applegate with a bug eyed toothy grin and said. Before you turn out the light, you better look under the bed, and in the closet. Then Applegate got a bad and ominous feeling of dread and nervously replied why? Cornwall...Because one never knows where the boogie man may be hiding ha..ha..ha..ha..ha.. That's not funny... It wasn't meant to be... and through a wry leering grin he uttered the words good night in a chilling Cameron Dillard was positioned on his front porch steps facing his little group of malformed task force members organized at his behest just two weeks prior as a sort of neighbor hood watch commander moreover than an actual task type force. He sat there in a stoic gaze at his little volunteer army that served as the only immediate line of defense the little run down housing section had. And by now had increased in ranks by several men due in part of the events that transpired from the previous night. What we need to do now is designate specific duties to each member and draft some type of action plan in case of another occurrence, and there will you can bet on it, be one. And just as Cameron was about to start another sentence in his capacity as group overseer Dusty came slowly and apprehensively strolling up the oil cinder laden road towards the group. Hey everybody...look who it is!! And to what do we owe this honor...Downtrodden, Dusty raised up her head to reveal a somewhat disturbed frightened expression on her face exclaiming, can we please just skip all the goading and the I told you so's and just get on with what needs to be done here? Why Dusty how could you possibly think I'd subject a long time friend to such a petty, juvenile form of public display and indignation, especially given the nature of such grave and imminent circumstances. With a frightened and imploring look on her face she exclaimed...What the hell is going on here? Cameron said I don't know all the specifics I spoke to several police earlier this morning and was only able to get fragmented bits of information pertaining to some freakish green substance they found the bodies of Myrna and Smokey submerged in. Myrna and Smokey are dead? Yes I'm afraid so the police found them both in her trailer house at about five or six o'clock this morning. Just then Dusty put her face in her hands and began sobbing uncontrollably.

Cameron put his arm around her shoulder pulling her closer to him as two other members of the group came over in attempts to console her in a calming manner. This is like some kind of nightmare!! She hollered hastily wrenching her head up from her hands in an almost angered like sense of composure. Did you hear all that shit last night? Cameron Yeh…I got so scared I got up and threw all the deadbolt locks on my doors grabbed my .38 and sat huddled by myself in a darkened corner of my living room listening to those distant God awful sounds and the whole freakish and bizarre episode.

Dusty,.. I don't own a gun, I hate guns and just the thought of even touching one scares the shit outta me I have a big stick. Well in light of the present circumstances I think your gonna need more than just a big stick, you may have no other choice but to put your personal feelings aside for awhile and force yourself to learn how to use one. I could take you to one of these surrounding open fields around here and set up some empty paint cans and 40 oz. glass beer bottles and teach you. I don't know, I've always had an aversion to guns… I've never actually fired one you know, and to be perfectly honest with they scare me, and I hate the potential mayhem they possess. And to tell you the truth I don't want to be lumped into the same category as some flag waiving, paunchy cigar chewing old farty bozo that belongs to an elk's lodge consisting of a bunch of old blow harded gas baggers recounting their old service day's on a regular basis, and almost as a form of ritual go's bowling every weekend and holds back yard barbecues every 4rth of July and Vet's day. And doesn't feel like a complete man unless he's totin' a shootin' iron of some sort, and what's more has nothing better to do than to go out in the woods on the weekend in an old pickup truck looking for another pair of ateliers to hang over his fireplace or as another rug for his den. Cameron' whew talk about reinforcing old stereotypes! You know instead of whacking me over the head with such cliché's you should seriously consider the violence this thing whatever it is represents hah. Look what it did to our two neighbors and friends. But I don't know I…

look this won't be like that and I don't consider my self any kind of gun nut either the only thing I've ever put a hole in is a tin can. I actually found a couple of old revolvers left over from the nineteen thirties or forties in an old wooden strong box somebody forgot about and left in my cellar when they themselves moved out, they were in kind of rusted and corroded condition at the time and I had to dismantle them and sink the parts in some kind of chemical solution with an acidic base to clean 'em up. I keep them well oiled and secured in a locked strong box and only take one out late at night when I'm alone and don't feel safe. I dunno I…Do me a favor just think about it ok, I could even give you the thirty two it's an old breach loader too and is very simple to load and you could use it for protection at your house. But I live with my mother and little brother I don't think mom would like or allow it. Look things have drastically changed in the past few days she'll allow it. Or do you mom and sibling want to wind up the same way Smokey and Myrna did? She momentarily paused looking over at Cameron with an intent glare then while rolling her eyes lowly muttered no, not really, Cameron look do me a favor let me think about it first, ok? Cameron…just don't take to long, time is something I have a feeling is going to become a precious commodity in the coming weeks and months ahead.

Later on that day the run down allotments indigent gossip mongering residents were busily milling about conversing among themselves in strange disturbed reference to all the weird noises and commotion heard on the previous night. Nosey residents congregated on porches or in the road caught up in a perturbed excited mode of conversation about the disheveled crime scene the police investigation and as to what the possible cause was of the two neighborhood friends that were found dead in their home. It was a hot sunny day and the sound of an approaching train engines car like horn droned in the distance as several children played barefooted on the dirt and gravel road as a little dog ran past through the dilapidated housing allotment. The railroad tracks were in an adjacent field a few hundred yards away that consisted of meadows with scraggly high weeds and patchy ratty type vegetation. And on a typical hot summer day on a walk through the field one was typically deluged by scores of big dragon flies and tobacco spitting grasshoppers, punctuated by the occasional white butterfly or two. The kids frequently took the massive field as a shortcut to the general store or to sometimes walk along the railroad tracks to access neighboring residential areas or shopping centers to buy music, or eat at a fast food restaurants, and the field had several dirt paths cut through it for this purpose. A cheap nineteen seventies transistor radio crackled over the airwaves with staticky local news broadcasts depicting events of the previous night as well as the impending police investigations into the baffling and bizarre circumstances surrounding the two deaths. Dirty, and shabbily dressed in soiled cut off jeans and sleeveless tank tops. Portly middle aged and old men stood by intently listening sitting on old wooden hand railings and rickety chairs. Momentarily looking upward and conversing among themselves as wives or girl friends walked out swinging screen doors bearing cold glass's of lemonade or small bottles of beer.

This kind of activity persisted for several more days until the momentum sparked by all the drama and intrigue finally subsided giving way to the usual doldrums of daily life and culminating to a sedentary state of business as usual. Dusty Moors came slowly up the old dirt road accompanied by her seven year old brother whom she brought along as a type of security blanket until she reached Cameron's old dilapidated wooden back porch that was in desperate need of a fresh coat of paint and a restructuring job on the hand railing. As she reached the screen door she began to knock loudly. And it made a rattled bonking like sound as you could hear the door hook jingling around as her fist repeatedly struck the old screen door. As Cameron appeared in the darkened rear kitchen doorway he smiled when he saw it was Dusty. Hello this is unexpected have you come over to pay me a visit? I've got a pot of coffee on do you want to come in and sit down? She stared expressionless directly into Cameron's smiling face and uttered the words I'm ready…Just then the smile left Cameron's face and somewhat taken back said, ready for what? You know what we talked about last week, you know what you suggested…Cameron' Oh that… are you sure? Dusty' Yes I've given it a lot of thought and this point I'm willing to consider just about any suggestion in the way of possible safeguards. I'm scared all the time and I don't feel safe in my own house at night even though I live with my mother and little brother.

Cameron paused for a moment with a serious gaze on his face jerked his head in an ushering fashion to one side and said ok, you wanna step inside? Creaking of screen door opening, and slamming shut. Sorry about the mess I haven't Had the chance to clean up. Sit down how would you like your coffee? Just cream…this your little brother? Yeh..what's his name? Brandon..I don't think I have anything I can give him wait…I think I have a little box of chocolate covered doughnuts. Here ya go kid, just go eat these in the living room I'll even turn on some cartoons for ya, I think huckleberry hound, Yogi bear or Magilla gorilla or something is on. Then as he came back into the kitchen Dusty sat there sipping a cup of discount brand coffee at the small little card table surrounded by rickety aluminum auditorium like folding chairs that this poor man had as his dinette set. Well we might as well dispense with the preliminaries and get to the first order of business, he tossed one of the old handguns down on the table in front of Dusty as she shrieked Wa-ah!!! It made a dull clinking thud as it hit the table. Then Cameron in a firm masculine tone barked…pick it up! A startled Dusty just sat there looking at the scuffed up old pencil lead gray nine shot Colt .38 breach load revolver over the rim of her steaming coffee cup. She just sat there nervously contemplating as to whether or not to actually go through with this and was starting to have second thoughts about having come at all. And just then Cameron's facial expression suddenly changed from warm friendly and hospitable to a stern unwavering glare. You heard what I said pick it up!! He barked this order at her at close quarters almost like an Army Drill Sergeant. It's not going to load itself, fire itself or clean and oil itself or defend your home against an imminent danger just sitting there on that table now is it…. PICK IT UP!! Just then her little brother came running into the room to see what was going on. Brandon go back in the living room and watch television.. I SAID… NOW!! She looked down at the gun not really wanting to touch it all she slowly and apprehensively picked it up. She was immediately taken back by it's weight and bulk. It's heavy it's really heavier than I thought it would be, why is that? Cameron' Oh don't worry about that your not getting that one anyway

I'm giving you the .32 it's lighter and smaller. Press down on that latch there on the side, and as she did that the barrel and cylinder fell forward exposing a nine shot cylindrical chamber. You see that's where all the bullets go. After you fire it you really should clean it…Dusty' hopefully I won't ever have to, "Cameron" Oh you will, believe you me you will I'm not just gonna turn that proficient in it's use. And the first and foremost cardinal rule is, always keep it locked and secured somewhere out of the reach of little curious and prying hands but easily accessible to you should the dreaded occasion arise! And never point it at anything you don't intend to shoot. When do you want your first lesson on it's practical application? Dusty' Whaah,…you want me to actually fire it!! Cameron' in a mocking mimicking tone, yeah I want you to actually fire it…how else do you plan on defending yourself against Mr. Fedders? By throwing spitballs at him?….that makes a lot of sense now doesn't it? Gee I dunno…boy you sure do have a no nonsense approach to this don't you. This is a no-nonsense situation and that calls for stern and drastic measures!! And the handling and use of firearms is serious business!! It's not something to be taken lightly ya know!! And one screw up is one screw up to many that could result in someone getting dead. You just may be called upon one day here soon in the sudden rescue and salvation of my bacon.

And ya know as often as I've handled, cleaned, and fired them, just the sight of a loaded one yet to be fired is somewhat unnerving to me it gives me the shakes every time even though I was once in the Marine-Corps. I've fired just about every thing there is to fire, automatics pistols revolvers, assault rifles and anything else you can think of. You'll see… once you actually use one for yourself you'll understand what I mean, It's not like T.V. Dusty' Well I've never as much as even touched one until now, I just don't know I'm starting to have second thoughts about this whole thing…Well start having a third thought about it and don't worry it's a little scary at first but the bullets come out the other end. Dusty your just gonna have to bone up to the plate here and do what's necessary to safeguard your house and maybe even your neighbors at night. Your just gonna have to learn to trust me in the fact that I know what I'm doing.…And from where I sit I don't see as how you have much choice. Ya know some things were required to do in life at times are no doubt unpleasant but nonetheless were called upon to do them anyway. Look at it this way your mother and little brother are going to depend on you for their security at night. And on that note he slapped the bottom end of the .38's five inch long barrel clicking it shut. I'll pack us all a pick nick lunch just in case we get stuck out in the woods for very long.

Shouldn't you be getting your brother home first? No, I want to bring him along as sort of morale support. Well just make sure he stays in back of us at a safe distance and outta the way, I don't want any unforeseen accidental occurrences…Don't worry I know enough along those lines to undertake precautions. I've got some empty paint cans and some empty glass bottles in a big plastic garbage bag we'll use as targets. Just give me a few moments to go out back and get em' and we'll be on our way. It was a warm sunny day as the trio proceeded off the back porch of Cameron's shabby little white house to adjourn to one of the outlying fields for the sole purpose of Dusty's indoctrination. It was a beautiful day as the threesome strolled down the center of the housing allotment toward their destination of the sprawling fields and meadows near by. All the while there the conversation centered on the looming threat that stalked the outlying communities and the baffling circumstances holding the principalities in a grip of fear. After a while Cameron attempted to alleviate some of Dusty's apprehension by shifting the topic of discussion away from the disturbing occurrences and the grisly discovery of the days prior as he could plainly see it drastically raised her level of anxiety. Then they walked approximately three miles or so through abandoned dirt roads, sparsely wooded areas and paths until they finally reached a secluded clearing that was just past a rise Cameron frequented this spot for the sole purpose of uninterrupted sessions of target shooting. As they walked over this elevated ground that was shrouded in thick high weeds and dense, scraggly vegetation scores of little white butterflies circled around them before coming to rest on some ratty white field flower or two. The surrounding area was deluged by tobacco spitting grasshoppers, big dragon flies, and huge bumble bees or multi colored beetles that had a dark green and brown colored armored like shell on the outside that were known to occasionally fly in ones face. The loud chirp of locusts resonated especially about ten in the morning on or until around one or two in the afternoon. The occasional large black bird circled high overhead, a cawing crow or hawk in a perpetual scavenging mode. And their unobstructed view from such an aerial vantage point was unopposed in scoping out some injured or disabled prey on the ground below to descend upon, a squirrel a rabbit or maybe a possum in some mode of distress. As they got closer to where Cameron frequented for this purpose sat a massive downed oak tree lying on it's side riddled with bullet holes and broken glass and old smashed paint cans lying about. The very sight of this unsettled Dusty as she knew there was no backing out now, her little brother carried the black plastic garbage bag full of the various targets turning it on it's side and spilling out the conglomeration of discarded contents onto the ground. I used to come here as a kid with my friends to fly kites play base ball or mess around with fireworks in the woods. They've all grown up since and have moved away I don't see em much anymore but they still keep in touch by phone or mail now and again. Dusty' I wish we were only coming here to fly a kite,…Cameron' awe common now it's not as bad as all that now!! Then he told the boy to line up as many targets as he could on the side of the downed oak tree and go back up the hill and sit down on a tree stump and don't move. He unfastened the two straps securing the big brown leather satchel that was strapped over his shoulder that contained the two fifty year old revolvers, as he held one up to examine he chimed, boy they don't make em like this anymore! The larger of the two was a colt.38 manufactured sometime in the mid to late thirties that had a five inch long barrel. He knew this was an unwelcoming and disconcerting prospect that gravely unnerved his friend. So to try and ease some of the fear and apprehension she had in regards to actually firing it. Cameron in his way tried to make light of it sort of chuckling saying Elliot Ness's gun, I have a revolver that one of the untouchables carried. Dusty was not in the least bit taken or amused by Cameron's lame attempts at humor or in the elated way he dispensed with it. She just sullenly looked off to one side with a somewhat despondent look of disparagement on her face exclaiming can we just get this over with please…I have to get back in time to fix dinner tonight. Cameron'...look this will go a lot smoother if you'd just try to relax and loosen up a little, your to tense for your own good you'd better be less scared of these guns and more scared of whatever did all those horrible things to our two friends, and besides I didn't go out and buy them I found em in my cellar shortly after I moved in. Dusty' Then sell em!! Cameron' Oh yeah that's just BRILLIANT!! What a plan!! and how then do you propose we defend ourselves against the crater face? Throw it a bouquet of flowers? Oh I know a gun when you pull the trigger a stick shoots out the end and a little flag rolls down that say's BANG!!...Ha,..Ha..Ha,.Ha,...C'mon get real. Dusty, There's no need to get mean or ridicule me!!...Cameron' then screw your head on straight and get with the program, don't you know that horrid thing is playing for keeps!!...Wryly grinning he exclaimed we'll get you acquiesced to firing a gun sooner or later... not excited about or thrilled with mind you but accepting and compliant...And besides I'm far from what you'd call an enthusiast anyway, I just come out here sometimes just for something to do, I don't have much in the way of a social life and I'm just proficient in there use that's all. Dusty? Yeah.. Were kinda like friends aren't we? She looked over at Cameron and said yeah I guess so.. Cameron'...What I mean is friends can ask each other stuff and it's not considered to be outta turn right...You been sleepin' ok these past few nights?...There was a momentary pause where she answered no...to tell you the truth...I'm stricken with insomnia...How bout you?....Not at all I was a lot closer to the vicinity of that God awful incident and I heard just about everything, I was in my house alone and sitting up all night after hearing all that bizarre horrid commotion and distant screams, shamefully I admit to have been to damn scared to move. What could have done that to all those poor people they've been finding?

I don't know I've been up all night for the past several nights trying to answer that one for myself. If not in attempting to reach a self based conclusion regarding it. I've either been plagued with insomnia or just trying to sleep with one eye open shuttering in fear at every little household creak or outside wind gust. And with that Cameron took out two boxes of shells from the big old brown cracked leather satchel. One was marked Winchester super X hornaday .38 special and the other was a green and yellow box marked Remington .32 caliber long rifle. The .32 was a lot smaller and was an old Smith and Wesson made sometime in the late forties or so a snub nose, with about a two inch barrel. Here,…your going to go first, your going to fire the .38 I want to dispel any preconceptions you may have from watching that all that misleading crap on television. Dusty was very nervous as she looked down at Cameron sliding open the box of .38 cartridges. The bullets were face up long and kinda fat, bigger than what she thought they'd be and the casings were a light brassy color and the lead slugs at the end were a copper ish dark brown. What's that mean? Dusty asked…What's what mean Cameron replied. Caliber, what does caliber mean? It just means that bullets come in different sizes that's all. "Dusty" Oh,…The one other thing she noticed and found very peculiar and unsettling was that the slug itself was hollowed out at the end. Why do the bullets have little like holes at the end? Cameron' their hollow points. Hollow what? Hollow points…there for stopping power they go in small and blast a big area out the back…Dusty's face flushed white cringed and contorted itself up in abject repugnance, oh that's just awful!! To many of those acquainted with her back in the allotment she purported a haughtily defiant exterior, and one that had exuded a stern unshakable mode of confidence in her outward demeanor. However in this instance the tough armor like shell that image portrayed was definitely beginning to show signs of cracking giving way to query resolve, revealing a petrified and flustered little girl. Dusty' do I actually have to go through with this!? "Cameron" mockingly replied Ya-a-as you actually you have to go through with this!! He loudly uttered in a curt and agitated manner, have you seen the television or read the papers lately? were gonna need this shit. Now bone up to the plate and getta hold of yourself!! And in a one handed brisk whipping motion Cameron flung the cylinder into the main housing frame of the old revolver as it made a clicking chinking noise the breech flipped closed.

And with the finger of his other hand it made a whizzing noise as it spun around handing it to Dusty here, it's clean oiled and loaded. I have earplugs here which we'll use later on. But first I want you to experience the full effect of this. There's the log down there, now pick something out cite in on it and pull the trigger, that's all there is to it. Coyly smiling my advice though is to use both hands in steadying it you'll see why soon enough. Dusty solemnly looked down the densely vegetative covered rise at the long downed tree below taking in innocuous breaths of the pungent smell of the bitter sweetness emitted by ratty weeds and wildflowers that permeated the surrounding country side air. Then she slowly and apprehensively raised her extended arm clutching that ugly old piece of wrought iron, forged so long ago scuffed up with about twenty percent of the bluing worn off, then as she stood there for several moments in a state of nervous angst before finally pulling the trigger. A loud thunderous BOOM resonated and echoed it's way through the whole countryside and startled Dusty, as well as her little brother who sat there next to the black garbage bag that contained all the targets. His little face winced as each shot was fired and the palms of his little hands were turned inward and jammed into little his ears. Her gun hand jerked backward from the kick as a bright orange flash shot out from the end of the barrel followed by a waft of thick grayish blue smoke that had the unmistakable yet pleasant aroma of seared gunpowder permeated the air. A paint can flew off the side of the log tumbling downward and hitting the ground in back of the downed tree. Hey you hit one and your first time too!! I'm impressed cheered Cameron.

But Dusty did not share in his level of enthusiasm or excitement she lowered her arm and said my God it's so loud it sounds like an atom bomb going off or something!.... And what's that weird smell it's almost pleasant. It's spent gunpowder it smells good don't it. Why...I... Try another one but don't be so tense this time remember all the dangerousness comes out the other end. And just keep in mind you may have to defend your house or others in this way. This is a grave stay of emergency and pending uncertainty you have no choice here but to get with the program. She turned her head towards the massive downed oak once again to dispense a final burst of shots, then again extending her arm raising it to fire several more times in rapid succession breaking a couple of the 40 oz. beer bottles and gouging away more bark and sections from the trunk of the old oak tree. Cameron immediately leapt to his feet and did a jig over to seize the revolver from Dusty. She gladly surrendered the gun to him shaking her head back and forth nonverbally conveying her moderate level of aversion and lack of enthusiasm to the whole thing as she went over to sit by her little brother.

Ok, now it's my turn, he was more predisposed to dispense with business as he somewhat enjoyed target shooting, just going out in barren desolate wide open fields and meadows and plinking at bottles and cans in his spare time, he had the veneer of enthusiasm as one who starred as lead hombre with a ten gallon hat, and spurs jingling as he blew in off the wind dusted range sauntering into a dilapidated old town deluged with tumbleweeds to confront the local near do wells in a pitted showdown. He was the proverbial Cisco Kid and one could almost iconically envision him dawned in a waist level patterned type of Mexican poncho replicating an ancient Aztec mosaic design crudely depicting horses and tee-pees moons and suns imprinted all over it as it lay draped over his upper body. And as he methodically stood there with an intent glare up from beneath the shadow of a thick wide brim of a sombrero hat. Then figuratively throwing down the gauntlet in a veiled challenge by briskly slinging his poncho aside exposing a holstered horse pistol. One could almost visualize a partially obscured sweaty brow hazily concealed from the intense heat of a hot desert sun high overhead. And completely unbeknownst to the local ruffian sect that besieged the town was the elusive and inherent fact of just what a lightning fast gun he was reputed as being. Then he through a taut and unwavering glare nonverbally dared them to pull their pistols at will on the stark edge of town. And just as he was about ready to quickly retrieve that 1872 Remington or Colt .41 pistol from his holster in the final and critical scene with the bad guys.

The picture from this sallow crudely filmed and unrefined old spaghetti western slowly fades to black. "Cameron" ok now!!…my goal here is not to try and turn you into some type of long distance sharpshooter. Any threat that is going to present itself is going to be at a relatively close range and is only going to require little more than shoot em from the hip skills. So therefore you are just going to undergo Cameron's general orientation program. I'm going to use your .32 I like the challenge of trying to hit a target far away using a gun with such a short barrel. Dusty you only have five shots here so make each one count. He turned his head toward Dusty oh I don't know if it'll put your mind at ease here any but the bullets for this are standard issue no hollow points and then he grinned. And with that Cameron raised his extended arm and fired in rapid succession with reverberating booms that were just about as loud as the larger caliber handgun Dusty used. Cameron scored significantly better hitting four out of five intended targets. He then surrendered the .32 to Dusty to test fire a couple of times to get the feel of it. Remember keep it clean oiled and out of little brothers reach somewhere only you and mom know about, and given the current state of affairs loaded and a box of shells right next to it. If something happens all your going to have time to do is retrieve it, and point it at the threat, whatever it may be and dispense with business. Dusty felt a lot more comfortable in handling and using the second gun as it kicked a lot less and fit in the palm of her hand a lot better than that big bulky cannon she used at first. She still felt an overriding aversion to the whole gun thing and remained ill at ease when it came to using one but like everybody else was scared of whatever was out there looming in the shadows at night and randomly killing people.

Just then the sky began to take on an ominous grayish appearance as it got eerily cold and gusty and small streams of lightning quickly flashed in the distant sky. Bushes and trees began to roll and sway in the intensifying wind gusts. Cameron uttered…uh-oh I think there's a bad electrical storm brewing and I think it's headed our way so we better pack it in and split the scene.

Then he fretfully gazed upwardly at the sky while exclaiming, I hope a tornado isn't in the cards as well or we'll be in a world of shit!!…There's no low lying ditches or gullies within miles we could take cover in as we won't be no-where's near safe from something like that in the barn I've staked out we'll be served up like a side of leftovers!!…Dusty terrified oh my God your scaring the livin' shit outta me so please stop it right now!!…Cameron' Oh will you just try and calm down a bit and try not to concentrate on the worst possibilities ok, but as leader of this group I've got to consider all the potential hazards…I'm sure we'll be alright ya know there really hasn't been a twister in these parts for more than twenty five years anyway so don't get your panties in a bunch!!. Lot's of sightings of funnel clouds maybe, but no real twisters so just try and relax ok?!. Anyway I can tell ya were really in for a bad one I can tell just by lookin' at it!!…We need to get under cover ASAP before any hail starts, And I for one ain't to thrilled at the prospect of being literally stoned to death out here got it!.., there's an old abandoned tobacco barn that's just about a mile from here I know of that's no longer in use. It was once owned by old man Hanley and his wife before the bank took possession and foreclosed on it after the economy got real shitty and the lenders called in all their papers. Dusty' oh yeah whatever happened to him. Cameron' well after his lively hood he so arduously struggled to build and maintain went down in a blaze of glory I think he just lost his marbles, went crackers or what have you and wound up in the state booby-hatch following the rank and file as yet another statistic chewed to bits in the crushing, oppressive insatiable jaws of capitalistic imperialism. Dusty just looked down and off to the side shaking her head back and forth chuckling that's very unfortunate. Cameron' yes it is and it's also an all to common a story, look if we hurry before it kicks up we can take cover in it until this thing blows over it has a big wooden latch you can swing close so it locks from the inside. I even brought along an old pocket sized transistor radio along so we can get weather updates. We can eat our picnic lunch there it's relatively intact and locks up and we can even sleep up in the loft for security until morning if we have to. Dusty don't worry the loft it's full of hay it'll make a nice soft bed.

Cameron turned each one of the revolvers barrel up letting the spent casings fall into a little tin can as he was so poor he had to reload the spent brass. And with a sense of distressed urgency at the impending electrical storm he quickly shoved them both into the leather satchel and threw the leather strap over his shoulder. Come on let's get moving!!… I don't want to get caught up in this. The little trio composed themselves as best they could before gathering their few belongings in a hurried attempt to access some form of shelter and to get out of the volatile and impending storm before they were either struck by lightning or became totally drenched. Dusty carried the food and her little brother carried the plastic garbage bag containing the few remaining paint cans and bottles they used for targets. As the group proceeded down the hill the wind slowly and steadily picked up gaining in it's verocity and momentum and the high weeds violently swayed back and forth in the volatile wind gust appearing to be pushed in as the storm increased in it's intensity. They moved frantically across several hundred yards of open ground under the clammy eerie dark grayish haze of a late afternoon sky amid the cold misty wind gusts that battered the little trio as they passed by the occasional abandoned decaying or dilapidated structure along the way usually an old silo, horse stable, chicken coup or an outhouse some of which the roof had collapsed by which would provide no security or safe haven whatsoever against forcible intrusion. And on their frantic dash towards the safe confines of the massive empty tobacco barn would provide before the heavy rains started and they got totally drenched. A loud clap of thunder that actually hissed afterwards sending Dusty and her little brother reeling and shrieking in abject terror as they all ran for cover. Come on!! Don't just stand there get your ass's moving!! Or were all gonna get struck by lightning out here, then we won't have to worry about safeguarding ourselves from a monster!! Just then the dreary hazy gray image of the old barn came into distant view. It was dismal old and shabby with much of the red paint peeled and worn away with the partial remnants of a mail pouch ad barely distinguishable.

But nonetheless it was a sight for sore eyes and it put Dusty's harried mind at ease, she knew they'd be safe in that for the night. It was just about four hundred yards off or so to the left as the rain started to fall. The threesome just stood there momentarily frozen in fear before suddenly making a mad dash toward the decaying old structure that had the faded etchings of the old mail pouch ad on the side and roof. And just as they reached the partially open doorway the rain suddenly began to fall in a massive downpour that would have totally drenched the three had they arrived much later. As the two kids threw the big 4x4 latch that barricaded the main entrance breaching it they were immediately met with the faint unpleasant remnants of stabled farm animals in a putrid cow manure type odor that had permanently seared it's foul aroma into the interior of the barn and it's sparsely hay covered dirt floor that still lingered about. The darkened entranceway was partially illuminated by the eerie dull bluish intermittent lightning flashes subtly highlighting raw, clammy, musty and uninviting accommodations. But when Cameron clicked on his little keychain flashlight further lighting what was only a dirty dismal run down abandoned barn with a number of Coleman oil lanterns, old wooden barrels, milk jugs, leather saddles, galvanized wash basins and other 50 or 60 year old farm implements such as rusty shovels and pitchforks strewn about or hanging from walls or propped up in corners. But regardless it would proved itself out to be a warm and much and welcomed site that would temporarily provide a warm safe haven for the night from intensifying harsh weather conditions and the possible intrusion of that heinous night stalking abomination that lurked about the countryside. Dusty' E-E-EE-G-A-A-D!!…What a cold, dirty, smelly, depressing shit hole!!…Are we really gonna have-ta' sleep in here tonight!!…Cameron' mockingly took a bow swaying his extended arm exclaiming,.. Ooh a thousand pardons your grace words alone besiege me, I humbly request your majesty's forgiveness in my grave oversight!!…You see when I called the president of the United States on such short notice to reserve the blue room on the west wing he must've given us Mr. Ed's smelly old hay bed instead!!… Then in a mocking sarcastic moan, ya were really gonna have-ta sleep in here tonight so put a cork in it will ya!!…Hey honey don't knock it, or would you like to bunk outside under the stars with trench face as your bedfellow in that romantic lil' interlude you've always been dreaming about while me and little Brandon here stay locked in here warm, safe and dry!?…Then he slowly retrieved a small beat up flashlight with a marred lens cover from his old brown leather arm bag and jubilantly exclaimed…see I always come prepared!! Cameron' Now this old barn hasn't been used in twenty years or so I know because I used to come here to play and hang around here with my friends when I was kid. You know my old uncle Elias was almost like a second father to me as my own had just cut out on me and mom when I was just about six, and besides nobody will know were here let alone bother us, Then with a peeved and aggravated look on his face he groused, now do you think you can you possibly find it within yourself to cut the crap for about ten or 15 minutes or so? Or at least long enough for me to go up top and scope it out to see if we have any uninvited guests hiding in dark corners or in the rafters?, then with a contemptuous sarcastic wide eyed gawk on his face chimed do you think you can somehow manage that for awhile!?... Then he reached into one his big bulky cargo pockets and retrieved a stale candy bar and handed it to little Brandon...Here ya go goofus, this outta keep you busy for awhile. Then he turned around to face the haylofts extension ladder while looking upward placing the hand clutching his old revolver in it on a lower rung steadying himself as he prepared to mount and ascend to the top level. Dusty just stood there dripping wet and quivering while sternly looking down at Brandon's bewildered cow eyed expression,...Once Cameron's muffled thud was heard on the tier above signifying he was there.

Dusty intently glared at her little brother and tersed, you just do as your told, you hear you little goof!!...comprende? And after about ten or fifteen minutes Cameron returned exclaiming, it's all clear' ..And then he and Dusty went back over to the breached entrance and proceeded to pull the big heavy barn door to the side until the entranceway was closed off and quickly threw the latch securing it from any possible outside intrusion. With that there was a sudden and intense muffled howling of the wind through the lofty eaves, and the open gaps and crevices of the warped, weathered, wooden boards comprising the dilapidated old structure. And the old corn silo magnified the winds howl as well that was positioned just about 75 yards off and vertically adjacent from the old barn followed by the harsh patter of rainwater droplets in a sudden heavy downpour. Whew' that was close, we just barely made it!!.. I've also taken the liberty of locking the two other windows and latched the door in the back. Were all gonna spend the night in here and that's final!.. The weathers just to bad to go on any further, the storm should be over by morning. Then he pulled a small rusty old battery powered auxiliary type florescent lighting unit from his leather satchel. It was an oblong aluminum panel that housed two florescent light bulbs, about fifteen inches long and about eight inches wide that had a metal protective grate over the unit covering the two bulbs, and was something typically used by campers of yesteryear lowly stating I'm afraid this is going to have to be our primary light source for awhile so we'll all have to just make the best of it and stay in a centralized place of the barn. He looked upward holding the old flash light partially illuminating the ceiling of the upper loft. For security reasons I think we should pitch camp up there. If by some fluke something does somehow manage to get in here it won't be able to get at us up there especially with the latter retracted. Dusty' this place gives me the creeps it stinks and I don't like it one bit!! Cameron' well get over it, for the time being at least your safe in here!

Then he turned to her and sarcastically tersed,…look I'm really sorry you don't like my choice of accommodations but I tried feverishly to get us reservations in advance at the Hilton Regency but they were all booked up and this is the only other thing I could come up with on such short notice, so quit yer bitchin!!…Then he lowered the flashlight turned to Dusty and barked, Look!!…we should be ok in here yes it's a little dark and scary but your not alone!. Or would you like to take your chances on the out side?… For one I sure as hell don't, that country side is just as creepy if not more so at night this storm was just unexpected that's all. So my only advice to you at this point is to just get over it and try and make the best of it for the time were gonna be here got it!!! And with that he clicked on the beat up old emergency light panel that provided light for a radius of about twenty feet outwardly from it's initial point and it was beginning to get very dark. I use this as well as some lit candles at my house when the power goes out during a thunderstorm… And Dusty sarcastically remarked, or on those frequent occasions when your power is shut off for lack of payment, huh?.. Cameron abruptly looked back at her shaking his head back and forth muttering fun-nee… you know that's just what I love about you,…your infinite indispensable humor at my expense. Then he leaned back against an old wooden barrel and let out a long sigh… gees …it's been a long day, and I'm getting kind of hungry how bout you guys? I think it's time to put on the feed bag. Dusty…open that bag of goodies you have there and break out with some serious grub!

Dusty stood up and with one hand swiping her long flowing hair backward and outta her face as she stepped over to drop the big brown paper bag of sandwiches and assortment of stale chips with some cupcakes bought at the day old bakery section of the country store. Let's see what do we have here ahh chicken salad, ham salad on wheat uhmm, uhmm…Dusty?…Brandon?…what'lya have?…In a jaded manner of crass sarcasm he said, don't everybody jump at once there's plenty here for everybody. C'mon dig in, ham salad, chicken salad, or pickle and pimento loaf and Swiss cheese. C'mon now I spent the better part of my morning preparing all these fixing's for this special picnic feast. Don't tell me now nobody's gonna eat anything? How about a can of this flat as a pancake soda pop I got ten cans for a dollar. "Let's see now here we've got a wide array of choices here, there's, gross out grape knee high, gag it down ginger ale, sickeningly sweet strawberry geez it sounds like you'd get type two diabetes just drinkin' it sorry everybody I forgot to pack an insulin chaser! Or how about armpit orange or choke it down cherry… again I apologize there's no ice you'll just have to try downing this crap warm, maybe it'll help some if you just hold your noses…Ha, Ha, Ha, Ha…Here Dusty how'a bout'a ginger ale? Dusty's just sat there in a dazed state of bewilderment with a despondent wandering expression on her face. And then all of a sudden her face winced up and she began bawling uncontrollably I'm scared…what's going on and why are we out here?

Then she put her cupped hands over her face and started sobbing in abrupt spurts, Then Cameron slowly came over and sat down next to her putting his arm around her in a consoling manner. Calm down honey, every things gonna be alright we just got caught up out here in this rainstorm when we were out on our little outdoor hiking excursion that's all Outdoor hiking excursion!? I was learning to use a gun!! Cameron' I come out here all the time to use a gun merely because most of the time I have nothing else better to do.!! Dusty' Well now I guess all that's changed now hasn't it? Why don't you go to Chuck-E-Cheese instead and take up put-put golf or something I'd gladly come along with you for that!!…"Cameron" Yeah well at least for the time being it has, and anyway we can't just bury our heads in the sand stuffing our faces with pizza or playing golf, that isn't going to help our desperate circumstances or safe-guard us in any way now is it?…Dusty just looked downward and indirectly at Cameron in a gloomy wavering stare as he further tried to talk some sense into her. Now you've got to calm down a little here and getta hold of yourself we can't cross open ground in an electrical storm you know that!! You'll run the risk of getting struck by lightning. You don't want to get struck by lightning do you? My grandmother saw an adolescent boy get struck by lightning when she was a little girl from a 100 yard distance in a wide open field as he lay sleeping against a tree line.

She said she saw the lightning bolt strike him and he just went up in flames, she said it was awful. I'm not worried about getting struck by lightning!! that's the furthest thing from my mind right now!! I'm disturbed at all the variables that brought us out here in the first place and the disruption and total upheaval in our lives these events have caused and still!! Nobody knows who or what is stalking and killing any of the people they've been finding encased in that freakish green goop!! Cameron' Look the local and surrounding authorities are looking into that, but for right now your just going to have to calm down and sit tight. Try and eat something in the meantime will you try and relax and take your mind off of it ok?... Now I'm going to go up above and scout out the loft for our prospective sleeping quarters, you two just stay here and don't wander off or fiddle around with these locked doors either!! Cameron left the small light panel on a dim setting with his two friends as they both sat there in the horse stable eating supper. He then proceeded to climb the rickety old folding retractable wooden ladder that led to the old abandoned hayloft above as distant rolling thunder subsided in it's volume and frequency. When he reached the top he stood there momentarily swiping and brushing away strands of hay from his soiled and disheveled clothes. Then he raised up his right arm clicking on the beat up old flashlight he brought along in case of emergencies. The loft had a number of various rusty old farm implements leftover from the 40's or 50's that looked as though they had been laying around idle for decades just hanging from walls leaned up in corners or laying about on the hayloft floor. There were also a couple of wooden wash basins with missing spats and a horse saddle and something that looked like an old wooden wine barrel with a rusty old pitchfork leaning up against it located in a far corner. Ahhh, a table and chairs Cameron warmly thought to himself.

As he further examined the upper level he noticed nothing out of the ordinary for a hay loft. He stood there with a relieved expression on his face and muttered to himself ahhh just a bunch of rusty old pitchforks, horseshoes and such. There's nothing up here but a bunch of worthless old junk before finally breathing a big sigh of relief. Then he noticed the upper window that was latched closed that looked directly out onto the country side below and the rusty corroded hardware securing it was slightly ajar and it's rusty and loosened hinges made a steady clattering cha-chinging noise as brisk volatile wind gusts battered it from the outside. He slowly and apprehensively walked over to it and abruptly pulled open the small metal latch, popping it open. He was immediately overtaken by a sudden waft of cold air and rain mist which rudely blew past his face. As he stood there gazing out toward the open ground that extended for several hundred yards into the distance that at best maintained only a minimal level of visual clarity on objects up to five hundred yards away. Otherwise the countryside was darkly infused with eerie and cryptic connotations of something imminent and lurking amidst the cover of pitch blackness inwardly making him shudder and struck him with a queasy feeling in his chest and stomach. As there was no visibility other than the stark and periodic flashes of lightning in the distant sky that overtly illuminated the countryside. Cameron just stood there frozen as rushes of adrenalin pulsated through his quivering body apprehensively gazing out the open window at the vacant wide open corn fields with rows of bent downed stocks highlighting the wooded areas that surrounded them. Whispering to himself yeah Dusty I'm scared shitless too…And as the lightning momentarily flashed at five to seven minute intervals it gave off the creepy illusion of grayish overcast broad daylight even if for a few seconds.

At a gauged distance of about four hundred yards from the barn Cameron noted what appeared to be a dark silhouette standing upright and moving about in a peculiar fashion it's outward form was not like that of a man but of some type of creature. It was milling about in close proximity of a sparse tree line in the distance. It didn't quite register at first but with a couple more lightning flashes he was fixated with the strange and creepy figure italicized in the distance. The way it walked and moved about,… it was clearly evident that it was something ungainly tall in stature, well over six feet,…and wasn't human..Cameron was immediately overcome with a sense of abject terror that momentarily paralyzed his entire body. What the hell is that is it Bigfoot? He thought to himself,…And it couldn't be a grizzly bear for one it's body would be thick and stocky with stumpy limbs no!!…And besides they weren't known to be indigenous to this region. He knew he couldn't make a sound he had to internalize this and in his aghast and utter revulsion somehow had to re-gain a stern and confident demeanor as the other two looked to him as their brave, solid and unfaltering stone cold sentry they could rely on in harried times. Although he was mortally petrified at what he just saw he couldn't lose it or go bananas now or show the other two even an ounce of fear he just knew he had to get them up here too as fast as he could. And on that blustering and sobering note he slammed the loft window shut and hurriedly threw the latch closed.

DUSTY!!.. BRANDON!!….A deep gruff commanding and masculine voice reverberated throughout the entire barn. You both had better get up here right now and bring up all the foodstuffs the backpack and supplies! you can leave the plastic trash bag of targets down there but bring up everything else

PRONTO!!…Dusty.. Looked up at him in puzzled bewilderment and uttered is something wrong? Cameron just do as I say, no discussion!! Just you two get yer assess up here NOW!! Cameron quickly knelt down on the old wooden hay loft floor with his flashlight while frantically retrieving the two handguns from the old brown leather satchel and frantically spilling the boxes of shells onto the old wooden floor of the loft, in a hastened and frenzied manner to load the two handguns. He nervously scrambled about bungling in a rushed attempt to load both of them at the same time. His hands were shaking uncontrollably while dropping bullets on the hay laden loft floor as he concentrated on and tried to figure out within his frantic and traumatized mind what in God's holy name he just saw. His heart pounded in his ears like a big bass drum at a thanksgiving day parade as rushes of adrenalin surged throughout his quaking body. Shaking his head back and forth uttering to himself thank God we didn't cap off to many rounds today before it started raining. He tried to figure out just what kind of freak of nature he could have possibly seen lurking around out there in that distant cornfield that sat by a sparse section of woods. Then he silently prayed to almighty God that it would just bypass this area entirely and that by some slim chance wouldn't come any where near the barn.

Then he went over to the edge of the loft as he was peeved to look down to see the two kids oblivious and dopey expressions with no sense of alarm or urgency on them. They were just about to climb the extension ladder clumsily hoisting the backpack and the bags of supplies behind them slowly fumbling along as they procured the bags upward in strained arduous attempts to avert Cameron's ensuing wrath quickly hurled them to the upper level floor of the old barn. And like a Marine Core DI barking taut commands at his platoon to climb a rope ladder up the side of a military transport vessel…C'mon move it your slow as molasses!! my grandma climbs ladders faster than you two!! Get the lead out!! Dusty was the first one up, stumbling as she entered the loft's floor

Cameron grabbed hold of her upper mid-section steadying and hoisting her tall lean well above average formed specimen of femininity into the safe haven of the old hay loft provided. This was followed by her fidgety little brother who was always in fifth gear as far as bustling activity and perpetual movement goes. Dusty… with a worrisome expression, is everything alright? You had a disturbing and unsettling tone in your voice, did you see a ghost? I don't believe in ghosts as he frantically pulled up the rickety old wooden retractable ladder into place and in a big letting sign of relief stated I just think it's getting late and we all need to start getting settled in up here. Dusty' your shaking something is wrong isn't it!! I'm just cold that's all!! Dammit enough with the third degree already!! Cameron's complexion was totally flushed white and in a wide bug eyed expression gawkily retorted,… ya know just because I want everybody up here now does that mean all of a sudden I have to undergo some sort of Spanish inquisition!! Then her head jerked over to one side in a worried expression loudly exclaimed…You saw something out that open window box down there below in the corn field that totally unnerved and scared you shitless didn't you!!…didn't you!! Now what was it!!…c'mon now don't lie to me I'm not stupid ya know!! Cameron lamely stated, C'mon now just stop it right now your beginning to scare little Brandon here and I for one don't like it!!. You know what?, you ask to damn many questions for your own good!!… "Dusty' snickering and looking downward shaking her head back and forth oh-please you don't think for one moment your gonna just blow me off like that!! I didn't just fall off a turnip truck ya know!!…I'm gonna get to the bottom of this now your gonna tell me what was it! And in lame and volleyed attempts to try and divert the focus of her attention he exclaimed. Dusty no body uses that corny old expression anymore that's something my grandparents generation used to say!! Dusty' Oh your not getting off here that easy!!… Now don't try and change the subject I wanna know just what you saw out there that was so horrible that you now seem to have a major full blown case of yellow fever!!…Cameron' I just wanna keep everybody in the same place and I don't want anybody lollygagging or wandering off and getting lost that's all…, Were suppose to be a team here and I'm responsible for you two you know? You know on maneuvers we used to call it setting up a secure perimeter… Dusty' now your beginning to ramble, now just what is it that are we securing ourselves against? I'm just looking out for the welfare of this group that's all maybe it's just the squad leader coming out in me I don't know. As he folded the tiers of the old retractable wooden ladder into place on the deck. He let out a sigh of relief and turned to Dusty, Whew…I was a squad leader in the Marines you know. Dammit!! will you quit bringing up the Marines!! They might as well be a million miles away and they're not gonna help us now!! My father was in the Army and he was always reminding us of that fact with little anecdotes every chance he'd get and…Oh sorry I didn't realize that I …your pale and white as a ghost something is wrong isn't it!! What'd you see!! Nothing!! this thunderstorm has just got me a little rattled that's all now just quit asking me all these annoying questions and help me get us set up over there in that corner…now just ferggit it will ya!! and in some lame attempt to elude and detract the intent focus of Dusty's attention he loudly exclaimed. I haven't gotten a chance to eat yet I haven't eaten all day. In a flushed complexion and shaking mildly he nervously chimed now where's that bag of vittles? Here I've got this area set up for us here in the corner there's lots of hay here now I think we'll be comfortable over here.

Then the three went over and sat down on some old wooden crates in that dark, dirty and dismal old hay loft that once served as wooden makeshift beds once designated for the hired help of so long ago. The three just sat there eating and quietly conversing for a while as the wind gusts from outside swept across the countryside and battered against the side of the old barn making a lot of creaking and howling noises. And suddenly without warning the steady lull of the nights serenity was obtrusively pierced by a lowly and pathetic moan repetitive in it's delivery and morbidly ghastly in it's outcry….alone….alone….alone. This distant and morosely terrifying wane eerily resonated itself in a dull lowly drone across the dark uninhabited countryside. It was almost whining imploring in it's anguished tone like that of an anguished old man And just as Dusty held her sandwich up to her open mouth to take another bite all the color suddenly drained from her face she then got a stark look of terror on it and dropped it in her lap. What in God's holy name was that!! I'm getting the creeps!! She whined,…Cameron looked scared too I dunno..It sounds like it's coming from the out side. And with a dorky grimacing expression in a lame attempt to calm and appease Dusty, said maybe it's just the wind howling in the eaves or the timbers. Dusty' your fulla' shit that wasn't the wind and you know it!! Unphased by the ungodly moans from outside Dusty's little brother started fidgeting around jabbering and banging his knees and elbows hurtfully into the lower extremities of the two young adults asking pointless and nonsensical questions in a loud aggravating tone. In that instant Dusty grabbed Brandon in a taut scornful manner picked him up shook him turned him around and plopped him down hard on the seat of his Dr. Denton's causing him to start crying, then she tersely whispered knock it off!! And shut your pie hole!! Just keep your mouth shut…hear!! Now just sit there still and don't move, understand!! Again the lull of nocturnal serenity was broken with that ghastly God forsaken bellow only this time intensifying in it's droning volume…alone… alone…alone….alone….Dusty sat there wincing when she began bawling and sobbing as Cameron shut off the light panel and reached

around clenching his big meaty hand over her mouth, .Shshhhshhsh…
be quiet it doesn't know were in here. And if by the slim chance it does
manage to get in it can't get up here…

Cameron reached down and clicked on the low beam switch to the
flashlight and aimed it at the satchel to retrieve the. Then loud banging
started at the main doorway entrance and the sounds of jimmying as
if something was desperately trying to get in when the doors pressed
violently inward as if the thing had slammed all it's body weight against
it. This went on for about ten or fifteen more minutes. Cameron,
chuckled that won't work either those big heavy doors would stop an
elephant their slid shut, their braced with a big heavy beam on this side
there's no give or leeway. And the windows too haha. There's no way it
can't get in. Dusty by this time was a hysterical blubbering mess..It's that
thing isn't it. she cried through a face full of tears, it's that horrible awful
thing that's been killing all those people isn't it!! Ahhahahh…Cameron'
Yeah I think so but were ready for it if it is. And with that she continued
to unravel going into shock. This is when Cameron slapped her hard
across the face. And in a low strained horse tone he tersed, Snap out of
it and pull yourself together!! I need your help here I can't do it alone if
your cracked up!! With that he slowly handed her the loaded thirty two
and said, if that thing does manage to get in here were gonna throw him
a welcome home party like he's never had before. Then the jimmying of
the large main doorway entrance abruptly ceased and you could hear
the thud of heavy impending footsteps going around the side of the
barn to the rear corner where the boards were somewhat separated and
warped with significant gaping spaces between them. This was one of
the structurally weak portions of the barn that was the result of poor
maintenance, neglect and long term erosive weather effects.

The large grotesque creature stood there momentarily under the
dull incandescent glow of the moon gawking down at the weakened
portion of the old barn for several moments in bizarre and vile
contemplation before grabbing hold of one of the unsecured loose
beams with one of it's creature-ish-ish claws and pulling and breaking
it away leaving a wider gaping space but still not nearly wide enough
for one of such a statuesque size to fit through. When the kids heard

this, it was all they could do to keep composed and quiet enough to not reveal their position. As they all sat there in pitch black blackness listening to this immense malignant pus filled monstrosity pulling away yet another loose and weather damaged board one of the few remaining structural remnants standing between them and this walking animated malformation of chemically putrefying malfeasance vehemently attempting to gain access by forceful means, as the little trio sat there in pitch blackness quaking and frantically listening to the racket this blackened ogre from hell persisted in prying away more wooden spats in furthered vehement efforts to enlarge the opening And with the tearing away of about the third or fourth wooden spat, this grotesque mutated charcoal gray monstrosity with pocked and pitted wrinkled leathery type wrapping finally managed to wriggle it's malformed way through the damaged opening. This dark grotesque mutated intruder emerged and stood their obliquely as this nights uninvited guest. The loud heavy thump of it's large creature-ish feet against the old barns dirt floor sent waves of terror through the three kids as they sat huddled in a corner of the old loft in frantic attempts to keep silent and maintain their undisclosed position in total darkness. Cameron still had his hand over Dusty's mouth trying to keep her quiet and from abruptly letting out a loud scream.

They heard the monster walking around down on the dirt floor below taking in large innocuous breaths making air filled grunting sounds much like that of a caged gorilla at the zoo. Then this thing,.. began to push and bang on one of the loft's main support beams in attempts to bring the whole thing crashing down making big banging like sounds in the process. Then all of a sudden Cameron vehemently shot up from a seated position and yelled that tears it!! I'm not scared anymore now I'm pissed!! He Switched on the light panel with one hand carrying the revolver in the other and lunged over to the lofts edge to get a glimpse of their overnight guest. Cameron's face immediately winced up and contorted itself in horrific revulsion as he could not believe his eyes. What he saw was surreal a graphically horrific image and one that the average mind couldn't possibly fathom in the conventional sense. The innately ghastly creature that towered there on the dirt floor of the barn, was a mutated version of something between a Chinese dragon a demon and a gargoyle. It was about six and a half feet tall with charcoal gray wrinkled and leathery skin covered with bumps lesions and what appeared to be crooked rib like bones protruding from it's back and head areas and that were broken off at the end. It's mid section was covered with big red and white boils and had big thick horns like that of a Billy goat or a ram that jutted themselves around huge marffed gremlin like ears in a backward fashion. The top portion of it's head had what appeared to be large sea shells sticking out of the sides of it. It just stood there with it's elbow leaning up against a support beam with one leg crooked in a Mr. Peanut like stance leering up at Cameron through wide open doll like eyes the whites eerily accentuated the dark black pupils that were distinctly prominent in their horrifying gawk and voracious stare.

As this thing just stood there Cameron exclaimed,…Good Lord!! What in the name of God Almighty!! Dusty keep your little brother back there and outta site!!…And just then he looked down at the horrific visage below as it stared back at him in a creepy intensified leer. And through a wide toothy grin eerily resembling that of an old 1950's sedans front grill emitted a bloodcurdling E-E-E-E-E-E-E-E in a low monotone motor like buzzing drone.!! Dusty yelled frantically what in god's holy name is it!! Just do as I say you two get back there now!! Then Cameron raised up his left arm and began capping off 38. caliber rounds in rapid succession. Eerie flashes of hazy blue light from the cylinder and the end of the barrel creepily lit up the entire barn as he pumped all nine rounds into the creature with master precision. The monster emitted a succession of blood curdling unearthly screams that would make anyone at a tough man contest shudder in abject horror, like that of some poor soul being stabbed to death with a butchers knife. Dusty at this point was in an utter state of shock and hysteria. Woah, woah, what is it!! Cameron what's down there!! The monster by this time was reeling from just having several rounds of lead fired from a large caliber handgun rip through it's body. And as it stood there in a hunched and crumpled over position with what appeared to be some type of white goop oozing from big gaping holes in the back of it's body. It almost looked like thick gloppy paste or white latex house paint oozing out the huge holes blasted out by hollow point rounds. Then along with what appeared to be steam that made loud sizzling and hissing sounds that preceded what looked like hot black tar that began to rise to the top of the wounds and in a sense closing them off. Oh my God this thing is healing itself!! Quick Dusty throw me the .32 let's see how good it's head holds up!! Dusty quickly tossed Cameron the .32 and then quickly began reloading the .38. As the massive creatures twisted and wretched form recouped from the barrage of fire only to stand up again, Then massive blobs of what appeared to be some kind of freakish olive green colored goop rising out of a number of orifices in the creatures upper back portions of it's vilely repulsive form.

The material greatly resembled The Blob but only this stuff was green it just swelled and got bigger and bigger everywhere all over the monsters body and then nauseatingly flopping onto the ground in massive piles. And as it opened it's vile putrid mouth mounds of this material flowed out from there as well as from the tips of it's claws gushing out everywhere in some freakish boogerized meltdown. Cameron Totally horrified and awe struck at the nightmarish surreal image he found himself embroiled in mortal conflict with was filled with total revulsion at what he just saw, wincing E-e-e-e-h G-a-a-a-ad!! He then raise the little snub nose and capped off a tightly knitted cluster of five rounds in it's head and face. It let out a shuddering blood wrenching scream only by this time it had sustained more immanent damage. Slimy and swirled colors of red, green, dark blue in a sickening gelatin like sludge poured from it's laid open head as it slowly staggered in a final and feeble but foiled attack mode directed at the kids who were nonetheless out of reach any way.

Dusty stood there in the corner of the darkened yet dimly lit barn clicking the breech closed on the .38 she just loaded only to notice the old Coleman kerosene lantern that hung from a hook and was mounted on the wall. She also noticed it was still a third of the way full of kerosene and lit and thrown in the direction of the monster would not only make a nice combustion able fire bomb but would no doubt furnish an amusing source as this evenings dinning and entertainment activities.

She immediately dropped the handgun and bolted over to the dark corner and lifted the old lantern from the wall mounting it hung on. She quickly raised the glass housing with the small lever latch lighting the wick with a plastic disposable lighter she had in her pocket and went over to the lofts edge where Cameron was standing. Here do you wanna do the honors or should I? Cameron…stood over to one side holding out an extended palm in an ushering fashion, if you think you can hit em' by all means be my guest..Dusty in a wide legged stance drew back her pitching arm as she used to be on the girls soft ball team when she was in high school with one swift thrust hurled this makeshift fire bomb toward the vicinity of this grotesque abomination. Still writhing from the intense aerial strafing it had sustained just moments before, it had now found itself on the receiving end of a firebomb attack. The wider rounded glass portion located at the base of the lantern struck the bold ignominious intruder in the upper portion of it's wretched vile form shattering with an explosion of fire. Lit kerosene partially covered it as well as lit streams of fire trickled down it's legs to displaced sections of the dirt floor. The monster by now was in a traumatized state of total distress as it hysterically placed it's hands over it's gaping laid open head with it's body totally immersed in combustion able flames ran screaming from the barn towards and out of the damaged opening in the far corner it had entered just moments before Cameron just looked over at Dusty and said thanks that was a quick thinking, you may have just saved us all. He then went back over to the little makeshift camp the three had set up in the corner earlier and sat down next to a flustered and quivering Brandon. And as he began rifling through the brown grocery bag of eats he looked up and said is there any of that ham salad left? You know will somebody please tell me how on earth a man is supposed to get anything to eat around here when there are so many rude interruptions?

CHAPTER EIGHT

A Chance Encounter On The Old Railroad Tracks

IT WAS A COOL SUMMER AFTERNOON JUST ABOUT FIVE O'CLOCK AND IT had just rained a cloud burst in fact and the sidewalks and asphalted streets had swirling mists of steam rising from them. The sky was eerily painted in an array of surrealistic pale orange-ish and blue hues aloof the soft fading sallow rays of the sun which streamed into the partially enclosed patio deck the kids were lounging in. The air was cold, clammy and resonated with the sweet pungent combined scent of daffodils, chrysanthemums and tiger-lilies. And the combination of these factors was very intoxicating, and exhilarating to the senses indeed. But it only temporarily afforded them barely enough remaining daylight to read their concert programs. As the sun was going to be going down soon, and setting a somewhat dismal overtone to the end of the day. And as Julie sat there on her patio lounge aluminum bench seat adorned with tacky floral patterned designs imprinted all over the vinyl seat cushions in a pair of crimson plush red velvet colored jogging shorts and an ultramarine blue halter top.

And through her nearly impeccable, well above average physical prowess of her attributes. She exuded a very intimidating presence especially to those male counterparts who were even remotely acquainted with her. And with one leg crooked and raised up on the seat cushion she sat there in her bare feet polishing her toenails. She began cracking and popping a piece of spearmint gum in her teeth and then with the tip of her tongue began pushing the tiny piece of gum into her cheek, and then insincerely attempting to blow a bubble while leisurely painting them a bright glossy florescent pink color with tiny gold-n-yellow speckles to match her fingernails. She coyly nursed a glass of fizzling ginger ale with ice in it that sat on a cloudy light greenish tiffany end table next to her under the awning of a partially lattice enclosed back patio porch area. She casually chatted about upcoming concert events with her two friends Crystal and Todd. The air had a cool crisp snap that inwardly exhilarated the positive sense of ones spirit of splendid things to come and was permeated by the distant yet pleasant scent of freshly cut grass, lit charcoal grills and a varying array of tree blossoms. They were listening to a local rock station on an old aluminum '70s black leather bound portable radio that emitted a tinny sound and it mildly vibrated as it played.

The two girls just sat there reviewing the lineup of various rock hair bands that were slated to play at the Paisley Arena out of a stadium program she recently got from a local ticket holder. The wind chimes that hung there from the corner of the patio awning gently clanged together in the soft gentle waft of a cool crisp evening breeze that signified the steady approach of autumn. They were a colorful arrangement of small simulated tiffany butterflies cast in a pewter border of various sizes that made a soft wistful chime that had a soothing and calming effect to just about anyone who'd been within earshot. The two girls gleamed as they leisurely sat there either avidly pouring over the entertainment section of the newspaper or just relaxing as a mild gust of wind blew past. She had prearranged going with Todd and Crystal but still didn't know if Sherri was coming along 'too, yet at this point she was undecided as she was not a big fan of hair band rock music anyway but was moreover the preppie type that leaned more towards contemporary pop or New Wave genre and anything harder than Gash or the hotels just made her subtly cringe. And she knew if she went along she wouldn't be anything more than just a fifth wheel and not get that much out of it anyway. And she was also not at all 'too thrilled at the prospect of being trapped there all alone in a cramped and stifled concert arena's restricted seating area that reeked of second hand pot smoke, cotton candy, and popcorn, or that of being trampled or mauled by scores of rowdy, wild-eyed, druginfused rockers frothing at the mouth. Although the lush droning of masterfully played and segmented guitar riffs afforded by mid to late eighties hair bands had undeniably innovated the arena of Rock giving it a much needed and long overdue facelift. It had in recent years endowed it with a heart wrenching captivating lush and hypnotic sound indeed.

Making such artists stand out head and shoulders above the bulk percentage of those who were just a few years before were stale sounding and developmentally stagnant in the area of Rock innovativeness and holding out at most a bare minimum of talent and appeal. Those of whom were inexplicably elevated to the pinnacle of the musical forefront then via a biased media in completely monopolizing it. Autobahn, Vanguard, Astra, Rapunzel, Blacksnake and Pocahontas to name a few were among those on the play list definitely making it an event most did not want to miss out on. Yet it wouldn't seem to bother Sherri very much at all to have to forego it nonetheless as it would only seem to strike her with a pervading feeling of outcast, a gnawing uneasiness at being totally out of her element. The two girls just sat there going over the program together and the three talked about their favorite bands and how they could hardly wait for the concert date to finally roll around. If Sherri decided not to go it would just be her loss. Todd just stood there with his arms folded leaning up against an old blackish tar brown early nineteen forties looking wooden bureau that had a number of old cigarette burns marred in the finish and gold interwoven designed dual pin type striping running all the way around the once elegant old piece accenting its ornate brass handles and broken key locks on the drawers and exterior edges that Julies grandmother had put out there for safe keeping to store various knick-knacks and family heirlooms of intrinsic value that were randomly commingled along with other various odds and ends tossed there at one time or another. It had a folded tacky red checkered plastic picnic table cloth covering the upper tier with a number of old household bric-a-brac sitting on top of it like a ceramic cat curled up in a seated position, and a bull frog sitting on a lily pad and an old corroded brass candle holder with half a candle in it they saved for the occasional power outages that sometimes occurred during spring time on those occasional electrical storms. As the kids conversed you could hear the low distant drone of an evening's lawnmower engines buzzing hum in the background that resounded throughout the neighborhood coming from about a block away or so as some wiry teenage guy or a paunchy cigar chewing shirtless old duffer wearing a ball cap and pair of worn faded cut-off jeans with a multi-colored sweat cloth allocated for his perspiring brow hanging out of one of the pockets was probably out mowing his bee infested rat patch once more for the year before autumn set in. Then suddenly…Todd' with a serious glare of intent on his face looked over at the girls and abruptly blurted out…hey, 'guys' have you heard?… they just found two more dead people besides that old tramp in the old apple orchard a month ago bringing the count to three so far…. Julie just paused for a moment and stopped painting her toenails with a stunned look on her face to glare up at Todd Crystal'…no I haven't heard anything about it at all, what happened? Julie looked over at Todd intensely gazing at him through those hypnotic large doll like corral blue eyes and cutting a figure that has been known to shut down traffic at midday…and in a low murmuring tone of voice replied. No, I haven't either. I just got back from a one week outing with some relatives of mine we went on a on a camping trip up in the mountains. We had some battery powered portable radios but I think the high elevation put us too far out of range to pick up any news broadcasts from here. Todd'…Yeah it's been all over the television and radio news stations here for a few days now. They found two more people in the same bizarre condition besides that grimy old derelict they found in the apple grove about a month ago or so, a couple I think…Crystal' Oh how awful!! I guess there was another freaky unexplainable disturbance the other night and the two they found the morning after were right there laying on their living floor as they were watching late night T.V. as a grisly result of it. Crystal' where did it happen? Todd' I dunno I think…in that old 'run-down indigent housing section I guess, you know the one we all avoid like the plague and make fun of all the time, Washburn I think. They were found in a run 'down old yellow trailer hitch encased in some sort of freakish green goop like before, and in a leering grin exclaimed,…

looks like the boogie-man has struck again!!…Crystal', Now that's not funny!!…I'm really scared shitless!!….You know it's totally freaky and it almost makes me not wanna go out at night anymore. Julie' it just makes me wanna toss…Crystal'…Ya know now I feel kinda bad now about the way we've always treated those people and just because they're poor… Julie' while stretching a portion of her spearmint chewing gum from between her clenched teeth and twirling it around at the end with the tip of her finger and then putting back in her mouth making an annoying cracking and popping sound before she resumed chewing it, "ya know it just gives me the creeps"…"she said, Todd' in a gawked wide-eyed expression, and the police are completely stumped!… And the towns mayor is now even making noises about enacting some sort of nightly curfew instructing that nobody is allowed outdoors past nine o'clock or some shit. The girls' oh gees…what-err we gonna do? Crystal' I'm scared…Todd 'yeah it's totally bogus I know…and the police just can't seem to get to the bottom of this or make head or tails of it or come up with any logical or reasonable explanation as to the whys or wherefores either… Crystal' I just hope they come up with something and soon, and catch this creep before the whole countryside is wiped out!!…ya know I'm even starting to have trouble sleeping at night and people on my street whom I've known and been friends with for years are flaking-out and doing things that are completely out of character for them, like becoming socially inhibited and drawing their blinds and locking all their windows and doors even in the daytime. There is definitely a strong sense of communal uneasiness that permeates the air and it stinks… ya know this neighborhood is turning into some type of half-baked flake-o-garrison or something…

Julie' what kind of depraved sicko goes around randomly killing people? And in the manner with which he does and then leaving them for others to randomly find? And Todd suddenly interjected putting a teenage guy's spin on it crudely replied; a two legged pus' filled pile of puke, that's what kind!…Serendipity! but I'll tell ya what though… I've taken out a little insurance policy of my own just in case. And the girls inquisitively looked up from what they were engrossed in to find Todd who usually only carried around a large folding jagged' toothed hunting knife stuffed in his pockets along with a vast array of other miscellaneous junk including old baseball cards and a rabbits foot that also had numerous keys clipped on the end of a long extended pocket chain that dangled down. The knife was fitted with a thick black six inch blade with teeth he used for utility purposes and protection. And anyone who was acquainted with him could notably observe that he'd since significantly lightened his load as he now no longer jingled or had a spring in his step as he clumsily approached. It was almost one of his identifying features as well as the focal point of many jokes and razzing he took by many of his peers, some kids would call him Mr. Bo jangles,…singing here he comes jingle jangle jingle. That change alone as well as a much more subdued, inhibited and guarded demeanor,… it was almost a wary covertness coupled by a moderate level of sternness about him that wasn't present before that was immediately picked up on by the girls and somewhat unnerved them.

Then he slowly, while mildly trembling, fumbled around and awkwardly reached into the back pocket of his BDUs and pulled out what appeared to be a very small, marred and scuffed up looking forty or fifty'-year-old very compact pistol. It was an old Colt .25 caliber semi' automatic that had a nasty and unpredictable habit of jamming or misfiring at any given moment and ultimately was destined to become just another obtrusive item in addition to Todd's already vast collection of worthless junk including a rusty old vintage corkscrew bottle opener combination from the 1960's, and eventually he'd become bored with and it'd just get tossed aside. And not exactly a sound or formidable choice when it came to the three kids' personal security either, on their occasional late night outings when they sometimes ventured out on foot in the boondocks. But it was easily concealable and wouldn't be noticeable or detected much less draw any attention by the police and it was better than nothing anyway. It also had the outward appearance of maybe having been possibly used by some seedy level of the underworld or organized crime from that era perhaps in the garment district of New York or the seedy docks of New Jersey or something like that. Yet in any case the little gun would've fit in the palm of a little kid's hand much less that of an adult's and then Todd in a fumbling tense manner of nervous angst almost dropping it on the ground as he bunglingly held it out for Crystal to examine. Crystal sat there dumbfounded with a puzzled look of bewilderment suddenly gazed up at Todd and mistakenly identifying it commented…what's this? a cigarette lighter or a cap gun?…I don't get it, is this a joke? you're going to use a cigarette lighter against what ever is attacking all those people if it should happen to come after you? Todd moderately incensed at her total ignorance on the subject as well as her obtuse reply tersed… No duffas for your information…It's a small hand gun, it's a .25 caliber automatic and the magazine holds seven rounds. It maybe small but trust me it packs a nice little punch and it'll get the job done should the dreaded occasion arise!! And that's what I'll light Mr. Boogers up with!…..And on that disquieting note Julie's head slightly jerked back as her face began to wince through a mildly contorted and pained expression on it. She glared in a gawked wide' eyed expression over at Todd biting her lower lip in an air of silent disapproval, moderately incensed at his blatant disregard for her well-known position on the subject!…And callously displaying a firearm in her presence!!…. How could he do such a thing! She thought to herself!…knowing full-well how she maintained an unreasoning abhorrence to guns of any kind for whatever the reason. She just stared at him for a moment as if she were about to lay into him at any moment with her militant views on the subject. It's old and was probably manufactured sometime during the second world war or even earlier than that. You see my uncle said it was really just a piece of junk and that he didn't want it anymore, and so he just gave it to me out of his collection. Then he glared over in Julies direction and chimed lucky for us huh?…in a taunting Cheshire cat like grin. He further added it might come in handy in light of what's been going on.

Crystal flailed her head over to one side as she wistfully brushed her long auburn hair out of her ravishingly beautiful swarthy face looking down and reaching for the little gun in Todd's outstretched hand. Let me see that for a minute, gees I didn't know they came this small, It's kind of heavy isn't it?…Todd, with a goofy grin on his face chimed oh gees!…haven't you ever heard of a derringer goof? They come about this size too but ya only get two lousy shots with one of those…And through

a wry seductive smile and laughing eyes giggled as she uttered aw…
it's so little and cute it almost looks like my little brothers cap gun and
placing a cupped hand over her mouth and squinting her eyes she began
to giggle. By then Julie was seething, she couldn't hold back her pent up
rage any longer finally brimmed over in what would've been figuratively
comparable to a corral of pent up snorting and volatile wild and crazed
black stallions repeatedly battering at the gates just busting to get out. she
immediately sprung into action like a wild mountain lion, pouncing on
Todd verbally lambasting him in vehement protest OK,..THAT TEARS
IT!!…I'll tell ya what's small your brain is!!…Oh-no, there's nothing cute
or funny whatsoever about something that's sole and only purpose is to
just blow holes in things!! Especially people, and what for!! goddammitt
hasn't there already been enough wars and killing and misery stemming
from the invention and misuse of those damn things in recent history to
last a millennium!! And for people to start waking up and call it quits!!
You know how I hate and despise them and everything they represent
and I don't care how small or conceivably cute they come, And yet you
have the balls to bring something as dangerous as that onto this property
and brandish it right in my face!!…Highly peeved and incensed she
contemptuously glared over at him and barked…Have you ever,…or do
you even know how to use one!? Todd just stood there mortified and
completely stunned, at her sudden unpredictable outburst was tongue
tied, just uttered uh…

And as she sharply turned her head in his direction went on in her
scorn fueled bent tersed. I thought as much, probably not, your just trying
to look like a big man as she gawked at him in a wide-eyed expression
on her face, sarcastically exclaimed and in front of us girls!!…Well right
now you appear rather small in my eyes!…You know what place do they
actually have in civilized society?…I'll tell ya, none!!… and it isn't like
pioneer times where you had to have one to hunt for food or ward off
a wild bear or attacking Indians from your log cabin or something,…
that's what the local grocery store is for! And I for one want no part of
um' whatever the reason… Isn't it bad enough the police have to carry
those damn things around but now your going to start walking around
with one in your pocket too…oh that's just dandy! You know if I wanna

possibly get myself killed I'll just simply step in front of an oncoming train or a bus or something. You know goof you must have rocks in your head taking that damn thing out here in front of me knowing full well my feelings on the subject!! I oughta bust you wide open!! Do you also sleep with a handgrenade in your bed at night too? Todd' ok that's quite enough already you know your really overreacting to this and your not letting me give my side of it or say anything....OVERREACTING!! What the hell did you think I was gonna do once you took that god awful thing outta your pocket and displayed it front of me!! summersaults!! Todd' well you know as far as getting killed goes...you just may get your wish if that thing happens upon us here one of these unsuspecting nights!! Julie' Alleged thing!! And that hasn't been substantiated yet, and at this point in time I'll take my chances. You know it isn't Dodge city eighteen seventy three, or prohibition era Chicago of the1930s anymore!...And so far this has been the quiet peaceful amiable town of Avondale, nineteen eighties and we don't settle things by going out to the back forty to trade paint with Clint Eastwood. And it's certainly not an open society where anarchy reigns and men strut down the middle of the street with one of those iron rungs holstered and strapped to their legs!.. And as far as I know carrying a concealed weapon in public...IS STILL AGAINST THE LAW!! And anyway your not Elliot Ness or Matt Dillon!!... You know goof...you're more like Festus,!!... Now you take your little gun and your cute little bullets that go with it and kindly remove yourself from my respective property this instant!! Uhh...Cisco Kidd!! And in a wide eyed Cheshire cat like leer taunted her lifelong friend with a parting shot...And do yourself a big favor and get rid of that damn thing before you wind up shooting yourself in the ass with it ha, ha, ha!! Todd' Now that's not only not funny but considering the current state of affairs it's really uncalled for!! that's not my intention here and you know it!!...It's for our protection!! It's for your inward male insecurities more like! Ya know it never ceases to amaze me!

Every time a guy starts to feel a little insecure or inadequate about his masculinity he's gotta reach for one of those things? Todd' that's totally irrational and untrue in regards to the serious danger we could and probably are right at this moment... facing...Julie' mockingly taunted Todd while nervously shaking her hands,.. oh quiver, quiver, quake, quake…Oh gees,…what the hell else do you expect us to do here? Throw it a bouquet of roses as a sort of housewarming gift? Hey Julie, maybe we could invite it over to your house one evening you know, and throw it a Tupperware party sort of welcoming it into the neighborhood. We could even have a theme for the party…"how to refrigerate your dark green slimy boogers in your very own creature shaped Jell-O mold", Ha, ha, ha, ha, ha. That's if we get lucky enough to get the drop on it first, miss hearts and flowers…Julie' now that's not fair!…I was just havin' a little fun that's all you don't have ta be so downright cruel!!… and that's not funny either…Todd'…well neither is that thing!!…And so far it's been nothing but downright cruel to every poor unfortunate soul it's come in contact with so far!! And the only thing I feel insecure about right now is our personal safety…We should've had one of these on us that night when we so foolishly threw all caution to the winds and just ventured out there on those desolate set of railroad tracks to the general store in the dark for that lousy cache of glorified dime-store junk we bought completely oblivious to the danger that lurked in the darkened hallows of that vast desolate countryside!!…We were totally vulnerable and unprotected and that that God awful two legged freak could have been hidden anywhere and just sprung out of nowhere and ambushed us!!… we'd have been toast!!, Boy talk about stupid but never again I assure you!! Julie' Then get yourself a big vicious dog or some pepper spray, or a can of mace, or a stun gun or something, Todd' a stun gun! Against a slimy-seven foot monster! You must be outta your everloving mind! That thing would turn us into a side of minced meat not to mention tearing a big vicious dog into little pieces so it looked more like a set of paper dolls!! And on an insincere and moderately sarcastic note mockingly suggested, how about a set of nunchucks or some Chinese throwing stars you know like the wanna be tough punks carry? Julie' in a wide eyed, leer sat there glaring at Todd…yah that'd be ok but no guns!! Todd' while rolling his eyes, in a raspy tone hemmed, oh you gotta be kidding…Julie' but if you wanna continue to be around me, nothing that makes a loud reverberating boom has a muzzle flash or emits blue smoke when it discharges and that's final!! I'd like to skip the theatrics here if you don't mind!!...Todd' THEATRICS!! You know you're really being melodramatic here!!...This gun could save our lives!! And there's nothing theatrical about that!! Julie'... you know bub, if I wanna see fireworks I'll go to the annual fourth of July picnic at least there I'll get potato salad, hamburgers and hot dogs. Todd just murmured you know when it's all said and done, you might just get served up as a complimentary picnic side immersed in green slimy boogers...Unmoved by Todd's speech she began shaking that head of dishwater blonde hair back and forth in a curt and close minded display of defiance, No way hose' they totally creep me out!! And besides an uncle of mine who was a cop that I was very close to as a little girl was killed by one in the line of duty. And they never caught the creep who did it either. He just got the drop on my uncle right there in some disease infested back alley and plugged him in the back like the brave little coward he was! He died right there like a mangy dog, and before the ambulance or any other help had a chance to arrive in the midst of overturned trash cans rats, piles of garbage and a heroin ravaged junkie sticking a hypodermic needle in his arm. Todd' Yeah I know about all that and I'm very sorry, but sooner or later your gonna have to let that go and face facts as they presently are! That happened in Chicago right... that's just how those big cities are, you know, they are notorious for harboring unsavory elements, as well as serving themselves to be primo breeding grounds for fostering and cultivating a whole host of enabling and adverse factors that run rampant like the sore lack of real job opportunities coupled with a high runaway cost of living, they are just vast open playgrounds for prolific misery and senseless, violent crime, but this is an entirely different scenario altogether. And just in case you haven't heard, they're finding more and more dead people, and that creeps me out!! And did you also read what the paper said about all the victims they found sunk in that freakish green sludge? Julie...no I didn't...I don't read the papers anymore their too depressing. Well as far as the current state of affairs goes, maybe you should start, it directly affects you now ya know. Julie just turned her head off to the side while smirking. It said that they all had a stark bug eyed like gaze on both their faces and the derelict they found in the apple grove too..

And they also had an anguished and contorted expression with a look of abject horror on them, as if they'd seen something so utterly horrifying they just died of fright. And besides the two victims they found in Washburn, the paper said that the dead guy was clutching an old four-ten gauge goose gun or something that still had one unspent shell still in the chamber. And Julie knowing next to nothing about firearms or their ordinance, asked Todd, 'what's that mean? spent shell' And he tersely replied it means they only managed to get off one round of buckshot into it and it still managed to survive and flee the scene. That's bad stuff!! The paper also said that they found telltale traces of some other kind of bizarre unidentifiable white goopy substance and the elements of it's liquid properties were foreign and unidentifiable and have yet to be determined. Todd 'and if a shotgun blast wasn't going to stop it what makes you think a vial of pepper spray a can of mace or a stun gun will? Ya know I'd really like to just walk around with a belt-fed Browning 30 caliber machine gun but I can't hide one of those in my cargo pockets that's how scared shitless I am... Julie'... and if it survived a shotgun blast as you put it. What makes you think a bullet from that glorified little pop gun you have there will?

And then she jokingly retorted, hey maybe we can sic the big vicious dog on it and it will bite him on the leg and disable his attack instead! ....ha, ha, ha, ha, ha, ha, And as time went on it was becoming more and more readily apparent that the otherwise passive spontaneous unassuming nature of the three individualized personas the kids maintained up till now was slowly being eroded away by the eerie disturbing circumstances surrounding the imminent crisis. And replaced by chronic stress and conflicting heated debates such as this as to a mutually agreeable course of action had become commonplace. And the prior focus of such beloved pursuits such as music, suped up muscle cars, frequenting the mall for rad clothing styles and New Wave music became oppressively impeded. And attention was now slowly shifted to the imminent threat that damn thing surreptitiously imposed against their occasional clandestine nighttime excursions and furthermore collective attention had concentrated itself to frantic and desperate efforts in safeguarding themselves against the potential danger. And the ensuing element of cohesive dissent that had fragmented the efforts of little group into a non-collaborating ineffectual unit. The present course was streamlined with ongoing dysfunction that had hampered a once mutually agreed upon decisive plan of action leading to an effective resolve. And it only spawned ongoing friction and contention among themselves,… in that these three kids possessed about as much knowledge in the area of proficiently or qualifications in the handling, maintenance or dispensation of fire arms of any sort much less any predisposition thereof, as a one legged man has in a butt kicking contest.

Todd' loudly resounded, and from now on I would greatly appreciate it if you would kindly cease and desist with any and all forms of your so called levity, …Julie, this is no laughing matter we could in all likelihood and probability are as we speak be in serious danger and your sitting there making jokes!! I think you are in need of a serious attitude adjustment. Julie just glared over at Todd and defiantly barked And just who's gonna give it to me you? Todd just looked off to one side in a wide eyed and dumbfounded expression well…it just may be that thing, you better hope it's me instead. And in obstinate defense of his unwavering position on what had by now become an ongoing unresolved and hackneyed debate, in a whiney and imploring tone of voice loudly exclaimed, what else can we do here? Carry around some kind of a bazooka or flamethrower like the Army would use everywhere we go? Or drive around in a sixty ton tank! I think that at the very least that just might draw some unwanted attention from the police don't you? Look I don't really consider myself some type of gun nut either, And I think the NLA are just a bunch of, red necked, beer bellied radical, blow harded, crackpots and that if any of those arm chair wannabes ever really did encounter some kind of realized formidable danger most of em' would probably grow a yellow streak a mile wide up their backs and wet their pants. But in light of the present circumstances we've really got to consider other more potent and effective measures of defense other than just a stun gun or a can of mace. What were up against here is something the papers deem very dangerous and life threatening.

The two girls just gazed at him intently as he continued to plead his case. And I'll feel a lot more secure and at ease especially if when were out walking out at night and as far out as we went like we did before if we have at least one of these on us…And besides I won't in a bum rush just aim at it's body in a fit of frenzied hysteria like they probably did, and were only able to get off one shot. It'll get an almost instantaneous seven round burst. And just in case this thing, this freak of nature whatever it is, has some type of bizarre recuperative abilities within it's rancid and vile system. We'll just see how good it's head holds up when I cap off a few these hollow points into it's freakish face…and at having just said that Todd grimaced as his face turned red. And in the event we actually do run into something, at night, I don't want us to just be easy pickings and made mince meat of. You know we were damn lucky we got away at all that night ya know Julie?…And for the life of me that fact still totally escapes me I've mulled it over a thousand times in my mind…and its a complete miracle were even sitting here at all. She just sat there biting her lower lip contemptuously leering at him taking all this in in a silent mode of disconcertion, feigned tolerance and restraint, attempting to absorb some of what he was saying. You see I'll carry four extra full magazines here in my zipped cargo pocket. Looky here each one is no bigger than a small plastic disposable lighter. I also have a box of shells in this elastic ankle band with fifty extra rounds just in case we get pinned down. And if the situation gets really hairy requiring a higher dispersal of fire causing a number of magazines to be spent. I'll just push down on this little button right here below the trigger housing to eject the empty one onto the ground and then right away. I'll slam a full one in to continue firing there's no way it could survive that. And if and when we do decide to venture out at night together we'll be more amply prepared for real trouble. and as they say in the infantry I'll act as sort of a point man…Heh, Heh.

Julie' Ya know that doesn't exactly make me feel at ease. It's almost like your beaming with anticipation about all of this and can hardly wait for something to actually happen ….so you do actually get a chance to use that damn thing, And I must say I find it particularly disturbing and I don't know if I like seeing that in you it at all, Todd' Look Julie… this pocket knife I've always carried around here is not going to cut it, smiling as he caught himself, added sorry, no pun intended. And in reference to the pistol, he further added in a more confident tone of voice stating. Look I'm not asking for either of you to pick it up, handle it, or even use it. All I know is that sometimes we go out walking to dark desolate places at night, and if you two don't agree to take on more appropriate measures and added precautions I'm afraid that's gonna have to stop right here and now. At least for me it is because I'm just going to have to refuse to go along with you guys anymore if you two are foolish enough to keep doing so. And if something grave does happen who are we going to call for help in that instance…huh? And I refuse to be one of three ducks in a row. Julie I know we've been friends for along time now but I am not going to put my ass on the line for you or anybody else for that matter in the way of taking unnecessary chances. I don't care who it is! regardless of any longstanding friendships or extremist views! Why should I? Anyway there's no need to! The girls just stared at him not saying anything…And they are starting to find more and more dead people and that scares me a little, no it scares me a lot. Frankly I'd just like to walk around with a Thompson and a bandolier of hand. grenades to use against that horrid thing. Or don't you two remember all those strange and weird noises echoing from out there across that dark creepy meadow and into those distant woods we all heard that night coming home from the old general store? Or how we all had to run like hell the last two miles or so down the yellow streak road coming back here about a month ago don't you? Julie'…Yeah I remember.…I was so scared I thought my heart was literally gonna pound it's way right out of my chest. And that night all we did was hear creepy unidentifiable noises,…the next time we all might not be so lucky as far as getting away at all. Julie' yeah I know but that could have been just about anything at all out there in those woods we heard that night and we really don't know for sure at all do we and if…Todd 'What does it take here!!.. A ton of bricks to fall on your head!!?.. Look we don't know nor do the police at this point nor does anyone else for that matter just exactly what this could be and I for one don't wanna take any more unnecessary chances. When it comes to our safety or imminent danger I'm not going to waste any time speculating!!.. You nor anybody else for that matter has the right to demand it!!…And nobody that has actually seen it has lived to tell the tale. And I must say I haven't been sleeping very well these past few nights, I've been having a string of garish nightmares every other night since as well as keeping all my doors and windows locked, things I've never done before. And I'm still haunted by those creepy unearthly God awful sounds we all heard out there on those old tracks that night coming from those distant woods. And they weren't just the rustling of leaves or the snapping of branches or the howling of the wind through the hills or a hoot owl in the trees. They weren't the result of a collective imagination on our parts either. We all heard those eerie ghastly cries echoing from those distant far off woods and you can't deny how scared we all were either.

After thinking about this I firmly believe there was something lurking about out there that night. And intensely glaring over at the girls uttered something catastrophic, something dangerous, and something insidiously evil. This statement sent chilling ghastly waves of fear through the girls and they both shuddered as they thought how lucky they all really were that they may have averted a visually unspeakable horror by a slim and narrow margin. As they were both now becoming more open to what Todd was saying, not accepting,…open…Look all I'm sayin here is that when and if we ever do go out walkin in the boonies together again I think we should be better prepared and have some thing more in the way of a more solid and formidable backup that's all… I must say I was pretty creeped out by those eerie ghastly moans and that bizarre succession of cackling noises we all heard emanating from across that darkened countryside. It just scares the shit outta me every time I think of it. And the beauty part of this whole system is in that it's so small and compact it easily fits into a cargo pocket and no-one will ever know I have it on me. Or unless you guy's wanna start drivin everywhere we go from now on or restricting our travels to the limits and bounds of corporate city and forego all walks in the countryside day or night from here on out until this thing is resolved and who knows how long that will take. And my only question here is why should we change our life's routine?… You know that big hair band concert is coming up here soon and you guys wanna go see it right. The girls' Yeah… Todd' well you know there's no other way to access the town we gotta catch the bus in to get to the concert but by having to walk that desolate five mile stretch along those abandoned old railroad tracks and then several hundred yards more through that open field. Ya know anything could happen on route. Julie just glared over at Todd in a disturbed mode of query resolve. And I've been anticipating this for a couple of months now and I'm not backing down just because of some unseen threat heavily shrouded some veiled curtain of cryptic mysticism reputed to be lurking about the countryside at night. And just in case it just happens in on us one of these times! Were going better prepared from now on and no ifs ands or buts!! AND I'M AFRAID THIS IS NO LONGER OPEN FOR DEBATE!!…it's this or no concert and our travels become restricted to the immediate vicinity. So what's it gonna be?

The girls just looked at each other mildly contorting their faces in compromised and fuddled expressions as if they were both put in some sort of logistical half nelson at a loss for words.

Todd' hey this gun is for our protection not just mine, as this will serve as our main and most effective line of defense if we actually do run up against something in our travels, you two just try and keep that in mind will ya? Then Julie sheepishly asks how bad do you think this will get? Todd' bad…really bad, more people are gonna die… and if were not all better prepared than we have been us…Julie ' …so just what are you trying to say here…that this could be some sort of monster realized? And in a grim morose pensive glare Todd paused to look over at Julie said… yes, I'm afraid so,…that's exactly what I'm saying it's deadly serious… from here on out, beware…

The very next week was concert week and Julie, Todd and Crystal had another meeting to discuss all the preliminaries they had to undergo in preparation for a much anticipated arena rock concert. And on the part of the local kids, that was long in coming. It was to be held at the neighboring town of Fayetteville to play out at the Paisley Berkheimer arena it featured all the big named hair bands of arena rock as well as couple early eighties bands like Van-guard and Scallion. They say everybody and his brother in Biscayne county will probably turn out for the big event. Todd said it's getting late now and I've got to go home and get ready for supper or my ol' lady will ride my case again if I get back too late and quite frankly I really just don't wanna hear it tonight. Crystal' you comin with me? No I think I'm just gonna hang out here for a little while longer you go on ahead. Chrystal' Suit yourself, Todd' You two just think about what I've said ok? The two sat there dumbfounded just looking at each other in a sort of bewilderment, and then up at him through a somewhat intense fretful glare for some glimmer of comforting reassurance that things weren't at all as bad as they seemed and together gently nodded. I don't think we should chance venturing out that far again at night or the next time we could all be caught with our respective pants down. And just like yesterday's wash we'd all be hung out to dry. And in rebuttal to Julie's ongoing chastisement Todd vehemently replied.

And for that matter I'm not going to step up on any self infused soapbox in attempts to justify my position here or dispense with any lengthy or flowery speech's here either. For one there aren't any and for another the situation has become grave enough and doesn't exactly warrant it. I've just merely stated the cold hard facts here and if your minds are still closed to the subject of using deadly force so be it! Then I see I'm going to have to take over the reigns as the voice of reason here. I am not going to just stand there either and throw rocks at this thing whatever it is in some kind of half assed attempt to preserve our friendship or appease you in your extremist anti gun views as he intently glared over at Julie. And until the authorities get to the bottom of these bizarre and horrific events and gruesome finds, that from now on if and when we do decide to venture out anywhere that's remote or isolated together especially at night we as of now go lightly armed and that is the status quo as it presently exists, case closed!…end of discussion! Oh and Julie if you still want to bring along your can of mace or your stun gun by all means do every little bit helps in the way of armaments. Julie ' lowly murmured yeah, ok…Todd ' just make sure the thing is charged and the mace or pepper spray cans aren't empty you may at some point may be called upon to save my respective bacon for all we know…and having said that Todd beamed her a warm, wry and reassuring smile conveying to her without words that every thing was going to be alright. And as rock music at an audibly low volume emitted from the tinny black portable radio that sat on the patio table next to the girls, Todd turned away and began to walk off the concrete patio deck as the evening sun began to go down and away from the lounge area that the garage was adjacent to.

And as he came out from under the shade the awning provided onto the grass he sullenly set out for the direction of home. The girls relegated docile demeanor at this point remained transfixed. And their inward aversion towards the possible use of lethal force remained steadfast and un wavering even in the midst of a possible night stalking monster lurking in the shadows. They were both unphased at his pressured attempts at swaying them to come over to his side of the fence. They remained uninfluenced by his glaring intimidating attempts at staring them down in persuading them. And they found themselves mentally and emotionally frazzled by his obstinate and unrelenting predication on this matter he subsequently maintained throughout the whole discussion by way of strained contention in the debate they just had with him. Julie and Crystal attempted to divert their attention from the present stress surrounding the crisis and as best they could and try to focus more on hair band rock. They resumed their interrupted conversation while pouring over the arena rock concert program discussing the arrangement details. The two sat there as they both tried to come to grips with the unsettling fact that their longtime and otherwise unassuming happy go lucky childhood friend was now going around with an automatic pistol stowed in his back pocket just as dusk began to set in. The evening air bustled with the busy and stray sounds of children's voices together with their audible laughter tried to go about their daily activities in as normal a modem as possible in mere attempts to get in as much playtime out in the streets as they could before they were summoned in for the night by their now troubled and worrisome parents.

He was escorted on the dismal walk home by the occasional street light flicking itself on accompanied by the low hiss of an electrical fizz from each overhead post as it suddenly shed it's ghostly incandescent light on him as he sullenly passed by that were fixed on the side of telephone poles high atop overhead. His walk home for the most part consisted of darkened and dead end streets punctuated by the occasional overturned trash bin, barking dog or screeching cat that typified this and like neighborhoods. And it's frightened and inhibited residents were dauntingly beginning to get settled in for yet another night of insomnia tic watchful eyes and pensive fear. He became somewhat startled at the sudden and abrupt burst of dull glowing incandescent light that was almost instantaneously shed on him, almost signifying a dreaded and impending omen.

Todd's outward demeanor was one of sullen, and frantic dismay and the furthest thing from his harried and distraught mind right now was the upcoming hair band concert that all the young kid's were anticipating. This was definitely becoming the dark cloud that was beginning to rain a downpour on his parade, and at this point there didn't seem much else he could do about it. Aside from starting to carry a compact sized automatic pistol in one of his pockets as well as a couple hundred rounds of ammunition distributed elsewhere on his person. Even the fact that he was now armed held very little consolation and it didn't grant him much in the way of feeling much safer or sounder either, as he was always nervous and scared all the time and had a sick queasy feeling in the pit of his stomach that reverberated and he was starting to have trouble keeping meals down. And he was for the most part inundated by a torrent of bleak and dismal thoughts of gruesome and catastrophic outcomes that seemed to be somehow imminent. And the underlying fate held out for he, his friends and the townspeople at large was to be in the hands of some veiled and elusive garish monster, a cruel freak of nature that had somehow metamorphosed itself from some remote slime pit and was on the prowl. But he knew that somehow, someway he was going to have to become an unfaltering buttress of stability, a rock of Gibraltar the girls could look to for solace and emotional strength during this foreshadowing crisis. As it were it faintfully appeared that he was the only viable candidate waiting in the eaves randomly selected and appointed to their service as their proverbial knight in somewhat dented and rusty armor, saddled with the monumental task of slaying their slime spewing dragon. And hopefully a .25 caliber sword was going to be sufficient enough armament to do the job should the dreaded occasion arise. And furthermore hopefully he thought to himself, he wouldn't wet his pants in front of the girls in the process.

Yet though he as everyone else was baffled and rendered completely clueless as to the bizarre and unseen force responsible for the disturbing recent course of events. Inwardly he just couldn't fathom just what it was that could possibly have a hand in besieging local and neighboring principalities in it's vehement and horrific reign of night stalking terror. What could such a being look like? he thought to himself…it had to have taken on such a ghastly and horrific appearance that would beggar description and boggle the mind. He inwardly shuddered at the imaginative prospects. All he imminently knew was this was undeniably an insidious force that was going to have to be reckoned with sooner or later and that he or someone else was going to be elected to accomplish the unpleasant task. And what in God's holy name was that awful green goopy sludge and why do they keep finding dead people encased in it. This and a whole host of other like minded questions remained unanswered and continued to confound his by now frantic and bedeviled mind. And the police are no closer to solving this thing than they were a month ago. Yet as he drew nearer to his house he inwardly concluded that everybody meaning the community at large was now in it for the long haul. And he was at least for the time being going to have to attempt to just put it aside at least temporarily and try not to focus on it constantly. For one constantly internalizing on it wasn't healthy and for another it wasn't in the best interests of getting a good nights sleep.

And it was beginning to appear that all community members were now going to have to band together to form a sort of unified front in a collective action to safeguard themselves against this insidious and unseen danger. As he walked up his front lawn he dismally surmised that from this point on he was now going to have to be more wary of his immediate surroundings and devote more attention to broader aspects of his personal security from here on out. The next morning Homer Griswold sat on his little white wicker chair with one leg crossed over the other next to a matching table of the same sort on his front porch. It was about ten o'clock late in the morning and the sun was beginning to dissipate the misty early morning dew from the surface of the lawn as well as the floral accented hedges located in the front of the house. The immediate and surrounding air resonated with the sweet aromatic scent of jasmine and honeysuckle from the outlying shrubs that bore flowers on them. And as the morning sun set it's soft and subtle ray's on the neighborhood scape very large bumble bees hovered around various bulbs settling on one and then another pollinating and busily gathering nectar for their honey production. Homer was wearing one of those on golden pond type soft hats for shade retirees commonly wore when they were out tending their victory gardens. He was in the process of drinking his usual cup of morning brew thick rich and black as he took it right before breakfast and was also smoking his pipe that contained his favorite brand of black Cavendish tobacco when he unfolded the morning edition of a local newspaper, The Moncreef County Dispatch thusly placing it down on the table in front him beside his coffee. The heading immediately jumped out at him, Two more bodies discovered in Washburn early this morning; authorities baffled.

After having mentally noted the startling headline and briefly skimming over a few more sentences from the top paragraph of the article he reached up and grabbed the end of his pipe in his hand sort of shifting it to one side of his mouth and simultaneously taking a short drag from it, abruptly emitting small puffs of smoke through pursed lips as he slammed through the first couple of pages with his thumbs to see if he could find any further written editorials pertaining to the front page headlines. Then he abruptly turned his head backwards and in a horse and whiney tone of voice called into the house through the screen door. Claire'!! would you come out here for a moment, I've got something I think you oughta see! Just then an audibly loud and domineering yet muffled shrill pierced the tranquility of the morning air what!!… What is it!? came from inside the darkened front entranceway as a surly heavyset woman in her early sixties with a soft pale complexion, graying hair pulled back in a hair net with big blue eyes burst through the squeaking screen door having just been interrupted from a busied morning drudge routine that constituted rustling up a breakfast laden with coffee, toast, jam, scrambled eggs and bacon. As she leaned over her husband's shoulder to glare over at the newspaper's current heading she began drying her wet hands on a dirty white apron she was wearing. He took the pipe out of his mouth while looking up at her and blurted out the words look at this headline. After having briefly scanned the headline and top portion of the front page briefly taking in some of the sketchy details she stood upright wringing her wet hands in that dirty white apron she was wearing and with a startled wide eyed expression on her face loudly exclaimed what type of preposterous fallacy is this!! she exclaimed. Homer' haven't you heard?

They've been finding a number of dead people at varying time intervals in the last couple months or so under very strange and bizarre circumstances too… and the police have yet been able to piece together anything as to what the underlying cause may be. Homer ' with a rhetorically mocking winced expression on his face whined people are starting to say it's some sort of boogie-monster. Ha, Ha…Claire' A whaaat!! You heard me the first time a boogie-monster. Claire' I can't believe you would call me out here just to interrupt my busied morning routine with such utter claptrap!, how absurd!, don't you have anything better or productive to do with your time!? what kind of half witted idiot do you take me for anyway!! Like a long-shore-man she barked …Ya know ever since you retired I've been the one paying for it!!… Homer' wryly grinning through his pipe and clenched teeth that's what their saying, and in as stern and commanding tone of voice a man of his slight, demur and unimposing form could conceivably muster in a lame attempt to wear the pants and put his foot down even for one savored moment, whined Listen here ..From now on I want all the doors and windows around here locked at night, and that's final understand.? With a constraining, intimidating wide eyed glare on her face she tersely barked AGAINST WHAT!! And Homer waning in his initial stern and more commanding tone shrank back in his assertion and reverted to his usual timid and docile mode. And in a faint reply he took on the guise of a more neutral position on the matter to placate his domineering wife in an answer he hoped would deflate some of the mounting intensity of her unwarranted hostility in that instance and stave off what he could see coming as yet another belligerent outburst he would no doubt bear the brunt of. Nothing in particular dear, I just think that we should be safe that's all. And with that she sort of rolled her eye's in a sort of jaded affirmation shaking her head back and fourth simultaneously emitting a snickering noise as the tip her tongue jutted to the roof of her mouth. Ya know I've still got a full day of housework ahead of me and have yet to get breakfast up and ready, do a wash among other things. And if you want to just sit there vegetating in some sort of moronic self deluded stupor like some drooling, sophomoric idiot entertaining yourself with garish notions of hobgoblins lurking in the night that's your business!!… But don't ask me to go along with it comprende!!.. Homer' in a sarcastic whine muttered that's one of the things about you I fell in love with, your ingratiating warmth, openness and sensitivity. Claire' don't push your luck buster or your going to find yourself left to the devices of Regis' diner for your early morning breakfast delights for cold stale toast, rubberized bacon, fake eggs and some of that famous two and a half hour old coffee that tastes more like paint thinner!!…And with that she turned around to resume her household duties drying a wet dinner plate she had in her hands on a small kitchen towel and setting it down on the table in front of Homer and then with a peeved expression on her face through a sarcastic glare resounded "Boogie-Monster indeed" How ridiculous and then bustled her way back into the house to resume her daily work regimine.

Homer leaned back in his chair for a moment thusly, taking a few more short drags from his pipe. And with a pensive glare on his face sat there for a moment in a racked mental state and jittered nerves to quietly reflect on those disturbing and frightful events that he experienced in the previous month in his mind, just as he was inadvertently taking out the trash one night. It was an incredulous question as to whether the whole thing was just a product of a fervid imagination on his part or if what he thought he actually saw was real. It was from this somewhat shaken and unsettling standpoint within his harried mind he recounted that opaque and morose nocturnal image, that of a creaturish looking outline, silhouetted against the old withered wooden siding of a neighbors rickety old garage hunched over and prowling the night. A wretched form a hideous Grinchnode if you will, wrought in a besieging twisted, contorted and deformed frame hunched over in some freakish visually pristine night time composite and back dropped against that which served itself as a crude makeshift movie screen with an approaching cars headlights serving as the projector. With it's goonish exaggerated bodily proportions with its wretched arms and claws stretched out and extended creeping alongside a neighboring garage in a shutter stock motion.

And as the passing cars headlights served to further distort it's gruesome and mutated knarred characteristics. Its ghastly image grossly exaggerated by the approaching cars fluttering headlights before disappearing altogether... Thusly in presenting itself in a surrealistic blackened silhouette had clarified its dreadful, ominous and elusive image, in a visual nocturnal confirmation finally seared its eerie cryptic and indiscriminate connotations to the hazy ill defined bounds of the human imagination. Or those unexplained heart pounding, waning and mournful cries and moans that besieged the sedentary calm of the night time silence, awakening slumbering residents from the sanctity of nocturnal bliss, almost imploring ....beckoning impending doom. Seemingly coming from some distant and unknown location, that he was the only one privy to that night. He did not go to his wife that night in urgent forewarnings of these stark revelations because he did not want to scare or cause her undo alarm. As she would know he was telling the truth, he'd rather she'd remained dubious surly and belligerent, instead of a believing and frightened, emotional wreck and terrified for as long as possible.

And although he had never lied to her about anything of significant importance in the forty years they'd been married. She also knew him not to be the type for pulling practical jokes either especially ones of such a juvenile nature as it just wasn't his nature or style. And her seemingly outward skeptical reaction to all of this in her loud boisterous reaction to newspaper reports. Or her harsh brand of belittling him or scoffing at the supposition on the part of others in the community at the prospect that some type of green slimy monster lurking in the shadows at night is what's culpable here. Or that may just be an outward façade on her part in a contrived attempt to mask an element of truly underlying terror and a self inhibiting degree of apprehension that may lay within. He still tenaciously held fast to his earlier secretive precognition that what he saw was real and not just a figment of a lurid imagination and that he now he had to unwittingly appear to be as surprised and taken back as everyone else was going to be to any further stark revelations by local authorities or in public disclosures by the media in leading up to the source of these bizarre and mysterious incidents in any matter of descript form in further disclosures to his wife

He was going to have to do this in more subtle ways without arousing undue suspicion or a full blown panic on her part. And thus so doing he was going to have to cite newspaper articles and television broadcasts to Claire in a surprised and unassuming way and when she starts asking him why they were beginning to do certain things? And by no means could he divulge any details of the events that transpired that night in relative close proximity to his home about a month ago. He would also have to get involved in the upcoming neighborhood watch that was instigated and headed up by Gifford Fugates an old textile mill retiree who resided at the end of the street, on the corner of Crandall and Willow street. Willow was an old dirt and gravel dead end road which ran along the edge of the housing allotment and into a field of high weeds. It was called Willow street because on the other side of the road in the direction away from the, houses were fields of high grass that ran into swampy areas whereby you'd sometimes see men or adolescent boys standing in the shallows or in little row boats fly fishing.

There was a great big willow tree with a pond in the center that some of the neighborhood kids played in and around. The pond was home for various wildlife such as big carp that resembled extremely large goldfish as well as huge bullfrogs and painter turtles in the sludge of the green murky pond, and some of the kids captured these various types of wild life in the more shallow portions of the water and kept them as pets. After awhile some of the parents forbade their children from frequenting the pond any further as there were reputed sightings of water moccasins rising on the waters. The neighborhood watch meetings were typically held in the town hall and bore relatively high turnouts due to the rise in panic among residents in the local community, usually marked by paunchy old windbags winding up in shouting matches as to what they thought was at hand in causing these disturbing and frightful events. Everyone seemed to have an expert and conclusive opinion as to what they thought the root cause could be but no one seem to accurately pinpoint the cause or come even remotely close to minimizing the gap or narrowing the margin of neighboring doubt or unbridled suspicion. This also spurned a sharp increase in handgun sales of local sporting goods stores and pawn shops. Women stocked up on mace or pepper spray commuted in groups or were afraid to walk the streets solely or altogether, past evening hours at dusk unaccompanied. Homer just sat there for the better part of the morning outwardly perplexed in what was seemingly an inescapable mental quandary before he was granted a temporary reprieve by venue of a warm sunlit and comforting morning accented by a newspaper black coffee and a bacon and eggs breakfast his wife invariably bestowed upon him every morning like clockwork pretty much throughout the duration of their forty year union. This at least momentarily freed his troubled and distraught mind and distracted his attention from whatever it was that was rooted in these disturbing sequence of events and their bizarre and inexplicable nature.

The kids were really hyped up for the big arena held rock concert that was coming up in a few days as they had to catch a bus to the neighboring town of Fayetteville where the Paisley arena was. They had to travel at least six miles from their home in Avondale to where the bus station was. Five miles on the tracks and one in town to reach the location of the greyhound bus terminal for their stay at a budget type motel the night prior in order to arrive there on time. They were going to have to do this via the railroad tracks as there were no outlying or official roads that accessed the bus station from their home town. To do this they were going to have to leave for their destination early in the morning to arrive at the bus terminal in the neighboring town of Lehighton. And Sherri said she wasn't going she had to baby sit for some neighborhood children whose parents were going out of town to visit some relatives. Besides she wasn't a big hard rock fan anyway and needed the money as she was trying to save up for a car. So the following morning Todd, loaded up with a backpack containing a couple of changes of clothes some foodstuffs a toothbrush and a razor and some shaving crème to meet Julie at her house. She loaded up with similar items and they both ventured out to go pick up Crystal. The walk to Crystals house was a quiet, scenic early morning jaunt consisting of tree lined streets and birds chirping ushering in the dawn. When he arrived at Crystals door she looked like something the cat drug in sleep still in her eyes her hair mussed and disheveled overall and practically begged Todd to let her go back to sleep.

They were both wrought with that sick sleep deprived feeling but Crystal a lot more so you know the one where your forcibly rousted from a deep slumber for some usually lame aggravating purpose like school or a fishing trip or a first shift or odd job or something and had no other choice. That of which was coupled with that raw cold slap in the face blast of that early morning air that seems to wrap itself like a tight band around your forehead and combined with that dreaded almost out of your body feeling that it's early morning dawn and you knew that anyone with any sense at all was still in bed…and one which was often times accompanied by the foisted early morning roust initiated by the reverberating bull horned bellow of grandpa windbag or uncle blow hard on one of those dreaded annual visits. And the harsh stringent conditions that were clearly outlined in the stuffy annals of the book of old worldisms that dictated, one had to rise at five or six o' clock in the morning or it was going to throw all the planets in the solar system out of kilter from their perfect axis rotation or something. This was a crucial element in going to work in some sweatshop setting like a smelting plant or coal mine or a cow and chicken farm in some economically dilapidated post depression era setting. You know the fostering elder's, who instilled us with the old world fallacy as children that if we put enough pennies in our piggy banks and didn't at some point let them burn a hole in our pockets. And that if we duly exercised an above average level of self deprivation and sacrifice that Grandpa just knew we had within ourselves and didn't go to spend them they would accrue some sort of fictitional value, and that one fine and momentous day in the far off and distant future, we would awaken to find we'd have saved up enough capitol to be able to secure a qualifying interest in Microsoft or something.

And over the years they had become so conditioned to this archaic and unsubstantiated ritualistic form of non-sense no doubt taken from the book of preposterous old worldish myths. The crude backward mindset held in this regard taken from a drudge laden work ethic that was staunchly purported by the hot air balloon sect due in large part to a what had become a diminished sense of viable purpose in later on in life. In that these men were so conditioned to having reported as lackey underlings to some brutish iron fisted shop foreman for twelve and sixteen hour stretches for a number of decades in some grimy dreary factory setting that they found themselves totally unable to flip the outmoded switch in their obtuse minds to the off position. And then later on at ungodly early morning hours and without compunction felt the necessary overriding need to aggravate you with it demanding the same of you as well. And in all my years since, and aside from just needlessly taxing and expending the precious commodity of limited energy of some poor unfortunate. I have yet to clearly see one shred of viable evidence substantiating such unfounded and inflated claims in that of early morning rising making anyone much less one these old gassers, any healthier, wealthier or wiser. At least as I vaguely recall, it was a needless, burdensome and unpleasant exercise I had to repeatedly endure as a kid anyway on those annual visits I endured by uncle blowhard. But nonetheless, the blunt edge of that sleep deprived feeling was somewhat taken off by a stiff pot of black coffee brewed at Julies house. And Todd wholeheartedly took advantage of that as she got ready. Their trite and meaningless small talk on the way to Crystals house mainly centered around Todd's narrow and bias inclination towards hair band rock music alone that left no open or objective margin for anything else regardless of it's merit as if it was the only credible or legitimate music form in existence.

Julie somewhat touched on the topic of music but interjected other things into the discussion such as small insignificant events in her life as well as recent interactions with friends and family. The main focal point of conversation did not however shift towards anything pertaining to the recent turn of events regarding the seething crisis that loomed. Nor just what particularly had been threatening the community at large other than what has been reported by the news media. Neither did they call into question those creepy noises that were heard in a low pathetic moan from the hollow of that dark stretch of woods in the distance the month prior as they all frantically scurried home along the railroad tracks coming back from the old country store that ghastly night. At least for the present time the topic shifted to other things so as to try to alleviate some of the dreaded prospect and their inward anxiety they held regarding this whole thing. The kids primary focus was on just getting there and for the moment just relishing in the synthesized acoustic upbeat guitar riffs and lush droning undertones the harmonious singing voices hair band rock music afforded it's intent listening fans…And at least for the time being it furnished them an appealing and comforting version from that horrible nights talking thing. But that at least for the time being all was well, the drama that preceded on the communal level at this point had diminished and was beginning to lose much of it's excitement and appeal and was replaced by a guarded sense of wary subterfuge. And by now the overall fear level in the kid's les' the town at large had somewhat subsided, this was due in part to their youthful naivety, as well as a long held in a mistaken hopefulness toward the positive they fervently held to the faint notion this would just all somehow eventually go away like some bad dream that just came out of the misty fog of some long, distant and far off place that could no longer reach out and touch them and that they could just finally move past this and put it all behind them. After they picked up Crystal they headed in the direction of the railroad tracks that accessed the bus station. As they all slowly came up on the rise the early morning sun fully appeared setting it's light on tree lined foliage and the remaining landscape. The early morning was relatively cool with light yet steady breezes that slowly gave way to rising and sweltering mid day temperatures thusly evaporating wet dew that rested on leaves and grass. At a distance while walking on the tracks they all observed the waves of heat rising from the ground on the distant tracks on the horizon ahead giving off the illusion of rushing water. And in the distant sky at a very high altitude marked by a steady stream of white smoke billowing from it's end one could markedly distinguish the faint image of a passing jet.

Yet as the little group came onto the tracks Todd kind of stumbled around in the gravel before he actually set foot in the center of the old tar laden railroad ties that reeked of the same. As they looked out at the distant early morning horizon and taking into account what was inevitably going to be a long arduous march trudging miles on these old and decrepit set of railroad tracks in what would soon be a steady and oppressive mid-day sun they all stopped and paused momentarily considering what was going to be physically required of them. Then their once held collective enthusiasm at the prospect of having a wonderful time among thousands of their fellow rock fans screaming and cheering in that big old coliseum slowly began to diminish giving way to an emotional letdown. And after all they were not professionally trained athletes or regimented infantry soldiers either, yet although they were all young and relatively fit they really weren't cut out for an unnecessary and rugged eight mile trek over such harsh terrain as this in the hot midday sun with full packs and a timeline they were going to have to meet. In consideration of these stressful and burdensome factors they all stood there attempting to decide if the pro's far outweighed the con's. Was all that really going to be worth it and not even mentioning possibly running into that thing along the way…

After all they could all just sit home and watch it on either MTV or VH1…. But they had to come to a unanimous agreement and soon, they had to decide as to whether or not they were all physically capable enough to for all intents and purposes really be up to this. And for about ten or fifteen minutes they all stood there engaged in group discussion raising advantages and weighing in the disadvantages against them one being the physical stamina and preparedness they were all going to have to exude and the obstacles that lay before them they were gonna have to usurp before they reached the bus station. But Todd had the final say, stating let me be the voice of reason here. We'll take it slow and steady, not rush, and drink plenty of fluids along the way, rest at intervals as it's only five miles there and we have until night fall to arrive there safely.

So they agreed, they've come this far and why should they all turn back now just because the trip there will be somewhat uncomfortable

After taking a long draw of water from a light brown canvas covered hikers canteen and dapping the beads of sweat from his forehead with an old red and white patterned head bandana scruffy rangy bearded Harley bikers wore with sunglasses as they rocketed down interstate highways in the early to mid nineteen seventies. It bore an intricate white design resembling the back of a playing card and typically came in a varying assortment of colors. Thus of which he had shoved in one of the cargo pockets of pants that were about two or three sizes to big for his slender wiry frame. Todd returned it to his backpack and slung one of the harness straps over one shoulder and led the little group further on their way down the railroad tracks and acting as he earlier unwittingly put it…. "Point Man". And unlike the trip to the farmers market the month before the unassuming, playful, and jovial manner in which the three kids conducted themselves that day was now somewhat hampered and replaced with a more solemn and guarded appearance much like that of a wary squad of infantry soldiers struck with the thousand yard stare out on patrol in some dense jungle foliage anticipating the sudden outbreak of combat brought on by an insidious enemy unit ambushing them and erupting into a volatile firefight at any given moment.

Yet as they slowly made their way down the tracks the somber early morning light began to give way to a hot and humid midday sun. Todd in a lethargic manner motioned his two friends off of the steep rise the tracks ran atop of over the side and down through a deep gully. The three arduously trudged through rocky and uneven ground almost tripping and falling down along the way and up yet another hilly incline that onlooked more sparsely wooded acreage. The vast open ground was dotted with the occasional abandoned farm house or yet another deserted cow pasture with sparse scraggily weeds and vegetation, punctuated by downed or dilapidated barbed wire fences that were overgrown with high weeds and wildflowers paying silent homage to the long ago work inhabitants that were rooted in a moderately thriving and lucrative socio-economic times. And on their way to their mutually agreed upon resting place they passed by an old rusty farm implement that looked as if it belonged on display in the Smithsonian Institute. It appeared to be a little old fashioned steam propelled tractor that was frozen stiff in it's tracks and just left there. It was wrought in thick plated rusted cast iron even the wheels, and when they came to where they'd finally take a rest Todd ushered them to fall in under the shade of a big massive oak tree. The rough ground below that surrounded the tree was partially covered with big tufts of weeds and ratty vegetation as well as large rocks with which the kids could lean up against or set foodstuffs on as they ate. The trio by now was physically exhausted by the distance they'd covered in the hot sun and in resting for about a half hour or so began to adjourn for a lunch of assorted deli meat sandwiches, corn chips and potato salad Julies grandmother made and a box of chocolate cream filled cup cakes for dessert. Todd pointed to the rusty old tractor saying God I wonder how long that's been sitting there?

And as the little group sat there in the shade taking out the rations of sandwiches from their backpacks. They each began to take long insatiable gulps of cold water from their canteens and wiping the sweat from their tired and withered brows with whatever cloth type material was available, as the waning car like horn from a bypassing train engine droned in the distance and Todd suddenly chimed up... hey watch it with the water supply!! I don't know when or where were gonna be able to replenish it! Crystal lowly and abruptly replied maybe there's a river or stream nearby, and Todd said yeh but we gotta make sure the water supply isn't contaminated and clean enough to draw from and not some glorified cesspool do you know how to do that! Crystal somewhat startled by that statement paused and ceased gulping from the nozzle of her canteen slowly lowered it with a one handed gesture abruptly capped it and returned it to rest on her hip. Yeah whatever you say Yule Gibbons. The distant trains horn continued to bellow until it finally faded away, but they knew it was on another set of tracks miles away and would not be coming by in their direction as this set had not been in use for a good number of years now. Not since light to moderate level industry in the surrounding areas had moved to other countries, closed down or just disbanded. Then the main topic of discussion slowly shifted back to the freakish disturbances and the mounting level of collective fear suffered at the communal level.

Or in the rising number of murdered victims that were subsequently discovered in wooded and remote areas of local principalities by authorities, or the bizarre state in which they were found. Todd asked the other two if they'd heard any thing more on the subject by way of local news broadcasts or if there were any further developments. The girls just said no in the way that they really didn't follow the news much anymore even in matters of grave significance. But Crystal stated that at night she started drawing the curtains in her living room as she sat there watching T.V. she said she got the creepy and overwhelming intuition that something was leering in at her from the outside. Then as the three sat there finishing up their sandwiches and chips they slowly began to feel full saving those cream filled chocolate cupcakes for later, and then just sat there for about a half hour or so and then an additional fifteen or twenty minutes more for the food to digest in their stomachs. As Todd sat there under the shade of that massive oak tree and chewing the last remnants of his chicken salad sandwich he waved and swiped his hand about shoeing a flying pest out of his face maybe a bumble bee a big mosquito or a fly or something and then he abruptly crooked his right leg up while looking down he reached in to retrieve the shabby, worn looking little colt semi-automatic pistol that was stashed in his big oversized cargo pocket on the side of a pair of drab faded olive green BDU'S he was wearing. He just sat there simultaneously chewing his sandwich and holding up the little gun with an extended arm with one eye squinted closed and an intent expression on his reddened pock marked face. He began pointing it in the direction of the rusty old abandoned railroad tracks as if he were actually sighting in on something. Then he drew back his arm to eject the magazine before pulling the slide mechanism to expel any unintended shells that may have still been in the chamber while shoving the other half of his chicken salad sandwich into his face. Julie' just sat there wincing, and shaking her head from side to side exclaimed...do you have to take that damn thing out here right now...in front of me? Todd' just doing a service check on our saving grace that's all.... I just want to make sure this baby is smooth oiled, and operational. "Julie" a cold lifeless piece of steel is your baby eh, what about something that can love you back like a nice, soft, warm girlfriend instead? Todd abruptly halted his inspection of the shabby little pistol dropping his hand over one knee turned his head to leer at Julie…a girlfriend huh? Are you available? Julie just rolled her eye's in a disgusted gawk and contemptuously exclaimed E-E-E-GAAD!!…Oh you've got to be kidding that'll be the day!!…Todd' anyway that won't save us from Mr. Borgus Weems…now will it? Julie' Borgus Weems?… Who pray tell is Borgus Weems?,…Todd' the boogie man you know that's what I call him Borgus Weems, Julie' OH-GAWD!!,…you mean to say that you really still believe in all those grossly embellished and far fetched superstitious childhood fallacies we were force fed as kids by all those old farty aunts, uncles and grandparents we had? Ya know I think I stopped believing in the tooth fairy and the Easter bunny when I was about eight or ten or something, and anyway nothing even remotely pointing in that direction has been proven or substantiated yet…Todd' well how about all of those alleged bug eyed twisted and contorted stiffs they've been substantially finding encased in that gross green sludge or is all that just a figment of collective overactive imaginations too? I dunno about you but that certainly clinches it for me, or does an avalanche of one ton boulders need to fall on top of that pretty little head of yours? Julie' f-u-n-n-e-e, well wise ass, just the very sight of that hideous little piece of heinously forged wrought iron and the knowledge of what it's intended for makes me sick to my stomach, and I cringe inside at the very sight of it. And anyway this is not an emergency so put it away! Todd' And just what intended use is that "bright eye's?! Julie' KILLING!! Todd' moaned…Oh Gees….you know that's getting to be a one note tune you keep playing there on yer ukulele sister Sara, do you know any others? How' bout tip toe through the tulips or something? That would surely be a refreshing change…Julie's mildly contorted facial expression suddenly changed to one of moderate hostility as she sensed she was never going to get anywhere on this issue with Todd as the chances of converting him over to her side were slim to none.

And her feigned silence was her most effective modem of nonverbal protest at conveying her level of utter distain and contempt she inwardly felt on the subject. But this heated and ongoing debate had reached a mutual point of futility in an ongoing exasperating stalemate and at this point and had become a very tired and worn out form of ritual between the two. And also one that could've been compared to some backward and uneducated old world couple who'd been married for fifty or sixty years and had no redeeming matrimonial objects left but to derive some sadistic backwards form of gratification in their dysfunctional sniping and bicker some co-dependant relationship. Or even that of two old world clipper ships with cannoned bows facing off with each other in some pitted standoff at close quarters on the high seas mutually engaged in close pitch exchanges of volatile cannon fire barrages in vehement hopes of demoralizing the other into a decimated pile of smashed rubble and fiery wooden planks in a pathetic heap of smoldering ash descending it's way down to the lowly depths of the lost and forgotten trunks of DavyJones locker. Todd' just looked over at Julie and momentarily pausing from his mock target session and loudly retorted. Well ya know some people just have a lot of fun just target shooting like plinking away at big aluminum cans or glass bottles in a field on a dull sunny afternoon for instance and there's absolutely no killing of anything whatsoever involved!

Crystal' timidly looking on as he resumed squinting his one eye and grimacing sighting the tiny little gun in on something else in the distance while clicking and dry firing it and whispering pow-pow-pow under his breath just as if he were actually engaging real targets, then she suddenly interjected' you know I don't know all that much about guns but I have heard that doing that is bad for the firing pin. Todd' stopped and paused for a moment dropped his hand that was holding the little pistol in down and looked over at Crystal with a somewhat annoyed expression on his face.... tersely replied is that so? And then slightly nodding his head in a slightly agitated and broken reply muttered well yah yer right you don't know that much about guns. You need to stick to the things you do like New Wave music and being a preppie mall rat. Julie' You know if I had it my way all the appropriate figures in authority at the integral points of the earth would all come together on a grand massive scale in a mandatory collective action to confiscate every gun, tank and flamethrower on it's face big and small and take them all to a centralized location for the explicit purpose of having one giant sized meltdown in some sort of gigantic smelting pot to incinerate every one of them! And at having just said that she leered over at Todd with a bug eyed grinning expression hoping she'd struck a nerve or pushed a button or two almost gleefully awaited an incensed response. Instead Todd just began to laugh not only at the total ludicrousness of such an idea but in how unrealistic and implausible such a statement was... ha, ha, ha, ha, kind of an extreme and a somewhat impractical position don't you think? Julie displayed a moderately incensed expression on her face at his amused reaction.

And what do you propose be done with all those godless, lawless criminal factions located in remote corners of the earth whereby horrific acts of genocide are still being carried out by backward, apish, Neanderthalic organizations against what in many cases are almost entire populations of innocent people not to mention the tonnage? of smelted metal I mean? Should the world just ingratiatingly go in and bestow upon them a nice big bouquet of flowers from the FTD man or go over in, in full strength with fighter bombers, tanks and guns to dispense with business until such elements are completely eradicated from the earth?!...Or should the world just turn a blind eye and sprinkle it with some of your magical, mystical fairy dust Julie and maybe it'll all just go away,.... Julie' just got an incensed look on her face at first which was then superseded by a distant gaze and said in a semi-sarcastic and rhetorical reply, Well to your first question I don't exactly know that's a tuffee I'd have to spend a little time to think about it first...Todd' you do that...Then in a wide eyed glare she exuberantly chimed up,... but to your second,...perhaps,....perhaps maybe they could construct a massive iron bridge that would stretch across the entire length of the globe that would connect the continents and join together the fellowship of all mankind or maybe even build a stairway to the stars.....As he randomly pointed it to various objects out in the vacant old cow pasture whispering pow, pow and tilting the little gun back as if it were actually kicking as he fired it abruptly stopped turned to her and shot a look of total disbelief and loudly retorted Oh you gotta be kidding!! Have you been smoking opium!?...Ya know Ms. Peanut I just think you've been out in this hot sun to long and it's slow roasted your brain, Guns are only an inanimate tool, an enabling byproduct of existing chronic adverse social ills regarding the human condition. Julie you know the world doesn't constitute some half baked candy land with the tooth fairy or mayor McCheese giving us the key's to the city before were all led down the yellow brick road ya know, it always has and will be, since the dawn of time be plagued with man kinds self-manufactured woes and chronic misery. It's just something we all over a period of time must come to accept and learn to live with ya know.

And no measure of armament confiscation or destruction thereof facilitated by any ant-gun radical minded people would prove successful in eradicating that common denominator from the human equation, and I don't care on how grand a scale it would be imposed. Julie' yeah... but there'd be no more wars, no more gun violence in the streets of big cities. It would bring an exemplary end to a lot of this worlds misery. Todd' Yeah but there'd still be bad people and they'd just seek out and find other modes to keep purporting their badness, and as for misery it goes back to the dawn of time. It was here long before us or the inception of guns and I have a feeling it will be here long after. Julie' sarcastically exclaimed ooh boy your just a bastion of knowledge and infinite wisdom aren't you? You just have a convenient and ready made answer for everything don't you. "Oh thou great, wise and noble one...well I don't see the rest of the world lining up at your doorstep for any of your so called words of wisdom. Todd' no, they aren't but I have done my homework that's all...Julie' and it's not much, and boy you sure have, they are just all the wrong answers....that's all...Crystal' with a moderately worrisome expression on her face suddenly asked. Do you think that little gun will do anything to stop whatever has been committing all those horrible attacks on people if we should by some chance happen to encounter it out here? it's awfully small and it doesn't look like it would actually do very much...Julie' whaddaya mean!! after all it's a gun that shoots bullets isn't it of course it'll do much to whatever it is out there!! Tex here is just gonna draw his shootin' iron, and bear down on it like it's an approachin' sidewinder and blast it full of holes aren't ya there? Duke!! Todd' aggravated exclaimed, oh will you just finally put a cork in for a while and give it a rest dammit your getting on my last remaining nerve!!

And then he turned to Crystal and muttered I sure hope so or were all gonna be in a world of shit if it doesn't. I just don't know what else to do here, we all just can't be further victimized and totally isolated from each other by this thing and otherwise restricted to the corporate limits and bounds of the town or imprisoned in our homes and never seeing each other or going out anywhere or doing anything can we? We all might just as well be dead. Crystal' I guess so but I still don't feel safe even at home and I am always scared all the time and have a big lump in my throat and a queasy feeling in the pit of my stomach. Todd just grinned and said jokingly, maybe you should stop eating in so many of those fast food restaurants you do all the time before you and your stuck up preppie friends go the mall and tapping into the inexhaustible reserves of mumsy and daddy's money on like totally rad Preppie and New Wave styles and conventional pop records and tapes….ha, ha, ha, ha…Crystal' infuriated, that's not funny!! now I'm going to be pistol whipped in the back of the head with old worn out clichés' and stereotypes!! I mean it I'm serious here!! it's from all this pent up anxiety that keeps mounting at just the thought of all those awful news reports. Todd' oh honey I'm just trying to get you to lighten up and laugh a bit even if it's at yourself so you won't feel so bad all the time that's all. And then Todd paused and sat there for a moment and somewhat pensively looked over at Crystal and said….well ya know there's always one other way to put your mind a little more at ease,…. have you ever fired anything in the way of a gun before? Crystal' in a shaky and timid reply murmured no…I mean well….. I've used my little brothers Daisy Red Ryder B-B gun before shooting at some tin cans in the woods behind our house,…does that count? Todd' no sorry Sis' I'm afraid it doesn't, while leeringly grinning he laughingly stating, ya know and up until all this started happening neither have I, I've never pulled the trigger on anything more than a plastic squirt gun cooling off with friends in my back yard or a water hose to relieve the searing heat of a midday summer sun. I guess your gonna be one up on me, ha, ha, ha, ha, heh. The girls totally flabbergasted by this stark revelation retaliated in a scornful and infused manner shouted what!! Your going around with that thing in your pocket and you don't know how to use it! Todd' I never said I don't know how to use one I just said I've never actually fired one there's a difference.

But I do however have a thorough and proficient knowledge of their make, various calibrations, trajectories and inner workings Ya know I can completely field strip a stock M-14 clean and oil it and put it back together again just as well as any marine recruit in basic training. Julie' sarcastically… oh that just puts my mind totally at ease and makes me feel a whole lot better now! Todd' well anyhow I learned all this stuff from my uncle who's an avid gun nut and collects em' you see Julie I really don't have much of an affinity for them either I've never actually got around to firing one it's just never occurred to me and I've never really had any inclination to actually do so, I just wanted to appear interested in one of my uncle's hobby's even though I'm not really into it myself, you see he and my dad are really close. And this is the only thing I can think of to feel a little safer when we come out here in the boonies on a trip somewhere like the old general store. It's also the only thing I can think of as a potent and effective measure of security for us against this looming and unseen threat. I don't want us all to get caught out here in the middle of nowhere completely vulnerable and unawares ya know. Girls… I've never actually seen one being fired either except on T.V. and in that format I've often heard it's rarely acoustically depicted in true life accuracies. Todd' You mean like those phony Hollywood sensationalized gunshot sounds from those corny old 50's and 60's western and war movies?…Crystal muttered yeah like those…Todd no I'm afraid this isn't going to be much like that at all. I don't want scare you or anything but the sound of actual gunfire especially if you've never heard it before is kinda' creepy.

Then Crystal was suddenly filled with a cold pulsating adrenalin rush welling upwardly from within to where she felt a throbbing knot in her throat and a queasy feeling in the pit of her stomach. Julie' Oh, my God No!! Todd' Crystal would it put your mind somewhat at ease if you actually used it to see what it actually does? Julie' in a frantic excited tone of voice exclaimed Oh, No!! not here, not now, not in front of me!…don't you even dare!! Todd' OH FOR GOD SAKE'S TESS WILL YOU JUST PIPE DOWN AND PUT A PROVERBIAL LID ON IT!! were not gonna use it on you duffas! now get holda yerself, getta grip!! Crystal' inwardly she was utterly terrified she had never even touched a gun in her whole life and didn't want to do this at all,…I don't know, well maybe… what about conserving bullets? Todd' what? I've got a box of a hundred rounds and a full magazine in the chamber as well as four additional loaded clips in my other pocket. And besides were not deep in the jungles of some banana republic waiting to engage a band of Salvadorian guerrillas in some random firefight, it's not going to hurt us if we cap off a couple of magazines at some targets. This was apparently going to be something completely out of character for the three young hair band rock fans who's main interests only consisted of music and rad clothing styles. And it just didn't fit the profile for them to do so, and it was something that held out about as much in the area of appeal for them as a string of pearls would to an ape. And especially for Crystal she was going to be a fish completely out of water…Crystal' what do I have to do? In that instant Todd tossed the little gun over at Crystal and it bounced off the outer portion of her thigh and landed on the ground beside her as it was significantly heavier than it looked. Ouch that hurt! hey watch it buster that damn thing could go off!! Where's your head at? Todd' boy you sure don't know that much about guns do you… the safety is on. "Crystal looked down at it with a bewildered look of nervous apprehension on her face and exclaimed oh….as she slowly reached over to pick up the little gun to further examine it. She'd seen stuff on T.V. but this was not something she was predisposed to doing.

And it was totally out of character for her as she had no curiosity nor any inclination to handle or discharge anything other than a water hose at some flowers or one of her little brothers pellet guns at some empty tin cans in the woods. Those just made a pop when they discharged sort of like a blown up plastic bag or a balloon bursting. And she knew this was going to be very loud and very scary and just knowing what it was actually intended for scared the daylights out of her. And it was also readily apparent that the other two were not really gauged for something like this either, and for the most part it was going to be a feigned contrived exercise at best. But she trusted implicitly in Todd's judgment and background knowledge and proficiency he held on the subject in that it would be a safe exercise under his guidance and supervision. Yet she unabashedly displayed a grave lack of enthusiasm in doing so. But at this point she was game enough to try just about anything as a countering measure against that horrid predatory monster. And it was also going to be the only thing that was going to quell her nagging fears and anxiety as to it's potential power of effectiveness against that elusively horrid thing should it suddenly manifest itself. After all her immediate interests extended only to the limits and bounds of New Wave styles, contemporary pop and hair band rock music or that of being a narly rad and fashionable valley girl-mall rat, and this really wasn't in her preppie girl persona as she felt the sudden and cold surge of adrenalin in her throat and chest as her pulse began to throb and the blood in the fatty under portion of her forearms began to run ice cold.

She felt her stomach wrench itself up in nervous surges and waves of mild nausea., not only at the unpleasant prospect of having to discharge a firearm for the first time in her life but being a second hand party to the emission of gun smoke and that strange creepy smell she'd heard it had. It almost served as a signatured underscore of death itself. But the prospect of that horrible thing coming upon them in their travels or even invading one or more of their homes one night was beginning to take an emotional toll on her out weighing all other inhibiting factors.

And at this juncture she was beginning to regret having come along at all and that maybe she should have just stayed at home barricading herself in her house and just waited for the police or the National Guard or something, or somebody else to hunt down and destroy that dreadful thing. And for the papers or television news reports to produce concrete and physical proof of that before she went on a trip like this again she thought to herself but as of now it was to late. As she was fraught with nervous anxiety and couldn't wait until this unpleasant and disconcerting exercise was all over in desperate hopes she could put all this out of her mind at least temporarily. Worrisome she glared over at Todd, in a momentary pause of nervous apprehension, and in a timid tone of voice murmured, aren't you going to use it too? Todd' leeringly grinned over at her then in a maniacal tone and a gawking bug-eyed expression mockingly exclaimed, No-way José not me Noctrina!! guns literally scare the crap outta me!! Crystal aghast abruptly lowered her arm and cried, Why you lousy, rotten toad!!.. I outta' shoot you instead!!...Todd',...now honey, you see that little latch there above the handgrip take your thumb and press down. And with that there was a little click. Crystal' startled exclaimed...what was that? Todd' that was the safety my dear it's off. Crystal' oh my God!! Todd' com on now honey don't wuss out on me now you're almost out of the starting gate now place your finger over the trigger guard and pull back on that little slide receiver mechanism there on the top until you hear a click. But don't put your finger on the trigger until your actually ready to fire, My dad told me that, that old thing goes off if you just look at the wrong way!! Julie' looking on at this totally aghast watched as her friend

Crystal prepared to fire the decades old worn and scuffed up automatic pistol that was discarded by his uncle and manufactured so long ago that looked as though it could've been used by some seedy inner city crime element perhaps in the garment district or on the NJ. Docks of the post war era. "Crystal another clicking sound what was it? Todd' through a sardonic grin chimed, that was a bullet going into the chamber. Crystal' Oh God' her face totally flushed white and paralyzed with fear, began to shake mildly, imploringly looking over at Todd for his next authoritative directive. For God sakes get hold a yourself it's not an anti-tank weapon or a flamethrower or something, and it's not gonna blow up in your hand like a grenade with the pin pulled!!...Now site in on that old rusty yellow no trespassing sign posted on that old sycamore tree over there and cap off that magazine. Ya know I've always had a soft spot in my heart for those damn things and the dumb ass prick landowners who feel the imbecilic need to put them up.

They think they own the whole earth and even it's nature too just because of the temporary power a little money grants them in this life. I'll tell ya, I would like nothing better than to pepper one of them instead of these rusty old targets if one were around. Then Crystal shifting her focus of attention suddenly said, how about that rusty old tractor sitting further on down on the rise there? Todd' barked, no, no, no…that damn thing is made of solid cast iron you know what'll happen if you pepper it? Bullets are made of soft lead and they will fatten out and possibly ricochet back towards our direction and maybe hit one or more of us oh no! You might as well shoot at a tank and besides you gotta have a special type of ammunition for that! Some type of armor piercing rounds or something I think, but that shit is for psycho's and nutcases who usually belong to one of those whacko radical white supremacist hate group organizations that have amateurish armies and hold mock training sessions in the backwoods of Louisiana or Mississippi and have warped self delusions about the government and overthrowing it in some preposterous counter revolution or something. Then he started grinning and laughing at the ridiculous thought of the total construct of lunacy those racial anti Semitic groups actually entailed. And in doing a double take at the statement he made regarding it, and then told her just stick with the sign for now.

Then Crystal, her face flushed white, slowly and nervously raised her arm to recite in on the rusty old yellow property sign that had been posted there about twenty five years or more ago. It was at least fifty or more yards away and was just within range of that junky little pistol. It hung in a sparse section of moderate sized maple and sycamore trees with rusty barbed wire fencing hung from rotting and dilapidated wooden posts protruding from the ground running through the tree line. And with such a gun with just about no barrel as this was and with such a low trajectory, which was really meant to be used at close range and was really a very poor choice for a security weapon much less a target gun. And for such a passive and docile soul such as Crystal was, who wasn't geared for something like this anyway, for her it was gonna be like trying to hit a bull in the ass with a banjo. It was definitely gonna take an act of divine miraculous intervention if she were to come any where's close. Then Todd yelled over at her better use both hands! I've heard a twenty five kicks a little. Then as she placed her other palm at the base of the hand grip and not seriously aiming at anything abruptly fired off one round as there was a louder than expected cracking bang followed by an inadvertent rapid succession of eerie pops and flashes of light from the end of the barrel as the spent casings flew out the breach end of the little pistol. The pistol was set on automatic and the shots echoed throughout the vast countryside mimicking the sounds of a distant firefight to the unassuming passerby who may have been a on a trek somewhere else in the desolate landscape. Three out of the seven that were fired miraculously struck the sign.

And the last one blew it right off the side of the tree. Somewhat startled by the shots Crystal quickly lowered her arm as a thick wave of grayish blue smoke billowed out from the end of the barrel. Julie wincing with her eye's tightly closed and the palms of her hands covering her ears in a mellow dramatic display of oppositional defiance and disapproval to the whole thing. And in a clumsy display of sole exuberance not shared by the other two. Todd sprinted over to where the little sign had landed with a spring in his step doing a little jig as he went over to look down and examine it, exclaiming three out of seven not bad for your first time at the ranges!! And there's two holes in the sign as well! Ha, ha…and at a target fifty yards away ta boot, Then he turned towards her squinched up his face and while winking at her with one eye he jokingly asked…Is there something your not telling me? You're an expert!! Are you sure you've never done this before? He knew she felt bad inside and he in his awkward and unrefined way was just trying to relieve some of the overwhelming tension, anxiety and ill feelings she constantly had. Oh, but…I think that for the time being we should leave the firing to the proficiency experts from now on, in that instance he turned his head as the smile left his face. Then he lowly stated but in all seriousness I'm afraid were gonna have to do a lot better against that monster should the occasion arise,…each and every shot is going to have to be dispensed with careful precision no margin for error ya know?…Because it will only prove out to be very costly in the end you know.

And just as he went over to Crystal he put his arm around her shoulder in a mild form of consolation to her as he ushered her back over to the big old shade tree to clear up, where a visibly shaken Julie who was poised there in a flustered state. Crystal just sullenly gazed down at the ground and he resumed smiling knowing full well within himself any strikes that were made to the old sign were a total fluke and purely a matter of dumb luck and had nothing to do with real proficiency or skill and asked her, like to try that again deadeye? she mildly shook her head back and forth signifying no holding out the little pistol in her extended hand …And in a somber tone she murmured I didn't like that very much and if you don't mind I'll let that be your department from now on…yeah I gathered that,…ok? Todd' slightly jerked his head to one side and replied sorry to hear it! I guess we all won't be doing any target shooting in the future as a form of group recreation or mutual bonding huh? I guess we'll all just have to stick to back yard barbecues and hair band concerts, ha, ha…sorry honey I don't have one of those corny old kewpie-dolls handy to give you for blowin that stinkin' sign off the tree like they give out at those late evening two-bit country outdoor carnivals used to, so how about this pack of ho-ho's as a consolation prize ha, ha…. Julie' who was in a harried and agitated state by the whole thing yelled knock it off!! that was just awful that's what guns actually do it's much worse than I thought. Todd' Oh it wasn't that bad but I'll tell ya what'll be even worse than that though is just the thought of what that horrid thing will do to us if we don't have one in our possession. Todd' asking Julie in an insincere joking manner biting his lower lip sarcastically commented well I guess an enlistment in the Army or the Marines isn't going to be in you guyzzus future agenda huh?

They'd have to drag you two off kicking and screaming to the rifle ranges and then send you both home on a medical Ha, ha… Todd looking back over at Crystal, Still think it's just a mild, ineffective little pop gun? She slowly nodded her head back and forth signifying no. Relieve your mind somewhat? Feel a little safer? She slowly nodded her head up and down. Todd' sighed and looked up and groaned everybody get enough to eat? The two girls murmured yes under their breath. And Todd said now that the show's over and done with I think we've all wasted enough time here for now so let's wrap up today's amateur shooting lessons by Todd and pack up our shit and get going we've still got a lot of ground to cover before night fall. And I don't want to have to camp out here in any of these woods tonight build a fire or have to have each one of us stand watch in shifts while the others sleep!! And in a collective manner of lethargic chagrin each one rose up off the ground in slow drudging succession dusting off the seats of their pants and legs thusly composing themselves and slowly gathering their cumbersome backpacks containing essential provisions before resuming their long arduous trudge further on down the center of the old dilapidated railroad tracks. Then in a dismal and morose manner they all stood around appropriating their backpacks and slinging the straps over their respective shoulders and making sure they had retrieved everything in the way of leftover foodstuffs as well before proceeding onward any further.

Just then Todd suddenly remembered asking Julie Oh yeah, did you bring your can of mace and your stun gun with ya? Julie replied in a sullen tone of dismay lowly murmured yeah I brought them, but now I have serious doubts as to what good they'll actually do now after having seen your star-spangled fireworks display. Todd' oh don't you worry about that you just keep them handy and close by anyway we may need them too as backup ya never know…and from here on out your officially my point man. Crystal' anyway, on a more pleasant note, what's for dinner tonight some kinda' soup? "Todd in a terse sarcastic reply…answered

Oh no you have your choice here of either steak or lobster tail dipped in butter baked potato and sour cream with a hot buttery dinner roll and a luscious garden salad entree' with your choice of thousand island blue cheese or ranch dressings…doesn't the mere thought of such tantalization of your taste buds with such sumptuousness make your mouth water to no end just thinking about the fine banquet I've prepared for you girls?!!… I've even brought along a vintage bottle of chardonnay how does 1973 grab everybody? I've sparred no expense here, nothing is to good for my lifelong friends. I think it was an excellent year but it has to chill first before we sample it I have to pull out the cork first to let it breathe. That's how us real wine connoisseurs do it ya know. Julie did you bring along the hors d'oeuvres like I told you to do back at the house? This fine delicacy can't be fully experienced unless it's capped off with a fine assortment of crackers and expensive cheeses ya know. Julie' And you sure don't spare us from a hearty buffet of your seven course selection of jaded, cynical, sarcasm….Todd' Yeah goof, soup!! what the hell else? how's clam chowder and saltines sit with everybody? My mother makes it homemade she prides herself on a long time kept family secret recipe handed down through the generations of us Peterson's that all the soup companies have been after her for years to disclose.. But we'll have to go on up further to see if there's a more inhabited and safer spot closer to civilization we can pitch a camp in. Then very sarcastically he stated, I wanna be somewhere were it's safe enough for me to relax and indulge my pampered taste buds relishing in such a fine delicacy... Everybody bring a blanket or a sleepin bag? It's gonna get awfully chilly out here tonight so we'll no doubt have to build a fire to stay warm and heat up this crappy soup if we get stuck out here in the freezing cold.

Then the frightened little trio still somewhat uncertain of their ability to counter a possible attack even with a firearm in their possession were starting to have second thoughts about undertaking this whole venture. And by something reputed to be so malevolent and dangerous that has up to this point remained to be seen at least by anyone living was a ghastly fact in itself for one to digest. Yet they still managed to drudgingly muster up just enough feigned energy and inner fortitude to resume their rugged hike along the tracks with the smell of hot tar and rotting ties wafting upwards in their faces proceeded slowly on foot for at least a few of more hours stopping to take a couple of ten or fifteen minute breaks along the way and periodically resting off to the side under the shade of some sparse tree line. The mid day sun began to dissipate giving way to cooler crisper air as autumn and it's exhilarating connotations began to slowly set in. The sallow light of an evening sun set it's harsh sallow rays upon the landscapes foliage, as it was going on about five o'clock in the afternoon. Then Julie suddenly interposed the ongoing and steady group conversation by asking Todd, how will we know when were getting close to the town we gotta catch the bus in? "Todd" there'll be a huge bluish gray water tower off to the right in the distance with the word Lehighton written on the side of it in bold white letters. Ya know were just about half way there now Todd said... Then suddenly Todd noticed a hazy and indistinguishable form in the distance of a slowly approaching figure coming towards them in the center of the railroad tracks at a distance of maybe three or four hundred yards off. Todd with a spontaneous burst of giddy, excited energy chimed up look girls, we've got company there's someone coming this way jumping around like a fidgety kid full of bully beans squirming around in a church pew on a Sunday morning that couldn't find it within himself to manage to keep still.

Oh it's probably just some old derelict or something that lives in a makeshift tent that's actually a blue tarp propped up by four tree branches stuck in the ground in some hobo camp somewhere in the woods along with other of his homeless comrades that cook dinner over an open rusty fifty gallon drum, washes his clothes and bathes in the river and hops railway box cars, all day to get leftover foodstuffs like rotten apples or turnips that spill outta wooden crates onto their deck…. Ha, Ha,. Heh-heh. Crystal' oh whatta a cruel and heartless thing to say! Don't you have even one shred of compassion in that scraggily pock marked, pimple ridden, carrot topped body of yours at all!?… Todd' Wincing sarcastically, Ooooh that's harsh, I do by the way you just gotta' dig deep enough that's all, but for all intents and purposes it usually rings true. Yet as the hazy indiscriminate figure drew nearer it began to take on an eerie sense of imminent danger, urgent in it's gaining momentum that was readily picked up on by the kids, Terror began to set in when they all noticed it rapidly approaching in an ominous and imminent sense of verocity. And with a grave sense of alarm Todd began to realize something just wasn't quite right about what it was that was fast approaching them. He began to feel a sudden adrenalin rush coupled with a newfound level of terror he'd never felt before. Yet as he even from a distance noted a large stature peculiar in it's form and was not markedly human. He immediately alerted this fact to the girls and sternly ordered them off to the side for cover. Julie!! Have your mace and your stun gun ready! I think this is it! It's the real thing!! "Julie" What's wrong? Just tell me what's going on? Just shut-up and do what I tell ya if you wanna live!!…Now git goin!!…MOVE yer ass's NOW!! Get down below and off the friggin rise!! Crystal was lying down there huddled with Julie in the gravel with her hands over her head as she began sobbing. And as the girls came to realize in that something was gravely imminent, and that some type of covert danger that was dark and impending was rapidly closing in, and also that it was apparently not human.

Then they both began to panic were struck with an overriding rush of hysteria began to go into shock. When the figure at this point was about one hundred yards off, and in a nervous rush of adrenaline Todd began to markedly distinguish the image of some kind of grotesque mutated nightmare on two legs. At that point he knew they were all in very deep shit as he desperately thought to himself oh my God I wish I had my uncles M-14 from his collection. Yet even from that marked distance he could visually distinguish the unnerving freakish resemblance of something between a very large gargoyle a demon and a dragon as he felt his blood run cold and he could hear the deafening pulsating pound of his heart whooshing in his ears. It's movements were fluid and it's advances where almost mechanical and robotic as it tilted it's big hideous beastly like head from side to side simulating a visually articulate garish dragon design displayed on a mock float or some extravagant head dress typically worn at a Chinese fiesta type parade. Only the appearance of this was more perverse and nightmarish and was a dark charcoal grey, as it almost seemed to float in surged advances then abruptly stopping momentarily to stare through wide open doll like eyes with solid black pupils. First emitting a ghastly waning cry, alone…alone…alone…as it quickly lunged toward Todd's position this two legged freak that must have somehow been paroled from the depths of hade's… in a rapid forward advance tilting it's hideous head from side to side cried out in a freakish rapid stream of succession

Ballada!..Ballada!..Ballada!….sounding almost like a turkey buzzard as it vehemently rushed Todd in it's vile and putrid attack mode. And when the creature was about fifty yards off…. Todd began to back up franticly reaching into one of his baggy cargo pockets to retrieve what was now the only thing standing between him and certain death. The small automatic pistol his uncle previously gave to him as he got the sudden gnawing sensation in the pit of his stomach that this little gun was not going to pack enough of a punch to debilitate this putrid malignancy. And yet as the creature got within striking distance and better visual clarity and also one that Todd could more markedly distinguish in greater detail it's gruesome contorted features and grotesque physical characteristics he exclaimed with a wincing expression on his face, loudly exclaimed good Lord!! what in the name of God almighty is that!! The girls were by now relegated to a horrific state of frenzied hysteria, crying freaking out and babbling incoherently while on looking in total awe at the unbelievable and surrealistic scene that was now unfolding right before their eye's. Then Todd carefully took up a combat stance aiming with a grimaced and determined expression facing the hideous creature and simultaneously pulling back the slide receiver on the top of the little pistol he'd by now placed his last remaining hopes on while thinking to himself thank God I have this, chambering a round and readying it to fire. When the creature got within about twenty five yards of Todd's position he cut loose with an almost instantaneous seven round burst of shots in rapid succession that invariably found their mark. The pop, pop, pop, startled the girls as they were now evermore aware that they were now locked in a mortal struggle for their very lives with a far more than formidable adversary.. Then the monster let out a succession of ghastly blood curdling screams like that of some poor despondent soul in the process of being stabbed to death with a butcher's knife. It's towering and imposing form staggered about there in the center of the railroad tracks flailing about with it's gnarled deformed and twisted limbs in the air in a herky jerky fashion as streams of white pasty goop resembling pus spurted from small holes in it's front and gaping open craters in it's back and spewed out of it's vile and putrid mouth flowing downward onto the tracks. It almost looked as though someone had come by and dumped a gallon of partially solidified lumpy white latex house paint all over the tracks.

Then the monster stood there poised, pausing momentarily in a stark frozen state in the center of the railroad ties just glaring at Todd as steams of this sickening white paste gushed from it's open wounds. And Todd just stood there clutching the smoking little pistol in his fist in a state of shock and total astonishment, he was totally aghast at the surreal horrific and unbelievable sight he was actually gazing upon as he thought to himself nobody would ever believe me if I told them. Then suddenly white foggy steam came hissing out of the open wounds as a black tar like substance bubbled surfacing it's way to the top of each one appearing to close them off and making the horrific blackened mutation appear even more gnarled wretched and ominous, giving off the stark harrowing illusion of them healing themselves. By now Todd was mortally terrified upon witnessing this as he now knew they were all in very big trouble. Anticipating this malignant compilation of chemical garbage that had somehow assumed a freakish mutated life form would resume it's heinous putrid rampage he'd ejected the spent magazine onto the ground and hurriedly chambered yet another full one. At this harrowing point he was wholly riddled with reverberating waves of terror and intensive adrenalin rushes in which by now he knew that gunfire of any kind was only going to be little more than a temporary and futile measure to stave it off. Then the color had totally drained from his face as it turned white and was then replaced by a flushed a beet shade of red as he suddenly turned to and yelled to the girls to make a run for it

As the distance between the two combatants began to close tighter, his face turned a beet shade of red with a grimaced and exasperated expression on it as he once again took aim with the intent of dispensing yet another seven round burst from the tiny automatic pistol into the advancing creature as it's eyes lit up suddenly in a greenish yellow glow while opening it's grisly, vile and revolting mouth, in a lion like roar vomited out a massive wave of bluish green goopy sludge that resembled chunky partially solidified Jell-O and that simultaneously was vented from the palms and tips of it's claws in poor Todd's direction totally immersing his poor slight frame in a sea of translucent dark green boogery ooze... Upon witnessing this horrific and surreal scene, the girls already by now's state of unbridled and paralyzing terror that had irretrievably reached a fever pitch as the stark reality set in that they were now all alone in this and were going to have to face off with this thing in one final showdown and other than just hurling rocks at it, had just a can of mace and a stun gun. These items were by now the only line of defense for them against this wretched, mutated abomination, as they were out in the middle of nowhere and their frantic cries were at least ten miles out of earshot in any direction and that there was no one to help.

Then they both began to scream uncontrollably at the unbelievable sight of their poor friends contorted body struggling and writhing around in what was now soon to become a solidified and inescapable rubberized sarcophagus. As the creature slowly turned toward them with it's vile and malignant intent on further carrying out it's repulsive and putrefying attack, Julie while shaking violently quickly reached down for the only thing she had as a last line of defense from a pocket in her back pack a little black stun gun that had a substantial and incapacitating electrical charge for it's size. Crystal by now a blubbering mess looked over at Julie in a highly agitated state of disbelief that she would actually consider such a futile attempt to implement to a totally lame and ineffective defensive measure cried out Oh my God!!...you gotta be outta your ever lovin mind!! what do you think that little toy is going to do against that horrible thing?!! Julie' hysterical, shut-up!! just lay down there and shut-the Fup!! And in a sudden frantic and furious motion whirled around to Crystal to bark further instructions. When I give it a blast from this stupid thing you bolt your ass down this rise and run like hell into the woods you got it!!

Crystal was blubbering hysterically and not hearing even a word Julie was barking at her. Then Julie slapped her hard across the face in a frantic and exasperated attempt to bring her out of shock and yelled you got it!! If I somehow miraculously survive I'll meet up with you down there, and then like a sergeant in the bush taking enemy fire and barking orders at his men yelled...now get ready to move! and Julie with no real anticipation of it actually debilitating this freakish chemical mishap sat there poised to dispense an electrical charge into the approaching two legged nightmare. And as it came closer towards the two girls with it's revolting and nauseating intent to kill Julie slowly aimed her stun-gun at it as it stood towering above them casting it's bleak narly and elongated shadow over them, it just stood there momentarily gazing at them with those wide open doll like eyes, whites fluid in a fixed gaze just staring at the girls. Then it started to make a rocking swaying motion from side to side while jutting it's creepy vile little tongue in and out of that revolting cavern that was it's mouth. The two girls frozen stiff with fear just looked on in total aghast for awhile as this thing seemed to be doing some type of bizarre hypnotic dance in some freakish form of bizarre boogerized ritual. Then suddenly this goopy blobby olive green material began gushing out from numerous orifices all over it's body amassing in sickening piles on leveled out portions of it's body such as the tops of it's shoulders, back and head. Then nauseatingly flopping to the ground when they piled up to high, then this thing leered over at the two girls and opened it's jaws part way in a freakish grin emitted a low pitched reverberating E-E-E-E-E-E-E-E-E and then in a herky-jerky fashion it reached down and scooped up some of this green slimy boogery material and lifted it up in one of it's claw like hands as this goop slithered and streamed between the digits on it's mutant claws.

And as it opened it's vile mouth more of this slimy goop gushed from the roof of it's mouth over it's jagged teeth and onto the ground. Julie frozen in shock, gasped as she witnessed the horrific display of freakishness she got a sudden burst of courage which some say is only fear turned to anger. She yelled I hope you get a charge out of this you vile pus filled abortion!! And then she pulled the trigger. It made a clickety clack sound as it sent a paralyzing electrical charge through the monsters knotted, twisted and contorted frame. And to the total relief and astonishment of the girls this surprisingly incapacitated the horrid chemical abomination at least for the moment, stopping it in it's tracks as it just stood there in a comatose and frozen state motionlessness with that stark blank gaze on it's nightmarish and freakish face as that boogery olive green slime dripped down and flopped off it's mutated body. "Julie" Gad what the hell are ya!?....I think I'm gonna throw up!! Crystal ' never mind that for the life of me I don't know how but I think you did it the electricity actually worked let's just get the hell outta here!! We'll discuss it later!!...Then Julie abruptly turned to the railroad tracks winced and sobbed poor Todd...Then she grabbed Crystal violently shoving her down the rise causing her to tumble and roll downward ass over tea kettle over the hard jagged gravel almost losing their backpacks along the way and clutching that little black stun gun for dear life. The loud sounds of panting and frantic gasps and sobbing were superimposed by that of small rocks being tread underneath hiking boot soles or being kicked about causing a miniature avalanche of scores of others to roll down in succession off the side of the steep rise. There was not a solitary sole within twenty miles that they could turn to for help.

Then when they both reached the bottom of the rise that the old set of railroad tracks were set atop of. Julie looked back toward the direction of the electrically tazed monster to see if it was pursuing them but saw nothing. For in that instant it would seem that the battered remnants of this little trio had prevailed against overwhelming odds. Tearfully she abruptly turned to her friend and violently grabbed Crystal by the upper arm almost dislocating it yanking her to her feet and then pushing her in the direction of the outlying woods as she quickly followed behind and together in a mad dash accompanied by the loud chick-a-chin of locusts from trees and outlying brush and the distant sound of small bats chirping and flying about overhead as the two swiftly hit the field of high weeds and meadows dotted with randomly swirling fireflies in aimless ditzy flight as they frantically fled on foot for their very lives in a hurried and frenzied retreat from their once held position they were so vehemently dislodged from. Wholly exhausted as they both sought the temporary refuge in the partial concealment of sparse tree lines and dense vegetation that the outlying woods and ravines provided, just as the evening sun was beginning to set.

CHAPTER NINE

Anatomy Of A Wretched Mutation

After about two months had passed from the initial point the bizarre disturbances began occurring throughout the two neighboring communities. And the strange ghoulish nature in which the bodies of deceased victims had been discovered coupled with the sketchy details of those freakish unidentifiable substances were no longer being regarded as a matter of question and were followed up with varying points of clarification. By now the main focus was in just safeguarding the community as a whole against the roaming, indiscriminate and malicious cause. Most people began to reach a collective consensus that this was not the handy work of some deranged serial killer that had access to warped sophisticated implements, or a group of sadistic misguided youths with to much idle time and nothing better to do but had to be at the hands of some kind of garish monster. It wasn't something that was openly mentioned but was moreover subtly intimated during the normal course of conversation or was nonverbally conveyed that was something that was mutually understood.

People who'd as a general rule before who'd been up til' now outwardly congenial and unassuming were now becoming morosely inhibited, guarded and wary of their surroundings. Doors were being locked in the day as well as at night and fewer and fewer people were seen milling about even on quiet tree lined streets during the day. News reports from radio and television broadcasts as well as syndicated newspaper columns waited with baited breath for the next gruesome find so as to be first in line to go forth and bring it to public no longer a matter not to be taken to seriously and those of whom had been typically known for their jovial lighthearted nature by others poking fun at the ironic and innate redundancies of life, had totally become sullen and subdued losing or losing their sense of humor entirely taking on a sullen, morose demeanor exempt from any and all gayety. The air was thick and heavy with a grim level of morose fear and suspicion, people anticipated when and where will this thing strike next? And it was clearly evident that the frayed atmospheric state was about to shatter or explode at the slightest jarring or disturbance from the outside. A fragile atmosphere was noted among those of whom by now was reduced to a shadow like community of a twilight existence. And those who had not succumbed to mass panic or mistrust, walked on egg shells and it was clearly evident that it had culminated into a huge bubble of fear and suspicion, and one that at any given moment was going to burst and when it finally did, it was going to burst big. Cameron sat there on his porch inattentively listening to a local classic rock station on the radio and drinking a cold beer in feigned attempts to calm his frayed nerves. He waited for the latest news broadcasts or for Dusty to show up or call to recount the details of the harrowing events that took place from that stormy pastoral outing of the prior week and their overnight stay in that old tobacco barn so they could possibly sort them out and try to make sense of it all.

He hadn't seen or heard from her since that horrific encounter with that godforsaken thing that night which nearly cost them their lives. And just about every other night since he'd been on pins and needles and plagued with insomnia and experiencing garish nightmares of that grotesque mutation they had a run in with in that old mail pouch barn. As well as suffering from acute anxiety as he was grappling with inner conflict as to whether or not to go to the authorities with the story of what happened and maybe risk being locked up for being taken as some kind of a kook, or just take his chances and try and resolve the matter himself after all they had already faced off with the monster and he had done battle with it himself accompanied by his formidable comrades in arms. Yet from what he saw that night they'd already got the best of it and dealt it a pretty severe dressing down and maybe the thing was dead and this would just all go away. And for all intents and purposes he and Dusty could just relax and finally breath a collective sigh of relief and start getting a good nights sleep again.

And if this wasn't the case he knew he was going to have to come up with something more in the way of solid and concrete proof if they were going to be believed and not written off as a just a couple of crackpots by local authorities and the community at large even at this late stage in the game. Just then the paper boy rode past on his bike retrieving a pre-rolled edition of the afternoon paper in a taut rubber band from his big, dirty, worn orange nylon bag he had slung over his shoulder and tossing one onto Cameron's porch as he sped by. Cameron quickly rose up off of a rickety old wooden chair he was sitting on to go over to where the paper was thrown to pick it up and unfold it so he could read the grim and startling headlines. Another deceased victim who has later been identified as twenty year old Todd Peterson of Dorchester township the third deceased victim in a grim wave of terror was found encased in more goopy green sludge by local authorities yesterday morning three miles down on old abandoned Kunkletown railroad tracks. After having read this Cameron got a sudden rush of adrenalin and his heart pounded in his ears in a steady, rapid pulsating course. As he panned further down, the article read, Two dazed and disoriented girls in their late teens or early twenties who were later identified by family and friends as Julie Schaffer and Crystal Parsons. The two who were earlier believed to have been in the company of the victim and on their way to an upcoming rock concert in the neighboring town of Fayetteville. The two girls were found in a frightened and disoriented state wandering around in the nearby woods by two local hunters whom just happened by. They were promptly rushed to the local hospital to receive preliminary medical treatment, and later transferred to a state psychiatric facility to undergo a grueling battery of tests and further evaluation

Yet upon their initial questioning authorities have not as yet been able to illicit any pertinent or useful information regarding the mysterious and disturbing circumstances surrounding these two victims or the condition in which they were discovered. As yet the two subjects frightened and catatonic state remains unchanged as they are being held over for observation by staff psychiatrists at state level facilities pending further investigation by local authorities.. Police have so far been unable to uncover any tangible leads or divulge any further useful details at this time. After painstakingly skimming the article Cameron's face angrily contorted itself as he abruptly folded the evening edition of the paper containing the disturbing headlines and slammed it down on the old wooden table next to him almost spilling his beer over. He did not have to do any reading between the lines here or engage in any guesswork as he knew full well what hand was responsible here. It was that slimy, putrid, despicable thing, they had a run in with in old tobacco barn that night, and they'd dealt it some pretty severe blows too that were profoundly significant…and yet it had somehow miraculously survived to attack and victimize some of his peers. His nerves were totally frazzled by this point at by what he just read as he started making his way back inside the house to call Dusty on the phone.

And before he could reach the front door he overheard some of his neighbors congregating about again. With nothing better to do than buzzingly engage in yet another one of their usual idle group gossip sessions. The topic being the day's newspaper headlines regarding the latest sludge victim. Once inside he quickly went over to the scuffed up marred old seventies style beige colored wall phone in the kitchen to call Dusty. But before he could pick up the receiver to start dialing her number the phone began ringing. He hastily grabbed the receiver right away. A faint and distraught voice on the other end resounded… Hello.. Cameron? yeah it's me, Dusty' and in a loud audible sobbing tone of voice bellowed, Did you read the papers yet? Her words were shrill hysterically whining and half crying, I'm scared…the phrase was almost muffled but the tone was intensely reverberating, and it really unnerved Cameron giving him a cold, vapid chill in his chest, a slight ringing in his ears and muscle spasms twitched and writhed in the inner portion of his forearms. There was a momentary pause on the other end Cameron' do you still have that little present I gave ya? Dusty ',… yeah but now I don't know how much good it'll actually do now? I still don't feel safe anymore, that awful thing lived after everything we did to it and it attacked another group of people, whining Dusty cried what the Hell are we gonna do now? How the hell could it have survived being set on fire? What in God's name is it? This is like something out of a nightmare and then she began bawling. I'm scared outta my mind!!… Cameron' First of all your gonna have to get a grip and pull yourself together. Truthfully I'm scared too… I'm scared shitless remember I saw that awful thing too! And up close and personal, it was garish and horrible, but it isn't going to do us or our neighborhood friends any good if we for one internalize on it, or cave in now is it? We've still got each other and were gonna have to start thinking out of the box here…Dusty' what does that mean?…It means were gonna have to start thinking on a different level than we have been and forego all post conditioning and conventional norms that go along with it, especially when it comes to our approach to destroying this thing. Maybe we should try and focus our combined efforts on finding some kind of inherent weakness it may have, for all we know it may be something thing, so blatantly stupid, or obvious we may have just overlooked it, and right there under our noses, an Achilles heel if you will…. Dusty' what's that? "Cameron" It's weak or vulnerable point to attack or just what it will be that will play an integral role in it's ultimate undoing. Evidently it's not going to be gunfire of any kind, but you just keep your revolver anyway it's going to be the only line of defense for your house as it is mine at least for the time being, and it's better then nothing just unload on it's face if it shows up here again. And keep all your doors and windows locked at night!! "Dusty" you know if we all weren't up in that hay loft that that awful night that horrid thing would've killed us all!! …pause…Cameron' in a sullen tone…yeah I know…Dusty' Don't you think we should go to the police or something over what happened and let them handle it? You know just tell them that we've personally seen and battled some kind of boogerized creature at closed quarters? Cameron'

And just what'll we use to back up our story with, air pudding? What proof do we have? We'd be the laughing stock of the whole neighborhood, no!! the whole town!! They'd take us for a couple of wacko-nutso's or something that we escaped from the local booby-hatch, and then we'd both probably find ourselves in adjoining padded cells! Dusty' so what are we gonna do in the meantime just sit on this? Cameron' Yes!! That's exactly what were gonna do!! Just let them find that out for themselves in their way and in their own time besides the police have guns too...they are no better or worse off than we are at this stage of the game or anybody else for that matter. Maybe this thing can be fried or electrocuted or something. Let me do a little personal research into a few areas on my own and just let me see what I can come up with first then we'll go from there.

Just then Dusty suddenly started whining tearfully,.. what are you going to try and do next? lay your hands on a tank with a flamethrower or how about some hand grenades to use against that awful thing,... and then she totally broke down, and began bawling on the other end of the phone. Cameron ' now, now, that's not gonna do either of us any good and you know it! We've got to pull together as a team here and form a unified front you've got to bone up here and take on a more hard lined approach to this thing "Dusty" you mean like some kind of infantry soldier or something? Cameron' yeah something like that. Dusty' well I'm not....and not all of us have the luxury of having been big tough ex-marines now do we? "Cameron" that's secondary we've got to combine our efforts in finding and exploiting some weakness it may have, and we can do it, if you can think of anything between now and the next time we talk, by all means let me in on it, for all we know it may turn out to be the stupidest thing that it will take to spark off it's ultimate undoing. Like it or not were all each other has and we can not maintain an effective countering edge if one or both of us cracks up now can we?..... I really don't want to do this alone, now you've got to pull yourself together if not for your own sake but for your mother and little brother's they are counting on you right now, remember we're the cutting edge...Dusty. Cameron' before I let you go how much ammo did I leave ya for that little revolver of yours? "Dusty" the box is almost full we only capped off about thirty rounds from mine between target practice and that horrible thing,

Cameron' in an attempt to soothe her harried mental state and calm her down somewhat said. Whew!! Using the slang terms and everything!! now your talkin like a veteran shooter I like that! Dusty' I'd Say there's about seventy cartridges left. Cameron' good save em were both to poor and can't afford to just go around and keep buying that crap all the time anyway. Do you feel you need any more practice? "Dusty" no I'm good. Cameron' great now if that awful thing comes around to your place you know what to do! Now you won't just be sitting ducks there in your house!... Does your mother know you have it? "Dusty" Yeah but she doesn't like it, but all things considering she said she is in no position to disallow it. Cameron' good! Now just remember to keep all your doors and windows locked at night ok?

Dusty I appreciate for your concern but...Dusty I care about ya I've come to think of you as sort of a member of my family, kinda like a sister or something and I know you don't have much left in the way of an extended family anymore. And I don't have much in that regard either and what little I do have left live states away and I hardly ever see anymore so I'm glad to have an opportunity like this and I'm going to do everything in my power to safe guard you and yours. Dusty thank you for all the help and moral support you've extended to me so far I don't know what I would have done without you up to this point. I just hope we can come up with something soon that will stop this thing from killing any more people and possibly us. Cameron' don't say that..were gonna kill it you can bank on that... one way or the other we are going to put an end to the vicious reign of terror that mutated, putrefied, goon has unleashed on this community, were going to put it permanently out of commission if it's the last thing I or we ever do.... On that you can count on!! And on that note the two concluded their discussion and hung up with each other.

After the despondent and heartfelt conversation with Dusty and his repeated attempts to placate her fears and stave her off from completely buckling under such intense pressure, but in also hastily going to the authorities with little or no viable proof and what may outwardly appear to be a too rich and too imaginative a story too soon to be believed at this point would in all probability culminate itself into a huge fiasco. And in his moderately discerning conversation with her he did not shirk in his civil and moral obligation to conceal any underlying truths to her about the ominous situation at large in that it was as grave as it was or that this thing was as dangerous as it was. Cameron just sat there in a dazed state of agitation, wholly perplexed as to what would be a viable effective means to resolve to this mounting crisis. He was also going to have to come to terms with what was going to be demanded of him in his part of what was to ultimately be the grim and daunting task he was to be ultimately girded with in circumventing this sudden augmentative level of danger threatening the community. Now it was on him to try and figure out how to become a deadly and capable instrument in combating and finally decimating this seemingly invincible and unstoppable force once and for all. He has had a very difficult time in coming to grips with and still could not fathom that anything walking, breathing, sitting or standing could not only have withstood what was meted out to it that night in the old barn. And the intense barrage of gunfire directed at it, and at point blank range too nonetheless, and from two handguns of moderately large calibers, not to mention having undergone a baptism of fire from highly combustion able kerosene. Yet after having taken these factors into accounting the grim reality hit Cameron like a ton of bricks. What they saw that night in the old barn would've reduced the incredible hulk to a quivering mass of jelly and sent him running for the hills with a yellow streak up his back a mile wide.

At that point the came to the stark realization that the community at large was in grave and imminent nocturnal danger and something had to be done A, S, A, P. It was not going to be safe with even a marginal degree of accessibility to firepower and the level of carnage was going to be imminently apparent. Cameron with a grave sense of dread surmised that this was not a flesh and blood type creature that could be killed in the conventional sense of the word and what they were up against here, but some kind of sub animal type of monster chemically based if you will, with no heart, no central nervous system, and no blood to speak of, just white pus coursing through it's constricted mutant veins. And whatever it did have in the way of a brain it was vilely predisposed to only one thing, killing....He also knew he was going to have to do something and soon. And it was also readily apparent that it retained some type of internalized self healing or regenerative system that lay dormant in it's freakish anatomical composite and was activated upon sustaining injury. And it was also clearly apparent at this juncture that this thing whatever it was, was not going to succumb to gunfire of any degree and any and all such efforts along those lines would serve to be ultimately futile and only temporarily stave off the inevitable.

And if one inadvertently throws into the grim equation a hypothetical pitched battle between it and a seven foot, two thousand pound grizzly bear or an eight hundred pound gorilla and not to mention the alleged yet infamous yeti or Bigfoot if you will, which hails from the vast regions of the Canadian wilderness, no doubt large formidable creatures that could all be realistically brought down by a steady stream of gunfire of sufficient calibers. It would also appear that in a proposed throw down with any one or all of these very large and imposing beasts one could unequivocally reach the disheartening conclusion that in such a proposed match to the finish, would no doubt result in one or all of them being reduced to a side of mince-meat. And in weighing in these unsettling factors at once into final analysis Cameron's blood flushed cold as he felt a sudden reverberating rush of ice cold adrenalin and the whooshing pound of his heart in his ears began to intensify as the gravity of the situation became more starkly apparent. Maybe it was going to have to be reported to the authorities after all and the National Guard was going to have to at some point and time summoned to intervene. Surely this thing wouldn't stand a chance against hundreds of hardened, armed infantrymen with guns, tanks, flamethrowers and hand grenades could it? He'd been having freakish three dimensional nightmares every other night since, ones of him standing there in pitch blackness and all of a sudden a light going on from some undisclosed location in the room only to illuminate that wide eyed grotesque mutation's face up close grinning like a maniacal Cheshire cat leering at him, frozen in mortal terror!!…. enough to abruptly cease one's heart from beating. News paper reports of the victims and the boogerish cocoon they were found encased in or the nature of the bizarre material was freakish enough in and of itself. A steady and relentless parade of grim shadowy nightmares permeated his sleep in a cruel regularity just about every other night since that run-in with that hideous thing in the old tobacco barn. And he did not know how to get rid of them. This too, and upon further consideration hitherto, it became more and more apparent to him that this maybe something he and his little band of amateurish army recruits may not be sufficiently capable or equipped to handle

He also concluded through the slow process of elimination that this may be the sole and surviving remnants of some type of chemically spawned mutation that had somehow metamorphosed itself from some slime pit of long ago nineteen seventies industrial age as a forgotten toxic waste dump site hidden away in some remote location as a moss ridden wet swampland somewhere undisclosed to John Q. Public, a cesspool or some putrefied chemical dumping ground that somehow managed to amass, develop and emerge only to inadvertently make it's way into the dark, obscure nocturnal fringes of society. In an insidious campaign of surreptitiously stalking and terrorizing it under the cover of darkness in the shadowy and of visually repulsive opaqueness of an inherently grotesque life form it had inexplicably assumed. In that of some kind of pus filled, malignant and cancerous tumor that had the breath of life mysteriously breathed into it' from some far and distant unknown source. It was thus able to get up and walk around randomly menacing and snuffing out those poor innocent lives around it as part of it's putrid and vapid existence. Cameron was still haunted by the wretched, unspeakable images of that awful thing that tried to kill him and his two friends in the loft of that barn that dark stormy night and was the main subject of frequent and ongoing nightmares since. Reoccurring, stark and horrifying visions of that night reoccurred that of it's twisted gnarled limbs resembling thick black licorice whips or those hideous red, white and blue boils on the lower side of it's deformed torso and the sharp protruding bones from various extremities on it's repulsive body, broken off at the end. Or those huge marfflin like ears making it take on almost a gremlin like appearance. And one of the creepiest physical traits of them all, was the wide open gaping doll like eye's with the darkened pupils in the center accentuating the outlying whites around them. Thus gravely intensifying to the onlooker a frozen and stark level of terror to one's very core in it's panning and freakish gaze just prior to going into it's rancid and putrid attack mode.

He also began to assess within himself that if this thing was spawned from chemically based derivatives that maybe this was quite possibly the key factor he needed to focus in on and examine more closely as it may very well be the answer to the whole mess. If he could somehow by way of diligent efforts on his part and through the arduous process of elimination isolate some type of bio chemical abnormality or deficiency in it's immune system. He could then hone in on some existing internal vulnerability it may possess. This would most surely disclose at least some of the answers to these ongoing evasive and perplexing questions as to it's seeming outward invincibility. He would then stand a much better chance of single handedly overwhelming and defeating this clear and evermore present danger that has been menacing and holding the community at large in it's constraining grip of abject fear. The only question here was how was he going to get close enough to this thing to do any tests without it decimating him, that was the problem. In jest he surmised the possibility of shooting it with a tranquilizer dart, and then when the thing was out cold he could just move in and personally conduct the necessary testing and evaluations…ha..ha.. Then muttering to himself he said Stop it Cameron' your babbling like a wholesale loony-tune here knock it off!! Yet the notion of getting this vile freak of nature defanged and within the confines of safety and secrecy was no doubt a very appealing prospect to him. And one that would surely bring these series of events full circle to a point of culmination, and finally end this malevolent and insidious reign of terror. In lieu of the present circumstances Cameron was personally committed to in bringing under control to ultimately eradicate. He solemnly took a few moments to silently dismiss within his harried mind all troubling and burdensome thoughts regarding the mounting crisis at large. Momentarily drifting off towards a very calming place in his mind that constituted things, that were of a soothing and lighthearted nature. The seventies pop rock he listened to for instance and the fashions of the times to name a few. He fondly reflected on those distant childhood memories of himself as a kid growing up in Milford Pa. knocking around with one or more of his parents in the back seat of his father's old metallic gold nineteen sixty three Chevy Impala an old runabout work car that for many of his childhood years was all they had. The old car was even used in periodic moves hauling everything from furniture to the kitchen sink. It was a mammoth oversized dinged up and rusted around the door jams and rocker panels with thick gaudy corroded pocked and pitted trim. In that in later years was the target of an undue amount of lighthearted razzing in reference to it's size condition and lack of sporty aerodynamics by a local group of neighborhood teenage boys of whom had a pension for only two things hard rock music and supped up muscle cars. They shouted things like "Aye, aye!!... Captain, This here's a hot rodding port!!...Now you just take that oversized barnacle barge of yours out to the harbor to drop anchor!!...." or, Sorry sergeant you can't bring that tank through here this is a demilitarized zone! and then they would all resound in collective laughter as he passed by. As they themselves rocketed down the street in far more sleek, compact and customized rides of the time that were as the kid's put it totally Boss!!...as they obsessively fawned and fussed over them constantly. Typically jacked up in the back or on all fours sporting a set of mag wheels with customized aluminum rims, a hood scoop and traction bars in the rear, and the tackily iconic leopard skin dashboard cover and the pair of colored dice hanging in the rear view mirror.

Nearly flawless in their characteristics and makeup, and impeccable to a "T" in their customization and appeal, and ones that so typified the ever distant and faded image of the bygone era of supped up roadsters and muscle cars. The Chevy Nova's, Ford Mustangs and Plymouth Barracuda's were among some of the many highly prized pet peeves that came to so stylize the amateur do it your self motor heads of the period. Yet as he drove down side or back streets on his way home from the drudge laden 10 and 12 hour shifts of his grimy dismal old factory job or on some menial grocery store errand, almost immediately the upon the sight of that great big oversized, rusty and dilapidated 1968 sedan by the neighborhood hot rodding sect found himself on the business end of a relentless barrage of neighborhood razzing and taunts by them. Dad just grinned and took it all with a grain of salt and chuckled at some of the comments that were made in passing. He occasionally countered with some clever rhetorical comeback of his own in rebuttal to their hot rodding muscle car fetishes. It almost became a substitute form of greeting they had for each other in passing, this taunting form of oneupmanship, They'd say things like hey!!.... Hey Pop,...we saw you at the filling station the other day gassing up your oil tanker, then as I was watching the National news last night the commentator frantically proclaimed there's an imminent oil crisis brewing in the gulf,...The Wan-Valdese has completely dried up!!...now is there any gas left at all for anyone else? Yet this was not something that was done with malicious intent but rather in lighthearted fun. And he really didn't much care what a bunch of adolescent boy's thought of his shabby oversized work car that got bad gas mileage anyway. And he didn't have to travel that far as it was, it ran and got him from point A to point B and that was really all that mattered. After convivially recalling those fond heartfelt recollections of far more lax and simpler times and summer days gone by. The family exploits in that old jalopy that his father maintained for years afterward and almost into his retirement stuck out like a rusty corroded nail or a sore thumb to most of the other cars in the neighborhood as this habitually continued until the boy's grew up and eventually moved away.

This daydreaming of sorts, in revisiting former childhood haunts, momentarily afforded him at least some form of solace from the overwhelming stress and mental anguish he presently found himself ensnared in. And at least for the time being it served as a temporarily an escape hatch, And even if for a short while they were able to put a wry comforting smile on his face and a bit of laughter in his heart. It was a momentary reprieve from the present turmoil and mental anguish at least for a while put him somewhere else psychologically. And as for the one thing he knew at least for the time being...he was scared, and scared but good. And although he was still somewhat shaken by the front page headlines and the unsettling story content of the local newspaper. This prompted him to focus his attention unduly calling into accounting other memories that of which struck a cord of unspeakable and abject terror in him. The stark and unnerving prospect of having to venture out in the family car with his parents on the occasional night time outing were anything at all but endearing or pleasant. Those as a backseat passenger in that big oversized rust bucket that really belonged in one of those old multi car demolition derby's he sometimes watched on television as a kid on those sometimes lonely Saturday afternoons when he couldn't find any of his friends or anything else to do.

This was yet to become another faded icon from the archives of the early 1970's that has long since dissipated from the annals of the American red-neck sports arena of the period like motor-cross or funny-car racing. Those old wrecks had one tire on the track and the other in the junkyard and were crudely painted with very large numbers and sometimes the confederate flag on the doors and hoods of scores of these jalopies. They were fitted with roll cages and slated for systematic destruction in the center of some bumpkin orchestrated crash elimination contest held for the sheer delight of a stadium packed with those culturally starved wayward Neanderthals and backwoods bupkis who had only about four or five teeth left in their heads, and of who still proudly hailed the confederate flag and thought that Three dog night's The halls of Shambala or Lynyrd Skynyrd's Sweet home Alabama were the national anthems. Stock car drivers got in em' and they all drove around in the dirt center of some primeval stock or funny car track stadium in some off the beaten rural path where as they intentionally drove about crashing into one other until the last man who's car was still running was ignominiously deemed the winner. Such a crude and baser sporting event was a typical form of entertainment that appealed mainly to a lower unrefined class or a teenage mentality of the time like roller-derby or fake wrestling.

And at the very best that held out all the refinement and social amenities and appeal as a beer bellied belching contest that would comprise only those aimless and shiftless members of the rural ruffian sect of the time who more often than not proudly hailed from the University of Southern Comfort and chronically unemployed. And at the lowly risk of reinforcing old stereotypes they typically had little else better to do with their Saturday afternoons than to grow out of the center cushion of some shabby old sofa like some type of a giant self animated mushroom with a zero level of life ambition in some run down rural off the beaten path trailer park. Just sitting there in a soiled smelly old T-shirt with the logo of some local dive bar or hard rock band emblazoned on the front of it. Sporting a whole host of amateurishly etched tattoo's of morally questionable taste and that so crudely stylized the rural ruffian sect of the time, and that were also partially visible through some of the holes ripped in them.. Such crude and unrefined character traits that came to typify a rural class's sect.

And one I was all but to familiarized and acquainted with as a kid growing up in rural northeastern Ohio at that time. They were as iconic as the semi truck or the bearded Harley rider was on the highways of the early 1970's was in that many weekend afternoons were frittered away just sitting there watching those tackily dressed kids flail themselves about in bellbottoms on the dance floor of Bandstand or watching Super host's afternoon creature feature with those corny low budget 50's and 60's monster flicks like attack of the giant tomato or mushroom people or something, and among other things fake wrestling on those old black and white portable TV's. Those of whom also painstakingly perfected a refined level of social graces in such a methodical and skillful level of proficiency in exhibiting such class attributes as the innate ability to belch or pass wind in rhythm, or playing the National anthem making cuffed hand and armpit noises through a ripped T-shirt or crushing an aluminum beer can in one clenched fist or on their head. These crude and unrefined claims to fame which in the end had come to epitomize the likes of such a socially renowned and elite class of the time, as the shiftless and chronically unemployed, the laid off factory worker, as well as those discriminating beer connoisseurs and habitual wife batterers. And how it was by grace and grace alone they had in being personally endowed with such prodigal skills exclusively bestowed upon them and them alone by the dear Lord above. Yet on a fond and comforting note in just recalling the ongoing razzing he and dad took from the local adolescent hot rodding sect, and the fond comforting knowledge that it was all done only in good fun as they felt very endearing towards his father. It was a diversionary form of amusement that somewhat eased the boredom of long sweltering muggy summer evenings with not much else to do but the same old drudgery of having to get out there and mow the lawn, wash the car or water the vegetable garden to say the least, and it granted him a temporary deferment from the everpresent stress and turmoil of the imminent crisis at hand.

And at least for the moment granted him a warm comforting feeling inside and the ability to laugh a little taking some solace in those hazy distant memories of the old neighborhood. Although that was in the day and they lived in the suburbs then. But night time however was an entirely different scenario for little Cameron and posed a harrying prospect for him later on especially when the family relocated to a more rural area. In looking back he could remember the overwhelming sense of dread he felt when he was told by parents they were all going out somewhere in the car that night and he had to go along too. He would've much rather remained at home even if he was left there alone. He remembered begging his parents to stay home…He'd even promised to keep all the doors locked and not let anyone in as he'd only sit there in a great big old chair in the living room not moving until they got back watching night time western series that were popular favorites at the time on T.V. like The Wild, Wild West, Wagon train or Gun smoke on the local television stations. Nonetheless his desperate and imploring pleas fell on deaf, unreceptive ears and were insensitively ignored by his parents in steadfast obtuseness, they would just continue in manhandling him to later on forcibly install him in the backseat of the family car. And despite his frantic and repeated pleas not to do so. In blowing him off they'd say things like oh your acting silly now will you just let me get your shoes and socks on!!…or your being ridiculous, c'mon now there's no such things as the Boogie-Man now put your coat on and let's get going!! And in these statements alone sent icy cold waves of mortal terror that resonated throughout his chest and upper body at the ghastly prospect of being forced to venture out in the car after dark. This was an all to common scene that routinely played itself out in the Dillard house prior to their occasional night time outings.

His parents many times had to physically restrain him in the living room as he flailed about on the floor kicking and screaming. They had to put on his jacket and sneakers and forcibly drag him to the car and thrust him bodily into the backseat of the car. He was utterly terrified at what he perceived to be out there at night and concealed as a dark and sinister presence lurking amidst the shadows of darkened hollowed out entranceways of semi deteriorated old homes or buildings which were reduced to creepy old decaying historical landmarks, set in a row on some semi deserted or darkened streets on a disturbing route his parents commonly took on night time outings. Areas that from a distance were vaguely distinguishable in their outward features yet their visual characteristics by night were grossly exaggerated, embellishing a silent and eerie note to a profound historical significance by what the dull greenish blue moon or street light had shed. This furthermore lent itself to an already elevated level of morbid apprehension at their sight, thus of which was already deeply seared onto his traumatized psyche.. Ones that in the passing by of these dark cryptic nocturnal settings so far from home, on looking what at that time were a cluster of pre dated and decrepit depression era houses or buildings with dark opaque masses of ratty overgrown vegetation or tall knotted trees with massive branches reaching upward toward the iridescent glow of an autumn moon.

The dilapidated wooden white picket fences that adorned these once stately residences lent a gloomy moroseness of solitude to the overall setting as it stood silent tribute to a pre-dated era of a darker socially unenlightened enigma. This was outwardly apparent in the designed execution that haughtily boasted an elaborate level of ornamentation wrought by a Provincial Victorian style of architecture in it's staunch regimentation subtly enhanced under the greenish blue moonlight amidst vast spacious yards. Caricaturish in their creepy elongated shadows they cast by night stretching out across dimly lit yards giving off a distorted sense of the true proportions they actually posed in broad daylight. Marred by time and weathered by the elements these longstanding historical landmarks took on eerie and creepy nocturnal connotations that almost took on an animated aura of their own. And in an unsettling harkened disquiet served only to compound a small boy's morbid fear and apprehension further traumatizing to a highly impressionable psyche in a grave level of isolation in a fortified wall of silence to immediate family members. Habitually imprisoned in a despondent mode of quiet resolve void of all reasonable and logical aspects of conveyance in any manner of descript form to them. . that of an abounding dark and abominable presence looming in the shadows, malevolent and diabolical in it's inherent and vile intent, cryptic and elusive in it's nocturnal habits. That by which he inwardly held at the subconscious level to be a stark and inescapable fact in his inwardly held perceptions which rendered him to an abject state of feigned silence and desperate sense of solitary isolation. In that unspoken underlying knowledge of it's pure unadulterated evil and invincibility he chronically languished in mortal terror. And his fear of the boogie-man was that much more compounded by the grave element of it's dark insidious elusiveness. This disturbing and unsettling notion steadily resigned itself to the very depths of his inner core bringing with it a stark and graven level of terror whereas he'd felt as if his chest was a reverberating mass of ice, his tongue swelled up in his mouth and his head pulsated like a bass drum with intense blood and adrenalin flows in an unbridled state of paralyzing terror in his spine turning to ice.

Something obtrusively taking up residence in it's hazy, nondescript form far removed from society and elusive from sight, to perversely inhabit the dark hallows of these nocturnal haunts. He could feel the muscles and tendons in his face wriggle and twitch like the taught strings of a pick instrument or snap in two like that of piano wire drawn to tight in excessive tension. That of the mere prospect that the boogie man may possibly be lying in wait for a chance to physically manifest itself in the raw indiscriminately without warning, lurking about within these hallowed dark and morose cavities. And that as a child this fear steadily mounted itself from within in a slow steady parade of ghastly partial zed visages subtly indicative of stark goonish horror. And in their insidiously vagrant format took hold in a tenacious grip instilling an overwhelming and debilitating sense of silent anguish in him as the family car slowly passed by these stark, vacant and morose nocturnal settings. And as the family unwarily set out on the occasional night time errand or the dreaded, sudden spur of the moment whim of perhaps stopping at a local Manner's Big Boy for a late night take out bag of hot sandwiches, fries or a milkshake, but with only one other possible exception thereof to this day still gives him cold shudders to the very core of his being and paralyzing his central nervous system, frozen in incomprehensible terror just at the mere thought of, something hidden, outwardly unseen but sensed in a grave level of uneasiness at an intuitive level something he knew to be matted in dark green sludge, monstrous and invincible was there, seething from within darkened cavities of objects of night time shadows. And now he has finally and first handedly had his intuitive fears realized

CHAPTER TEN

Ghastly Finds In Hallow Valley

THE TOWN OF AVONDALE ITSELF WAS GRIPPED IN A HEINOUS REIGN OF night stalking terror in for what had over an extended period of time became all inclusive of a rare form of predatory invincibility of ill designs. A prolific and malignant scourge that up till now had remained wholly unseen plagued the local populace in a despairing continuance instilling such a grave element of fear in that some had dubbed the boogins and others, the night creeper. A dark insidious force cloaked in an enigmatic shroud of maniacal secrecy had seeped it's way into the far cavernous regions of the subconscious mind. And as it elusively beset itself upon those terror stricken unfortunates in hovering over the wary intuition of the random individual. Thus prompting him to subscribe to and exercise a wholesale level of subterfuge in restricting his movements from dusk onward.

And as the darkness fell it set a dreadful tone for a steady reoccurring succession of ghastly visages personifying macabre and prolific goonish horror set upon a partially obscure nocturnal stage and faintly illuminated by a faint bluish incandescent moon glow that eerily accentuated a nightmarish dreamscape thus rendering it cruelly inescapable. Night time from that point on was collectively regarded with an overwhelming sense of dread. It had been irrevocably transformed into a darkened surrealistic realm of ill perceived boogie monsters cast in a grim ensuing cons cape who's darkly silhouetted, mutated and bumpy forms suddenly emerged deep from within the blackened portholes of one's ill laden subconscious mind lunging outwardly in a steady succession of creepy nightmarish visages. And with wretched and mutated outstretched arms they eagerly attempt to seize their victims in a ghastly clenching embrace horrifically symbolic of yet another unnerving and putrefying nightmare. And one of the most horrific aspects that surrealistically stylized these embellished nocturnal ghouls was in how they were faintly accented by an indiscriminate misty glow of an eerily haunting blue iridescence outlining their dark mutated and silhouetted forms. These kinds of internalized personifications were widely rampant, and one's that especially presided in children who were more prone to be the subject of such cruel torment and mental anguish were by no stretch of the means exempt. A bleak and damming undertone had subliminally exuded itself outwardly from darkened objects silhouetted against a dismal evening dusk-scape, subtly indicative of a darkened aloof presence in a looming and pervasive communal sense with the steady accompaniment of subtly diminishing sallow evening rays that had slowly transcended itself upon the little town and it's surrounding principalities.

And as it progressively undermined what had otherwise been up till now a relatively copasetic and damningly unimpeded nocturnal perception it had otherwise maintained in the past. A grossly disproportionate number of those whom had undergone a heightened level of palpable fear were also predisposed to a perilous sense of grave uncertainty. Outlying principalities were also diligently struggling to cope with and come to grips with the stark possibility of something so grievous and utterly repugnant that it beggared outward description in that it may suddenly and without warning manifest it's ominous black silhouette. He could just imagine with a grave level of intensity it's terrifyingly vile and nondescript form slightly hunched over like a big ape highlighted by the dull greenish glow of the moon suddenly lunging out from amid the shadows towards him at any given moment,…But this was not an ape, this was something of a very grave magnitude, a vile pus filled malignancy so maniacally horrific that to the limiting constraints set by the bounds of the conscious mind were all but to frightfully inconceivable to even begin to attempt to successfully construct in forming a clear mental picture of what such a proposed mutated goon could possibly appear as in the stark, raw and unnerved sense in the harried realm of ones augmented mind. And this was something that if given the chance would just rend you to pieces. The utterly terrifying prospect of being caught totally unawares coming around the corner one evening and meeting up with a dark leathery mutated visual perversity inundated with bumps, lesions, raised skin contortions, and various sized bone like protrusions overall it's ghastly form just standing there leering at you in a paralyzing gawk Yet at the mere possibility of a realized visage of such a vile and repugnant manifestation would undoubtedly stricken one with complete and utter revulsion. Moreover as it steadily and progressively pillaged any and all remaining objects of inner peace and security. Insofar as a dark elusive embodiment of evil had subtly transformed the region into a shadowy dreamscape host only to a steady parade of ill conceived specimens of contorted and wretched form in such a wide arrayed spectrum of profound goonish horror at the wholesale level. Individual citizens wholly internalized garish self conceptualized images in morbid anticipation of such prospective and frequented visually repugnant manifestations.

This however resided itself in stark contrast to the generalized consensus maintained in morbidly indicative level of speculation once held by the local populace. Yet in it's grossly exaggerated connotative essence had subtly cast a bleak and elongated, caricaturish shadow over the vast countryside. Eerily indicative of the surrealistic connotations it held out that stirred the more lurid aspects of one's untapped formulative imagination. And to what had become all inclusive gravely accelerated all dreaded aspects regarding the of fear of the unknown.

A dark leathery and gnarled mutation with a violently contorted frame, twisted limbs and a freakish gawk had indiscriminately emerged deep from within the darkened hollows of such dismal nocturnal haunts as vacant churches, old annex buildings and other decaying historical landmarks to prowl the streets in an unceasing wave of indiscriminate terror. Mercilessly lurking about seeking more unsuspecting innocents randomly attacking in it's vile and putrid form in what had up until now remained silently indicative of a lurking goonish horror. A freakish mode of macabre crypticism had established a foothold in the minds of many slowly etching away the very cornerstone of an otherwise tranquil and unassuming town demeanor. A vile and prolific scourge had besieged itself upon the towns inhabitants in an unrelenting nocturnal campaign of mortal subjugation.

And in it's putrefying and malignant propensity to exact unfounded and baseless retribution by way of cruel and systemic mayhem. The creepy, wretched aura that presided over the town and it's inhabitants hung over in a bleak and dogged haze and as they haplessly scrambled to sequester themselves away in a desperate series of ongoing fateful nightly rituals. Hastened and erratic attempts were made at fortifying themselves behind the self perceived false security of dead bolted doors aluminum ball bats and large vicious attack dogs that in the end only proved themselves out to be temporary stays of contention. And for yet another night of surreptitious and insufficient measures against what unseen and ill perceived threat that inexorably seeped from deep within a darkened nightmarish shadows cape and was potentially outside one's door, like the steady unnerving blast of a distant foghorn droning outwardly in the night ominously signifying imminent doom with the approach of dusk. Many just sat poised in the dreaded anticipation of that horrid thing possibly emerging from within the shadowy cons cape of the towns vacant and decrepit landmarks this particular night. Only to possibly show up outside their door or window attempting to violently force it's way in. This factor in itself prompted the streets to slowly empty out becoming all but deserted, and taking on the grim omnipresence of a modern ghost town ignominiously relegating it's terrified inhabitants to an isolated twilight existence. A somber tone had gradually transcended itself into a profoundly macabre shadowy dreamscape, subtly symbolic of a prolific goonish self contained insurrection that lay hidden and waiting,…peering outwardly from a distant and undisclosed location. One might eerily sense a weighty uneasiness as they were out for an evening stroll in being beset upon by the stark gaze of a pair of goonish wide open doll like eyes gawking at them from a darkened hollowed position that may have sent a wave of ice water up their torso prompting them to pick up the pace to a jog. It's vile repugnancy was a gruesome prospect that had yet to manifest it's lurid form out in the open.

A horrific visage that had yet up till now remained a dark enigma, a mortally terrifying experience able to be conveyed only by those who met with such vile and despicable ends. It's oppressive aura was a prevalent factor and deeply traumatizing to ones inner subconscious and frayed central nervous system, subtly indicative as to what was potentially concealed in the bushes or lurking around every corner. It was also one marked by a pervasive uneasiness that gnawed at the pit of the stomach in a morose ambivalence and accompanied by a collective sense of communal fear of impending doom. It was a dreadful tone that presided over the local inhabitants especially it's elders thus of whom nonetheless wholly subscribed to such old world notions founded in superstitious lore anyway, warily relayed urgent and alarming warnings to it's youth in beseeching and unnerving pleas to remain inside and not to venture out after dark for any reason whatsoever! An underlying and malignant scourge had staked out a foothold as the whole countryside was in the sinister grip of some bleak and evil siege. And from the chaotic fallout of it's chilling aftermath, to the gruesome articles contained in it's grisly wake, thus resulted in hastened and erratic responses of unprecedented proportions by way of sporadic hysteria to the sudden rash of brutal and systemic mayhem. And to those who may have preordained such dark and morbid notions within their morbid psyche may have invariably sat huddled in dimly lit corners of dismal rooms at night flinching in terror at every little sound, such as a tree branch snapping from a sudden gust of wind on the outside, or a barking dog or perhaps glass shattering in the distance.

These noises became frequent nocturnal prompts for unbridled and paralyzing fear in the night that typically sent one reeling in frenzied terror. And it spawned a imploring outcry from it's citizens aimed at local authorities to remedy and bring a swift end to the overall danger and the rash epidemic of bizarre and unsolved mayhem. Thus prompted a significant degree of social inhibition on the part of many demoralized individuals to internalize, nightmarish and abhorrent self manufactured conceptualizations. This in turn spawned a widespread sudden and inclusive rash of ghastly repugnant perceptions of what such a creature could possibly appear as, steadily offsetting the unwary minds of many. Stark and elusive premonitions of a vague partial zed mental image of some statuesque mutated creature grossly disproportionate looming with outstretched arms silhouetted against a creepy nocturnal backdrop. Varying mentally indistinct conceptualizations were eerily haunting and presided over a collective host of traumatized psyches. As one put it, you could almost mentally envision such a being perhaps standing there loitering about one cool evening in someone's backyard slightly hunched over next to a dark green dilapidated old garage with collapsing doors and a crudely fenced in cabbage or tomato or some other type of rat patch garden setting adjacent to it morosely vagrant, indiscriminately lurking about in a misty partial zed haze subtly illuminated by the sallow rays of an evening sun in a profound sense, stylizing a stark and horrifying enigma. This and similar visages where all to often reoccurring and unfortunately one many had to apprehensively come to grips with, and contend with on a regular basis. Bizarre and harrying mental visages such as these in a constant and steady stream plagued and tormented countless scores of hapless individuals. And even to those one's who would be considered as possessing a morbidly rare and perverse mindset were no exception. Yet these elusive factors alone wholly remained outwardly concealed, but wholly presiding in the figurative sense. Thus confounding any real potential for successful investigative measures by local and regional authorities. Turn of the century lore referencing that of such a dark enigmatic presence had mentally figmented itself within the collective minds of the townspeople in a dreadful consensus as a whole.

And it was a demurring aspect to all the basic activity levels of the local townspeople. By night put them in a perpetual wary some defense mode of nocturnal covertness in that by day initially took on intensely guarded levels of basic and essential movements brought on by a wary inhibition followed by erroneous suspicion within regarding even their close neighbors and a grave uncertainty regarding the imminent future. The townspeople at large were plagued with ramped fear and indecision scurrying about in confounded and erratic attempts to carry out even basic elements of functioning. And as neighboring communities would set in for the night, petrified residents were forced to come to grips with such a pervasive and overriding fear of the night that signified the elusive presence of a night stalking boogerized mutation. A morosely guarded level of inhibition the towns people had embraced only resulted in ambiguous and ineffectual responses to a sudden and inclusive rash of the horrific in a macabre sequence of events. And in their strange and baffling format had left many of it's victims in either a semi-catatonic state of hysteria or writhing around in a freakish mass of slimy bluish-green ooze. These series of freakish night time occurrences of which had recently transpired have left the surreptitious townspeople mercilessly stalked by an insidious air of grim and malevolent doom, and one never knew what was going to be waiting for them around the corner of their own house or garage should they just haphazardly walk around outside in their yard one unsuspecting evening. Basic movements were becoming drastically minimized and either short distance travel was exercised or eliminated altogether, and despite those who unwarily ventured out and about after dusk was one maniacally shrouded in fear...the fear of something in the dark and visually elusive and outwardly concealed from sight, at least to anyone living.. The local and surrounding regions were ignominiously turned into a nightmarish surrealistic scape of stark and garish interpretations

Steeped in self conceptualized images of potential Boogie monsters that may suddenly lunge from the shadows of darkened hallowed places to ominously lurk about indiscriminately looking to slime another victim. And those old abandoned railroad tracks and distant woods were now viewed with an elevated sense of palpable fear and abject horror stemming from the bizarre incident weeks prior by immediate and surrounding residents. And with the onslaught of dusk brought a grim rush to judgment as fear levels rose and wholesale levels of terror that gripped it's citizens in morbid and paralyzing degrees. And as an innately evil aura vehemently seethed deep from within the darkened hollows of such outlying objects as decaying landmarks and massive trees in wide open clearings in gloomy moon lit night scapes. Thus unduly cast it's ominous and foreboding connotations over a nocturnal setting morosely unsettling one to the very pinnacle of their psyche. And as alarmed residents resigned themselves to the stark realization of a potential manifestation of the incomprehensibly enigmatic may very well be well within the realm of imminent possibility. Yet as neighborhood streets progressively became more and more deserted at dusk, one was undeniably forced to come to grips with what had to essentially be done in safeguarding themselves against that horrid thing. And like busied teams of bees in a hive or field mice setting in for the winter they scurried about to carry out their basic daily functions in fretful preparedness before nightfall.

Tasking in morosely sullen ways before they hid themselves behind chained and dead bolted doors with big wooden sticks and big vicious attack dogs at the ready, as they also locked their widows. There were also those who sat there alone in semi lit living rooms in rocking chairs at night peering out darkened windows either through partially drawn curtains or Venetian blinds with an eerie intuition gnawing at the pit of a queasy stomach in that some unseen and undisclosed inherently evil presence was observing them in a freakish gawk from the distance of some darkened secluded hallowed location unknown to anyone on the inside. And in that, that some creepy statuesque and bug eyed goon whom had staked out a regional claim was just standing there fixated stare garishly leering in and sizing them up for that next ghastly home invasion. Many of it's resident's just sat there huddled in dimly lit rooms behind chained and dead bolted doors quaking in fear at every little thud, snap, wind gust or household noise that inordinately manifested themselves late into the night in nerve shattering anticipation of bludgeoning and volatile attempts at forceful entry by some evil green slimy ogre from the other side. And as they sat there in fervent and despondent hopes that a baseball bat, a long butcher's knife or some type of worn or substandard firearm would have sufficient stopping power to disable it.

CHAPTER ELEVEN

Evil Reclamation

HALLOW VALLEY WAS A PROFOUNDLY EERIE AND CRYPTIC PLACE INDEED that was virtually unexplored by most and hikers viewed it with an abiding consensus of ominous dread, as those on foot in many instances chose to skirt or it bypass altogether in singling it out as opposed to other possible routes. As one was immediately struck with a grave sense of ominous and imminent doom emanating from the location. It was a remote five mile stretch of uninhabited countryside situated just on the edge of Perrydine County and located several miles to the outskirts of adjoining towns Dunmore and Avondale. It's baseline was a moderately wide low lying gully that snaked for miles through desolate hills and was shrouded with four foot high sallow yellow weeds and punctuated by creepy wretched knotted trees.

And the prospect of venturing it alone, especially with the ghostly howl of the wind through it's hills at night coupled with the rustling sounds of willowing weeds, was one that would most assuredly send a yellow streak up the back of even the most surly type ruffian a mile wide causing them to shudder to their very core. And in furtherance of it's creepy nocturnal ambiance, among other things, one could hear the howling of wolves or the distraught barking of wolves or coyotes in the distance against the grim pale blue backdrop of a dully lit moonlit sky permeated with puffy dark silhouetted clouds. Some of the terrain in Hallow Valley leveled off to a more even keel and served to accommodate modest sized cow or horse pastures for adjacent sparsely located farmhouses built sometime in the 1930's located just a few miles away. These animal pastures were few and far between and were usually enclosed with old dilapidated barbed wire fences with withered and decaying wooden posts sunk in the ground. The grassy vegetation within these enclosures was usually chewed down to the bare soil and especially on a hot day the outlying area always stunk like manure and when it rained it became a depressing miserable sea of mud inundated with puddles of water. For the most part these animals were neglected and unkempt, rarely fed unless there was absolutely no grass at all to graze on or the occasional cow was to be slaughtered for it's beef.

And in lieu of it's alarming history and ominous repute Hallow Valley had been irrevocably branded as taboo by remaining older surrounding residents and local historians alike. It's ill connotations rooted in old wives-tales originating from the late 1800's that channeled their way upward from the dark & dreary annals of the early 1900's. It was reputed to have been the site for a series of grave tragedies and a well renowned one in particular spoke of a family of lowly drudge laden prairie dwellers who resided in an aloof dilapidated old log cabin set upon the hilly rise. It is said that the a result of such insurmountable catastrophic events a site can seemingly inherit the spiritual residue of other such like occurrences that result in an ominous karma radiating a powerful sensation of grave imminence. And if severe enough will transcend their ghastly auras into the physical plane of a site thus possessing it and prompting it to droningly emanate the overwhelming sensation of a dooming ambiance to those whom just haplessly come upon it. Legend has it that a work laden wheat farmer by the name of Cyrus Coburn who in a grave state of inconsolable despondency over a series of insurmountable and grievous circumstances encompassing mounting life's adversities, some of which comprised two or three consecutive seasons of failed or unsold crops, a series of bank notes he was unable to re-pay and an impending eviction and foreclosure on his farmhouse and acreage that had culminated to such an irretrievable degree in that he was wholly unable to circumvent or offset, one evening took his old Henry rifle in a harried & anguished state grievously offed his wife and four hapless children and then torched the house. He was then subsequently discovered hanging from one of the rafters high above in the barns hayloft of the adjacent horse stable later on. And also not mentioning that the immediate and surrounding location was also the site for earlier tragic occurrences involving an unprecedented series of roving band Indian attacks and grisly massacres perpetrated on other hapless prairie dwellers whereby victims were typically maimed, mutilated or strung from trees… And ever since the turn of the century has became an eerie enigmatic site shrouded in mystery and tales of woe and one fraught with a grave omnipresence. ill-advised by presiding authorities as one that should definitely be avoided at any and all costs and by-passed by John Q. Public.

However upon the transpiring of a series of more recent events on varying late night occasions residents from the immediate and outlying countryside have reported as having been garishly rousted from late night slumber by a frightfully disturbing series of unearthly low droning whining like moans followed by a succession of bizarre cackles like that of a wild turkey buzzard running about emanating from the huge creepy gully that had left many reeling in a frenzied and flustered state of pure unadulterated terror and literally shuddering in darkened sitting rooms and beds. And all too often these unearthly drones which had frequently echoed from the huge creepy gorge spooked many to such a profound degree it abruptly prompted a good number of them to hastily scuttle up all their belongings in boxes and move away leaving those remaining few behind that were brave enough to stick around. Legend also has it that these types of late night occurrences were reputed by local and surrounding inhabitants of the 1920's and 30's in similar fashion and holding steady to a dark cryptic and eerily enigmatic connotation. Old wives-tales and folk lore shrouded in aloof crypticism held over have been carried on and passed down by the few remaining old timers of the period that were still left. And even surrounding authorities upon conducting much investigation were completely and utterly baffled and apparently unable to reach much in the way of a plausible conclusion as to a possible source, other than it's just reputed to be haunted. And during daylight hours wary travelers who were commonly youths slowly plodding their way on foot through the rough passageway of the massive grassy gorge have alarmingly reported some strange and peculiar milky white substance which seemed to have the same properties and consistency as paper-mache' or an old bucket of chunky clumped up 10 year old expired white house paint. This coupled with some other olive greenish type goop was frequently discovered strung through and hanging from the branches of old knotted trees or strewn about the immediate grounds and surrounding areas subtly making reference to some bizarre representation of astrological signs and symbols in triangular shaped or semi-circled patterns or in sketchy crudely shaped pentagrams. Eerie and disturbing evidence held over as ghastly remnants of a mysterious unknown source. These disturbing findings were initially made by those who were enough to venture through it. And yet maintained little to no apprehension in that regard despite the frantic and desperate pleas of a wary-some local authority's grave and imminent warnings to John Q. Public at large to fervently heed it's advice in just bypassing it altogether.

The large grassy gully had also been the general site for other strange and particularly unnerving findings in the way of not only a substantial number of animals such as cows pigs and horses that were reported missing by their owners, but others as well such as those in the wild like wolves, coyotes and foxes alike had also been discovered totally encased in the same type of bizarre, freakish dark green semi-translucent sludge like material. All animals which were randomly discovered were described as all frightfully peering outwardly from within the strange greenish semi-transparent rubbery material they were permanently encased in. Each one frozen in an eternal death mask of extreme horror and mortally stricken with the same stark bugeyed gaze on each one of them….As if they'd seen something so surrealistically horrific prior to death that it literally caused them to go into shock and succumb to heart failure.

Various types of farm animals were frequently discovered in such a state within the dilapidated barbed wire fence enclosed pastures or in the cases of horses, pigs or sheep, corrals. Upon such horrific daytime discoveries of not only their missing and ill displaced livestock farmers and sheep herders alike were so frightened and unnerved by not only

that but those god-awful unearthly whining type moans and strange
cackling noises coupled with the howling wind late into the night
emanating from that huge creepy gully. In that the combination of
these dreadful and unnerving factors prompted many to scurry about
scrambling to somewhat fortify themselves out of fear against whatever
it was out there roaming around at night in summoning local authorities
to come out to conduct a lengthy and ongoing investigation to no avail.
But also installing motion sensitive floodlights in key positions on their
properties and obtaining large dogs renowned for being trained in the
attack as well as being notoriously vicious, such as pit bulls, Doberman-
pinchers or German Sheppard's and stockpiling various types of
hardware such as handguns, rifles and ammunition regardless of make
model year or condition so long as it was able to chamber a round and
fire

CHAPTER TWELVE

The Dismal Site of the Old State Asylum

THE ROUTE TO THE MONTCREEF SUSSEX STATE MENTAL HOSPITAL WAS as an unlikely destination for Cameron and Dusty to set out for as the Bahamas would've been for Frosty the snowman. But in lieu of such grim and imminent circumstances, the two perilously set out for it that morning as it was one that had become an essential and key element in resolving this looming crisis and was one that was unavoidably going to have to be made out of grave necessity in desperate attempts to deviate from their present course of wayward perdition. And yet unlike it's more sophisticated present day counterparts hailed from a more darkened enigmatic era of unenlightenment in that it was once crudely and unabashedly referred to as an insane asylum. And then much later on a more appropriate and euphemistic derivative was more overtly readily applied to it, a sanitarium accompanied with it, it's grave and longstanding effects.

Yet it was a facility who's patients in many instances required close quarter supervision. And up until the late nineteen seventies with great strides in practical application in the field of mental hygiene and psychiatry most patients due to that fact as well as cut backs by government agencies funding them on both state and federal levels. These institutions that were once slated for long term facilitation were reduced or eradicated altogether. This transition made it only possible for residents to be held on a short term basis only. The days of permanent or long term stays were slowly phased out entirely rendering that type of application obsolete or passé'. On a warm sunny day the front lawn of the facility was marked with a sense of leisured business. It was usually one marked by the facilities supervisory staff such as nurses, orderlies or doctors bustling about pushing residents around in wheelchairs in a quiet and relaxed mode all dressed in some type of drab white, light green or gray hospital garb in what was to become their recreation area. This was sort of a reward for those patients who didn't act out or tapered off in their sudden and violent outbursts or no longer had to be physically restrained and subdued by teamed groups of specially trained staff. And to those whose outward behavior became more docile, manageable or copasetic in their demeanor or who in taking their prescribed psyche meds showed signs of marked improvement. A day could be spent outside just to relax and bask in the warm summer breezes and comforting rays of the sun. Or one could choose to just sit there sullenly to stew in their own juices in wheelchairs if they chose to. You could stretch your limbs and go for a leisurely walk around the compound. But in any case it was going to be a lengthy, dreaded unpredictable sojourn nonetheless, and most of which was going to have to be undertaken on foot.

And although these were modern times there were no roads directly leading to the old facility from any point of proximity of Washburn. It was located in the Perridyne region of Pontiff county and was a good twenty miles away but once he hit town he could take a cab to the area where the open ended ravine was located. He was unfortunately going to have negotiate and cross that dreadfully eerie and creepy gorge to directly access the facility itself which was not outwardly visible from that vantage point...But all he knew at this stage was that he needed answers to pervading questions that only those two girls could give him and he was prepared to go to great lengths to get them. He was also going to have to set out early in the morning to arrive there in time before nightfall as he didn't want to get caught out there in those woods alone, armed or not. He was also going to have to physically undertake at least eight miles of rough hilly country side terrain which mainly consisted of vast open fields and meadows overgrown with tall grass and weeds and was more than likely snake infested. Also of which was going to require the implementation of a heavy duty pair of hiking boots and a good old fashioned bowie knife. Yet as Cameron lethargically sat there drafting a plan in his mind on his porch that afternoon listening to the local news station on the radio and weighing in a host variety of potentially adverse factors he was more than likely to be bogged down with, the weather being one of them, and with an overall sense of dread as at this point he didn't want anything to offset his plans. He inwardly considered as to whether to go or not, as for one he didn't even know the girls and was unsure how they'd react to him.

Yet he maintained a nagging recompense that the benefits of what the girls would divulge far outweighed any looming drawbacks. Although he inwardly knew he was going to exact some kind of harrowing tale depicting a mortally terrifying run in with that slimy two legged boogerized malignancy. One thing was for certain though, he was going to tell the girls of his grisly hair raising account in that mortally grave stand off they'd had with that putrid thing, As at this point he knew deep down inside they had a run in with it to and if it was anything like the closed pitched battle he and Dusty were embroiled in he knew they were put through a grueling ringer. If this was most certainly the case it would insure that this would prove itself out to be a beneficial and fruitful endeavor thus yielding the much needed results. Or when he finally arrived there was it just going to culminate itself into just another fiasco? As it stood now, this looming crisis has already begun to take it's toll on him and the community at large. He'd become distant in his guarded interactions with immediate friends and had developed a short fuse in that the slightest little things began to set him off. He was going to have to volley and exact a productive and successful result and soon in resolving this. And before any more people died. All he knew at this particular juncture was, that God awful thing they saw that night survived everything they threw at it and it was still out there…Lurking, stalking and insidiously preying on innocent souls from within the murky shadows of distant decaying historical landmarks that remained ominously haunting and unapproachable at night, vacant and eerily ensuing to the occasional passersby. And as it stood he had a pretty good chance of running into it again further on down the line and he was more than likely going to be by himself this time. But he knew that at some point of grave finality it was going to have to be ultimately reckoned with and if not by him, but by somebody else, and by any and all means necessary. For one as this was going to be an eight mile trek and much of which constituted rough and inhospitable countryside terrain. He also knew that he was going to have to pass through a rugged stone laden ravine, a gorge that stretched a good mile from end to end and thus went up a steep rocky incline at the mouth of it's entrance. Even then he didn't know if he was going to be able to get in to conduct his own personal interrogation with the girls once he got there. Or just how lucid or coherent they were going to be at this point, but he had to try.

And too, he was somewhat unsure of how stringent hospital policy would be regarding security or the admittance of surprise or unannounced visitors would be received. And in such instances that staff might strictly regulate that aspect and turn him away entirely, He was then going to have to concoct some type of ruse stating that he's a distant cousin or something sent by relatives who came in from Connecticut for a concerned visit and hoped they'd fall for it. Then once behind closed doors he could then proceed with what he had to do. And anyway it wasn't as though he was intent on doing the girls any harm by accessing them under such false pretenses he was on a noble mission. And what he had to do had to remain secretive because at this point he had to try something, anything. He just had to find out just what the girl's saw and particularly just what took place that evening and if it was that vile, putrid composition of living breathing garbage was behind it. And he was pretty sure it was, and also in just what they did in their intense battle to ward it off in such desperate efforts to preserve their lives and why they made it and their friend didn't. It was now going to be up to him, as he bore the brunt of resolving this whole thing in that the overwhelming burden of it has now come to rest on his shoulders, Dusty is a mental and emotional wreck right now and may become a viable candidate for the same if she doesn't snap out of her catatonic and traumatized state and soon. She not only won't receive anybody right now, she's so wrenched up from this whole thing, she won't leave the strict confines of her home, so she's not going to be much in the way of any real help at least not for the time being. And now it appears, that the ball was in his court and that this was going to be a tough job somebody had to do. And that as of now became his own personal and private property and exclusively his to resolve.

"What a lonely and disparaging thought he murmured to himself "shaking his head back and forth in a solitary display of moderate level aggravation as he was now at a personal crossroads and perilously approaching a wits end. "Yeah" Cameron once again gets elected here to get saddled with all the bullshit!! But despite the present and seemingly insurmountable odds were, the underlying obstacles marked the path of the monumental task that was ahead of him. One of which was, just what this things weakness was and what it is going to ultimately take to bring an ignominious end to it's vile existence. He also knew from what the papers outlined in that railroad tracks confrontation they'd most likely had, had a run in with that same putrid thing that he and his friends did in the barn that stormy night engaged in such a vicious, pitted battle at close quarters with that invincible monstrosity, and quite obviously their little trio didn't fair nearly as well. The state hospital was located in a remote and desolate location miles away from the outskirts of the town of Perridyne and was erected in 1834. It was first allocated as a state prison, housing mostly the unsavory elements taken from the low ends of society. The dregs, if you will, the violent and unmanageable, habitual petty and hardened criminals, rapists, murders and the like much as it is today. Then later on it was slated to be a long term facility for the mentally ill of the time, in what they used to call an insane asylum a term that was used then, but by today's standards as a crudely unenlightened term, mildly crass and outdated. It strictly housed violent unmanageable mental patients years later when it was dubbed The Sussex state hospital for the criminally insane positioned a way's back from the woods and the Sussex Madeline, Dartmouth river that runs along side it. It eerily sets remote and isolated on a steep rise majestic and stoic in a dismal silent omnipresence in an open clearing.

Yet through it's dreary brownish gray massive stone and brick mortars in that each block was a mammoth nine by nine foot block at the base of the foundation of this ominous and foreboding structure each weighing a good five tons or so, in that they were incorporated into the majestic 19th century style of architecture of this towering historical landmark. It seemed to possess a grim and dismal aura in and of itself, almost animated as though it was peering outwardly out over the vast hilly countryside through the dark cavities of the iron barred windows taking on the grim morose appearance of sullen eye's leering back in a fixed gaze at an approaching unwary onlooker. And in exuding a menacing air of dark foreboding, starkly intimidating much as a stone faced troll like sentry in all it's physically repugnant exuberance standing there intently poised to exact a toll and silently defying one to pass. And to one who would just happened upon it in the clearing, was met with a bleak and menacing omnipresence, marked by a nagging sense of uneasiness in that it seemed to possess an inherently sinister entity deep within the bricks and mortars of it's historical conclave. This stoic grayish stone exterior rose a towering four stories high. and was one of the few remaining relics that paid silent homage to a darker, cruder, and socially enigmatic period of a distant past. That by which was wholly committed in it's somewhat primeval methods and limited means, to contain and sequester the undesirable elements of the day or the chronically troublesome and dysfunctional elements taken from the low ends of society.... And one had to cross the Sussex county Madeline river on foot through low lying and shallow portions steeped in rough terrain while negotiating rows of huge flat rocks steadying one's self with a long wooden staff usually a tree branch or makeshift staff to balance them selves in crossing it prior to access it from the banks of that awkward vantage point. This massive stone fortress boasts a broad occupancy of about two hundred and fifty rooms or more and just about as many windows on the outside as well as an extensive below ground floor level reserved for permanent hospital staff. Local legend has it that in the late eighteen scores of countryside inhabitants were sent reeling in fear behind locked cottage or cabin doors at night huddled by the dim light of candles and oil lanterns, as word went out over the eerily desolate landscape that "there'd been another crazed escapee from Sussex house and the subject was being sought after by authorities as they were on the loose prowling the countryside"!

One could almost envision a strait jacketed bug eyed drooling goon from the distant past leering back at them upon unassumingly opening up one's locked door on a cold dreary moonlit night. It has since undergone a number of structural renovations and upgrades like the removal of iron bars on the facility's interior that were once used for prison incarceration as from the doorway entrances of each unit and replacing them with a thick heavy iron like security doors with a one by ten inch window located towards the top with a section of wire mesh running through the center of the pane of glass. The old facility still had iron bars and grates over the exterior portions of the windows and pretty much to the casual observer took on pretty much the same externally creepy appearance as it did back in the eighteen hundreds, the only difference is it is now it's significantly more advanced and sophisticated in it's procurement of practical application. Yet upon viewing it by pure happenstance one could become almost hypnotically captivated and entranced by the dark ominous aura it exudes.

The building itself evokes an eerie omnipresence and one of solitary uneasiness and one may find themselves involuntary drawn by an inherent interconnection to the past at almost an intuitive level. Especially from under the yellowish green illumination of the moon which inadvertently sets an eerie tone when panned from a distance at the faint sallow yellow light emanating from various window openings. And in panning this dismal historical stone monstrosity from a distance of maybe a few hundred yards off or so especially from the sparsely wooded vantage point across the river one is stricken a sense of sullen invasive uneasiness that's hauntingly captivating. And one particularly familiarized with the darkened era could almost hear the ghostly anguished cries in the night, and the imploring pleas, or the tormented bellows of volatile out of control inmates reverberating from within those towering, massive, dreary stone walls whose crazed shrieks and guttural moans of a hundred years ago eerily echoing their way throughout the countryside in a muffled yet audible tone which have long since fallen silent. One could almost mentally conceive a vague image of such scenario's playing themselves out, as harried groups of inadequately trained and crudely equipped nineteenth century medical staff haplessly scramble to restrain and subdue a mentally deranged and out of control subject on a sudden violent rampage and unpredictable outburst upon other patients or institutional staff. And one could almost visualize from a panned view overhead as a group of frenzied doctor's and nurses frantically scurry about to retrieve leather restraint devices or crude sedative drugs. And in the administration of such experimental drugs was often accompanied by the archaic and barbaric implementation of oversized hypodermic needles and cold water submersion techniques, leg shackles or leather types of crudely fashioned and primitive restraint devices in their ongoing and exhausted quest for ultimate submission and containment of chronically out of control subjects whom were medically and socially deemed as a danger to themselves and others. Scenes such as this were commonplace in like institutions of the day in that they of themselves were victims of their own unenlightened perceptions and inept methods of procurement by such mental health practitioners as these in their post theoretical stumble in the dark. As this compels more pensive minded persons to reflect in silent contemplation such unfortunate events that transpired marking a darkened age of social awareness and enlightenment which sorely lacked the bare essentials of far more sophisticated and practical modes of application in what were primarily contrived methods of implementation based solely on experimentation. And wholly left to it's own crude and primeval devices in their long term treatment and short term remedy of the mentally ill in the bleak and long forgotten darkened hallows of this age old historical landmark that stands dismal testament to a somewhat harrowing, disparaging and institutionally unchallenged, volatile past.

Cameron was packing some things in an old olive green rucksack he had from when he was in the Marines for the long haul to the State hospital. He had to decide what items that were going to be essential he had to include in getting ready for the trip. He knew he had to include basic items like a couple of changes of clothes, bar soap, and some food stuffs. And a box of wood stick matches and a small can of kerosene just in case he had to start a fire to keep warm at night out in the woods, and of course a shaving kit, so he wouldn't draw wary suspicion by looking to rangy in front of the institutions staff or receptionists at the front desk when he attempts to gain visitor admittance. As they'd probably just take one look at someone like that and dismiss them as some unauthorized or unsavory character attempting to enter the facility without legitimate reasons. Thus forth in that instance he'd undoubtedly be forcibly removed and escorted from the premises by hospital security. And in that event it would render the whole endeavor a colossal waste of time. And yeh of course, the thirty eight and a box of shells. He was not going to take any unnecessary chances this time so he also included a thick bowie knife with a ten inch blade with razor sharp teeth notched into the top portion of the blade as added protection against that thing if by chance the ominous circumstance that may potentially arise warranted it. He was going to try and cover most of the distance in one day and stay at a cheap motel when he got within the corporate limits of the town so an overnight stay in the woods wouldn't be necessary. One thing was for sure though he didn't want to meet up with that God awful thing again as he was fairly uncertain as to how he'd fair with it this time.

The paper said the victim from the last attack was clutching a small automatic pistol in his fist when they found him as well as a spent magazine about a few feet away from the body. That told Cameron that the poor guy had managed to dispense at least one full magazine at it and was more than likely in the process of dispensing another seven round burst when he was cruelly and abruptly cut down in his tracks. And like all the others he was immersed in that freakish green goop. And just the very thought of running into that thing again struck a sense of mortal terror in him at his very core, and he wasn't going to be afforded the luxury of being in a safe overhead position out of reach like the hay loft this time. Nor was he going to be able to reign down an unceasing barrage of gun fire or throw Molotov cocktails at it like before either. He was going to be on foot this time and most of his maneuvers were going to have to be evasive ones in the way he was plain just gonna have to run away from it. For one thing he knew it couldn't run at all as it didn't move very fast either it sort of trotted at a brisk pace in some bizarre freakish slow moving pursuit but would not be able to keep up with a relatively young fit thirty five year old guy at a full sprint,

That was the only advantage he had over it at this point. Yes he could still fire upon it but he knew that would only serve as a temporary measure to slow it down and he couldn't find himself on the business end of that deadly green sludge that booger spewing mutation launched from it's putrid arsenal to subdue it's victims or this time he'd be ultimately finished. One thing was clearly evident at this juncture was that this was not going to be a pleasure trip by any stretch of the means, but one of grave necessity and one he had no level of enthusiasm to take. But he had a strong inward sense of moral obligation to see this thing through to the end. He not only owed it to himself but to those girls, the town and Dusty. He had to do something to stop this thing from further stalking and terrorizing the countryside. He also knew he just had to get into see those two girls and at least get a sketchy account of what actually happened between them and that thing on the railroad tracks that fateful day and why their friend didn't make it, and why their lives were spared. He was just about finished packing that old green canvas rucksack when he herd a faint knock at the front door. He looked up over across the cluttered unkempt and dimly lit living room pausing as he leered over at the front door he suddenly got a sick queasy feeling in his stomach and a heart pounding tight feeling in his chest at the unsettling prospect it may be Dusty. He hadn't seen her in the two months since the brutally pitted confrontation in the old barn that night as she wasn't at all bearing up very well emotionally or psychologically and she not only wouldn't take phone calls but wasn't receiving visits from friends either. As far as he knew she was held up in her room in a sullen almost catatonic state which was perplexing to her mother who handed her daily meals through her bedroom door. He figured she would eventually come around as maybe she just needed some quiet down time to fully come to terms with what happened that night in the old tobacco barn that stormy night. He sat there still, frozen on the sofa for a moment as he held onto the same olive green backpack he was issued and once used to trudge along on those grueling eight mile hikes fully loaded they took in the hot blazing sun on Paris island. He was in the process of snapping one of the main flaps along the top closed and zipping up all the smaller cargo pockets on it when he heard a timid, and wispy female voice through the door.... Cameron,...Cameron,.... are you there?

He sat there completely dumbfounded as he recognized Dusty's faint and quivering voice muffled but identifiable from the other side. His overwhelming sense of anxiety was immediately superseded by a warm calming sense of relief...Dusty!!....is that you honey? And in a muffled sounding reply through the door she answered...yeah it's me, can you let me in? And with that Cameron immediately leapt to his feet and letting the strap from the backpack slide off his shoulder and fall to the floor simultaneously as he bolted towards the front door flinging it open. What stood there in the doorway was the wretched and pathetic remnant image of a much thinner gaunt and somewhat unkempt specimen of a once pretty young girl now haplessly reduced to only a shell of her former defiant and confident self who'd been so physically and emotionally ravaged by the surrealistically horrific events that took place that night she was rendered barely able to carry out even the most basic of functions. And whom since he'd seen last her, had lost about twenty or thirty pounds in the process was un bathed and he could tell she'd probably wore and slept in the same clothes for at least a week or more straight. Yes it was readily apparent that something had mercilessly just ate her up inside and just spit out the bones. Her hair was filthy and askew and she had the mauled and disheveled appearance of a wet dog who'd been kicked about by it's owner. Dusty'? is that you?....Cameron intently implored as if she was that unrecognizable through all the wary subterfuge they exercised in regards to evading the dangers of the creature. Dusty!! What the hell happened to you He was immediately taken back and totally aghast by the stark emaciated and distorted image of a once beautiful girl that stood there in the doorway before him.

A young girl who'd been so gravely terrorized, emotionally battered and put through a horrific ringer that she couldn't bring herself to eat a decent meal for days on end. Dusty' I'm not doin so good...Cameron' yeah I can see that! Well the first order of business here is going to be a bath, a clean change of clothes and a hot meal in ya!! "Dusty" I just don't feel like…..And Cameron grabbing her by the upper arm and forcibly leading her through his living room barked….I don't care about what you feel like doing your going to get in that tub or do I have to strip you myself and put you there? She just muttered some inaudible ramblings as they entered the bathroom and Cameron jammed an old rubber stop in the bottom of the wash basin and while briskly turning the knobs jutting out hissing, spurting blasts of hot water into the tub. Her weakened feigned attempts to resist a forced bath were immediately put down as he continued his strong armed prompts to submerge her in a hot bubble bath as he quickly began pouring the last remnants of fragrant beads out from the open end of a generic box marked lush lavender into the running water. Just then he stood in an upright position and said are you gonna get in there or am I gonna have to put you there?…And using some kind of intimidating reverse psychology he barked,. I mean it now, we can do this the easy way or the somewhat more demeaning hard way it's totally up to you, and quite frankly I don't give a shit which, so what's it gonna be? And knowing this was one round she was going to most assuredly lose….she said ok just leave and close the door, Cameron' good here's a towel I'll set it here on the toilet seat. You just get your bath and take your time and I'd better hear water splashing and sighs coming from this bathroom or you and I are gonna tangle comprende?! I'll start dinner and bring you a fresh change of clothes we might have to bury those in the back yard.

After about a half hour or forty five minutes a reddened and somewhat pruned Dusty emerged from a hot steamy sauna slowly strolling into the living room with a large oversized beach towel wrapped around all the important parts. She just stood there with steam rising from her physical and emotionally wrought and emaciated body lowly awaiting for yet another one of Cameron's stern, confident, authoritative directives as in just what to do next. She looked almost like a pitiful wet canary her skin pruned, flushed red and white and just standing there dripping before Cameron as he sat there seething at the kitchen table. He cast a somber gaze over at her shook his head and said your clothes are on the foot of my bed in the back bedroom, I just hope they fit somewhat I still have some of my clothes from when I was about fifteen I don't know why I still keep them but they do come in handy in emergencies such as this. Dusty' said what did you do with mine? He sarcastically replied…I sent them out to be fumigated…Dusty' was that supposed to be funny or some kind of a joke? Cameron' no actually it wasn't not only have I completely lost my sense of humor but am now in the process of slowly and surely losing what few marbles I started out in this life with as well. Dusty' well I'm sorry to hear that…Cameron' just go get dressed and get ready for dinner and from the looks of you that's been a long time coming. Cameron went into the small shabby semi clean kitchen area where a buffet of pot luck was set out on top of the stove consisting of a partially opened loaf of cheap stale bread, a pan of honey baked beans and some type of tuna noodle concoction along with a small pot of something that vaguely resembled some kind of succotash sat steaming in a set of non matching worn, beat up looking aluminum pots that looked like they'd been cast in the sixties and were strung to the back bumper of a car and drug over about five miles of rough pavement. It would be a safe bet that they were probably found in a cardboard box someone had put out at the curb on trash day. And the kitchen stove they all sat on also looked like it had been picked up from a local scrap yard.

The old faded and marred yellow tackily designed patterned tiles covering the floor seemed to silently proclaim "this is a poor mans house". The shabby but serviceable furniture in the living room as well as the brick-a-brack, the sofa and the mismatched beds and dressers in the two back bedrooms were all found inexplicably discarded at one time or another. And Cameron would randomly come upon them going through more affluent neighborhoods each one at a time throwing them or a box that contained old vases, statues or figurines that were in moderately good condition but had no redeeming monetary value. Like a running flea market or rummage sale dealer this was partly how he made his living, he'd enthusiastically toss such items on the bed of his old seventy six F-150 pickup truck that was thinly framed in rust to either furnish his old dilapidated makeshift house or give what he didn't have any more room for to neighbors that had next to nothing in the way of furnishings for their houses as he figured it was better to give these articles away to those in desperate need rather than that they just needlessly get wasted in the back of some smelly old trash truck. It was poor but it was cozy and it was home and besides old furniture had character and a past that he derived a warm comforting feeling from it almost at a level of companionship as he lived alone and only had a big old Siamese cat named Benny that always sat up on the window sill and slept to keep him company. And notably newly manufactured furniture was structurally to uniform in it's design as well as being oversized overpriced and too cold and clinical in it's outward appearance and devoid of certain aesthetic qualities he sought in that regard....And besides the price on the furniture he got, aside from the minimal cost of a couple of dollars for some sand paper, furniture nails paint or stain that it sometimes took to repair superficial scuff damage, was well within his budget; it was free...Even though he owned the old house it was hard enough on a month to month basis to put food on the table and pay the utilities on his modest salary from his job at one of the few remaining old textile mills he worked in for the past ten years or so, and that at often times proved out to be unstable as he often found himself laid off for months at a time during down times

Dusty slowly made her way into the kitchen in a timid and inhibited fashion with a flushed complexion she got from a lengthy submersion in a tub filled with hot water and the scent of fragrant bath oil beads permeated the air. The clothes Cameron gave her to wear were a little to big and were for a guy but they were clean and so was she and that's all that mattered. And as she stood there looking down at the pot luck that was going to be tonight's supper. She took the palm of her right hand and swiped her long dampened locks from the side of her face and said "this looks good I'm starved". And Cameron heartily retorted ya I'll bet...at this point just about anything would I guess if you've gone without food as long as you have....and anyway who's fault is that? She abruptly stopped in what she was doing holding a big serving spoon and a dinner plate glared over at Cameron and said...mine I suppose... Cameron' why? You mean to tell me that, that thing that happened that night has got you so wrenched up your starving yourself? Dusty' not starving myself I just haven't been very hungry or eating very well lately that's all. I just don't think about food anymore that's all. Cameron' well your either going to be a prime candidate for anorexia or the state booby hatch and at this point I'm not sure which. Dusty' I've almost totally lost my appetite, and replaced it with a grave level of anxiety you know. I haven't been sleeping very well either since it happened. I've been having freakish nightmares just about every other night since and my mother is worried sick, she keeps asking me what's wrong and I just say nothing, what do you propose I tell her at this point? That I saw the real boogie man and he tried to kill me…Oh that'd just go over real big with her hah…. Cameron' well for one thing you could try to get a more level head about you and try and function on a more even keel….but for the time being do you think you can somehow manage pull yourself together enough to help set the table for this sumptuous dinner I've slaved over a hot stove for the past hour while you were indisposed to prepare?

And I won't even mind if you ask for seconds. And Dusty looking around at her modest surroundings replied oh gees can you spare it? Cameron' f-u-n-n-e-e, yeah I can spare it…As Dusty stood there at the kitchen stove with a plate and a big serving spoon getting ready to spoon helpings of Cameron's makeshift Duff's smorgasbord onto her dinner plate she casually glanced out into the living room to see Cameron's olive green backpack overturned sitting there on the floor by the sofa appearing as if it was dropped there by someone in a hurry. And with an inquisitive voice asked…what's that doing there? The abrupt question startled Cameron as he got a flushed expression on his face. It's all packed up are you planning to go somewhere? Cameron got a fluttering feeling in his chest and stomach as he knew Dusty wasn't gonna like the answer and there was definitely going to be an outburst of some degree or magnitude. But he knew he was going to have to do something to divulge potentially valuable information that could assist him in ultimately destroying the creature, as this was not all just going to go away and that he'd eventually have to tell her anyway he responded, I have to make a trip…Dusty' oh yeh, were to? Cameron' the old state mental hospital in Perridyne. Dusty' what? What are you going there for? I wanna get in to see those two girls they found wandering around out there in the woods and question them. Dusty'…What!! Now let me see if I got this straight,…you wanna question them!! are you outta your mind? You don't even know those girls!!

And just what makes you think they'll even let you in to see em? I've heard that place is locked up tighter than a renters purse strings!! I think you've been out in the sun too long or maybe it's a form of heat prostration held over from those long eight mile hikes you had to go on in the Marines and the end result is that you now have a shriveled brain that's been reduced to the size of a walnut. "Cameron" will you calm down now let's not blow this all out of proportion! Dusty' Why? You know your going to have to walk most of the way there? That damn thing is still out there somewhere and all your gonna do is get yourself killed and nothing else!! And after having said that she wincingly fumbled with her half loaded up plate then dropping onto the counter and just started bawling…Will you stop it? I knew this was gonna happen I shouldn't have said a word and just said I was going hiking with some friends up on Santee's trail. Now getta hold a yerself!! DAMMIT!! This shit isn't just gonna just go away if we just sprinkle it with some fairy dust you know…. we've got to do something! I've gotta do something!! Dusty Yeah!, your gonna do something alright your gonna die!!

And having said that she slammed her cupped palms into her flushed red teared up face and began bawling uncontrollably. Cameron mildly incensed at this point at her many tearful display's of defiance to his course strategies up to this point and was at a loss as to what else to say barked snap out of it!! Getta grip!!…I'm going to be ultra careful and take precautions I'm not gonna get killed!! Dusty sobbing and her face hot and wet with tears and partially obscured by her cupped hands and looking up through the spaces between her fingers cried…how do you know that?…Cameron' I just do that's all…And Dusty in a sarcastically mocking manner mimicked I just do that's all…And then Cameron some what perturbed replied ok that'll be quite enough if you can't support me on this than I suggest you keep your personal observations to yourself. You've done little more than dissuade and hinder progress since this whole thing started and I have got to tell you it's past the point of aggravation. Fear and apprehension isn't going to help us here and it's not going to stave off the inevitable and it's not going to do anything to remedy or offset the clear and present danger now is it? Dusty' And neither is you getting dead either...Cameron' look I just have to find something out about what happened to them out there on those tracks that's all and how they managed to survive their run in with Mr. Fedder's that's all...Dusty' then call them on the phone don't try and go it alone on foot you'll run into that thing again and this time you'll probably get killed, and your revolver won't do you any good against that festering chemical garbage dump covered with those revolting boils!! Cameron' Look!! That thing has got to be destroyed and as it stands now I'm the sole and primary candidate that's standing in the lime light elected to do the job. Dusty' you don't have ta do shit!!… let the authorities find him and then they can have the Air Force drop a hydrogen bomb or some napalm on it or something why don't you just stay the hell out of it? Cameron' well for one thing we are among the few living people who have seen it and nobody else thus far has any inkling of just exactly what it is yet and a lot more people are gonna die before this thing is over or that thing is finally revealed on a grand public scale and I just can't let that happen if I know one thing I'm not entrusting anything like this to these local bupkis!!…they would almost certainly screw it up in a hastily bungled Gomerized action!!.. And in any such instance it would only prove itself out to be total unbridled chaos of mass proportions spilling out in the streets. Dusty' and just who are you some kind of proverbial white knight or lone ranger or something set out on a white steed to save the world? No but I do however have some moral semblance about myself in the way of having some indirect level of obligation to my fellow man, look!!, I'm not gonna just cut and run here!!…for one thing I'm not made like that and I should also hope your not either!!…Dusty in a lowly disconcerting glare just looked at Cameron as he spoke.

And besides I firmly believe I or we do however maintain the upper hand in this instance in the way of having the element of surprise strongly in our favor in regards to stalking and centering in on it's elusive and looming nature, all we gotta do is lay back and stay outta sight and all that could all be lost to us in some not very well thought out public action which would no doubt be carried out in a frenzied fit of blind haste resulting in mass pandemonium and hysteria and in all probability and likelihood we would only just end up losing that edge. "Dusty" what do you mean we? Oh no!!...your not draggin me back into this shit again!!...you just get that thought right out of your head right here and now BUB!!...You must be on some serious drugs!! DO YOU GOT SOME KIND OF A DEATH WISH OR SOMETHING!!!... You gotta be outta yer ever-loving mind if you think I'm ever gonna come within fifty miles of, or ever face off with that horrid pus filled abomination again. Oh you will you know how I know? Dusty' no but I can hardly wait to hear..."Cameron" well for one you love me, and two you'll greatly reduce your chances of getting killed by it yourself here in the allotment one lone and unsuspecting night when the Avon lady incognito rings the doorbell with a personalized sample bottle of perfumed dark green slime specially allotted for Dusty Moore's. And just by you contracting me out as your personal bodyguard you won't have to run the risk of such unpleasantries as maybe having to undergo the needlessly annoying experience of such a high pressure sale!!... HA, Ha, Ha, Ha...Dusty' mockingly ha, ha, ha, ha, ha,...fun-nee, and I'd also miss out on all the benefited privileges of constantly hearing a steady stream of such ironic and cleverly articulated analogies colorfully illustrating the pukey circumstances were in. Or in how you seem to feel an overriding compunction to foist them on me every chance you get!!...

So don't push your luck that love is starting to wear a little thin and you must be psycho or on some serious drugs if you think we stand a snowballs chance in hell against that blackened invincible two legged horror!! What chance do you think the two of us could possibly have against that indestructible pus filled slime sputtering pile of garbage? Well I'll tell ya none that's why I still think we need to notify the national guard or the proper authorities or something with what we know...Cameron' No way Houssay!! I want this to be as secretive and covert as possible and for as long as possible until I find out just what it's hidden weakness is. As it stands now we are among the very few who know about just what it is let the authorities come on to this in their own good time. Their no better or worse off than we are at this point, and as it stands now it would appear that all the guns and all the bombs in the world may just be temporary stays and ultimately useless against it. Because if we sound the alarm now it could result in disastrous consequences with mass unorganized, and hysterical pandemonium in the streets and it will take the National Guard alone just to curtail and bring something like that under control. The way I figure it at this point is it's gotta be something that is completely obvious that we are overlooking a chemically based derivative if you will something that it will take to neutralize or disable it's slimy ass!! Dusty' Go figure…I knew it, I just knew it…. Cameron' what do you mean? Dusty' I mean I'm going to get drug right back into this crap again whether I want to or not aren't I… Cameron' smiling wryly, what do you think? Dusty' you just can't let this thing go can you? Cameron' no I can't it's stuck in the back of my crawl like fly paper hanging from the ceiling at a cheap diner, and the one and only thing that's gonna dislodge it is when that thing is completely and permanently discombobulated once and for all!!

Then the mismatched duo proceeded to down at the little card table in a grave air of dread and uneasiness attempting to ease some of the pervasive fear and apprehension stemming from the looming danger and uncertainty the impending doom that lurked in the shadows held out. And in resuming to consume the odd variety of assortment the piecemeal Cameron put together earlier consisted of. The two faint and disconcerted allies that were haphazardly thrown together against this elusively dangerous and unnerving crisis. The rest of the evening was spent discussing the plans detailing all the why's, where's and here-fore too's regarding the grueling trip to the state hospital. Cameron just sat there chewing and vulgarly mumbling through mouthfuls of food while outlining the best route to taken there and what supplies were going to be needed, while Dusty looked on with a disparaging look on her face. Are we taking guns this time? She muttered…Cameron somewhat startled paused for a moment glaring at Dusty at first and daunted through wincing eyes as he was somewhat taken back by such an unexpected question from her as this which reminded him of the gravity of the situation suddenly got a sick queasy feeling in the pit of his stomach at the grim and unsettling prospect of a repeat of earlier events nervously flinched and murmured... yeh I guess so,... what the hell else are we gonna do? In all seriousness, I don't have a grenade launcher or an anti-tank weapon handy to use on that horrible thing. And he wasn't laughing or joking when he said that either.

Dusty just looked at him in doubt mildly shaking her head back and forth in dismay. Cameron' well at least this shit's better than nothing. My aim here is just to get us within the corporate limits of the town and stay overnight at a generic motel so we're not caught out in the woods in a vulnerable position at night. There's only a distance of several miles we have to cover on foot by daylight to reach a safe-haven. Dusty' safety!...Is any place really safe? Those two people in that old run-down trailer park were indoors...and they had a shotgun too...Cameron' well were more aptly prepared and ready for it than just a double barreled ten gauge shotgun and anyway they were caught totally unawares. Dusty' oh yeah what if we really do happen to run into that thing again along the way, then what huh?...Fancy pants, Cameron' well we can always make a run for it...Dusty' MAKE A RUN FOR IT, THAT'S YOUR PLAN?...

Yeah,...All in all that thing moves at a relatively slow pace, I've noticed that we can outrun it if we have to. Dusty' And if we have to stand and fight then what? we can't outrun that river of green slime? Then we will, but I'm telling ya I don't think we'll have to, and don't worry about the slime were not gonna get close enough for that. Ya know it's not like were gonna be cornered like we were in that barn that night and it's going to be daylight. That thing is a creature of habit it's primarily nocturnal I think we stand a very remote chance of encountering it in broad daylight if we play this book by the rules I think we'll be safe all the way there and back. And with any luck we won't run into him at all. Dusty' ya know I just think your pretty much off your rocker anyway the paper said that, that group of kid's were on their way to a rock concert or something and ran into it on the railroad tracks. And it was reported that the incident happened around four or five o'clock in the afternoon. Cameron' yeah so,...Dusty' well that still constitutes daytime doesn't it? The sun is still out at that time, ya know?...Cameron' technically yes, but your still forgetting one thing this is mid-autumn and that really puts that time frame at dusk, just before the sun goes down. If we start out early enough we should have ample time to get the jump on him. Besides were going to be far better fortified this time if we do. Dusty' Oh yeah how?

And just then Cameron slowly reached into that big old brown leather satchel with the weathered stained and cracked surface to retrieve a cache of fireworks including a bundle of roman candles a bag of M-80's and some stumpy yellow and olive green aluminum rocket canister shaped items with odd oriental markings on them resembling crudely fashioned Chinese communist type mortars or hand grenades as well as a whole host of other goodies. Dusty' Whaah…is it July the fourth of July or something already? what's all this shit gonna do? Blow us up!!…Cameron' laughing No, hopefully blow him up!!…To kingdom come god willing, since gunfire doesn't seem to have any visible disabling effects,…I dunno maybe it'll scare the shit out of him eh?… Then in a mildly exuberant tone it's backup,…something we didn't have before and probably nothing that those other poor kids had either. Their lack of preparedness proved out to be very costly in the end now didn't it?…You see all I have to do here is light one of these roman candles and point it in the general vicinity of that slimy thing and light it's ass up like a Christmas tree!!…He'll look like just the dancing tinsel man from Oz,…Heh,…Heh,…Heh,….I've got everything here I'll need to do it with, short of fixing a light up star on the top of his repulsive beastly head!!…It'll have a similar effect as one of those phosphorous grenades we had in the Marines, and while slightly nodding his head back and forth snickering and biting his lower lip, he muttered through a pitied expression…boy the poor bastards that got lit up with one of those damn things suddenly found themselves in a world of hurt!

Dusty haughtily replied subtly conveying a moderate level of cynicism to the whole thing in a disconcerting tone of dissent, boy you x-military people never seem to outgrow your affinity for any and all types of armaments, explosives and things that go BOOM!!…do ya… Ha,.Ha,.Ha,. and then on a cutting, sarcastic and ridiculing note she chuckled while uttering, kinda' like those NLA extremist wacko's huh? Cameron, mockingly grimaced Ha,..Ha,..Ha,..what?. Dusty, you know the gun nuts heh, heh, heh, Then in a moderately aggravated tone he tersed, yeah I heard you the first time and their not gun nuts, THIER JUST NUTS!!…Then he proceeded to go off on another cynical, grousing, bent at length in rebuttal to her thoughtless and callous statement hastily and thoughtlessly casting him into such a radical extremist fraternity, this really rubbed him the wrong way as he paused momentarily. Then he abruptly turned upward intently glaring at Dusty in a contemptuous scornful scowl with his bottom lip pulled back over his bottom row of teeth and through a moderate gape tersely began to admonish her for her blatant comment; You mean the National Lunatic Asylum?!…Dusty laughingly retorted No silly, The National Long-Rifle Association, …Cameron' No actually I had it right the first time their a convention of lunatics that by rights should not be in possession of or retain any delegatory power over anything as dangerous as firearms. You know if there's one thing in this life that never fails to burn me up to no end it's somebody that blindly makes snap judgments and final decisions on people without even bothering to scratch below the surface to see what's really there or get the actual facts before they draw any conclusions or make callous statements such as the one you just made. And don't you for even one minute try and lump me into the same Neanderthalic category as that convention of socially antagonistic malcontented paunchy, turnip brained, blow harded, Duke Wayne wanna-bee's who not only harbor a dive bar, pool hall, or bowling alley mentality but a whole host of insecurities mainly in regards to their own masculinity as well…Most of them never saw a day of active service peacetime or otherwise in their whole vapid, pathetic and washed-out existences. And as far as Billy Ray Bog's or Bobby Jo Bumpkin go, they typically have got nothing better to do with themselves on an idle Sunday afternoon than to just go out in some rural back wooded area in an open field in some pre-arranged publicly staged display of apish brawn and homegrown backwoods intelligence much like a big smelly gorilla thumping it's bare chest with it's fists and swatting at flies. Only to blast away at some old ringer washer or TV. set that has a blown picture tube with an AR-15 or a Mack-ten or something to try to look ultra-he-man-ultra-macho in front of the cameras. Or in blowing away some poor, defenseless deer rabbit or other docile type of wildlife in it's tracks just for the fun of it and typically just leaving it lay there to slowly suffer and die. But in all reality these men of minimal substance in doing so only reaffirm themselves to the masses as the socially erosive antagonists they really are. And through an annoying series of banal invariably contrived propaganda they diligently attempt to lend credibility to in their stale, distorted and unfaltering position to purport it as a well founded and profound solution to a prevailing host of chronic social ills by subliminally imprinting themselves in the publics mind as the nations noble & essential guardians, self appointed of course,…gallantly standing active sentry at our nations helm. And under the watchful eye of the cawing American eagle hovering high above in a constant state of continual protective surveillance over all the rest of us lowly and vulnerable underlings with a screaming wide open beak and an intense scowl upon it's face. And an AR-15 firmly grasped within it's gnarled claws majestically swaddled up in an ornately designed ribboned banner with some tripe, nauseating and corny slogan like, Don't mess with my freedom, faith, family, firearms!!…Now, all is right with the world,… BARF!!…The only fortifying buttress standing between us and certain imminent foreign invasion, civil insurrection by unsavory elements such as inner city gang types who exist on the fringes of society or some other far-fetched and contrived bullshit.

Then in a wide eyed cynical and contemptuous gawk he awkwardly stumbled to his feet while mockingly placing his hand over his heart and sarcastically exclaimed, I must say I'm profoundly moved by a strong resurgence of long lost patriotism I can feel welling up from deep within!!….Oh no my mistake I think that's my lunch I feel welling up from deep within!!…They invariably hammer this tripe home by constantly harping on and grossly distorting and abusing the true meaning of a long since outdated article known as the 2nd amendment that gauged by today's condition of standards is entirely irrelevant and unfitting. And by twisting and contorting it's original purpose completely out of shape to further the goals of their warped, insipid and delusional ideology of ultimately arming every man woman and child and stopping at nothing short of even the blind or replacing a rattle with a small automatic pistol packed in the waist band of the diaper of a little babe in a stroller. And the rhetoric drivel which is constantly and systematically regurgitated through an unrelenting and inane drone via public media bullhorn at every turn to the point of utter nausea!!... But in actuality they only represent just more of the same old stale cake with different frosting in just fanning the pervading, irrepressible fires of social ills and instability. They bring nothing more to the table than a very old, very tired and very worn out solution to remedying a longstanding condition with something that's already been tried and tested time and again to no avail and with no viable end resolve in sight.

A country that on a whole has been chronically plagued with lethal street drugs lack of real opportunity and senseless short fused violence in what otherwise only serves to further aggravate a longstanding condition. Dusty' boy your certainly have a very strong aversion for that organization of glorified crackpots don't you, I take it then your for gun control?...No gun regulation, No wind bagged idiot control and regulation. It doesn't take a mental genius or a rocket scientist in deducing the dormant and inlaying fact that nobody has any long term intentions of banning or confiscating all guns. That's just more of their fabricated hyped up martyrdom bile they invariably regurgitate every time there's one of those mass shootings just so they can appear victimized by the liberal sect or federally proposed emergency legislative measures to safeguard the public. Or for that matter in hearing any more of their lame predictable gun grabber rhetoric they always refer to or that 2nd amendment manure which has for quite some time now been a dead horse laying on the ground that has literally been kicked and beaten to a pulp!!... And I'll tell ya when it gets right down to the nitty gritty most of these articulated buffoons shouldn't even be allowed to own a cap gun much less give public lessons on how to use a real one!!... Ya know you gotta pass far more stringent requirements just to be able to operate a motor vehicle!!...And it's not entirely unheard of for a very intelligent highly competent person to fail the test numerous times prior to and have to repeatedly reapply!!...But authority holds out very little in the way of sufficient safeguard measures to society as a whole against selling something as dangerous and lethal as a firearm to any potentially mentally deranged lunatic that lollygags into a sporting goods store that appears with it enough upstairs to check off the right answers and is willing to plunk down enough greenbacks!!….You should have to pass some kind of thorough and extensive psychological battery first to even be considered!!…

Dusty just sort of hemmed while shaking hear head back and forth making no comment as she passively stood by as he continued in again getting more than she bargained for in hearing him vent further wholly indicative of his utter disdain for life in general. I just don't think, nor does a vast majority of other rational minded people believe that anybody needs to and should be able to attain legal access to any type of military hardware unless their a trained combatant in a ground war against a corrupt politically unstable warring regime that adheres to a pointless aggression type philosophy mainly against legitimate peaceable governments. It's asininely stupid and as far as I know we don't live in an open ended society where vigilante type anarchy reigns!!…and I think all of that type of needless lunacy should be banned through governmental legislation and made inaccessible especially to these radical loony's who are so tenaciously bent on setting society back 150 years to the old west, and this kind of shit should be made be punishable by harshly enforced laws!!… Dusty' That all sounds well and good, but how are you going to stem the tide of it nefariously flowing into this country from say the black-market there genius!?…By instituting some form of constraining marshal-law in regards to it, AND FOR ONCE AND FOR ALL REALLY CRACK DOWN ON IT AND STOP MOLLYCODDLING AND JUST SLAPPING IT ON THE WRIST THAT'S HOW!!…. Sorta' like having to reprimand a spoiled rotten tantrum throwing little child by taking away the very object it took supreme delight in cruelly tormenting his little sister with, there would seem to be no other way!!…Head em' off at bordering shores with strict armed patrols of naval and coast guard units confiscating any illegal weapons caches and ill gotten gains discovered on board merchant vessels followed up with stiff fines and harsh imprisonment all across the board.

And if governments actually did what they should've been doing in the first place which is to form an international coalition and finally get serious about this kind of crap by imposing stiffer preventive measures in regards to it instead of just mollycoddling it and coming only half way in appeasing these juvenilely minded nutso's who never attained the maturity level of thirteen, in allotting them free reign with little more than a slap on the wrist in some lame half assed measure a lot of this shit would stop!!…Ya know it's just too late when this organization of left-wing radicals gets to big for it's britches and scores of innocent people are haplessly cut down in their tracks in a public place in just going about their business!!…Dusty boy you really seem to have all the irrefutable information in your slanted aversion to them don't you… Your damn right I do because they want to eradicate any and all proposed regulations and restrictions in regards to it and they even want to have the ATF disbanded!! And then those who haplessly find themselves in the wrong place at the wrong time innocently just going about their business will then just be left to their own devices to yet another rampaging out of control crazed psycho who got up on the wrong side of the world one day and decided to carry that internalization over to a crowded public place with a clip fed automatic weapon he was able to get his hands on!!…And these are the ones who usually wind up paying the ultimate price in the end!!…And to the president of the NLA, I'd just like to pose this pressing question, HAS SOCIETY AS A WHOLE REALLY LAPSED INTO SUCH PITIFUL ALL TIME LOW THAT IT HAS NOW BECOME NECESSARY FOR ONE AND ALLTO BE HARDWARE CAPABLE OF RIDDLING A POSSIBLE NOCTURNAL INTRUDER ON THE FAINT CHANCE ONE MAY CLIMB THROUGH A WINDOW ONE NIGHT WITH A BRUTAL AND EXCESSIVE WAVE OF MACHINE GUN BULLETS IN THE PLODDED COURSE OF CONDUCTING SUCH WARPED EXTREMIST LOGIC IN WHAT ONLY AMOUNTS TO A POINTLESS RIDICULOUS EXCERSICE OF BURNING DOWN AN ENTIRE BARN JUST TO KILL A RAT?!… Then he sharply turned to dusty and tersed,…Can you please shed some light on something for me that has had me completely stumped for quite some time now!!…Dusty,…Yeah if I can what is it? Then he sarcastically grimaced and crassly posed this question to her in a wide eyed glare,… How it is that in all this time that we ever managed to remain relatively safe in our homes at night our whole lives up to now without the pressing overbearing public influence of the NLA or the retention of their prescribed cache of elaborate and excessive firepower!!...WILL SOMEBODY PLEASE TELL ME THAT!!...Dusty slightly jerked her head off to the side while suddenly expelling a puff of air through her mouth and nostrils in a slight grin at the comment and lowly uttered gees I dunno...Then rolling his eyes through a wandering glare he looked downward while shaking his head back and forth slowly shuffling his feet and kicking stones about on the ground in addressing his first question. BECAUSE IF IT HAS,... I'LL TELL YA RIGHT NOW I JUST WANT TO WHOLLY RESIGN FROM IT ALTOGETHER AND JUST GO UP INTO THE HILLS AND LIVE IN A DIRTY OLD CAVE WHO'S ONLY INHABITS ARE MANGY BATS AND TURN INTO ONE OF THOSE KNARRLED, WITHERED GRIMY OLD HERMITS DESCRIBED IN ONE OF THOSE OLD GRIMME'S FAIRY TALE BOOKS WITH A LONG WHITE BEARD AND WEARING A SHABBY BROWN CANVASS CLOAK and CLUTCHING A TWISTED OLD WOODEN STAFF. Dusty timidly and sheepishly just looked on as he spoke offering up no comment. Dusty just sorta' rolled her eye's in his direction while slightly pursing the corner of her mouth together as she lowly uttered chuckling boy that's a real cliché' if I've ever heard one right out of the annals of genuine classics. Cameron' irked, Clip fed military assault rifles are designed for one purpose and one purpose only, by that of a professionally trained combatant for anti personnel use in the unfortunate event a ground war is called or for a civil defense action by that of a qualified National guard member or a swat team!!.... Otherwise they are to be stockpiled and housed in a heavily secured and fortified governmentally regulated armory!!...And out of the reach of juvenilely delusional psychotic and unqualified hands!!...And most certainly not just so the glorified boy scouts can go out in the woods and play cowboys and Injuns!!... And what this organization of pompous, arrogant, wind bagged, intellectually stunted blowhards with a prepubescent level of maturity's biggest longstanding issue would seem to be is in just finding more practical, worthwhile and productive ways to make better use of far too much idle time and expendable energy. AND WHAT THEY REALLY NEED TO DO IS TO JUST GROW A

BRAIN and GETTA LIFE!!... And what never ceases to amaze and incense me is how they seem to be under the self deluded notion that they are somehow separate and above the law, no above the rest of us in holding some kind of delegatory position of authority!!...And are not in any way shape or form going to be told what to do to any degree under any circumstances by anybody! Even the senate, members of congress or the house of representatives even the president of the United States!!... And in their ongoing endeavors to be able to secure the legal right to exercise free and unrestricted reign only after having connived, pestered and finagled their bent and pointless life's philosophy and inane agenda deep into the halls of state legislature to be able to legally attain any and every piece of hardware and type of ordnance known to man under the sun to their hearts desire with impunity. All in some bent out and ludicrous extreme, stopping nothing short of a guided missile. IT ONLY REPRESENTS A PSYCOTIC SELF DELUSIONAL AND IDIOTIC BRAND OF WACKO, RADICAL, EXTREMISM AND THERE'S NO LEGITIMATE CAUSE, JUSTIFICATION R VALID REASON FOR IT AND I'LL TELL YA WHATS EVEN MORE LETHALTHAN A NUCLEAR WARHEAD IS, IT'S THE NLA!!...And what is the most galling is how they constantly persist to circumvent congressional and senatorial branches of the governments proposed legislation to supersede and override the authoritative governing faculties of this country!!... well their not!!...Is there really any valid or legitimate reason John Q. Lunatic should be able to legally obtain a banana clip fed military assault rifle!?...Nooo!,...there is none!!...Not even from a hunting or target shooting enthusiast standpoint!!...IT'S ALL ABOUT ONE THING AND ONE THING ONLY WITH THEM AND HAS IN ALL ACTUALITY VERY LITTLE IF ANYTHING TO DO WHATSOEVER WITH BEING A GUN ENTHUSIAST OR PRESERVING ANY RIGHTS TO KEEP AND BEAR ARMS,...AND ALOT MORE TO DO WITH UNDERMINING THE LAW BY A JUVINILEY MINDED and TRIFLING BRAND OF ARROGANCE IN A PERSISTANT and REPETITIVE ACTION OF ONEUPSMANSHIP IN DOGGEDLY PERSERVERING TO CIRCUMVENT ANY AND ALL REGULATORY and SAFEGUARDED EFFORTS TO INSURE THAT UNDUE, AND

EXCESSIVE FIREPOWER IS MADE LEGALLY INACCESSABLE TO THE GENERAL PUBLIC BY GOVERNMENTAL AND LEGISLATIVE AUTHORITY. AND YET THEY STILL SEEK TO BECOME COMPLETELY SEPARATE AND ABOVE THE LAW AT ANY AND ALL COSTS!!... IT'S ABOUT THE COMPLETE AND UTTER DISCARDING OF RATIONAL DOWN THE MIDDLE OF THE ROAD THINKING IN REGARDS TO IT, IN JUST FLAUNTING THEIR FLAGRANT DISREGARD FOR AUTHORITY IN GENERAL AND THUMBING THEIR NOSE IN THE FACE OF IT IN AN EXALTED EXERCISE OF UNMITIGATED GALL PERIOD!!...And that's really it in a nutshell...And to tell you the truth I'm all but sick and tired of constantly hearing their lame, repetitive and distorted gun grabber 2nd amendment rhetoric through the written or televised media every time there's another one of those mass shootings, to the point of utter nauseating bile!!...And they never once make any reference to the victims even if their kids!!...yet they invariably purport this tired worn out drivel on some gaudy bought and paid for public media platform with their irrelevant, warped and extremist views. They also conveniently fail to mention that when that particular article was drafted in the late 1700's!!... I'm pretty sure it refereed to a black powdered musket that chambered one steel ball and one shot was all you got. It was a very clumsy, cumbersome and slow process just to recycle the damn thing just to be able to re-fire it. Hell, it was little more than a very accurate slingshot!!...Nor do they mention the country was in the midst of a gradual Colonization of a vast untamed wilderness by those that had to hunt for their food, fend off attacking Indians or engage in a conventional war with invading England, not the resettlement of an already development and supposedly civilized society that should have evolved far beyond that crude darkened stage. And one that is now inhabited by a vast population that should be comprised of far more intelligent and sophisticated people than that of the period in question.

But what has evolved into since then is an automatic weapon that chambers a 30, 40 or 50 round clip capable of rapidly dispersing up to 20 rounds a second and that since WWI has been directly attributable for the augmentation of world misery. Something that can easily maim and butcher scores of innocent people in a single pass and is usually only sought after by John Q. Psycho who is nefariously bent on acquiring one. Automatic weapons belong in the hands of qualified trained combatants for use against insidious warring factions around the world. Such as middle eastern terrorists who live in a constant state of war or roving bands of guerrilla fighters wearing tiger stripes and cut foliage attached to their jungle attire in remote jungle regions of some Godforsaken banana Republic not in civilized society!! And just what does John Q. Public need with an A-R 15 or an A-K 47 anyway? I dunno you tell me…To be able to do as he damn well pleases and not have anyone on the face of the earth tell him otherwise in only flying in the face of and defying governmental authority at every turn of the screw PERIOD!!, THAT'S WHAT!!….FREE MEN DON'T ASK PERMISSION,…WHAT A HIGHLY SIGNIFICANT and THOUGHT PROVOKING GLISTENING GEM OF PROFOUND WISDOM!!…MY SENTIMENTS EXACTLY!!…EASY STOMACH TAKE IT EASY UH, GAG BARFORAMA!!…DID THEY THINK THAT ONE UP ALL BY THEMSELVES OR DID THEY JUST ROB A FORTUNE COOKIE?!!… Boy I can just envision a group of em' getting together and staying up all night long burnin' the midnight oil thinking of that witty little slogan…. Hello that's what laws are!!…being told what to do by those in authority and it's usually for a pretty good reason!!!…To look big and impressive to the public!?…Well I'm not impressed!!…And strictly speaking from a target shooting standpoint they don't require any level of marksman skills at all, they just spit clustered bursts of rounds and mow down anything directly or indirectly in their path you point em' at a blind person couldn't miss with one, and what element of sporting ability or fun is there in that!!…I'll tell ya none. And there really not designed for hunting either, they are for only one real intended purpose,…anti-personnel use, to kill people like the gangsters did in 1930's Chicago. And a hand grenade, a claymore mine or a field piece belong in a war and I personally don't wanna live next door to some hyped up self delusional whack job, or crazy as a loon crack-pot who now by foisted legislature and minus legal ramifications now owns one!!…

And I think if the founding fathers knew what their crude invention has evolved into those same historical figureheads that drafted that particular document so long ago would in all likely-hood call for a retraction. And if very many of these Gomerized bumpkins' were put in an actual war setting they'd probably grow a yellow streak up their backs a mile wide and piss in their pants!!…And finally just the thought of one of these hyped up arm-chair cretins armed with anything more lethal than a squirt or cap gun living in any close proximity to yours truly, just gives me the willies'….Dusty' Here! Here! Cameron' gun's me personally, I can take em or leave em, Ya know I've fired just about every type of ordinance and piece of hardware there is in existence except a shotgun!!…I was even a qualified sniper in the Marines, YA know I can hit a relatively small target pretty consistently at three or four hundred meters off and without a scope much less!…But I don't constantly come out and make a major point of it in publicly broadcasting it to the rest of the world all the damn time!! So what!!…who cares!!…and aside from the current state of affairs or maybe that of maybe being attacked by a grizzly bear or Bigfoot or something it really wouldn't affect or matter to me at all if they were all just banned entirely. Those words warmly enamored Dusty as she gleefully smiled exclaiming you know that's a very healthy well balanced attitude, to bad so many other men don't feel that way!…this gravely troubled world would be a much better place if they did!…. Cameron nervously smiled at Dusty went on to explain, now these are M-80's and they sound like a hand grenade when detonating and will most likely scare the shit out of slimetard! This stuff combined with the two revolvers outta give us an ample line of security. Dusty just sat there smiling mildly and appearing a little more relaxed and at ease on looking

Cameron, taking inventory of the vast oddity of wares in his crude makeshift little arsenal while inwardly questioning their actual potential degree of effectiveness against that repulsive thing,.. I'd like to just go saddled down with a browning .30 caliber machine gun with a couple of belts of ammo and a large bandoleer of hand grenades. But he in his ongoing terror he knew inwardly that wouldn't prove out to be very effective at all in ultimately debilitating or putting that horrid thing permanently out of commission…But he didn't want to scare or alarm Dusty anymore than she already was with that sobering fact. So he tried to seem as comforting and reassuring as possible in his exemplary display and their potential effectiveness of the wares he did have as opposed to any type of firearms in attempting to somewhat put her mind at ease. Well I couldn't manage those and there's no way we could conceal em' anyway without drawing attention to ourselves, so I guess this is going to have to do for now…

And at that statement Dusty just looked over at Cameron in a sullen look of dismay as she finished her plate and began clearing the table. "How are we gonna gain entrance to the state hospital with all this crap? Don't they have a metal detectors or something at the door's entrance? I mean won't they search us or something? Cameron' yeah probably…but we can always stash the satchel in some bushes or underbrush nearby before we go in and retrieve it when we get out I'm not really worried about that now. We shouldn't have any trouble like that at a dive motel we can just take it in with us it's not like were going to use this stuff for nefarious reasons anyway, it's for our security…Dusty' when are we leaving? As soon as possible…. You know I really wasn't figuring on meeting up with you again this soon or even you coming along but for our mutual benefit I think we should put it off for a couple a more day's so you can better compose yourself, increase your strength level and get more comfortable with this…Then he beamed her a serious look and barked, you really need to view this with a lot less fear and a lot more as a job of necessity that has to be done and focus on the immediate task at hand. You outta be a lot more incensed at the inane disruption this has caused in your life than scared I know I'm getting to be. You know I'm not exactly thrilled at the prospect either but I'm not going to internalize on it or let it keep me up nights or tear me apart anymore. Don't give this thing such a high level of importance!! for one thing if you do that it's already won half the battle. And for another it doesn't deserve it! your important!…I'm important! The only true importance that thing holds is in the lethal level of danger it poses to society period. You know it's really just an oversized termite that needs to be expunged and we are the Ortho men, that's all!! You've gotta start putting this in it's proper perspective and keep it separate 'and be more detached or we as a unit will become ineffective got it!

And all of a sudden at hearing that line of reasoning Dusty was overcome by a somewhat warm comforting feeling as she smiled in a mildly sarcastic reply in attempts to ease the tension and fear they were both under, yes first sergeant now can I bunk down now for the night? or do I have to pull fire watch first. Cameron suddenly got an amused look of surprise on his face, grinned and sort of chuckled fire watch? How'd you know about that? I told you my dad was drafted into the Army at the tail end of Viet-Nam and he was always conveying every little aspect of it he could to us kids all the damn time. Oh yeah well I guess you can bed down out here on the couch,... uh, lance corporal, then he satirically said that is only of course if your mini-14 has been properly broken down, cleaned and oiled and reassembled and your low quarters have been buffed to a glistening shine!!...and of course if that head is standing tall. Then they both laughed and hugged each other as this kind of joking sort of eased the grave level of fear and tension that was constantly looming overhead. Cameron said he'd fetch her a blanket and pillow from the back bedroom for the sofa and that he was just too exhausted but she could stay up and watch TV for awhile if she chose to and she said ok. It's an old portable black and white TV I've had for years now with a broken antenna and staticky reception as he told her it's a little beat up but it works good enough to watch the local news or afternoon or late night movies on and for all intents and purposes and that's all that mattered. He also told her that there was a couple of late night movie stations on UHF she could tune into that were still on with all night movies if she didn't mind a little snow in the picture and that was as good as it would come in.

She said yeah I suppose so, and just before he adjourned to one of the back rooms for the night he left Dusty just sitting there in a darkened living room by the dull blue glowing light of the TV until about one or two in the morning when she finally fell fast asleep.

On the morning they were slated to leave a slopped together breakfast of bacon, eggs, toast and home fries was hastily prepared and consumed over broken and hurried conversation and the second hand noise of morning newscast from the portable black and white in the living room. Yet in the brief forty five minute time period the two had to eat they took the partially soiled plates and just tossed them in the sink afterward and left them unwashed. Then as they both stood in the darkened disheveled living room slinging their backpacks over their shoulders Dusty turned to Cameron and said…I guess this is it, the big day has arrived! have we got everything were gonna need? Cameron' yeah I think I've carefully packed up all the essential weaponry so there's no need to worry…Dusty' oh I'm not worried about that I meant food… do we have enough food I don't like going hungry…

Cameron' while contorting his lower jaw and biting his lip sarcastically uttered; well you could've fooled me that didn't seem to bother you very much before back at the house now did it? Dusty' you know things would go much smoother here if you didn't read to far into or overanalyze them once they've already been brought out onto the table and discussed…Just then she abruptly turned her head in the direction of the backpacks they were to carry catching herself and loudly exclaiming Oh…'and also is there enough bar soap toothbrushes and clothing changes for the trip? Cameron' yeah goof we've gotta nuff food and personals…boy you beat everything you know that…we might have to face off with the creature of the black lagoon and your concerned as to whether there's enough grub packed or not tisk..tisk…well for your information sister Sara, I've saved some money aside to insure we don't run out once we get there Ok…Now I think we've wasted enough time here we and need to get the show on the road. We've got a lot of ground to cover before sundown and if you don't mind I don't want to run the risk of meeting up with Mr. Congeniality along the way get it? Now let's get on with it! And with that the two exited the little old house locked the door behind them and proceeded off the dilapidated porch and down the gravel laden street through the center of the poor old run down housing allotment towards their destination that warm sunny morning amid the random sounds of barking dogs and the usual shrieks of children playing as one soiled and shirtless four year old little boy with shorts on and no shoes ran up to Cameron with a half of a torn up peanut butter and jelly sandwich partially shoved in his mouth holding up a toy airplane as the big red propeller slowly spun around in the gentle morning breeze loudly mumbled through that messy sandwich hey Cameron look what I just got for my birthday! Cameron stopped momentarily looking down and grinning at the child while palming the back of his head mussing his hair as he slowly bypassed the child and said that's nice Damon as he brushed passed the boy and the two proceeded further down the road past the casual inquiring glances of neighbors just standing about inadvertently looking on. They were in ardently met by the occasional…hey Cameron, where you and Dusty goin?

And as the two strolled down the middle of the petrol smelling little tar laden cinder road Cameron just grinned and waved at children playing and his neighbors while slinging that old leather satchel over his shoulder repositioning it so it didn't slip off. He looked as if he didn't have a care in the world as heartily exclaimed, were going on a little nature bound excursion out in the bold and beautiful outdoors…among the birds- n-the bees and the big tall trees, he heartily chuckled that's all'…we'll be back in a few days. Then as they both began to slowly cross the open field laden with wildflowers to incept the railroad tracks that would enable them to access the town they had to catch a cab in to get to Perridyne. Their figures of the two slowly began diminishing from sight as they got further away from the old housing allotment and the further away their distancing figures got they finally disappeared as the morning sun was rising.

CHAPTER THIRTEEN

Crossing The Ravine

IT WAS BY NOW BECOMING READILY MORE APPARENT AT THIS IN CRUCIAL stage of the game, that in the face of such bleak and ominous circumstances that had recently taken place thusly of which stemmed from such bizarre and horrific events and the like combination of the two It became more evident as the day progressed that the kid's initial surge of enthusiasm they had when they set out earlier that morning was slowly beginning to wane giving way to a temperate mode of somber inhibition a wary reluctance and a taut uneasiness that began to set in on the two. It was all they could do just to generate a moderate level of strength and momentum within themselves to maintain an even keel sufficient enough to see this thing through to completion. The total schematic was grim and shrouded in a misty fog of wary subterfuge and uncertainty at the daunting task that lay ahead. And as they both found themselves solely chosen as the only viable candidates standing in the spotlight. It was going to require a mode of methodical covertness in sort of flanking or ambushing this thing for any success in destroying it.

They for now at least stood in the limelight surreptitiously elected to see it through. And as a more realistic and broadened scenario of the grim schematic as a whole began to play out and manifest itself within their harried and bedeviled minds. It was also going to be clearly all to evident that this contrived effort at possibly getting into see the two remaining traumatized victims that were now presently in a semicoherent state and confined in that glorified maximum security fortress as a grim result of that ogre-ish railroad tracks incident the papers so colorfully spoke of at the very least was going be a constrained and uncertain one. And in just considering their probable present state of mind and any success in exacting the least bit of useful information from them as well as having to negotiate much of what was to be rough and grueling terrain and possibly running into that putrefying thing on the way there or back was at least going to be a frightful and debilitating prospect, and was going to be a daunting obstacle that eventually had to be overcome. As the incursion of any potential outlying risks that were going to be necessary and unavoidable were nonetheless ones that had to be negotiated regardless.

And in the final analysis they would undoubtedly serve as a viable means in curtailing the impending and ominous threat bringing a well sought after end to this looming and horrent crisis, as well as providing valuable insight and prelude of things to come. And by no stretch of the means was this trip going to denote many intrinsically pleasurable aspects or instill one with a positive note of reassurance or elevated degree of self confidence less personal security, no this was only to be purely, a fact finding mission one a miffed with morbid apprehension…. and a very risky one at that, Cameron just had to find out just what those two girls experienced in their horrifying confrontation with that repulsive chemical aberration on those dual sets of desolate railroad tracks on their way to that big hair band concert they never made it to. And God only knows what went down in their horrific and surrealistic encounter with that thing, It had to have been just horrible he thought to himself and those two girls must have been frightened out of their minds. And that poor head dude with only that tiny little pistol to try and fend it off with. I'll just bet if he really knew what he was actually going to be up against and the level of danger it posed he'd of probably along taken a .44 magnum along instead…but inwardly he knew that against that horrid putrid invincible thing even a gun like that wouldn't have made much of a difference either. Then in a hearty exhaling sigh he groaned. Oh I guess it's to late now for any concrete or conclusive speculation along those lines for that poor bastard eh? I guess it's just all water under the bridge now. I just wish I could've met and got with him before all that happened! Maybe we could've joined forces in this. But in a war there are casualties and this is a war of sorts with a very dangerous and elusive enemy, he thought to himself, and that thing is playing for keeps. As he and Dusty walked through the meadows with high weeds and wildflowers he held fast to the fervent hope that maybe just maybe he could somehow stumble onto the key that would unlock the door to the aloof mystery to some hidden and inherent weakness or vulnerability it may have that would lead to it's incongruent undoing. He also knew he'd have to do it soon and undauntedly, diligently persisting in rooting it out. As he'd hate to consider the bleak and dismal alternative having to face the grim consequences of someone who'd potentially fold and just cave in under such pressure. Just the mere thought of the level of grave peril the local and surrounding principalities would be put in if this thing were able to continue in it's blustering rampage unchallenged, it would just be catastrophic.

Yet the thought alone of what that monster actually looks like and what it alone is capable of would be sufficient enough reason to make most of us shrink back in the face of it's bleak and unyielding nights talking terror. And the imminent level of danger it posed and should one potentially shirk from an innate sense of moral responsibility and obligation in the lending of much needed assistance to his fellow man or at least frantically sounding the alarm.. Or just what the long term ramifications on the community at large would be from someone who was not only morally deficient in that regard but displaying such modest levels of inner substance and proving themselves out to be nothing but a shiftless coward in that same respect.

Cameron was afraid, mortally terrified all the time in fact and although this was overtly apparent it inwardly stemmed from deep rooted childhood fears held over. And yet the only thing that distinguished him from the aforementioned was in that he was not just going to turn tail and run. He was going to stand his ground and oppose this threat no matter what it took or to what degree his nervous system had eroded to. No he was going to set up an outlined perimeter, dig in and fight. He was going to draw a chalk outline around the vicinity and when that thing stepped into it, he was toast!! He knew it was just going to be a matter of time and that much of what he was going to have to do was going to have to be behind the scenes not in just rooting it out and confronting it face to face. It has been said that bravery is cowardice turned to anger and at this point he was just mad enough to compose himself enough to go after that thing with just his bare hands. Maybe even run up on it from behind and put some kind of submission hold on it and break it's lousy neck! But he knew the grim reality was that, that was not going to be the least effective much less a viable option. He also knew he had to appear as a solid unfaltering rock presenting a strong unfaltering rock like persona for Dusty.

Though as a kid he could vividly recall a stark and unreasoning fear of the "Boogie-Man" such that he would not go outside the house with his parents in the family car after dark and he literally had to be physically restrained from flailing fits of frenzied hysteria at the mere utterance thereof and then having to be forcibly dragged kicking and screaming from the house and installed into the backseat of the family car by both his parents. For he knew if his feigned armor began to show any chinks or began to crack now she would undoubtedly follow suit and then in that instance they both might as well just turn around and go back to their respective houses lock all the doors and hide under their beds and let the police or the National Guard try and contend with it. But Cameron strongly felt at this point that was not an option, he believed that, that would have gravely adverse affects that would lead to a chaotic state of civil anarchy and mass pandemonium were by scores of innocent people would be trampled under foot in blind haste in a massive wave of catastrophic insurrection to this thing. The city would no doubt undergo some stringent form of marshal law the and local Army National Guard would no doubt intervene. And in such a case a bold rush to judgment would undoubtedly ensue brought on by hastened and unprepared public disclosers that in Cameron's mind would no doubt spell civil and authoritative pandemonium. No this thing had to be dealt with covertly and methodically and by someone relatively calm and level headed enough to insure success and by somebody somewhere who had the brevity and balls to meet the ensuing threat head on. And although the absence of raw human emotion were markedly distinguishable character traits of someone who'd been subject to some initial form of military hazing was adept at.

It'd been ten years now since Cameron's inception of such brutal indoctrination as a Marine Core infantryman, whereby they completely tore you down stripping you of any and all inward inherent emotions that are attributable to any warmth tenderness or human kindness only to rebuild you from the ground up as a hard, cold feeling less, mechanized machine a tool of sorts who's internal components are cogs figuratively cast in iron and steel and who's basic function is for one thing to kill. But he really didn't know if all that was going to help him now in any way in trying to stand up against that horrid thing. Which just upon the sight of that freakish wide eyed gawk and that beastly head tilting back and forth with that vile tongue jutting in and out, would no doubt strike mortal terror to the far innards of the most brutal and hardened drill instructor in known existence sending him fleeing and scrambling for his very life one way down the yellow brick road!!…And although he'd mellowed out a great deal since, he really wasn't hard core grunt material anymore and by now he'd steadily lapsed into what was little more than a great big teddy bear like state. But he knew he was at some point going to be called upon to recall and draw from what he was trained for, to fight in a war, and this was a war of sorts. A freakish bizarre one with a blackened chemically mutated invincible and abominable nightmare he and Dusty were going to have to stand off with sooner or later and he'd have to at some point steadily brace himself to be hit by an oncoming freight train. Hell he'd even recouped a good percent of his raw basic unassuming human emotions in recent years to a moderate level of warmth and receptiveness he'd been stripped of in the Core.' He was really no longer "born again hard"…And much of what he was stripped of and re-conditioned with since then had by now greatly dissipated, such as the hardened ability to flip an internal switch to the off position not showing fear, compassion or much of any other kind of raw or basic human emotion was all but gone. As a grunt in the field in as many ways possible you were trained to kill period and not much else and to show little or no emotion when you saw others die. He'd learned early on in an unsettling and non-evasive sequence of events was forever branded and instilled with a grueling set of very hard lessons, in that under extreme or adverse conditions emotions were only a trap,…a quicksand trap, and in being an effective countering agent one did not give in to em' and that was pretty much the extent of it.

Although this was as a matter of course ingrained as military protocol a hardened trait in which all outward signs had all but completely dispersed over the years in having once been so brutally forged into some kind of human mechanized tool, a weapon in that for a long time after was a hard tempered mode he harbored and maintained with a refined level of continuity, and left with courtesy of a stone cold and cruel slant eyed Marine core drill instructor, the kind upon receiving a raw batch of inductee's, a quaking formation of Joe Blow's just off the streets. And who was well known for bringing so many of those reputed tough guys to a quivering tearful mass of jelly in stern formation. And one who'd also left an indelible boot impression on his ass in and around bay and compound areas of Paris Island years before. He still faint fully recalls the borderline torture of being rousted from only about three or four hours sleep. And how being awake a day seemed more like a week. Or those grueling P.T. sessions at early morning dusk and the slop they passed off as food or the eight mile trudges out there under the brutal and searing heat of an oppressive South Carolina sun. And many times you were laden down with about sixty pounds of equipment,… rucksack and steel pot, pistol belt and forced to sleep with carry and field strip that damn bulky M-14. As well as having to plod through slimy filthy murky southern swamps filled with water moccasins and leeches. Or that awful thick dry sun baked red sand you sunk in while your feet sweltered in those awful heavy black leather knee high boots that didn't fit half the time anyway. And that when kicked up went in your eyes and stuck to the hot sweat on your face and brow, went in your mouth, down your throat and poured out in a steady stream of hot liquid from your nostrils. And the harrowing experience of being bitten by hordes of those damn one and a half inch fire ants that stood up on their hind legs facing you ready to fight. And also that of having to physically exert yourself to the point you thought you were going to die right there on the spot as buckets of your own boiling hot sweat amassed under your steel pot and gushed down over your face and head as a cruel steely eyed, hyperactive psychopath wearing a Smokey the bear hat with a medallion of the globe an anchor and a rope wrapped around it inexhaustibly bopped around the formation barking vicious obscenities and degrading remarks at weaker members of the platoon and systematically proceeding to kick or physically abuse in some way anyone who well within their rights tripped or fell out from pure exhaustion. Or if they found even one small crease in the outer woolen blanket of your bunk that wasn't pulled taut. They systematically proceeded to throw it your locker and everything else out the window into the sandy bay area below and you private had the pleasant and abiding task of flawlessly re-appropriating it. Held over from that it was a markedly distinct and notable trait characteristic one was left with that afterward mildly exuded in the outward demeanor of, and was subtly indicative of an xmilitary person regardless of the branch of service one hailed from.

And it was one that was markedly distinct at even minimal levels of a stern persona that such an individual emanates. He began to wonder at this point if those taut hardened internal components he was once instilled with in such brutish and sub level of apish indoctrination was in the end going to help him survive and ultimately prevail against a hidden deluge of vicious attacks and putrefying designs of that vile unspeakable thing. And hopefully in this case those in such an individuals aura had integrally become second nature, a permanent byproduct if you will of their persona, even as a civilian it was ingrained and remained there much as the uniform itself did. You were never the same as you were before you entered you were forever hardened internally to some degree, even if you were some kind of a docile unassuming emotional marshmallow. They used to chant once a Marine always a Marine!! Well at least for now,… for him that no longer rang true and it's waning cry and imprint was now beginning to slowly dissipate, he hadn't been highly or even minimally charged much less motivated to even the slightest degree about much of anything since, let alone the physical and psychological drudgery of that damned core. And if someone did sound off they were highly charged or motivated they were either the worlds biggest liar or they had some cog was lose in their internal workings and usually found themselves relegated to a lowly ridiculed position by the rest who somehow managed to still maintain even a shred of normalcy in that insanity were rebuffed as merely an object of cynical contention .. I mean who in their right mind could sincerely or realistically get motivationally or highly charged cast in such a hardened brutal environment or having to fight a war for that matter. And for a great number of years now like many of us, he just subsisted from day to day.

By now he was thoroughly terrified of that horrid thing they saw and somehow miraculously survived in that old tobacco barn that night. And at this harrying crossroads he was beginning to have serious doubts as to whether having once been in the core was going to help him at all in bearing up under such insurmountable tension and stress. He was literally coming apart at the seems and scared out of his mind all the time, especially at night and had been plagued by a string of garish nightmares ever since. And he was by now at his wits end as to what could possibly serve as a course of effective action. He'd also had become so jaded and worn down in recent years by the big grindstone of life that in the way of once having the vehemence and fortitude essential to potentially be an effective fighting tool and countering agent. But he's never had to come up against something like this and as of now really he wasn't sure just what he was going to do. And in the area of maintaining those former hard core infantryman internal components went, he at this point was no longer even a reasonable facsimile. And all that bullshit GungHo pep talk was just a lot of hype, a diversional guise if you will, a smoke screen of sorts, put on for Dusty's benefit just so she would begin to lighten up and calm down a little bit and wouldn't be so damn scared and petrified all the time, or for that matter notice just how scared shitless he was,…That thing just appears out of nowhere and has an unmistakable air of invincibility about it….It is also gravely dangerous for anyone who encounters it!!…And he at this point was at a perilous crossroads when it came to drafting a viable plan of action. He really wasn't sure just where to begin, and it was also becoming a downright dubious fact as to whether any type of firearm at all or military training formalized or other was going to help them endure or ultimately destroy that invincible chemically mutated nightmare.

As it stood it was going to take every modicum of brain power he could summon to isolate and center in on a potential weakness or vulnerability to destroy that horrid thing once and for all and finally putting it out of everyone's misery. He was going to have to calm down, refocus and somehow regain his composure enough to draft and successfully execute a viable plan of action. As it stood now it was going to take every ounce of inner fortitude he could muster not to just crack up and fold under the extreme duress that was really not present in his by now nerve frazzled lethargic body to go the distance. Even enough to muster a minimal amount of energy or motivation that was going to be required to sustain an even keel in this bizarre campaign at even a trudging pace to see it through to the end. And Dusty was right the Marines weren't going to help them now. They were a million miles away and they were haplessly on their own out here in the middle of nowhere.... He was gravely despondent and mortally terrified all the time and it was becoming more and more difficult to outwardly conceal that fact from her. He'd awaken many a night from a dead sleep shaking with the cold sweats and was having trouble eating and holding down what little he could forcibly bring himself to consume, which was barely enough to sustain a chirping songbird, and most of the time he was barely lucid. He'd often times heard of how war time veterans frequently suffered traumatizing flashbacks or nightmares that brimmed over from harrowing battlefield experiences in what is called post traumatic stress syndrome. But this was something so completely different from that, and although he was a peacetime Marine, what he'd experienced first hand in that old barn that night was far worse than any war vet ever encountered against a formalized enemy on the field of conflict with exploding guns and bombs. That thing was visually and surrealistically horrific, it resonated a terrifying air of invincibility about it, especially when it droned forth at it's hapless victims paralyzed in utter terror with the force of an oncoming freight train.

And that unwavering fact alone gravely heightened the level of gravity and urgency in regards to any potentially feasible resolve of the situation. And the profound significance his nightmares had taken on in their dreadful severity and the progressive evil abscess was indicative in the sequence of their horrific format that paraded themselves by in his dreams as he lay there frozen in fear and many times was unable to wake up from them but wholly forced to beset his eyes on such horrific and ghastly visages while completely unable to close them or turn away. His nightmares were abominably evil, surreal, garish and all to frequent. And all that occupied his distraught and harried mind during waking hours was how in the world were they gonna expunge this seemingly invincible thing before it eventually wiped out the whole countryside...HOW!! as well as having to face up to this daunting task, the stark reality was that this was not just a man they were up against... not like an occupying and opposing enemy soldier, in the bush, an equal counter part that in formalized military preparedness you were trained to interface with and contend with in conflict. As it stood he wasn't sure how he was going to accomplish this. It was going to be difficult enough as it was to root that putrid out find it's point of vulnerability and ultimately destroy it, he was mortally terrified of it and If it was up to him he'd just assume to never see it again. But he knew inwardly that was just a pipe dream, a lofty aspiration to good to be true. Yet even on that minimally comforting and reassuring note to be called upon to have to go and fight in a war for anyone who retained even a modicum of the milk of human kindness or emotion would down right suck....But at least knew you stood a fair and even chance of coming out on top. For one you could either conceal yourself from in camouflage amid the thick dense foliage a pine forest or a jungle afforded. Or just partially expose yourself in mutual combat as you knew he was just a flesh and bones mortal, a man like you that could be successfully opposed. Hell for that matter you stood a far greater chance of survival going up against a tank with a flamethrower or a prolific serial killer. No this was some kind of dark invincible pus filled mutation with a yen for killing, people, dogs, cats or any thing else it

And in that very unsettling instant Cameron unwittingly thought to himself that in the midst of this wary and uncertain plight he's now found himself caught up and in the midst of. Was just that he must be outta his ever-loving mind not only in pursing such a malignant and dangerous course, and not just turning it over to the proper authorities but in bringing such a warm gentle soul like Dusty along with him as his point man on those covert boogerized patrols along the railroad tracks, open fields and through the woods. And the only element of safety realistically held out for them was going to be in their extreme covertness and methodical plodding. Yet that unsavory thought alone was abhorrent enough, as this was an abominable, wretched, horrid mutated freak!, a thing, a vile despicable conglomeration of putrefying chemical malfeasance that would surely decimate anything or anyone that stood in it's path it could wipe out a company of infantry soldiers without breaking a sweat. It was going to take nothing less than a freight train bearing down at a high rate of speed to destroy it. Hell for that matter the surrealistic and harrowing site of it would most assuredly rattle the incredible hulk to his very innards sending him fleeing for the hills with a yellow streak up his back a mile wide. No this was something that metamorphosed itself and emerged from the deep dark cavernous regions of a hellish underworld and that was undoubtedly spawned from the putrid bowels of Hades. Or that of some long ago forgotten toxic waste infested cesspool leftover from some smog ridden latter day industrial age and that had somehow had the miraculously ability to compile itself just enough to freakishly assume some foul and vile life form and as yet untested probably has the strength of about ten or fifteen good sized men. And if were ever placed in a cage with an eight hundred pound gorilla or a five hundred pound lion with razor sharp claws. Would in all probability viciously rend them into little bitty pieces like a couple of rag dolls. In that it's also seemingly endowed with as amiable a disposition as that of a volatile pcp or methamphetamine addict. It would also appear that it has the inherent and freakish ability to withstand a steady barrage of gunfire regardless of the calibration or the mechanism of dispersal, with little or no longstanding or debilitating effect and it would also appear to have some kind of flame retardant outer layer that can be set a fire with combustion able accelerants and recuperate from that as well to continue on it's heinous and nightmarish rampage of terror.

Cameron looked over at Dusty as they both slowly plodded their way through the scraggly meadow towards the distant railroad tracks amid the audible chirps of locusts and high weeds infested with tobacco spiting grasshoppers, dragon flies, beetles and off-bred white butterflies of various sizes in ditsy swirling and aimless fight. It was beginning to get hot as the midday sun was looming. The air resonated with the sweet pungent smell of weeds and ratty wildflowers. And then as afterthought Cameron in a fretful and agitated tone asked Dusty if she remembered to pack the .32 and she said yes but she really wanted to leave it at home for her mother but she subsequently declined stating she was to afraid of it and didn't like guns and refused to consider even touching it…. Cameron' moderately incensed from the mounting stress put on his flustered and constrained nervous system at the grim disparity that the whole situation posed simply snapped, what the hell!! do all you females possess this rash and unreasoning fear of guns or something!?

Dusty in her freshly showered miffed and disheveled state of appearance coyly grinned while brushing her bangs out of her face mildly jerked her head to one side sarcastically replied…Is that anything like a rash and unreasoning fear of the police? "Cameron" who at this point was beginning to get more and more unraveled was incensed at her joking lighthearted dismissal at such a serious and pressing matter of security squawked No it isn't! Well, I guess so…laughingly,…well it would seem so wouldn't it. Then she smiled and mildly sarcastic with an impromptu grin muttered I mean we are after all the fairer sex aren't we….and unless we have a big strong man like you at the helm to protect us most of us are just left in a totally desperate and vulnerable position otherwise aren't we…. I mean that does seem to ring true and be the general consensus among us helpless females now doesn't it an aversion to pop-guns and then she giggled…Then Cameron abruptly stopped walking turned and placed his palm firmly over Dusty's forearm grasping it firmly halting her in her tracks. And in a stern unwavering glare directly in her eye's somewhat incensed by her callous and mocking disregard in her remarks vehemently tersed your mother outta be a lot more afraid of that thing than a crummy old thirty two revolver. Ouch your hurting me! take your big oversized meat-hooks Offa me this instant! Dammit let me go!!...with a contemptuous expression on her face rolling in and biting her lower lip while vehemently attempting to writhe free from his grasp, exclaimed as she flailed her long auburn hair to one side. Your forgetting one other thing here! I saw that damn thing too BUSTER BROWN!!...And for another, I'm sure she'll keep all the doors and windows locked at night!! And besides my mother like most other people doesn't even know that thing exists much less what it looks like they are all still pretty much in the dark about this as I was. They just suspect something gravely imminent is looming but don't know just what. And until all this happened neither did I. I had pretty much the same views on the subject all the rest of us ditzy narrow minded batty broads have, And with a wide expression on her face haughtily and disrespectfully began laughing. This seemed Cameron as his face intensified with a stern look of disdain on it when he gruffly replied. You know you really need to start taking this thing a lot more seriously than you have been and look at it for what it really is!...A deadly serious matter instead of some temporary lame-ass bullshit to make jokes about all the time!!.. This is no laughing matter Sis' and it's not just going to just eventually vanish or disperse and if you keep it up it's gonna rise up unexpectedly one of these day's and bite you in the ass!!...So I suggest that from now on you'd better start putting your feelings in check, that is if you can come up with a more viable solution to this I'm all ears... you saw for yourself first hand what that awful thing was capable of and I don't see how your constantly able to make light of it all the time. You need to start focusing in on the clear and indiscriminate danger were even at this moment facing as we speak, that horrid mutated freak could just lunge out at us from nowhere at anytime or anywhere...It's serious!! Ya know this thing isn't gonna just disappear and go away like a bad case of the measles or poison ivy, you know were gonna have to deal with it sooner or later. AND I DON'T WANNA DO IT ON HIS TERMS,...COMPRENDE!!...So my advice to you here is to just cut the crap, ok?!!...it stopped being funny I think about five miles ago. And to tell you the truth it's really beginning to aggravate and work my last nerve and it borders on sadism!... And all things considering I don't think it's exactly fitting or appropriate here. Dusty' well EX-CU-SE me for living!!...Gees do you like always gotta be such a complete and total bummer all the time? In this instance yes, I wind up spoiling everybody's fun sooner or later....

Then he momentarily turned away and looked off to one side and raising up his forefinger to his nose while lowly muttering to himself, pensively now in our absence I just hope there's somebody else there in that the allotment that has at least a minimal access to firearms of some sort indirectly affording your mother and little brother some adequate level of security. And then she figuratively proceeded to sink the irons of her ongoing disparagement and discontent at life in general until they were glowing red hot in the burning flames of minimal worldly expectations in a vent of jaded cynicism. "Dusty" in a wide eyed sarcastic grin replied in a gaudy expression, WH-AA-T DID I JUST HEAR YOU CORRECTLY!!...You gotta be outta your ever loving mind!!...YOU GOTTA BE KIDDING RIGHT!? And from somebody who's lived there just about as long as I have nonetheless!...we are talking about the same allotment aren't we?...Washburn right? C'mon now you know better than that!...in that malformed contingent of rural rabble-rousers and backwoods ruffians? That's like saying I hope this elephant is gonna like these peanuts I'm about ready to throw him when your standing next to his cage about ready to feed them to him at the county zoo!!...Oh I'm sure that all of your ridiculous worries of Buford and Harley Hicks being amply stockpiled can most assuredly be put to rest if you just simply factor in the equation!!...And should the dreaded occasion arise he'll most assuredly be met at the door by a cache of armaments that could easily stockpile Fort Sumter consisting of a diverse array of shotguns handguns and hunting rifles all of em' trained on his green slimy ass!! Huh!!,...boy if Fedders happens in on that lot this time around God help em' cause they'll reign down on him in a monsoon of lead with a level of firepower surpassed only by your Marines, to the tune of Dixie over the allotments intercom loudspeaker system!!...Ha, Ha, Ha, Ha, Ha,.....Oh and I just know there's also gotta be at least a rusty run down pick'em up truck or two, in the lurch for backup with balding tires outfitted with hunting rifle racks mounted in the rear window...Hey!...and don't forget the famous greasy beat up old chainsaw with the 20 inch blade laying in the back of the truck bed with the big rusty holes in it strewn with empty beer cans and other debris they could no doubt successfully fend it off with too.

ha, ha, ha, ha,…

Cameron' Sarcastically winced, Ooooh, That's harsh!!.. Boy when it comes to redneck haven you sure don't pull any punches do ya!!… And then on a furthering note of mocking sarcasm exclaimed Ahhh yes indeed, Ms. Moors has yet again struck another blow for good taste and keen insight in tapping into that vast repertoire of her invaluable and prophetic seeds of vast witticisms to retrieve yet another thoroughly worn down to the nub and exhausted stereotypical cliché' to yet again bop me over the head with!!… And as Cameron went on in his insincere and satirical reproach of his friend saying, boy when it comes to some of our friends and neighbors back in the allotment don't you think your being a little to hard on them?…. Boy what on earth would I do without you?… just never give it a rest for one solitary moment do you? Dusty' Me!!…whatta-ya mean me!? Then she exclaimed…. Hey!!…Wasn't it you who just a little bit ago gave some long elaborate dissertation thoroughly lambasting that glorified organization of extremist crackpots!!… And views that are incidentally similarly held by many of our long time friends and neighbors back in the trailer park most of whom just happen to be proudly born and bred of Southern stock and still hail and pay credence to the confederate flag!!…who are doggedly unyielding in a longstanding antiquated and obsolete 2nd amendment stand to their inalienable right to be able to keep and bear an RPG a flamethrower or a belt fed 50 caliber machine gun mounted on a tripod with aerators cut in the barrel positioned behind their living room picture window just in case there's trouble!!…. Or a guided missile on the roof of their house if they so choose in their ludicrous and blockheaded position in distorting it's originally intended drafted purpose and meaning, and to exaggerate and exploit such an irrelevant and outmoded clause by present day standards of a document that was enacted in pioneer times by our founding fathers that referred to a black powdered musket.

And in how they tenaciously cajole, buffalo and extort their ludicrous designs from members of congress and safety and regulatory lobbyists to substantiate their warped and twisted and radical minded agenda so that continue to undermine the safety and security of all the rest of us underlings at any and all costs. You know one of em might wind up rescuing your respective bacon from the fire here one grave and unsuspecting night in the allotment. Dusty' or maybe Gomer, Jethro and Early will just wind up blowin me or my mom and little brother away in some hastily bungled, misconstrued and misconceived booze fuelled action more like! Just then she stopped and turned to Cameron smiling from ear to ear exclaiming in a haughty tone of jaded cynicism…I wish to extend my deepest and most sincere heartfelt apologies at all points of admonishment and awareness to all residing members of the peanut-gallery, and with undue regret I stand corrected sir! I didn't know just how unreasonable I was being, thanks for setting me straight…And while taking a bow in a figurative display of mockingly contemptuous disparagement. She tucked one of her tall lean lanky arms inwardly at the elbow and placing her forearm against her stomach caustically stating…I thank you and the countless thousands of little ones across the country that never attained the ripe old age of seven of whom haplessly climbed up on a chair while unsuspectingly reaching into a bedroom or hall closet hat shelf to retrieve mom or dads unsecured and loaded cannon and offing themselves with it thank you….Then she looked over at Cameron,…Ya know In regards to my own disheartening and disenchanting crossroads I've reached in recent years in my stunted level of faith in human nature reflects on the fact. In that if I didn't have such vast retentive inward powers of rationalization and a great level personal restraint. It's no small wonder so far that I haven't by now already positioned myself atop a high rise building somewhere with a high powered rifle myself,…Heh,..Heh…Heh… "Cameron" Ooooh boy!!….. Ok I think get the picture now…maybe I am a bit to overly serious.….I guess being to outwardly stern tense and intently focused all the time isn't going to help matters much either way I suppose. I'll try to relax and ease up some from here on out.

And as the two proceeded further on out through the wide open ground they were just about to come up on a twelve foot rise where a set of abandoned old dilapidated and deteriorating railroad tracks were set atop of, and that were inundated with ratty weeds. Dusty turned to Cameron and said,...what do you expect to find once we get there? I mean do you think we'll be able to get in to see those two girls? Cameron replied intently I'm not sure at this point it's still uncertain to me but the one and only thing I am sure of is that there's no other viable course of action we can pursue from a practical standpoint here to illicit a successful outcome but we've just gotta try, And from what the papers said, I just know they had a run in with that thing to. And they just managed to get away by the skin of an onion. And just then Dusty stopped and turned to Cameron and said well if you already know that what is the purpose of the two of us going there at all then? Because evidently they survived some sort of close pitched battle with it like we did and survived but didn't fair nearly as well, when the friend they were with was killed that's how. And do you know how I know that? Dusty just nodded signifying no. For one the state of extreme shock and disorientation the other two were found in that's how....When the two hunter's found them they were wandering aimlessly about immediate and surrounding areas of the attack with blank stares on their faces babbling, almost incoherent in their rambling statements to the police. And it was also clearly evident that, the long haired head dude they were with shot at it with a small hand gun he had on his person which was found just a few feet away from his body. Dusty' how do you know that? "Cameron" because not only were there several spent shell casings discovered scattered in relative close proximity to the victim, the gun also had the remnants of powder residue along the breach and trigger housing.

And just then he stopped and turned to Dusty and tersed now you should know all to well for yourself by now that, that's tell tale evidence that a gun has been fired! And evidently the gun also had a full magazine chambered and ready to go again but apparently that putrid two legged nightmare boogerized him before he got a chance to dispense with business. Dusty' groaned Oh that's just awful!! Cameron' yes it is,...it's ghastly and so is that thing. But you and I are gonna do something about that aren't we? Dusty just stopped and glared intently at Cameron for a while and said in a mildly imploring way, we are?..... if you already know all this what do you expect to find out from those two girls? First of all if they are still in a traumatized state what makes you think institutional staff will let us in at all? And secondly if they are still in that dazed condition how do you expect to illicit any useful information surrounding the incident? Were just gonna have to take that chance now aren't we and this is the only thing I can come up with in finding out the link to that putrid abominations internal weakness…Dusty just looked fretfully at Cameron as he spoke thinking to herself that maybe she got in way over her head agreeing to accompanying Cameron on this little fact finding mission. Cameron' I plan on concocting a rouse, stating that I'm a distant cousin coming in from Maryland on a concerned visit. Dusty' in a mildly sarcastic tone, oh that's a stroke of genius…that's why your in charge here!

Cameron' ok, ok knock it off that'll be enough comments from the satirical peanut gallery for now. You've gotta at some point start taking this a lot more serious than you have been and do a little bit more planning than we have…understand? Dusty' in a disheartening tone uttered, yeah I guess so…Cameron' pensively looked off to one side and murmured something happened after that I just know it, Dusty' inquisitively, after what? After those shots were fired I mean….and that poor guy was brutally killed. They managed to somehow successfully combat and stave it off momentarily disabling it long enough to successfully flee the scene and temporarily evade it. I'm thinking they must've had some other type of weapon with them other than just a small handgun that enabled them to successfully ward it off with….. There could've been no other way they pulled something like that off, but what?…Something other than a firearm. But what?…I just can't seem to put my finger on it that's what I got to find out. "Dusty" what kind of gun did the poor guy have? Cameron' I think the papers said it was a .25 or something. Dusty' that's a small gun isn't it? Cameron' yes to small…with a low velocity and trajectory. Dusty' Why didn't he use something a little bigger ya know with more stopping power? Cameron' because he could easily conceal it inconspicuously, nobody but his immediate friends would've known he had it on him at all. And he wouldn't have drawn any unwanted attention from the police either it was sound thinking on his part. Besides we both know a bigger more powerful gun wouldn't have made much of a difference either way in staving it off. That thing is some kind of chemical freak of nature with pus coursing through it's vile system, and seemingly invincible to any known ways of effective or disabling weaponry. Making it impervious to physical injury and totally devoid of the element of fear or emotion. Dusty' and just the very thought of that scares me outta my everlovin' mind!!...Cameron' Yeah I know well the sight of him doesn't exactly enamor me with a warm rush of love and admiration either honey...It's a graven threat that poses a terrifyingly unspeakable level of danger not like a flesh and blood beast like a bear or a mountain lion that would be susceptible to gunfire. They were probably completely in the dark as to the magnitude of danger that loomed posed.

Dusty' slowed down in her walking pace turning to Cameron and said aren't you at all scared that we might run into that awful horrid thing again unexpectedly in our travels? Yeah somewhat but that will be the intended purpose of our mission once we do now won't it...In that much anticipated instance Mr. Fedders will be a side of breakfast toast once we do find his Achilles heel. Dusty' and what if he doesn't have one of those?.... You know an Achilles heel I mean, then what?...smarty pants?. Oh he does you can best be sure of that, every living thing in existence does.... We just have to get out there and work very hard until we eventually find out just what it is...and we will all in good time my dear all in good time. "Dusty" coyly grinned, and giggled is that' a fact Cameron' yes that's a fact!...Dusty' well what's yours? I mean just what is it specifically is it that constitutes the famous Cameron Dillon's kryptonite? Just what is his weak and vulnerable point of attack? And just what is it exactly that completely breaks him down and depletes his will to go on any further reducing him into a cringing mass of grossly debilitating and agonizing pain?....Cameron stopped and momentarily paused in an aggravated state of cynical and jaded reclamation tersed, well off hand I can think of several prospective unsavory things...one being an involuntary second party to,... in being trapped like a mangy rat at close quarters and forced to have to listen to and lowly tolerate the borderline torture of the screaming constipation like singing voices of death metal, grunge rock, or the talent-less, vapid and insipid sounds of alternative or underground music.

Or being stuck in closed association with no viable means of escape with the sideshow self body mutilating socially maladjusted freak-a-zooids that have their heads shaved their earlobes opened up and stretched out like primitive native pygmies do. And are also covered with countless scores of borderline satanic and other like moronic and idiotic tattoos and body piercings that inexplicably listen to it. Then he turned to Dusty and paused while lowly grimacing as he was suddenly overcome with a stunned, anguished and disparaging look on his face as a very unsettling and disdainful memory churned from within as something so disparaging and insufferable lowly resurfaced itself within his stricken mind. He then went on to figuratively mount what could only otherwise be described as an intolerable gut wrenching, fateful, stalking, lying in wait opportunistic, button pushing and emasculating bitch to a cross, driving in big long colorfully descriptive nails as he proceeded to go into a lengthy crucifying bent in her honor. Beverly Aggravating or was it Aggressive or Ignoramus I'm not really sure which. Oh yeah now I remember it was Beverly Boomerang!!...Dusty' Boomerang? Cameron' Yeah No matter how many times I kept trying to throw her away she just kept whirling back in my direction anyway. Dusty laughingly expelled a few puffs of air through her mouth and nostrils while shaking her head back and forth. Cameron' my favorite pet sociopath!!...My ignominious blast from the past and the rejection queen and insufferable blabbermouth of the Gordon B. James Career center!...Or should I say CREEP Center!!...Or as I fondly call it the house of pain!!...Then he paused for a moment to reflect on those torturous disparaging memories while shaking his head back and forth in infused anger and disgust. And without realizing it he proceeded to go into an seething uncontrollable rage fueled vent at great length stemming from a wide range of pent up hostility and frustration. Yeah one day she suddenly just slithered out of nowhere from an obscure and undisclosed rock formation somewhere.

And of whom was grossly adept at honing in on and constantly refining the skillful art of minding everybody else's business but her own especially people she didn't even know.. And yours truly suddenly found himself starring in the leading role of a legendary 1950's B-rated sci-fi classic. Dusty just paused while solemnly looking at him waiting for the tersely delivered punch line. IN ATTACK OF THE 50 FOOT BITCH!! Ya know I just turned around one day to find that unbeknownst to me I was haplessly under observational surveillance of this gaping predatory weirdo of whom just suddenly and inconspicuously, inappropriately appeared out of nowhere and began hanging out in my classroom staring at me all the way from the other side of the room as if I had two heads or something, Then he abruptly turned to Dusty and yelled, DO I HAVE TWO HEADS OR SOMETHING!?…Dusty by this time was completely unnerved by his sudden outburst lowly and meekly muttered, well no…, And that I later on found out that hers was completely on the other end of the building about 75 yards away from mine in fact and she was also doing the same pestering shit to a guy across the hall from ours in a drafting class and when he understandably rebuffed her giddied amphetamine fueled pursuits she then went after me!!…He painfully winced as he went on to angrily state,…

AND I'M ORDINARY TO STAND THERE AND GAWK AT BY ANY STRETCH OF THE MEANS BY SOME MENTALLY DERANGED FREAK!!…and when I think back on it now it like just totally creeps me out!…Then he abruptly turned to Dusty and groused…What business did she have in a classroom that she not only wasn't assigned to but had no viable or legitimate purpose for being in, in the fist place?…And furthermore why wasn't she firmly instructed to go back to her own by a member of the teaching staff and stay there?…And as far as I know that's supposed to be part of their damn job isn't it!?…enforcing and maintaining some semblance of order and institutional discipline or is that just another one of many waning social pillars of the past that has been allowed to become completely broken down and scuttled off to the obscure realm of a bygone era. Only to be superseded by apathy, ineptitude and bungling incompetence!!…This isn't your classroom what are you doing here!!…you don't belong here go back to your own there's no valid or legitimate purpose for you to be here at all!!…Dusty suddenly taken back just sheepishly looked on as he spoke…Well I'll tell ya honey,…For one, a total lapse of discerning judgment or discipline on the part of an inept and incompetent teaching staff.

And for another she was a lookin' ta spread some of that thar ol' time home grown garden variety bitch venom my way, in her ongoing contingency plan for honing in on and refining her skills at just being an all around chronic, persistent and wholesale pain in the ass to any and all unsuspecting, well rounded and mentally balanced people that, that type seems to be so notorious for nefariously seeking out and foisting themselves on more fresh unwary victims that's what! Ha, Ha, Ha, Ha… Dusty just got a wide eyed stunned gaze on her face as he continued in his vent. I mean don't get me wrong I don't like to say that I've turned into some kind of misogynous in coming to despise all women in general, that wouldn't exactly be fair on my part now would it!…But believe you me I've met enough of em that fit that description right there in that inappropriate and unsavory setting that have made me at least guarded and apprehensive enough to the prospect of entering into very many relationships friendly or otherwise. But yeah some I do, at least those of whom have proved themselves out to be nothing more than worthless, sadistic, no-account button pushing bitches!!…Dusty' Well I'm a female do ya hate me too?…Cameron' Oh no honey of course not!!… for one your not a psychologically dysfunctional ignoramus who does little more than try to get under my skin unravel me and incite me to rage!!…And for another I wouldn't be around you for even so much as one more second if you did I'd just be a lookin' to boogie for the rear exit. Ya know she was, no they were definitely the type they had in mind when they finally got around to enacting anti stalking laws and restraining orders, she was the Ogre of my night mares alright!! You know her mouth was just like a broken water faucet.

Dusty's countenance relaxed and warmly lightened up a bit as she nervously grinned and swiped some of her locks out of her face as she leisurely strolled alongside Cameron while mildly turning her head in a whipping motion towards him and sighed,….Oh yeah and just how so?…Cameron' It never stopped running…As a matter of fact it dripped incessantly if ya get my meaning. And with an intent scowl on his face tersed, yeah I would've just loved to have been the given the golden opportunity to act in the capacity of the eternal plumber just to have been able to make a desperately needed adjustment on that that flailing out of control tongue of hers with a great big ol' pipe wrench with locking vice grip type jaws. Dusty in a sighing grin just shook her head back and forth Oh!!...Yeah I unassumingly awoke one day to find myself haplessly in the blind and bullying sights of a thoughtless insensitive oblivious and unreceptive steamroller blissfully ignorant and with a total sense of abandon to any and all objects of common ordinary decency or consideration for others. And if she really wanted to know my true likes, dislikes or innermost thoughts and feelings on any subject whatsoever really was, especially music, she'd of given-em' to me. Dusty' Oh come on now, she couldn't have possibly been as bad as all that!!...Now don't you think your exaggerating a little!...Cameron' oh no not at all and don't you try and lessen the degree of the severity of it either!!...I just had a gut feeling about her that's all, and then he abruptly turned to her and said. Haven't you ever had a gut feeling about someone in the way that something just wasn't quite right about them? A persistent, nagging, unsettling, queasy feeling in the pit of your stomach about them that you just couldn't quite shake or put your finger on? Somebody that you just didn't feel good at all about in being around?

Dusty just sheepishly looked over at him with big cow eyes with no comment. Well I sure as hell did and especially in this instance something was definitely rotten in the state of Denmark!!...And if there's anything else at all I've come to know for certain in this life is that you can most assuredly trust your gut instincts especially when it comes to those that emanate unusually peculiar, uneasy or bad vibes. Because gut feelings are usually correct and quite accurate in their ability to hone in on, sense out and detect one who radiates an unusually rotten aura. And yeah she proved out to be just that,.... INSUFFERABLY HORRID in her unmitigated gall!!...She was an insult to the intelligence of an orangutan and all lower primates as well as an effrontery to all that is good and decent!!...And what she did was inappropriate, intrusive, bullying, harassment at the very least!!...I was literally being stalked and pestered to death by froggy the gremlin with a bad attitude, bad breath and an even worse hairdo...Ha,..Ha,..Ha...

And lemme tell ya this there's nothing worse than being relentlessly pursued by a giant goonish looking frog that was in desperate need of an extensive psychiatric scrutiny as well as tasteful fashion tips!! Ha,.. Ha,..Ha,.. Dusty' Oh gees,...Cameron' Ya know it just stands to reason that if you are genuinely interested in and like someone you at least try and find some of these kinds of things out first to see if your even the least bit compatible or at least come half way and release the gates to a two way street open mindedly in considering new things and even adopt them yourself if they are truly an obvious and legitimate improvement before you proceed any further. BECAUSE ANYTHING ELSE IS NOT FAIR TO THE OTHER PERSON!!...But no she just saw fit to just corner and bludgeon me into a bug-eyed drooling disoriented stupor with her grossly warped and perverted reason and logic. And her persistent assailments which were unscrupulously directed at me were based on a deep rooted underlying immovable unreachable multi-faceted bigoted and ignorant life's philosophy launched from a sickeningly syrupy sweet veneer of false pretense. And ones I just didn't possess nearly the sufficient level of inner fortitude nor the stomach for, among other things that stale outdated, regurgitated, rehashed to death, bias and separatist manure. Dusty' Yeah I suppose so,...Cameron' Whaddaya ya mean you suppose so that doesn't just go against your eternal grain and flip a switch to the off position within your erroneous zones too?!!...Yes, that's how normal people do it stalking, intimidating and steamrolling doesn't get you anywhere with those who posses even a moderate degree of intelligence or inner substance!!...Because when the thin facetious veneer of ill intentions eventually dissipates it reveals only what is only a lame and empty exercise resulting in repeatedly being dumped. Or going through what usually proves out to be a pointless frustrating revolving door in a multitude of failed relationships!!...BECAUSE ANYTHING ELSE ONLY CONSTITUTES PSYCOLOGICAL HIGHJACKING and EMOTIONAL EXTORTION AND IS ONLY A PREREQUISITE TO FAILURE!!...And any level headed, rational minded person will just look for the nearest escape hatch the first chance they get!!...You know for all intents and purposes it's really a very vile and putrid form of molestation initially and any seemingly successful initial results will only prove out to be temporary. And it eventually unravels into a pitiful pile of ribbons on the bungling idiot that nefariously constructs and implements it!!…And it always will!!…Then she was going to try and get me strung out on idiot drugs and turn me into a grinning, blithering, brain fried retard like herself!!…

Dusty just pursed her lips together at the corner of her mouth and expelled a puff of air through her nostrils and mildly shook her head back and forth. Cameron' Ya know my mother had a very wise saying once that she told me years ago and I'll never forget it to this day. No three very wise sayings actually…Dusty' Yeah and just what were those?… One she said son when you see a steamroller bearing down on you the only thing you can really do is get outta it's way and let it pass!…And another one was. The only place that a one way street ultimately leads is to a dead end…And the third one which fits her and a large percent of the student body of that imbecile asylum to a T'…A closed mind is like a closed coffin, for the one who has it…And dip-shit after climbing inside the box took special care in added measures to vehemently drive as many long carpentry grade nails into the lid as possible!!…Cameron grinning wincingly,…And yet I still seem to keep coming across far to many stubborn lunkheaded oafs of whom still have a great deal of difficulty in just getting a handle on that very basic and simplistic concept!! Well in any case she later on found out the hard way that the one with the biggest mouth or blustered about didn't necessarily have the inalienable right to forcibly corner others in a stifling submission hold. I just dee-deed like hell for the nearest exit. He further went on in a wincing and pained sarcastic grimace on his contorted face,…yeah she was a whistling overbearing and promiscuous bullet that cruelly bore down on yours truly, and one to this very day I don't know how I ever managed to evade. Maybe it was through the merciful help of divine intervention I dunno. No in fact it was actually due to a highly concentrated series of intensified evasive and elusive maneuvers on my part in the way of doing a lot of running and hiding and the only divine aspect about the whole momentously asinine thing is that I somehow ever managed to finally get away at all!!…Ha,..Ha,..Ha,..Ha,..

Dusty just looked on with a sullen disheartened expression on her face while shaking her head back and forth as he continued in his crucifying bent. But miraculously I was somehow able to narrowly escape with what little sanity I had left and just by the skin of my wooly mammoth, from that godforsaken vocational school. The lid on a volatile pressure cooker of long buried and pent up anguished rage was now ready to burst. And the unsavory and disparaging memory of being the hapless recipient of such foisted ill and inappropriate designs of an all consuming ill-compensating and non-complacent social blob with no viable or legitimate purpose in the pointless course of her ongoing social endeavors had resurfaced provoking a lengthy verbal lambaste and castigation on his part as he continued grousing….Everywhere I seemed to run there she was arrrrrrgh!!…yeah she was definitely long on tongue and short on brain alright, you can best believe that!!…You know her mouth should've been registered with the FBI as a lethal weapon because just about every time she opened it she committed a heinous crime!!…. Hey, ya know something Dusty? I think I just may have without actually realizing it at the time stumbled onto the vast insatiable consuming innards of the Bermuda-triangle whereby entire squadrons of planes and fleets of merchant ships upon entering haplessly disappeared never to be seen or heard from again Ha,..Ha,..Ha,..Ha,…Dusty by this time was so startled and unnerved by Cameron's sudden lengthy and vehement burst of pent up rage. In that he was furthermore unable to keep the lid over what had been a festering, bubbling, boiling active volcano soon to emit a river of pure hot unadulterated hatred lava. And that for the first time she saw a raw surly unnerving side of him that she's never been exposed to before sheepishly uttered, ok you can stop now, I think you've said more than quite enough I got the picture now. Cameron' Oh no sis I've had to keep all this shit bottled up inside me for far too long, Now that I've got you here SOMEBODY'S NOW FINALLY GONNA HEAR IT!!…Now I'm finally going get the chance to air protest to that asinine stifling crop of intellectually deficient buffoons I was forced to remain in close quarters with and lowly tolerate. I'm just warming up to the plate and have barely scratched the surface here yet!!…Dusty' Oh Gees now I'm sorry I ever asked….but is it really necessary to turn her into a total and complete turnip!!...YES!! Because I was in the middle of a damn turnip patch!!...He further went on to vehemently state that her cavernous mouth was big enough to drive a tractor trailer into and turn completely around!! It was audibly indicative of a insipid mentality and of someone who upon rising one fine and momentous day in that just by sheer chance heard the sound of their own voice and fell madly and passionately in love!!...She had the bias shallow sieve like mindset of a toad-stool and all the social awareness and sensitivity of a piranha or barracuda that nauseatingly wrenched at the heart and gut of the random unassuming pensive soul who had the grave misfortune to be stricken with in earshot of it's blatant bullhorn blast!!... Ya know her mouth was just a festering Pandora's-box to a bottomless cesspool like pit of stale, unpalatable chunks to just about every kind of stereotypical bigotry, blind and blustering ignorance that stopped being funny I think about a hundred and fifty years ago that bounced off my stomach like a steady succession of tennis balls fired from one of those auto cylinders!! That were comparable to a piece of bubble gum with all the flavor gone and literally chewed to death until it had about the same taste and consistency as a blob of window caulk or silly putty, that was always in a state of perpetual motion and that brandished a tongue that was strikingly similar to a giant venom spewing anaconda slithering in and out of unwary social venues unwelcomed and unwanted just to spread it's malicious toxicity and ultimately in the end prove itself out to be little more than just a deadly bullwhip. You know Dusty?...she was really endowed with a very special gifted vernacular as so many others in this life are!!...My ex-father-in-law for one in just having the rare innate ability to miraculously breathe the breath of life into what would only otherwise be regarded by the rest of us common ordinary folks as run of the mill diarrhea and endowing it with a profound thought provoking and prophetic meaning almost to where it was,....soul stirring!!...

Then in a wide eyed gawking expression he sarcastically stated while putting his right hand over his heart, ya know Dusty, I must say I was almost moved to tears....Or was it to hurl?...oh yeah I remember it now it was to hurl!... And in having such a chronic and incurable case of the verbal Hershey-squirts as she was, for one, was completely oblivious to any deficiency in what otherwise should have been an openness to a well rounded sense of diversity and receptiveness to the blatantly obvious of improved musical innovation. And like a race horse with blinders on, was inexplicably a character trait she greatly prided herself on, she attempted to put me in the suffocating and stifling psychological and emotional stranglehold of a warped, twisted, bent reason and logic that was so deeply ingrained in an impenetrable and un-receptive head of petrified wood that I don't think even a sledgehammer would have so much as even made a dent in, and that she for some ungodly reason placed such great value on. IGNORANCE IS NOT BLISS!!...And then in a very cutting note of jaded cynicism stated, yeah she definitely possessed the inane ability to take a steady stream of it and miraculously transform it into profound and deeply thought provoking words.

Then in a wide eyed cutting and cynical expression exclaimed,...OH DUSTY HOW DID I EVER MANAGE TO LET SUCH A PRESCIOUS GEM SLIP THROUGH MY FINGERS AND GET AWAY!?... I MUST SAY NOW IT'S ONE OF MY MAJOR LIFE'S REGRET'S!!....Then he abruptly stopped and forcefully placed his hand over Dusty's upper left arm firmly grasping it halting her in her tracks and while sternly and intently glaring into her eyes he contemptuously exclaimed...Ya know I only come out and say this kind of stuff to people I think enough of and have come to somewhat personally value and respect and who I feel will be intelligent enough to be open to and receptive to it....Life is supposed to be a steady ongoing progression of growth and openness to legitimately improved new things and ideas not a lunkheaded discriminatory stagnated regression!!...People are suppose to already without having to be shown or told, have the presence of mind to be receptive to and posses an innate awareness on their own to the blatantly obvious of legitimately improved and better things and be open to and gratefully receive them, and not blockheadedly insist on cleaving to or remaining in a pervading state of unmovable stubborn BLIND and FOSSILIZED ignorance to what in many cases is nothing but stale worn out and clearly substandard or grossly inferior in comparative quality usually held out by the past just because it suits some bigoted close minded agenda, but to recognize it for what it really is, discard it and move forward!!. The cruder less developed and sub-standard objects of the distant past should be left there, in the distant past!! not brought forth into the present and adopted.....SHE WASN'T GROWING!!!..AND I DON'T MEAN PHYSICALLY!!... OR OPEN TO IT!!... NOBODY IN THAT GOD FORSAKEN GLORIFIED IMBECILIC GOON ASYLUM WAS!!... THEY WERE ALL BLISSFULLY OBLIVIOUS IN WALLOWING IN THE FILTHY PIG PENS OF THEIR FOSSILIZED BYGONE, OUTMODED RACIAL and ANTI SEMETIC BIAS AND IGNORANCE AND THAT TO THIS DAY STILL INFURIATES ME!!... And like the eight wonder of the world she for some god unknown reason maintained the asinine notion that anybody with even a modicum of a brain cell would lift so much as a finger to assist in substantiating it to further propagate it's banal stagnated idiocy.

And if her mouth had been a gun it definitely would've been a mack-10 or an Uzi. It had a hair trigger and was prone to commence firing at any given moment without warning, decimating anything in it's path with an I.Q. above the double digit range. And she literally had no compunction about using it on poor unassuming innocents like me. And the one thousand year old recycled short jokes braintard for some unknown and infuriating reason felt necessary to heist from among other such far removed obscure relics so deeply fortified in the dark musty vast maze of the tomb of King Ramses that reeked with that unmistakable overwhelming odor to them, was yet just another symptom of the terminal case of foot and mouth disease she was stricken with. Then he paused momentarily and turned to her on yet another cutting note,...you know Dusty? She must've thought I was something really special!!...Dusty' nervously smirked and lowly replied yeah and just how?...I mean in going so very far out of her way even to the very ends of the earth in sparring no expense especially mine, just so she could forcibly break into one of the pyramids or the Sphinx along the Gaza strip using a giant battering ram. And then unscrupulously ransacking it from among the other ancient artifacts, or even hijacking the dead sea scrolls for it. And like some giant mutated ear-wig with an asinine level of determination sought out to forcibly shove it my face, ram it down my throat, and nauseatingly turn my stomach in driving me completely and irrevocably outta my gourd with her seemingly unending repertoire of imbecilic and thoroughly worn out clichéd life's perceptions, insights and comments.

And in an utter state of giddy oblivion and\feeling no compunction in her overriding propensity to cruelly foist them on pensive and unassuming souls like me, were I think the last time I checked carbon dated as having their origins rooted in and around the pale azoic or Jurassic periods of time, like in early cave writing. And I'm pretty sure they saw their last hoorahs in the midst of corny third rate HAZZ-BEEN, stand up vaudeville type comedy acts who upon opening their mouths with this kind of rehashed manure on their lips got pelted with rotten eggs and tomatoes and then booed off the stage just for telling them in the crusty obscure annals of a distant and bygone era. And have long since remained among other moth ridden artifacts of the period just lying around and gathering dust and mildew in damp musty moth ridden trunks along with other iconic archival memorabilia like Charlie McCarthy, Mortimer Snerd from a long forgotten era. And anyone with even a fraction of a brain cell would see fit to just leave them there buried in the dust,… far and deep!!… and not only have they stopped being even remotely funny 100 years ago when Jimmy Durante & W.C. Fields were in the public limelight!!.. I'm pretty sure they have long since dissolved from the mainstream norm as the socially irrelevant context it presently is. And have long since been cast off to the wayside of antiquity and can now only be found in the hall of fame for dried up crusty, stale humor in poor taste. and are only further purported by those few remaining grinning, drooling and intellectually illiterate cretins with walnut sized brains who inexplicably insist on keeping it going!!…

Then Dusty's face suddenly turned beet red as she laughingly winced with tears seeping out of the outer corners of her eyes as she covered the corner of her mouth with the end of her sleeve from a shabby man's oversized dress shirt she was wearing with a partial fist and began giggling uncontrollably. Cameron' Wha?…you think that's funny uh?… Then he loudly and angrily groused, She was Gigantor! The teenage mutant ninja termite!.. and I was the wood pulp!…She had a voracious appetite for the ignominiously inane and an overriding pension for latching onto me and depleting any modicum of an upbeat spirit I may have had at one prior!!…in just whittling me down to my last remaining brain cell and nerve!!….God-dammit!!, you don't judge people by those shitty standards!! It's pukey!!… And I didn't want to hear it or her smelly music either for that matter!!…And what I was really in die or need of then was a last minute rescue by the Ortho man!!…She didn't insert humor she went on bombing missions!!…And having to listen to that stale worn out drivel for even so much as ten seconds hurt a hell of a lot worse than when my old man used to ball up his fist and bust me in the chops for no reason!!.. or even possibly being buried up to your neck next to a vast sea of ant hills and having somebody pour honey over your head!!…or having to have your teeth drilled or pulled without enough Novocain!!…And it's a queasy, nauseating brand of humor that's as dried up crusty and fossilized as King Tut's tomb!!…And anyone who insists on propagating it any further suffers from a terminal case of cranial paralysis!!…

Then Dusty suddenly winced up as she turned a beat shade of red and then her complexion flushed white as a sheet. Then her face got a stunned and startled look on it as she suddenly stopped giggling. This wasn't like the jovial lighthearted Cameron she knew at all and it somewhat scared and unnerved her to the point she was becoming somewhat fearful of him as he was now like a run-away semi barreling down a steep hill who's brakes had failed. And she wasn't quite at all sure just what he would say or do next in his rage fueled vent, then Dusty sullenly paused for a moment and lowly uttered, boy you really hate her don't ya!…Cameron paused for a moment as his face sarcastically contorted up and he lowly uttered,… Naaw,…We were actually the perfect couple, she was the bull and I was the china closet. And she wasn't entirely without any redeeming qualities at all,…I must say I have to give credit where credit is due, what she so sorely lacked in her repellently abrasive, pushy and overbearing personality,…she more than made up for in her bizarre warped and twisted logic and smelly value system!!…Ya know if there's one thing in this entire world that I can't stand more than anything else it's an unrelenting, brainless and disrespectful button pusher!!…And furthermore what never ceases to completely baffle me to the galling point of shear amazement, is how they think they are so cute and funny in their stale and nauseating brand of asinine humor or that the whole rest of the world is laughing and applauding them too. And boy you'd best believe they make sure in their psychological and emotional hijacking in tormenting and manipulating their selected victim under their thumb by trying to incite an angered and screwed up reaction they seem to derive some kind of sick and perverse psychological orgasmic pleasure from in that they always make damn sure they have the last word!!…Ya know not only is it galling and infuriating it's pus and filled just about as pukey as it gets!!…I don't know how much good it would've actually done at the time other than just driving home the point with a sledgehammer through one of their heads…but I guess somebody should have informed that crop of mental midgets somewhere along the line that, that outmoded brand of humor can now only be found in two places, one, currently residing in retirement homes for washed up corny third rate stand up comedy acts of a bygone era living on an old age pensions. And the others stretched out on a hospital gurney hooked up to an extensive critical life support system with a number of hoses, I.V.'s and tubes sticking out of it's mouth nose and ears just barely clinging to life when somebody should've just pulled the plug on it along time ago. But I guess in any event I was just gonna be cornered by it and hear it anyway,…whether I wanted to or not.

Then he turned to Dusty intently and said, ya know when you do little more than spend the better part of your life in just pushing other peoples buttons. And then in a wide eyed gawking expression stated, all you really wind up doing in the end is to push good decent and worthwhile people out of your life. Then with a scowl he tersed and furthermore nothing more than the summation of a total creep would notice, call attention to or address something like that!!…And only a brainless idiot would judge somebody purely on such criteria as race ethnicity or physical makeup in that they were randomly born with and had no say so or control in the initial drafting thereof. And furthermore in looking down on such and deriving some false delusional sense of self righteous feelings of supremacy from such an asinine brand of judgmentalism in that regard is truly unconscionable and appalling!!... Nonetheless I was haplessly cornered in an inescapable and oppressive stranglehold of a grossly substandard compulsory rate of an inept and apathetic public school system in a non-evasive state of forced association with those of whom at best shall we liberally say, were morally and intellectually deficient or for that matter totally bankrupt!... You know it never ceases to amaze me how these bastions of close minded and fossilized ignorance have it in their tiny little mind of minds that the whole rest of the world holds them in some type of high esteem, applauds, wants to hear or thinks it's funny too. Take music for instance using that as a platform of subterfuge in a subtle mode and guise to propagate and solidify nothing but a white racist and separatist ideological agenda,... HOW SMALL MINDED!! HOW SOCIALLY EROSIVE, AND INFURIATING!!...AND WITH ALL THE REAL PROBLEMS THIS WORLD IS GIRDED WITH THAT'S WHAT THEY CHOSE TO CENTER IN ON AND ATTACK WITH SUCH AN INANE DILIGENCE!!...DANCE MUSIC, NOT GRUNGE, INDUSTRIAL, ALTERNATIVE OR UNDERGROUND, STUFF THAT IS REAL CRAPOLA BUT DISCO AND FOR NO VALID REASON OTHER THAN THAT OF THE BASIS OF RACE AND ETHNENTICITY!!....BOY IF THAT ISN'T SOMETHING THAT DOESN'T WHOLLY EPITOMIZE THE TERM AND I DON'T USE IT LOOSELY HERE EITHER,...DIRTBAG!!... AND I THINK I CAN SAFELY SPEAK FOR ALL OTHER RATIONAL MINDED FREE THINKING INDIVIDUALS EVERYWHERE WHEN I SAY I DON'T KNOW FOR THE LIFE OF ME WHAT THE HELL ELSE ON EARTH DOES!!....AND IN NAUSEATING COMMEMORATION I JUST WANNA GUSH THE DIGESTED EATS FROM MY INNARDS and THEN BUST ARTERIES!!...Dusty?...Have you ever heard any of it?... No I can't say I ever have I favor New Wave, Punk and hair band rock ya know. Now ya see there that's just my point!!.. that massive contingent of grime-tards wasted no time in putting a kibosh on it before too many other people got a fair chance to be exposed to hear it and judge for themselves as to it's merit. It was colorful, magical, refreshing and exhilarating.

And the stuff they actually played at studio 54 was a very splendid and magnificent sounding music that got trashed solely on the basis of skin color!!...AND I CAN'T EMPHACIZE THIS ENOUGH,... IT'S CLOSE MINDED, CLIQUEISH, RACIALLY BIAS MUSICAL EXCLUSIONARY BULL,.. AND IT REEKS WITH A SPECIAL UNDENIABLE BRAND OF STENCH ALL IT'S OWN HIGH TO THE HEAVENS ABOVE!!...And without even hearing a good 70% of it no doubt and not that mainstream crap that most of the radio stations backed with a lot of hype in order to just drum up media dollars they literally played to death!!.. But the real stuff they actually played in the clubs, that only obscure urban based stations featured and not because of the sound quality or merit it had but solely on the basis of some kind of backward close minded bias to among other things skin color or ethnicity no matter how damn good a lot of it may have sounded!!...What was really wrong with it? Well somebody after all this time just needs to be honest and up front and finally come right out and say it!...It was just quite frankly the complexion of the whole thing!!....To much widespread adoration and enthusiasm was lavished on a fresh new music classification that was quite simply just the wrong color, black and Hispanic it was a fantastically exhilarating sounding music that put a lot of the stale sounding rock by that time to shame in comparison. And this same legion of low life, dirt bag trash rockers who in the latter portion of the nineteen sixties spent their waning hey days drifting aimlessly about, jobless and loafing in some self deluded, drug induced, psychedelic fog, bucking the system, resisting authority and eluding any and all forms of social responsibility, or obligation who took it upon themselves to decide for everybody else as to what they were gonna hear in the mainstream forefront and saw to it that nobody else heard it or enjoyed for very long!!...HOW DARE THEY!!... And why?... Well for all intents and purposes it was just a shade too dark for it's own good!!... And a massive hate movement insidiously loomed on the horizon that was soon organized and instigated by the dirt bag brigade who's soiled uniform comprised of an un-bathed unkempt set of jean materiel clothes consistently worn unchanged for weeks and months at a time. And this magnificently sounding music suddenly came under attack by this massive contingent of low life druggie type trash rockers across the country that got the ball rolling by joining their grimy rat paws together on a collective and unified scale. And of whom also took it upon themselves to make the final decision for all the rest of us as to what we were going to hear from here on out or how it evolved and then to completely eradicate this from the musical mainstream.

And what became paramount importance and top priority at the time was in painstakingly insuring that any and all music artists that stood in the media forefront were all the same color, no matter how sorely lacking they may have been in the area of talent or fresh sounding innovation by comparison WHITE!!...Dusty' hemmed oh yah I think I remember that now...you mean kinda' like hands across America or something right?....Cameron' Yeah but only this was low life burn out crud monsters across America with nothing better or productive to do with their idle time or energies than to come out and shine like the grimy pus bags they were...And it's not in any logical or rational sense of the word a valid or legitimate reason to organize, rally against, boycott or have an aversion to a very magnificent musical innovation or to try to intimidate others to do the same!!, DAMMIT IS THERE EVER GONNA COME A DAY WHEN THIS COUNTRY IS GOING TO FINALLY BE RID OF THIS KIND OF TRIFILING BACKWARD CLOSED MINDED CRAP ONCE and FOR ALL!!...THS IS SUPPOSED TO BE A FREE COUNTRY and WHY DO THESE KINDS OF GRUNGE MONSTERS INAPPROPRIATELY and WITHOUT PROMPTING OR JUST CAUSE SEEM TO CRAWL OUT OF THE WOODWORK AT THE MOST INOPPORTUNE TIME ONLY TO REAR THEIR UGLY DENSE PEABRAINED HEADS JUST TO POISON THE WELL WITH THEIR GRIMY FORK-TONGUED VENOM TO DEFAME and SPOIL SOMETHING THAT WAS SO, UPBEAT GLITTERING and MAGICAL!!...AND WHO WITHOUT ANY PUBLIC PRODDING OR SOLICITATION INEXPLICABLY PERSIST IN THEIR INSIDIOUS EFFORTS TO DENIGRATE and UNDERMINE THE DIVERSE FABRIC THIS NATION IS SUPPOSE TO BE BUILT ON WHEN THE OPPORTUNITY INDIRECTLY PRESENTS ITSELF. AND IN ATTACKING SUCH A REFRESHING INNOVATIVE SOUND IN

THE STEADY COURSE OF THEIR POINTLESS ENDEAVOR'S TO SABOTAGE THIS NATION'S RIGHTFUL HERITAGE OF DIVERSITY FROM WITHIN!!...AND AS FAR AS I KNOW THE CIVIL WAR HAS BEEN OVER FOR ABOUT YEARS NOW, AND I THINK THE SOUTH LOST!! AND NOBODY WITH EVEN HALF A BRAIN IS EVEN REMOTELY INTERESTED IN FIGHTING IT ALL OVER AGAIN ESPSICALLY FOR THE WRONG SIDE!!....AND SINCE WHEN DO I HAVE TO GET CLEARENCE FROM THE BODYODOR BRIGADE TO ADOPT A VERY MUCH IMPROVED AND LEGITIMATELY VALID FORM OF MUSIC!! Personally I absolutely loved it, RandB and dance music too!!...The bass guitars and bassy beats were off the hook and anybody who doesn't like me for it, to that I say tuff you know what!! It's great music and my vast collection of vinyl can attest to that!!...and so did millions of other people it was racially and ethnically based and that's really straight out of the book of who gives a crap!! A lot of it sounded magnificently awesome and it had a wide array of very innovative and talented artists that didn't get the wide range of praise and recognition they so richly deserved!!..., BECAUSE OF A RACIALLY BIAS MEDIA REIGN THAT FOR SOME UNKNOWN REASON WAS GRANTED FAR TOO MUCH POWER!!.... It was a fresh appealing sound to what had become at that time very monotonously stale and mediocre sounds of rock and roll!! And what was carefully hidden under a very transparent nauseating veneer lamely disguised as a valid, legitimate aversion to a type of music based on it's true merit or a deep loyalty towards rock music, was in actuality something as old as the confederate flag itself,

And as stale as the Twinkies, pies, and buns mom used to get from the day old bread store which should've been called the six month old bread store., and as smelly as the fenced in sulfur festering cesspool on the end of my street of a housing allotment I lived in as a kid!!.. and let's call it what it really was!! Small minded, bigoted racial bias and that is what really sucks!! It stinks to high heaven, and if you were a black or an urban type artist then you got one and only one kind of reception and treatment by those who completely controlled and monopolized the musical mainstream media at it's forefront at the time as far as fair and just exposure or promotion went,...EXCLUDED and IGNORED and banished to the dismal confining annals of musical obscurity now matter how you magnificently great you may have sounded!!.....A social travesty to say the least and one that was painstakingly orchestrated and purported by a vast disproportionate majority who monopolized and controlled a large segment of it's radio listening audience perpetrated by a methodically well organized clique of mental midgets who consistently disregarded it, or rather WHITEWASHED it over with invalid unfounded propaganda and grossly inflated hype with an extensive array of British contemporary pop or talent wise very mediocre and borderline rock artists just as long as they weren't black!!.... RATIONAL OPEN MINDED PEOPLE ARE USUALLY OPEN TO SOMETHING ELSE IN THE WAY OF FRESH IMPROVED SOUNDING MUSIC!!...AND THEY DON'T WANNA BE SUFFOCATED BY STALE TIRED WORN OUT MUSIC THAT HAS DOMINATED THE MUSIC FOREFRONT FOR 40 YEARS ESPECIALLY BY A BIAS CLIQUISH WHITE SEPARTIST CONTROLLED MEDIA REIGNING WITH A DIVERSIONAL SMOKESCREEN IN PAINSTAKINGLY ATTEMPTING TO CONCEAL AND SQUELCH THE GOOD STUFF,...BOOGIE-MUSIC!!...WELL IN THE END IT FLOPPED AROUND ON THE BEACH LIKE A FISH OUTTA WATER BIGTIME. BECAUSE I EXCLUDED AND IGNORED THEIR BIAS, STIFILING and CONSTRAINING MEASURES...And the only thing that was missing really in this asinine movement to suppress any and all exposure to the public those endowed with such vast well above average level of musical talent ingenuity and creative powers, was the hooded white sheets and the giant wooden crosses wrapped in rags just about to be soaked in gasoline UUUHG, GAG!!!.... BARF!!...Or those goose-stepping brown shirted SA men wearing those insidious swastika armbands who did the same type of thing in Germany during WWII by abolishing civil liberties, constraining intellectualism and burning books!!...And we in this country had better take notice and be on the alert and exercise special care or these types of radical supremacist groups are going to completely take over and censure any and all creative elements altogether. And this country will be rendered a controlled state just like Nazi Germany was...But I'll tell ya though they all got their come up-ins in the way of payback they so richly deserved a few years later with compounding interest for that!!...The cavalry finally did arrive in full force to save the day in the widespread adaptation and proliferation of RAP MUSIC that was methodically interjected into the musical mainstream and those who so tyrannically controlled and monopolized the airwaves in excluding bassy urban type or club style sounds suddenly had their power and public influence drastically diminished...Such that they couldn't manage to contain or suppress it when the flood gates on that finally busted open on it!!... And those same blustering low life grime balls that went about with the phrase disco sucks on their filthy sewers now found themselves on the business end of an assailing barrage of sonic reverberating booms and crass, vulgar and assailing lyrics of something that really does,...

And of whom suddenly got blasted with an unrelenting ear full of this crass and haughty crap at every turn as they either walked down the street or through a parking lot by menacing, gaudy and suspicious looking cars looming about with tinted blacked out windows with bad-ass ghetto boys at the wheel booming and reverberating their way down the street obliviously hipping and hopping down the avenue!!... Ha,..Ha,..Ha,..Ha...Serves em' right because they should have kept their filthy, lying, ignorant garbage dispersing sewers shut about DISCO!!... Because they really didn't have nearly enough information to know what the hell they were actually talking about in the first place to even make an informed decision about it in the first place!!...Ya know I love it when a plan finally comes together!!!...Rap music it's bold and beauteous!!...It can't be bullied, silenced, cornered or buffaloed nor can it's fans,...me personally I lowly despise it but it's a vast lush cooling oasis for what had been for so long a totally unfair, exclusionary racially bias media desert!!...And if ya ask me, it's been a long time coming!!...the far lesser of two evils finally prevails and it serves as a very effective bulwark and equilibrium against what was an insidious, outdated, baseless, unfounded racially bias monarchal media reign that so ruthlessly dominated the radio mainstream airwaves and Grammy awards ceremonies for to damn long. And the duped masses of whom compliantly let themselves be brainwashed, and led around by the nose by all the baseless inflated hype with blind, oblivious impunity,

And instead of doing what they actually should've done in the first place which was to boycott and ignore all the subliminal white separatist messaging in just cutting it off and booting out, and just start thinking for themselves if that were really at all possible!!…They just blindly adopted it!!…And in grossly neglecting to question it or take the time or personal initiative to go forth and scratch below the surface and actually investigative and research it on their own in making their own real and individualized musical decisions instead of just swallowing this garbage at face value. And in doing so, completely missed out on hearing a magnificently sounding alternative that was obviously far more innovative and much improved sounding over what was obviously significantly inferior by comparison that was forcibly being rammed down the throat of people like yours truly here in particular!!…but based moreover on true merit and not skin color or urban point of origin as if it didn't exist at all!!!…

But instead in just swallowing this trumped up, hyped up fallacy totally immersed in a by then a largely WHITE, contemporary pop smokescreen JUST AS IF NOTHING ELSE IN THE MUSICAL UNIVERSE EXISTED!!…WELL IT DID AND I MADE IT A SPECIAL POINT TO PERSONALLY BOYCOTT THIS INANE BRAND OF CLIQUE-ISH EXCLUSIONARY BULLSHIT SO BLOCKHEADEDLY ADHERED TO AND PROMOTED BY MAINSTREAM CONTEMPORARY POP STATIONS OF THE TIME AND I MADE IT TOP PRIORITY TO PATRONIZE ONLY CLUB STYLE DANCE MUSIC and THE URBAN STUFF IN SPITE OF IT!!….And yet the grossly lopsided percentage of the public still inexplicably let themselves be blindly led around by the nose like a massive herd of sheep with no sense of discriminating taste when it came to considering a blatantly obvious improvement!!.. And this was something that so insidiously typified the duped spoon fed masses of radio listeners and record buying consumers of the early to mid 1980's. And every time I think about it I just wanna spit nails!!…But the good news is now you can listen to just about any kind of music you want to, good or bad and nobody really cares anymore. And without the pressure or intimidation of that white separatist clique which is now passé' with it's blustering stranglehold monopolizing the radio and music media forefront in a dictatorial reign of the social media anymore. Now it's a free country in that regard!!... encompassing all the colors of the flag not just one but red and blue as well!!...It's poetic justice, and it is beauteous!!...

By this time Dusty was overcome with a wide eyed, stunned, timid and overwhelmed expression on her face at the sudden unexpected resurgence of such vehement hatred and resentment in finding herself in the direct line of fire of a steady barrage of long standing pent-up anger, frustration and animosity!!... and deep resentment stemming from Cameron's rare insight into such a blatant and disproportionately blind social travesty and injustice. Cameron' yeah it only lacked one other essential element to the casual unassuming recipient it was foisted on... Dusty with a moderate grin on her face lowly uttered, yeah and what was that? Cameron' furnishing an ample supply of Prozac to one who had any insight into it, and was unfortunate enough to have had to bear up under and endure it...Ya know blind, blustering, close minded ignorance is not an aphrodisiac it's a COMPLETE AND UTTER TURNOFF!!...Dusty chuckling while nodding her head back and forth, boy your terrible. Then he sharply turned to her and angrily groused no she was terrible!! They were terrible!! Terrible for anybody who wasn't a borderline retard themselves and was unfortunate enough to be in close enough proximity to and cornered by and within earshot of having to listen to it in feigned and futile attempts to stomach it's nauseatingly putrid green bile!!

And with an intensifying look of contemptuous disgust Cameron went on in his lengthy and colorful dissertation of his past time disconcertment of unsavory characteristics regarding a few repellant members of the opposite sex he at one time found himself haplessly cornered in a non evasive state of adolescent regression into infantilism. Cameron' that damn vocational school was a grueling two endurance test of one's inner fortitude!!... Eight hours a day Five days a week which seemed at the time more like an eternity in purgatory. This held over was the hapless state of affairs exemplary of a compulsory rate of education by an apathetic, sub-standard sorely lacking and inept branch of the public school system of the time. You know she not only desperately needed a doubly reinforced steel belted muzzle, but for some unknown and inane reason she inexplicably insisted on expending her malformed and misdirected energies in inappropriately foisting a whole lot of unwanted attention my way in her merciless bedevilment after the guy she was with before, understandably ran like hell for the hills from her too.

Dusty just shook her head back and forth and snickered,… boy your really quite the little Lee Harvey Oswald of character assassins aren't you? Cameron' Yes!!…they were all characters that richly deserved to be assassinated,… in the figurative sense of the word that is. Dusty' Ya know in all the years I've known you I still can't figure out how in the world you've come to be so jaded and infused with such an extreme battery acid strength level of hatred directed at so many people…Cameron' Hatred my dear, is a sad unfortunate, inescapable yet harsh fact of life that is often times justified and duly warranted… Some are just so unconscionably contemptible that they incite an uncontainable and irrepressible level of it!!…It is something that at least it affords one some minimal degree of compensation especially in such extreme circumstances such as these were,…and often times proves out to be very necessary because any compliance or acceptance to a reprobate element successfully propagating and flourishing it's warped, perverted and malignant, designs is one prospect I've never had much of a stomach for. Then with a sighing sarcastic insincere grin muttered, Naaw not really honey. Just perceptive is all, You see Dusty, I was really born with a special gift, a rare and discerning insight into the vast and seemingly unending realm of witless boobisms. And I couldn't have possibly done it without the eager co-operation of such a vast army lining up and for lack of a better term mentally deficient buffoons to pool from!!…And it doesn't really take a rocket scientist to see the completely obvious. No, I'm just statin' thee facts here, I jus callz em' az I seez em' Ya know, now that I really think about it I don't think there was enough collective brain power in that whole entire building to even snap on a night light. And her pea sized brain incepted gibberish was only unsurpassed by a nauseating, inexplicable and perpetual grin that was constantly painted on her face all the damn time, and that took every ounce of restraint I could muster to keep from just slapping it off!!!... AND IT JUST MADE ME LOWLY CRINGE EVERY TIME I SAW IT!!...And it was furthermore accentuated by a hyper enthusiasm for God knows that was undoubtedly fueled by some form of amphetamine abuse!!...DAMMIT!!...THAT DREADFUL PLACE WAS A HORRIFIC ENDURANCE TEST OF THE WORST KIND!!...And I'VE BEEN IREVOCABLY SEARED FROM IT FOR THE REST OF MY LIFE!!...Ya know the Army not only could've stockpiled her mouth but my x-father in laws as well in it's secret weapons arsenal for use in covert opts in the sudden and without warning emittance of some deadly form of nerve gas!!....Ha, Ha, Ha, Ha,.....Dusty' Boy ya just don't have anything good to say about her at all do you?...Cameron' Oh yeah sure I do I'm not entirely devoid of any shred of compassion,...she did finally prove out to have one redeeming quality that in the end I came to gratefully appreciate,...mercifully she's gone....

Dusty just pursed her lips together and mildly shook her head back and forth. You know my old man had a term he used for people like that and in that insufferable place there was a whole brigade of them. Dusty' bug eyed while lowly looking downward uttered, yeah and what was that dare I ask? Cameron' A grinning idiot....They never stop grinning or being a complete and utter fool. And what really infuriated me to the boiling point of aggravation was the fact that she had the monumental gall to get pissed if I didn't go around with that same nauseating, idiotic smile painted on my face too...Ya know when he first came off with that prophetic little gem I must've been about thirteen or something and I didn't think much about it then or even knew exactly what he meant by it at the time until much later on and especially having the wonderful and fulfilling experience of being cornered by that insufferable bin of intellectually illiterate grinning goons!!...Proudly I can boast I did prove him wrong about one particular thing though,...He just looked at me one day grinning sarcastically and said that's probably the kind of woman you'll marry,...Naaw dad not in this millennium nor the next no not ever!! I don't have any more tolerance for them than you did!...probably even less!!...And since then proudly I must say I've painstakingly gone to great lengths to make sure of that!!...And boy it sure rang true especially in a certain case of a blithering magpie who's mouth was unceasing in it's inane verbosity in having inappropriately chased after me to foist upon me more of her warped and twisted backassward logic and insufferable gibberish which rained steadily down in a cruel insipid Chinese water torture like river of liquefied manure like some insidious volcano, positioned over a putrid bubbling cesspool!!...Mt. Saint Flatulence was given to erupt at any point in time without warning in gushing a hot lava like river of diarrhea upon hapless random unfortunates down below, Then he sharply turned to her and chimed. Ya know I think if she was ever forcibly made to keep quiet for any longer than five minutes her brain would've in all likelihood undergone some sort of profound metamorphosis, her face would've been thunder struck with a with a stark bug-eyed gaze on it and her tongue would've went into catatonic shock and literally snapped off it's rollers!!...ha, ha, ha, ha, ha....Dusty' Oh how cruel!!,...It sure was!!,... cruel for anyone who wasn't a total imbecilic braintard themselves or for that matter possess a substantial level of inner fortitude to be able to stomach and listen to that regurgitated bile!!

Nonetheless I was however prompted to go fleeing and cringing, in disparaging and despondent anguish out of the room with my hands clasped over my wincing face as if I was in nauseatingly imminent danger of having what little still remained of my precious brain sucked out of my skull through my ear. Dusty suddenly busted out laughing and sarcastically exclaimed,...ya know you really shouldn't talk about your girlfriend like that!!...I mean you'll almost surely ruin any possible chances you may still have to get her back! Cameron' WHAAT!!...He tersed, My girlfriend!!... Oh you gotta be kidding!!...Are you outta your ever lovin' mind!!,...You must be on some serious drugs yourself if you think that!!...I would've rather done it with Sasquatch!!...or did the bump and grind with the Grinch or Oscar the grouch!!... Or even knocked boots with Lurch or Herman Munster!! Oh yeah sure.... they'd of just had to hold me down and pump me with an entire cabinet full of pharmaceutical type psyche meds to such a debilitating and

disorienting degree that I wouldn't have known what planet I was on!!…
Ya know if she just would've more kindly re-appropriated her perversely
malicious attentive energies to an even a minimal degree in redirecting
them altogether in either just haunting a house or at least somewhat
compensating herself in the grossly deficient area of basic personal
hygiene in the way of a perfumed bar of soap or instead of stalking me
stalking the mouthwash isle at the local grocery store. And what really
typified this crop of maladjusted cannabis smelling crud-monsters of
whom habitually showed up in the same set of jean material clothes and
death metal t-shirts bearing racial and satanic undertones and literally
going un-bathed for weeks and months at a time, with this baseless
creepy grinning leer on their faces that just made my flesh crawl along
in jittering reverberating spasms every time I was forcibly made to look
at stomach and contend with on a daily basis, which undoubtedly was
invariably the asinine result of being chronically stoned on goofballs.

Then his face winced in a contorted disparaged look of horrified
revulsion. And groups of these for lack of a better term turnip-brained
trolls would nefariously congregate in groups in the hallway standing
there in a moronic loitering state gawking at innocent people just trying
to go about their business and inappropriately accosting them verbally
with some imbecilic and asinine comment as you just tried to walk
through the halls to class or lunch. They constituted a rare form of a
walking two legged social malignancy carrying with them a wide range
of mental deficiencies and bizarre behavioral ones, that derived some
kind of perverse orgasmic psychological pleasure at an incensed or hurt
reaction by the victim in any pleas to cease and desist were only met with
stepped up and intensified action to do it even more by this imbecilic and
fungus based mindset with a walnut sized brain anatomically located
in a lowly place much further down that it shouldn't have been, and
definitely AS F-U-N-N-I-E-AS A CASE OF PANCREATIC CANCER
BARF!!…YESSIREE BOB, THERE'S NO MISTAKE ABOUT IT, I
WAS DEFINATELY TRAPPED DEEP IN THE CLENTCHED JAWS
OF WASTEOID CENTRAL!!…ARRRRGH!!… Ya know,… something
like that is just about as horrific and treacherous as having to go up
against Mr. Fedders!!…Dusty in a hemming expression clenched her

lips together and shook her head back and forth as Cameron continued in his lengthy verbal castigation.

And the only seemingly effective countering agent or antidote against this rare breed of assininity was for the victim to exude an indifferent or unemotional type of reaction to it, in the way a chemotherapy treatment would for cancer. You know whenever I think about having been an involved bystander even on so much as even a minimal level. I just want to crawl out of my skin and just go take a bath in lye or bleach or something. Those ravenous and insidious mutated termites despicably turned that two-bit trade school which should've for all intents and purposes been called the Gordon B. James CREEP Center!!...for the remaining small percentage of decent people that had no other choice but to have to attend it into glorified goony bin!! They were just the residual byproduct of such incompetent and apathetic authority figures who ineptly headed up that particular branch of the public school system in giving these animals free and unchecked reign of the zoo that was so liberally mislabeled a vocational school!... And what was outwardly concealed through a transparent veneer of excessive nauseating syrupy sweetness, was an I'll do whatever I please, when ever I please attitude that was the most potent and putrefying agent at the center of this sugar coated acid pill making it near fatal to ingest...Dusty' smiling coyly...oh please it couldn't possibly have been that bad...don't you think your being a little overly melodramatic?

Cameron' and with an insincere look of sarcastic and contemptuous intensity on his face exclaimed oh no not at all....you know I've always wondered in the back of my mind even for years afterward if Evil Knievel could've ever made that momentous jump over her wide open mouth.... Dusty' snickering while shaking her head back and forth,...boy your terrible...and while laughing jokingly said oh your gonna burn in hell for that. Cameron,...Oh no,...whatever misdeeds I may have committed in this life rest assured the debt is paid in full just in having endured that insufferable torture for two whole years!!.... Dusty?...Can't you see?... I'm irrevocably scarred for life!...you know there for quite some time there afterward I had been mortally stricken with some kind of half-assed inferiority complex I couldn't quite comprehend or fully grasp within myself as yet another long term effect of assininity from that miserable place that was a long time in writhing free of, in that I thought I was just some kind of loser magnet when it came to the opposite sex. And then he sarcastically grinned at her and crassly stated. You've heard of something called DSS or delayed-stress-syndrome haven't you? "Dusty' yeah but isn't that some kind of psychological trauma war veterans are stricken with after they come home from a war where they suffer from long term sleep disorders and wake up shrieking from horrific nightmares or something? Cameron' Yeah something like that but I suffered from something a little different but similar to that held over from my forced two year attendance at the C-a-r-e-e-r center,... something I call A-SS,...Dusty',...A-S-S?...Cameron' Yes, ASSINIGNLY STUPID SYNDROME!!...Dusty' snickering Ho Gees...For a long time afterward I'd wake up thoroughly nauseated and suffered from uncontrolled vomiting!!... Dusty just scrunched her lips in a crooked wavy smile while expelling a puff of air from her nose and the corner of her mouth and shook her head back and forth at his final cutting and cynical remark on that personally disparaging subject. Which brings me to my last item of aggravation!...Dusty' Oh god no,...there's more?!...Haven't you lambasted and ridiculed enough people to last the remainder of this millennium!?...No actually I haven't there are just to many bumbling boobs in the world who are severely stricken with a case of terminal imbecility with compounding interest!!...

Dusty' I just don't know how you can get such supreme delight out of mercilessly shredding people to that degree, I must say it's not like you at all and it's particularly cruel!!...Cameron' well that crop of goony trolls sure derived supreme delight out of holding me hostage and literally torturing the ever-lovin shit outta me and if that doesn't constitute unusual cruelty I don't know what else on earth does!!...Dusty' I'm to the point where I just can't stand it anymore, ya know you better hide the guns, I'm starting to get really depressed!!...Cameron' Come on now gimmee a break I'm just having a little fun that's all. Dusty' yeah and so am I,...very little. Cameron' Awe why do ya hav-ta be such a spoiled-sport all the time?. Ya know your starting to sound like my mother now and besides. How can you possibly say something like that when there is such a beckoning multitude of prime candidates lined up imploringly crying out from the idiotic annals of the past that deserve nothing less than the utmost care and attention I can give em' in the famous Cameron Dillon's very own jumbosize shredder which I lovingly call GIGANTER!!... Courtesy of yours truly the resident president, so just hang in there with me for the long haul honey the nights still young yet, so pull up a box of pop-corn and just kick back relax and enjoy. And anyway it feels really good to just vent a little and blow off a little steam with my basic overall ill-contentment with life in general what harm is there in that?,... I mean for the time being what else have we got to do on our way to that dark dirty broken down old pest hole were going to be staying at,? And aside from all the oodles of fun we as the solely elected resident welcoming committee are going to have in staging all the special details I have arranged for Mr. Fedders grand reception finale once we finally do get to where were goin' huh?...Dusty' How about a nice friendly game of stress and strife free checkers instead huh?... Cameron' Aw gees I don't think I brought a board along...Now I want to delve deep into the annals of workplace and governmentally incepted bipolaristic, obsessive compulsive trifling attention to menial, mundane & insignificant tasking matters. Yet another point of aggravation that has always been near and dear to my heart. The besieging and baffling complexity of the internal working components of on the job inefficiency, incompetence and expert bungling by those in charge that have so long come to characterize two outstanding government agencies and all to many places I've had no other choice but to have to work in.

And that I've always maintained a soft spot for over the years especially in the pit of my stomach in the way of an prorated ulcer. And ones my grandparents, aunts and uncles used to so fondly refer to as governmentally incepted bureaucrap! And incidentally ones that are so methodically calculated, instituted and implemented by an incurable, neurotic crop of arrogantly based, witless, petty minded, and booberish type mental deficient's of whom are typically appointed to such lower level supervisory or managerial positions. And of which in all to many instances are not only grossly unqualified to oversee a lemon aid stand or a pay toilet but obviously have nothing in the way of any real credentials in the way of formalized education past high school, not to mention anything in the way of real life substance to begin with. And how they invariably possess the inane knack with strict and unrelenting pain-inthe-ass time wasting diligence. In centering in on, concentrating on in elaborate and expounded attention to nonessential components of simple tasking matters nobody with half of a brain gives two shits about. AND IT NEVER FAILS IN THAT IN JUST ABOUT EVERY OTHER PLACE I'VE HAD TO WORK AT OVER THE YEARS THERE'S ALWAYS BEEN ONE OR MORE OF THEM STATIONED IN A SUPERVISORY CAPACITY TO PESTER, AGGRAVATE AND ANNOY THE SHIT OUTTA ME!!...And those who feel an overriding propensity to interfere, badger, and drive you outta your ever lovin' nut!! as well as inordinately waste vast amounts of corporate time and man hours in just pestering grossly underpaid subordinates with this nonsensical bullshit. who in just attempting to carry out what otherwise constitutes blatantly simplistic and mundane tasking matters by needlessly complicating them with an inundation of pointless, trivial and inane procedures and rules into regimented process's all must strictly adhere to as gospel by the glorified buffoons who institute them and are inexplicably appointed to key positions of delegatory reign!!...Such as a restaurant or department store manager or supervisor... JUST SO FOR LACK OF A BETTER TERM SOME PSEDUE ANUATED ASS CAN PLAY LET'S PRETEND LIKE WERE ACTUALLY DOING SOMETHING INTEGRALLY CRUCIAL and SIGNIFICANTLY IMPORTANT!!... And densely remaining steadfast and unwavering in the course of what has now been transformed into an arduous, ponderous mountain of inexplicably pointless bullshit in clause laden forms fraught with tripe stipulations and process's in duplicate, triplicate and idiot. And how they possess the inane knack for turning such things into a pointless, burdensome lengthy and cumbersome process that absorbs not only all your time and energy in what may have started out as a nice day for you winds up shot to hell leaving you overly distraught, frustrated and downright angry. And with their baseless idiotic nonsense to systematically aggravate you, a bureaucrappy system that is staunchly adhered to by governmental agencies like the state

DMV or board of labor and Industry's unemployment compensation board entails. I've always loved how they inexplicably drag their feet in the sluggish time wasting inept and inefficient wheels of pointless procedures that slowly grind you the way they do.

And in propagating such trivially oriented processes laden with baseless nonsensical and inane clauses incepted in such backwards logic. I'm not so sure that even the government bureaucrats themselves who incepted them understand it. And like the eighth wonder of the world they for some unknown reason elevate this to a place of such a critically exalted place of significance. I guess it's just so they can full-fill the self deluded, idiotic notion that they are somehow accomplishing a crucial and essential tasking matter of the utmost importance. And if and when you do find yourself in the unfortunate position to have to undergo the frustrating and futile experience of attempting to introduce even a minimal degree of reason, logic or common sense to say a postal worker, a member of the state dept. of commerce a librarian or some other type of governmentally instituted personnel serving in some lower to mid level capacity of the federal government your invariably met with a blind, droning and unreceptive retort of THAT DOES NOT COMPUTE!!…And in your hapless and fruitless attempts to penetrate a thick impenetrable skull your invariably left exceedingly angered and frustrated in conferring with what only constitutes a stiff regimented automaton that staunchly adheres to, in constant and unwavering dedication to back-ass-wards governmentally incepted doctrine THAT MAKES ABSOLUTELY NO SENSE WHATSOEVER!!…. In what only characterizes a stiff, droning, mindless and expressionless mechanized drone who couldn't possibly muster the ability to self manufacture an original or innovative thought on their own volition even if their very life depended on it!!…And if you were to pull their shirt off, you would probably find a clustered circuit board with a vast highly complex configuration of wires transistors and resisters located just behind a removable flesh colored panel on their back, carefully programmed to only recite statutory clauses verbatim frontward's, backwards and sideways or blindfolded if need be in some mindless idiotic drone. And who by have had far to much starch pressed in their little shorty, shorts and have probably never once gotten laid in their whole entire pathetic existences!!...Dusty suddenly grinned widely putting her sleeved hand over her mouth and started giggling uncontrollably....Cameron' oh you liked that one huh?!.... yes it's so thoroughly and utterly asinine it's comical!!...And in weighing in the overall scheme of things it does ring true!...And who with an exceedingly gross level of efficiently and almost down to a science painstakingly waste vast amounts of your hard pressed, preciously allotted time and in many instances money. Then they both just smiled and loudly chuckled,...

Then he turned to her and gruffed you once asked me before earlier just what my Achilles heel is? Just what exactly is it that reduces Cameron into a mass of cringing and agonizing pain? Wincingly he exclaimed well now you know, CLOSE MINDED BLOCK HEADED IGNORANCE, INEFFICIENCY, INCOMPETENCE and DOWNRIGHT STUPIDITY, And I'm not talking about things that are so philosophically, technically or mathematically complex that take some kind of rocket scientist or learned scholar to fully grasp, comprehend or adopt. But in simplified matters where some inept and incompetent goof just can't seem to get it together enough to even grab his own ass with both hands!!...I've seen it far more than I care to in my 35 years and I just think somebody like that outta be smacked around or beaten within an inch of their life or at least until the pilot light of their mind begins to flicker on!!...Namely, a few past time restaurant general managers I've had to endure!!... Dusty just glared at him with a stunned and bewildered expression on her face as Cameron raved on...With me it strikes an inner cord in the way of a raw open nerve!!...Unchecked and unchallenged it festers an all consuming cancerous like malignancy that will continue to grow and spread throughout the world stunting any and all outward sociological progression, you know sorta like that old movie the blob!!...

And when it's vile malignant scourge is located anywhere it should be rooted out and isolated immediately upon discovery and eradicated by any and all means necessary!!...Even if in the end it ultimately has to be dynamited out with a lethal powder keg!!...And in much the same way as that two legged boogerized abomination will once we find it and do what so desperately needs to done!!.... An uneasy and wide eyed Dusty was very much taken back as she sheepishly looked on as he spoke…Nonetheless I at the time had no other choice but to be forced into constant contact and stomach those who while wearing blackened race horse type blinders were blissfully content to bask, wallow, bathe, baste and immerse themselves in it's filthy disease ridden trough!!.. And the real social travesty in such instances is the significant degenerative ramifications it poses to a healthy organism and ultimately society as a whole upon any contact at length. What usually winds up happening is the healthy host rarely raises the diseased one up to a receptive, responsive and enlightened level of openness and awareness but just the reverse. What usually happens is that the morally degenerative organism doesn't cease in it's vile duplicitous course until it finally succeeds in attaching itself to and despicably draining it's spirit then reprehensibly dragging the healthy one down with it to wallow in the same filthy degenerative depraved level of degradation, right there in the same putrid and slimy pig pen!! Dusty' What a colorful and descriptive analogy highlighting something so awful!! Cameron' Yes it is!!…awful, horrible and terrible and anything else you can think of to describe it!!…It's also a very unfortunate and inescapable fact of natures inexplicably disproportionate schematic of checks and balances!,…It disparaging yes I know but it's just another unfortunate aspect of her pitiless cruelty that we all must try and learn to live and cope with and possibly avert whenever it rears it's ugly head as best we can. Thanks but I think you've more than said enough and I'm pretty sure I get the picture now, Cameron', you do? GOOD That really puts my mind at ease and I'll sleep a lot better tonight now knowing that!!…Because to tell ya the truth for a moment there I was getting a little worried that I wasn't quite getting through!! Dusty' Boy I sure got a lot more than I bargained for in your expounded answer there Bub,…I really wasn't expecting you to stand up there on some soap-box at such length!…

Boy you really rage like a wild fire when it comes to this particular subject don't you!…YES!!..YOUR DAMN RIGHT I DO!!…Come to think of it,…that just very well maybe what that putrid vile thing were after is,…Dusty' Whatta-ya mean? Cameron' You know that horrid awful pus filled malignancy is,…The total compilation of total unyielding, pristine blind and blustering ignorance, that somehow was able to manifest itself stand upright in some bizarre putrid physical composite. The pure unadulterated conglomeration embodying every vile, reprehensible repugnant aberration historically known to man that somehow amassed itself into some living breathing slimy freakazoid that we've both come to develop such a deep abounding love, mutual respect and admiration for, whereby whose next visitation we eagerly anticipated with baited breath!!... Dusty just mildly shook her head back and forth with the corner of her mouth turned up in a slight wry smile. Ya know that's a very heart wrenching and thought provoking statement. You know if you keep swigging from that jug of wretched cynicism the poison is gonna eventually kill ya... Cameron' coyly uttered ya but at least I'll die with some degree of contentment anyway all other things aside!!.... I can't let fear or apprehension hinder or dominate our mindsets or impede our efforts or proceeding further in just doing what ultimately needs to be done here. A lot more innocent people would die if people like us just sat around on our hands and just did nothing out of fear. Look!... I've undertaken all the necessary precautions. And I'll guarantee you that if I aim one of these lit roman candles in the general vicinity of his slimy boogerized hide, it will most assuredly cool his jets for a good long while.

And besides it's not going to be like last time when we were caught completely off guard and unawares. Now we now know somewhat more of what it is were up against and will be far more aptly prepared this time for what pus bag has in store for us and we won't just be taken totally by surprise. Dusty' what is this? Cameron's three step program for covert ops preparedness training or something? Cameron just sort of grinned and replied yeah you might say so...Anyway were not going to be open or outwardly direct in our movements or overtly expose ourselves in any way either. If we do we will more than likely be taken by surprise again. That thing would have a field day and we'd just wind up in another brutal ringer washer and hung out to dry courtesy of Fedders coin operated laundry-mat, only we won't just get a little starch in our shorts this time!!...and in the end were just going to have to do our damndest to root him out,...you know and then ambush him out in the open when he least expects it before he has a chance to react to the extreme force that will be used against him. Dusty' Oh yeah and just what extreme force monkey-shines?… those oversized sparklers and firecrackers you have there in your little bag of lame ass ordnances!?…How is giving that vile freakazoid that escaped from the bowels of Hades a fireworks display going to do shit in the way of warding him off or keeping him at bay, Huh!?…Come to think of it while your at it why don't you just forego all the amenities and just invite ol' Slime-tard over for the annual 4th of July cookout to roast marsh mellows afterward!!…He could even bring a huge sample of that dark green Jell-O mold a recipe that's made him so famous and hailed in culinary art circles around the world for everyone to savor and enjoy. Only instead of garnishing it with pieces of fruit and pineapples going through it he's substituted that with a variety of human body parts!!…

Ya know that famous recipe has even landed him on the cover of Creature cooking magazine standing there posed and holding a plate of his wares topped off with a generous mouth watering helping of whipped cream and wearing a big white chefs hat and an apron that say's The Cook in bold letters on it. Hey!!…we could even serve him hotdogs, hamburgers and potato salad with a little miniature complimentary American flag stuck at his place setting commemorating his most recent exploits!!… Cameron' lowly murmured ok that'll be enough already…Then Dusty in a leering sarcastic expression chimed up further adding even more insult to injury…Hey Sherlock! Better yet we could even hold a ceremonial corn roast instead with big juicy slices of watermelon and tomatoes like my aunt Estelle and uncle August did at a semi annual family reunion they once held for all the distant relatives to attend, ya know they that came in from far and near just for a sample of that sumptuous mouthwatering recipe of burnt corn covered with slimy, smelly charred residue wrapped in tin foil overcooked on an open flame we had back in Morgantown west Virginia years ago when I was a kid!!…That final statement as well as the level of sarcasm it was dispensed with coupled with a mounting level of anger and frustration sparked an uneasy sense of awareness in the back of Cameron's mind as well as the sobering knowledge that, that horrible thing was out there somewhere exercising a free and unbridled reign of terror across the rural countryside and surrounding Boroughs. And that not only could it suddenly and without warning just emerge out of nowhere from amidst the shadowy hollows of a creepy dismal nocturnal nightscape. But they knew that sooner or later that they were going to have to at some point be forced to finally contend with it once and for all and someway, somehow figure out a way to end it's vile existence. And this seemed to further underscore the apparent futility of the grave situation overall.

And this was more than enough to just completely go against his grain and send him over the edge grossly incensing him tipping him off to the boiling point and setting off a short fuse to an explosive powder keg, And at that point he just snapped from the combined pressure of such a freakish concoction of bizarre negative forces in which seemed to converge on him from all sides. God-dammit!!...I've just about totally had it with you and your constantly belittling and undermining my constant efforts at safeguarding us with your defeatist attitude and I'm telling you right now that I'm just about three steps away from just throwing in the towel altogether and just throttling the shit outta you right here and now!!...Jokes aren't going to help us out here one iota, and I can't take it anymore!!...Now will you for once just close down that unceasing wind tunnel emittance of cynicism and angst just long enough for me to say Whatta I gotta say....So just knock it off for one single solitary minute PLEASE!!...Now this is no laughing matter and needn't I remind you that were in serious shit here!!...And we better start foregoing all the bullshit and begin pulling together on this thing or else!!...Because sister Sara!, as it stands now all we've got is each other!!...And once we do find out how in an viable and effective way were gonna end his pathetic, miserable and vile existence,....and we're gonna do it, see.... By now a stunned and dumbfounded Dusty just kept walking along side Cameron as he started babbling solemnly trying to take in some of what he was saying in attempts to draw a minimal level of ease and reassurance in just how they were going to go about successfully applying some kind of lethal force to that elusive, invincible two legged nightmare, as well as any further insight into what he had in mind from his methodically drafted plans. Dusty' became mildly appeasing at this point tried to shift the topic of conversation to that of a more lighthearted and jovial nature,…oh you mean try and catch him off guard and ambush him taking him by surprise like some roving band of rag-tag Salvadorian guerilla type fighters suddenly lunging out of the jungle thicket to pounce on their prey huh?…having been banished to the snake ridden, leech and mosquito infested jungles of some Godforsaken Banana Republic,…right?

Cameron' grinned,…Ha, ha yeah sort a like that, I'm afraid that's the only way were gonna stand a chance here…hey where'd you pick up on such an oddball and fruity term like that? Ya know that's usually something only somebody who's been in the military is acquainted with or has at least has watched the national news in the 70's!!… Dusty' You know in history class about Castro and Viet-Nam in school and on the televised national news. You know how those chronically educationally and progressively stagnant and backward third world countries and middle eastern regions who always seem to be in a continuous state of ongoing religious upheaval or political dissent and insurrection and plagued by civil unrest and strife in the streets are?… Oh yeah we'll maybe you should quit reading and watching the news all the time ya know it's nothing but death, despair, governmental and economic non-complacency and corruption, famine and war. With very little if any variation, And the only thing that changes are the dates. Dusty' I don't, just sometimes. Cameron' and for that matter, why do you think were out here wearing brown and green clothes, for the visual aesthetics or the fun of it? Dusty' abruptly jerked her head to one side while flailing her long locks out of her face replied laughingly, I don't know camouflage? Cameron stopped and turned to her warmly grinning and said as a momentary form of diversionary comforting ease in that if they stuck to an outlined covert pattern of movement they'd be safe, outta sight… and outta the reach of Big Daddy long-arms….And with a nervous throbbing, clammy and prickly feeling in his chest and a queasy one in the pit of his stomach he chuckled nervously, right again ya know I'll make a soldier outta you yet…Dusty with the re-occurring image of that horrid thing resting on the back of her mind nervously joked through a crooked grin" just not a Marine I hope, and then a moderate sense of security in each others protection in that if they just laid low and stayed pretty outta sight they'd be safe. Then a temporary sense of warming comfort and ease swept over the two of them as they felt a sudden release of much of the overwhelming level of pent up stress, fear, anxiety and tension in a moderate rush of relief as the two began nervously laughing.

Random like minded conversations such as this haphazardly presided over much of the walk along the railroad tracks and onward for several more miles. They conversed on just about anything that came to mind memorable events from their childhood pasts among other subjects in attempts to divert their present focus of attention and to alleviate some of the ongoing fear & apprehension and to somewhat alleviate the ever increasing level of fear and anxiety stemming from the looming uncertainty that constantly hung over them in a dogged haze like a dark ominous storm cloud. Then as the morning chill began to give way to a brisk cool autumn breeze amidst the suns soft comforting rays that accelerated the crisp aromatic scent of fallen leaves. Dusty suddenly asked Cameron, with a worrisome tone in her voice what'll we do when it begins to get dark? Cameron made no comment as he continued walking along and his seemingly blasé' demeanor permeated the air and was apprehensively picked up on by Dusty. Then her voice suddenly shifted, and it cracked in an agitated tone as she tersed in an intimidating tone of grave anticipation, you do have some kind of a plan of action in mind now that were both out here now don't you big bad point man?...

And then she lowly uttered through a grin that further incensed her as he then carelessly stated, I sure hope so or else we are both gonna wind up as the hapless guests at a boogerized held pig roast held in our honor, and then he turned to her and jokingly stated and I don't think you'd look to appetizing at the end of a skewer with an apple stuffed in your mouth,...ha, ha, ha, ha, ha,... That crass comment sent Dusty into a rage,...Ok that just tears it!!...I've had it up to here with your lame bullshit and satire already!!...Then she sternly glared over at him in a threatening and intimidating manner and barked,...Now are you going to start letting me in on some kind viable and concrete course action plan you carefully laid out in that brilliant mind of yours!!....Or am I gonna have to beat one outta ya!!...Cameron somewhat rattled and a little taken back at her sudden unexpected display of aggression shrank back from Dusty, trying to calm her down loudly uttered, relax,...relax, I'm working on something,...I still just need a little more time to work out some of the bugs that's all.

OH I JUST THINK YOU'VE JUST GOT BUGS ON THE BRAIN!!...Well, you just better hope ta God you do because if not it's not going to be in you being served up as slime at one of Mr. Fedders cookouts your gonna have to worry about, it'll be in trying to sleep with one eye open all night Buster!!.. Now can you tell me where the hell we are. Cameron' To tell you the truth, well I'm not exactly sure at this point, but hopefully we should be well within the safe bounds of the towns corporate limits here soon. Whatta ya mean your not sure!? I thought you had at least knew this area and would've had a better idea of where we are and where we were going before we set out on this maniacal little excursion!!....I thought you would've been more prepared in the way of knowing a little bit more about this area before you felt the overriding compunction to drag me out here in the middle of no mans land!!...I should've known better than to let you talk me into coming out here in the middle of nowhere just to shoot from the hip I outta have my head examined!!...And I'm not exactly thrilled at the prospect of having to break camp out here on a rise or out here in these woods either, just to have to stand armed watch in shifts unless I have an anti tank weapon with a sack of rounds to do it with in case that horrid, putrid two legged chemical malignancy decides to grace us with another one of his grand appearances or for that matter have to build a fire to cook and I'm not exactly in the mood to roast hot dogs or marshmallows!!.... Then Dusty's face suddenly went from a scornful glare to an imploring and worrisome concerted expression,... That thing does have an aversion to fire doesn't it?

Cameron just wryly gazed over at Dusty and after a short pause carelessly and unwittingly stated yeah I think so...Dusty' Whatta-ya mean you think so!!...Either it does or it doesn't now which is it Sherlock!!....Cameron' well from what I gathered from that horrific barn incident I guess one would be inclined to draw such a seemingly apparent conclusion from that now wouldn't they?….but I'm not at all for certain. Dusty' caustically and in a mocking tone tersed yeah I guess that would've been apparent!!….and what do you mean, your not for certain? Are you sure about anything at all!?...Cameron' Well when we were up in the hayloft and you were in the final process of baptizing it with a housewarming gift of combustion able accelerants via a Molotov cocktail I was not exactly in a primo position to see the whole momentous event now was I, if you'll recall I was standing off to your side and towards the back remember?…. Crystal' tersed yeah so what…

Cameron' well I didn't exactly witness the whole splendiferous incident myself or it's exuberant reaction to having been baptized in kerosene and then immolated now did I? I just heard it's high pitched screams as it ran fleeing from the barn in flames, and from what I gathered was that fire would more than likely be a somewhat fearful and debilitating prospect in deterring it's putrid advances nonetheless. Dusty' Oh thank Gosh phew for a minute there I was afraid we had nothing here in our little makeshift cache of wares that would prove out to be the least bit effective in warding him off with. I'll sleep like a baby tonight now knowing that!...And I'm so glad were not going to have to tolerate Mr. Fedders tenacious will to once again impose his brash and brazen presence and rudely infringe upon our gracious hospitality with his obnoxious and atrocious table manners as our fond and repeat dinner guest. Then I'll have to go to all that special out of the way trouble to make extra portions and set out another placemat!!…. For one he just sits there and gorges himself like a pig and for another he drools all over himself and in his food and even more profusely when he's done it's really disgusting and I find it very hard to keep down what I've already eaten much less further maintain any minimal degree of appetite in just having to sit there and watch it….. Cameron' ha, ha, funee were all gonna die!!…. Well we all just might as well make a great big colossal joke about it at every turn while we still can!!...Then he proceeded to grouse in a moderately sarcastically aggravated tone, you know with such a brilliant insightful mind and cutting intellect as you have I think you've been grossly neglecting your inner talents. Ya know with such a vast forte' of cutting satirical tidbits of cynical life's insight and anecdotes that are so incredibly humorous. I'd just like to say that you really make this trip almost bearable, maybe even enjoyable, and I'm really glad no fortunate that I chose you to bring along with me on this mission, yesiree I'm one lucky duck in that regard alright!...And for another,...for the life of me I don't know why you just continue to idly waste them on the doldrums and drudgery of that crappy pizza-catering assistant, delivery drivers job you work in that crude, greasy, smelly third rate old world ma and pa spaghetti house and Italian eatery you've been fritting away in all this time for all that big money you make. Ya know I think you've definitely missed your true calling,.. you really belong on a roving circuit tour bus some where heading up a band of third rate stand up comics or you could just simply bump Carson out and just take over his slot as the host on the tonight show you know your material just puts his to shame!! And your far more witty, insightful and funnier than his stale writers or that sidekick of his McMahon is!....You'd most surely have em' in stitches just busting at the seams with their squinched faces flushed white and then turning beet red flailing about and rolling in the aisles.... Dusty' hemmed "aw-geez"

Yet as the two continued along the center of the tracks the evening sun began to dissipate painting the clouds a vibrant bluish-purple hue amidst the sky opening behind the clouds revealing a bright orange and yellow luminescence and setting a crisp autumn chill to the air scented with withered leaves. Dusk was setting in and it was beginning to get cold and dark. Dusty' suddenly chimed up in an intent and worrisome tone tersely whined, I thought you said we weren't gonna get caught out here in the open after dark? Cameron' yeah so...Dusty's face angrily contorted at his blasé' expression and abrupt dismissal of her wary concern and she mockingly replied yeah so,...is that all you gotta say? So then whatta you gonna do about it smarty pants? Is there another deserted barn, horse stable or farmhouse in your bag of magic tricks we can crash in on for the night that's even within ten miles of this depressing Godforsaken wasteland? Cameron' heh, no I'm afraid not, not along this route anyway...Dusty' looked at him terrified...whaaaa... whadda you mean.!! You promised you'd have us safe and under wraps before nightfall were completely vulnerable and easy pickens out here in the open after dark!! That doesn't worry you none that were probably gonna have our assess hung out to dry!!...You know were desperately gonna need the assistance of the 2nd Air Cav to lend us fire support if that damn thing shows!! Well are you just gonna stand there looking like the worlds biggest dork or are you gonna say something comforting and reassuring to yours truly?...or better yet just come through for us like you said you would in the first place, or is that to much to ask?!!... Cameron just looked over at Dusty dumbfounded as she went on in her verbal chastisement at length. Are you just gonna wuss out and totally renege on that promise now? Ya now I don't exactly feel like duking it out here in the open with Mr. Boogers tonight I've got better things to do! And anyway it might muss up my hair and makeup!...I mean it would like totally put a real damper on the rad time I'm having with you on this awesome fun filled excursion you've so thoughtfully planned and arranged for my benefit, as well as the possibility of having this evenings dinner plans totally ruined and like that would be like a total bummer!! Ya know this is like really crampin' my perfunctory style... And then in a cutting sarcastic tone she tersed you know I'm gonna have to call my travel agent over this I want a refund!! Dammit!! will you just for once put a plug in it and quit your bit chin for one single solitary moment and I'll tell ya!!...VALLEY GIRL!!... Just gimmee a chance here and I promise I'll see to it that you make it to the mall tonight!!... Then he grinned wryly,...I'm not exactly reneging here,...

At that point Dusty could see by the preoccupied dazed expression on Cameron's face he had something in the works. There's just no barns or farmhouses in this direction that's all....abandoned or otherwise maybe a dilapidated weigh station or an outhouse or two...but no farmhouses he lowly chuckled. Dusty' marginally incensed, well if your not reneging then just what would you call it? And where do you propose then that we go for cover? The Salvation Army or the Red Cross? Cameron' we'll if you'll give me a chance and cease and desist flogging me with that heavy bullwhip tongue of negativity and defeatism for one moment I'll tell you...Ya know it's starting to get old,...now there's two places I know of up about a mile ahead...Dusty' anxiously yeah?....But there...well one of em' anyway is not entirely secure..."Dusty" sharply turned her head and

glared at Cameron intently and nervously replied, whatta you mean!?…
not secure…Well it's breached, at both ends you see there's a long brick
tunnel about one hundred yards long and fifteen feet high that runs
through some elevated and hilly ground that was hollowed out through
it for the purpose of some type of big drainage port or something having
to do with the war effort and mining for ore by low to moderate level
industry and the railroad at the time that sits adjacent to it about fifty or
seventy five yards off from an old abandoned mine shaft that was built
in the mid 1930's or something just before the war. It's been abandoned
there since the early seventies…Dusty blasted Cameron, that's it!! That's
it!?…That's what you drug us out here in the middle of nowhere for!!
A tunnel and a mine shaft!? It's starting to get dark and were out here
in the open with our pants down!!…Were mince meat out here!…Are
you outta your ever lovin gourd!!…Then Cameron in a leering grin said
Boy I'd really like to see that!!…Dusty' see what!?…You with your pants
down…Dusty wincingly tersed only in your dreams Noctrina!!…Ya
know I think your brain went through a tunnel and then down a mind
shaft and got lost in the blackened innards of the great abyss!!…How
the hell are we gonna be secure in an open ended tunnel if that thing
just happens in on us huh!? AND IT PROBABLY WILL…Wasn't the last
time bad enough for you huh!? If Mr. Invincible Pus-Bag happens in on
us while were in there were gonna need a flamethrower just to ward him
off and keep him at bay with!! And a mine shaft oh that's just brilliant!!

Hey Einstein for your information old abandoned mines have a
nasty habit of just caving in at any given moment!! You know I must've
had rocks in my head in just letting you talk me into coming out here in
the first place!! Cameron' Will you just pipe down for one minute and
let me finish!! If you don't wanna try the tunnel the mine shaft has a few
below ground sleeping quarters units that were built for mining work
crews that sit adjacent to it they maintained at the time. There's also
two big heavy double doors at the top of the entrances of each one of
these that swing open and closed and a huge sliding wooden beam that
secures them from the inside you know sort of like a stockade or a storm
cellar. Dusty' Good!!…because it's gonna have to be strong enough to
keep the Tasmanian devil out!! Cameron' well we could take refuge in

one of those I'm pretty sure we'd be relatively safe there. You might not like the accommodations though their a little dark and dirty and are probably bug infested. And on that comforting note Dusty seemed to calm down a bit, a locking thick storm cellar door, huh? Good!!, now yer talkin' sense again that sounds a lot better and as far as accommodations go I'd rather contend with bugs than take our chances out here in the open with slime ball on the prowl!!... Cameron' anyway there's also cots we can sleep on and an old wood burning stove in each of them we can cook dinner on or burn wood to stay warm at night if we have to, we can hold up there until morning I'm sure we'll be safe enough there and we should have ample time to get our bearings and make the state asylum before nightfall the following day if we set out early enough ok...I've even brought along a little transistor radio so we can tune into ongoing news broadcasts and keep abreast of any further developments on that awful creatures movements. Dusty' well what are we standing around here waiting for let's get the hell outta here and get behind the safety of those big thick heavy wooden doors you so glibly spoke of before it gets dark and we run into Mr. Congeniality again and he tries to kill us or even worse, hijacks us of all our four star restaurant quality foodstuffs!!...

Cameron' Aw how nice, I come up with a safe place for us to stay for the night and all you do is cast aspersions about my culinary art skills!!...And with that the two briskly trotted toward the secure location of the old abandoned miners sleeping quarters and the safety they held out as dusk began to set. Much of the open ground they had to cross consisted of distant sparse tree lines rough and hilly ground impeded with high weeds, large rocks, ratty vegetation, and infested with large hairy burrowing type spiders and snakes. They were escorted by the loud chirps of crickets and locusts that resounded in the distance as crisp night air resonated with the sweet scent of wildflowers throughout the countryside and the night sky was dotted with distant stars and an arched quarter moon illuminated their frantic dash to safety.

And as they both warily approached the dismal and desolate mining area several small bats swirled about in ditzy and erratic flight overhead in the night sky sputtering and chirping as they passed by mildly spooking the two intended overnight inhabitants as they surveyed the proposed area. The quarter moon that sat partially obscured by large puffy masses of swirling misty clouds partially obscuring it allowing it to shed it's creepy bluish green glow on the dilapidated objects below in and around the mining area casting an unsettling morose nocturnal setting. Dusty' yelled Oh that's just great!! I don't have to worry about pus-bag I'm going to get bitten in my sleep by some mangy vampire bat or something and turned into a bloodless anemic....Cameron' grinned wryly and unwittingly turned to Dusty and said, Ya know I just think you've been watching to much Barnabas Collins and Christopher Lee on television. And those aren't vampire bats either, goof! There brown bats, Dusty' Whaat?...vampire bats are cave dwellers and attach themselves on sleeping cattle in that fashion not humans and they are also not indigenous to this region. Dusty' Thank you Marlin Perkins for that latest installment of wild kingdom. BROWN BATS, BLUE BATS, RED BATS, OR GREEN ONES, I DON'T CARE IF THEIR RUBBER REMOTE CONTROL ONES HONED IN ON SOME CYBER GEEKS RADIO HAND SET!! I DON'T LIKE THIS PLACE ONE BIT!! AND I'M LIKE TOTALLY CREEPED OUT BY IT UNDERSTAND!! "Cameron" I take back what I said earlier about making a soldier outta you. Well as the old saying goes you can't make a silk purse out of a sows ear. Or in this case draft a set of khakis from of a mound of chicken doo… The location itself was dreary and desolate and had an eerie surreal omnipresence of grim despondency especially under the bluish green light of an Autumn moon. As Cameron shined the dull light beam from the beat up old flashlight on the big wooden door entrance way to the abandoned below ground workman's quarters he solemnly uttered I don't remember this place being in such a shabby and run down condition. The secured doors were strong but weathered and dilapidated and overgrown with vines and what appeared to be compiled tufts of stray tumbleweed that clung to their exterior. The desolate area under the moon light gave off a somber and dismal ambiance that seemed to exude a gloomy existential aura. This place really gives me the creeps and I'm afraid! Cameron startled quickly turned to Dusty as she exclaimed do we really have to stay here tonight in a frightened and agitated manner.

"Cameron mockingly replied in a sarcastic wine, yes we really do have to stay here tonight! And besides the Hilton hotel there down the street is all booked up for the night so I'm afraid this is gonna have to be it!! Uh but don't you worry sweetie I've all ready taken care of everything here, when I phoned in our reservations in advance they said they had this luxury honeymoon sweet available just for the two of us. Room service has laid out fresh towels and linen and a complementary bottle of champagne we can toast our comradeship while we dine on a sumptuous meal as we watch cable television!! Dusty just looked at him in an expression of utter disgust. And anyways where the hell else are we gonna go!! Can you think of a safer place for us to stay that's ten miles within earshot of civilization! complain, complain, bitch and complain…you know that's all I've heard you do for the past hour or so I told you that this wasn't going to be comfortable or easy, look can't you just bone up to the plate here a little and see this thing through to it's finish!! Sometimes life is fraught with inconveniences and uncomfortabilities just deal with it. Besides you'll score a grand slam in the eyes of your fellow citizens and it'll be something you can tell your grandchildren about some day! Dusty' not if I get immersed in a sea of dark green boogers first that will definitely be uncomfortable! And I don't care about hitting any homeruns or scoring communal accolades! I just wanna get through this thing in one piece ya know! As the two stood there at the entrance of the double doors Cameron just rolled his eyes and uttered oh gees as he beamed his old utility flashlight at the iron latch that secured the big storm like doors closed. Dusty just stood there with a peeved look of chagrin on her face as he pulled at the vines and overgrowth away in a moderate and frustrating level of exertion to clear and wriggle the big heavy doors open and then shined the light down the rickety old wooden stairs illuminating the dirty dismal work quarters of the old dugout. He bowed and extended his right hand out in a sarcastically ushering fashion towards her grinning and very cynically chimed. Our luxury sweet awaits my dear should I now swoop you up in my arms and carry you over the threshold? She barked, Oh no I won't be bitten by a vampire bat I'll probably be bitten by a big hairy spider or a rattle snake down there tonight in my sleep! Cameron' Oh will you just knock it off and just get your ass down there and cooperate for once in your life before fart face shows up here with all the noise! And as for the big hairy spider goes I've come prepared for that too, I brought a huge can of Black Flag insecticide see here it kills everything from spiders to cockroaches so don't get your panties in a bunch and quit yer complainin' you know were damn lucky we have a safe place to stay at all tonight and you know it!!

Then as Cameron continued to aim the dull flashlight beam down the dilapidated old wooden stairs below that led to a dirty old wooden makeshift wooden floor with about four cots with old burlap covered mattress's and pillows and even a couple of musty old woolen blankets still on them. There was some crumpled up decades old newspapers, invoice receipts, liquor bottles and other debris strewn about the dirty old floor. As Cameron stepped downward he turned and flung his duffle bag onto the deck below and as it made a loud thud he turned back to look at Dusty and held out his arms in a receiving manner saying…well are you going to just stand there and wait for a prompt from fungus face or are you gonna do the right thing and take cover down here? Dusty' I suppose, what other choice do I have? Cameron' none…The stairs were a little rickety so Cameron grabbed hold of her as she negotiated the first couple of filthy dilapidated stairs at the top as he escorted her down into the abandoned old shelter. He then panned the gloomy night time horizon up top once more to see if that thing was anywhere in sight of a hundred yards. Then he grabbed Dusty's duffle bag of provisions and rolled it down the stairs on it's side. He gave the outer perimeter one last look before pulling the big heavy doors closed and latching them from the inside with the big wooden beam there these doors are strong enough to keep the jolly green giant out. We outta be ok here until morning, then he looked over to Dusty raising his brow in a stern questioned expression on his face stated, that is of course if nobody makes any loud noises or unnecessary outcry's that would almost surely draw a whole lotta' unwanted attention our way.

Dusty abruptly folded her arms and beamed an aggravated look at him and replied in a sarcastic tone of dissent, meaning me. Cameron said no meaning the Lucky Charms leprechaun bursting at the seams to bestow a generous well deserved pot of gold on us meager little ol' impoverished underlings. In a life long awaited rescue from our inescapable systemically mandated, indigent station in life, yes goof meaning you! Then in a haughty tone exclaimed, Ya know not to many people know about this place it's a well guarded secret among us tightly nit group of covert operators like me. Dusty just rolled her eyes and tersed oh you gotta be kidding, who the hell do you think you are you James Bond or something?…He wouldn't be caught dead out here in a filth hole like this!! Then he flipped the switch on the old campers utility light panel illuminating the dismal sleeping quarters and the dilapidated sticks of old makeshift furniture such as end tables with empty kerosene lanterns still sitting on them that were no longer serviceable and an old wooden dish cabinet in the room with just a couple of filthy broken dishes and a coffee cup still left in sitting in it. An old cast iron skillet and pot that sat atop the old wood burner was faintly visible from the dim gloomy florescent light the portable utility panel emitted. I see why as Dusty went over to the little dinner table struck a wood stick match and lighting a candle that sat there to further illuminate the room in a dull sallow light. And said as she sat down on the edge of one of the old cots and turned to wriggle herself out of her brown jean jacket. What kind of hermitized troll would care to know about this broken down old shack out here in the middle of nowhere? "Cameron" you'd be surprised,… we may be able to cook breakfast here in the morning on this cast iron stove, we'll see, but for now anyway were just gonna have to be satisfied with cold deli meat sandwiches and Doritos for dinner. I'm not going out there at night scavenging for wood to burn with Mr. Boogers looming about on the horizon.

As Dusty was shedding her jacket onto the cot in back of her she suddenly stopped and got a wide eyed sarcastic leer on her face and replied with a gleefully cutting note ya know that really shows good sense and puts my mine totally at ease…refraining from prowling around outside after dark with that Boogerized freak lurking in the shadows and all, just about to lunge outta nowhere and spring into action at any given moment!… Cameron' as he was reaching into one of the duffle bags for some stale corn chips and baloney sandwiches said boy oh boy you just never let up for one moment do you? You're the incessant flame under my boiling hot cauldron of agitation and frustration, or the pain in my ass I just haven't decided which. This form of sarcastic sniping was a sort of pressure release and momentary diversion from the overwhelming stress, and anxiety this constrained endeavor has held out for the two thus far as a wretched continuance that went on throughout much of the trip. And as he shoved a handful of those stale aftermarket corn chips into his face while simultaneously unwrapping the cellophane from one of the much to be desired baloney and cheese sandwiches grumbling through a mouth full's of food crumbs flew from his puffed checks and pursed lips. Ya know if you were any funnier I just don't know if I'd be able to stand it!! I'm just ready to bust wide open at the seams were gonna have ta somehow figure out a way to contact the local EMT'S from way out here to stitch me up again!!… Then with a chagrinned look on his face he tossed a wrapped sandwich and a bag of corn chips in Dusty's direction down on the dirty old table that he was sitting at and as they plopped down on the tables edge dust flew up and some stale chips flew out of the bag and onto the floor and he muffled the words through a mouthful of sandwich here work your jaw on some a this crap I made it myself special with just you in mind? Ya know we still have a long ways to go and your gonna need your strength, so eat up!…. And maybe it'll take your mind off all this other crap that's been going on. Strength! I'm gonna need all the strength and fortitude I can muster within myself just to be able to gag this shit down!

Dusty rose up from the beds edge shaking her head back and forth in an agitated manner of distain as she came over to join her comrade in arms in what was at the very best an amateur level of soldiertude in this bizarre theater of Boogerized conflict for night time chow. Then as she sat down at the table and began unwrapping one of the stale sandwiches to take a bite she exclaimed now I know why in the service they refer to eats as mess!! And this is definitely a MESS!! And while grinning at Cameron uttered,…Marine. Then as she sarcastically held up the partially eaten sandwich as if she was really making a champagne toast, glared over at him and chimed mockingly Semper Fi. Then as Cameron reached into his duffle bag and pulled out two more cans of that cheapo ten cent off brand soda pop tersed was that suppose to funny?.... You know I should be awarded the bronze star just for having to bear the brunt of your constant put downs and your brand of off color humor.... Here, you can wash that crap down with more of this cruddy flat as a pancake soda, then Dusty lowered the warm somewhat slimy and barely palatable baloney sandwich down while looking over at him and said you know it's already hard enough to try and pretend this crap tastes even halfway good without all the crude and unsavory comments. But do you always have to constantly remind us of how poor we are all the time?

Then Cameron leaned over to retrieve one of those outdated 9 volt battery powered hand held nineteen seventies transistor radios from a cargo pocket of his faded BDU's and set it up on the table. And as he nervously turned the little round dial on the side it popped hissed and sputtered with a muffled, tinny and staticky sound as he fretfully searched up and down the dial for a news station that would come in over the airwaves clear enough through the crude staticky reception to understand. Dusty satirically leered over at Cameron as he unbeknownst to her tried to hone in on some halfway audible news broadcast that would report any further public updates on that things current movements. And the nearest radio station from their location was about twenty miles away. She gleefully chimed ooooh AM radio with supper! Not only am I being wined and dined in such posh surroundings but I also get to be serenaded by staticky old farty music and news broadcasts as well boy Cameron you sure really know how to spoil a girl don't you? What next I wonder a freezing cold water bubble bath in some filthy old wash basin and a burlap towel to dry off with?. SHUDDUP!!...HUSH!! Listen this is deadly serious! Now pipe down for a moment, I'm trying to see if anything else has happened since we left. Then suddenly all the lights went out, all the smiling, and the jovial gayety of the moment as well as the fluid color left Dusty's countenance leaving a flushed stark look of terror on it. She just sat there frozen still in frightful anticipation at the grim prospect of hearing further developments and reports of terror and mayhem purported by that horrid thing.

This gave way to a very frightened and panicked look on a little girls face as a radio station local to where they lived was beginning to come in over the airwaves. The muffled staticky broadcast popped and sizzled in and out as the hysterical voice of the panicked commentator came in over the poor reception in a stern and urgent plea against a corny bleeping tickertape sound of an AM radio stations musical news broadcast introduction played. The newscaster frantically began to give a grave descriptive account of the latest events that transpired. Cameron quickly pulled up the small antenna on the side of the tinny little sound box and it came in a little clearer. The frantic petrified voice of the radio announcer came over the speaker in an urgent warning prompting those in the surrounding listening area to stay tuned for further instructions and station identification! We here at AM WKRZ 106.3 will pause momentarily in order for local stations to identify themselves......We interrupt this program to bring you this urgent bulletin!!...we have just received official confirmation by local and surrounding authorities of the discovery of what looks to be that of a small compact car possibly an old Datson, VW beetle or Rabbit driven by a group of youths in their late teens and early twenties, and it is presently undetermined as to whether or not they resided locally or came in from out of town. The car was discovered on a remote and desolate stretch of road early this morning by a random group of joggers witness to the horrific scene just happened by. The car itself and it's occupants were outwardly unrecognizable as being just that, due to having been encased in some sort of bizarre foreign substance of unknown origin. The material itself is described as a seven foot mound of bluish green ooze that had solidified into some sort of bluish-green semi-transparent rubbery material given over a period of several hours. The joggers as well as the police were totally aghast and filled with utter revulsion at some of the other freakish material found in and around the immediate vicinity of the car. It was also reported that some pasty white substance resembling paper mache' or spoiled latex house paint was strewn about and abundant amounts with some other sort of olive green blobby goop that lay heaped in mounds in and around the encased vehicle.

And it is now believed that some type of night stalking monster is at the bottom of these ghastly findings and the once collectively held consensus of the possibility of a group of local malcontents with a sadistic and perverse sense of humor was responsible has now been dismissed. Then as the hysterical tone in the commentators voice intensified it went on to instruct the general public….local citizens are as of now forewarned not to venture outdoors after dark as the local towns mayor has issued a state of emergency and has enacted communal marshal law! No one is permitted outside at dusk with the exception of police or local National Guardsmen! Dusty's face flushed white and her eye's protruded as her facial expression contorted and began twitching. She started panting and drawing airless breaths as she began to hyperventilate, she was now going into shock. Then the news caster's voice took on a stern fearfulness in it's tone as he delivered this imminent warning; All citizens!! please be advised to lock all your doors and windows at night we have just received official confirmation…the town and it's surrounding principalities are in imminent danger!!

Dusty went into a frenzied fit of hysteria of bellowing screams, flailing about knocking over the rickety old table and chairs as well as spilling that nights dinner rations and the lit candle onto the floor. Just then Cameron stood up and bum rushed Dusty tackling and quickly wrestling her to the dirty old wooden floor putting her in a taut submission hold while clasping one of his big meat hooks over her wailing mouth then as he squeezed her cheeks tightly together in a loud whisper Shut-up!! Will you Shut-your mouth!!….Do you wanna let that damn thing know were here!!…..Why don't you just climb up on a high water tower and broadcast our position clear across the countryside through a loud bullhorn!!….Your gonna give us away…Do you wanna get us killed!?….Now shut your mouth!!,…and get hold of yourself!!…..As the two lay there on the floor for several moments Dusty seemed to calm down a bit maybe it was due to total exhaustion from struggling to try to outmuscle Cameron but for now she was quiet. The dim light from the old campers utility light panel had cast eerie elongated shadows of the two kids extremities and other objects in the creepy old darkened miners quarters of long ago against the wall.

Cameron's big hand was still covering Dusty's mouth and her eye's rolled backward in a fixed and beseeching gaze at him. The little transistor radio had hit the deck with such force it shattered apart in cheesy little tin and plastic pieces all over the floor. Cameron just looked over at it with a chagrinned look and shaking his head back and forth said oh well I guess we won't be receiving any further news updates for awhile as he snickered. And just then he got a clever idea to try placate Dusty's sudden fit of frenzied hysteria and subdue her potential for further outburst and calm her down and maybe even make her laugh and relax a little. He then raised up his other hand to cast a surrealistic and amusing shadow of his hand on the drab crudely textured old wall. And then he stuck up his thumb and split his index and fore fingers apart in the center in an opening and closing fashion simulating the head of a barking dog. And in a high pitch whine he cried Dusty, Dusty bark, bark, bark, it's me Rover the roaming Dover I've been searching all along the countryside for you...Don't you recognize my voice? Then he let his forefinger drop down over his pinkie to simulate a-the wagging tongue of a loyal boxterrier in eager anticipation searching for it's owner as he satirically made panting sounds of exhaustion. Then her eye's sort of squinted with little beads of tears streaming from them and you could see she was smiling and her body mildly shook in his arms as she laughed through his clenched hand over her mouth. Then he slowly removed his other hand from over her mouth and made a partially knuckled fist in an attempt to simulate the silhouette of a fire hydrant. And the with his other hand he went into entertainment mode and put on a personal and private shadow simulation puppet show entitled, "The tinkling doggie" for his friend Dusty.

The next morning found the two laying there huddled on the floor together in each others arms as they had just fallen asleep there from sheer mental and emotional exhaustion instead of just climbing into their adjoining cots. Cameron was the first to wake,... moving about in a stiff groggy fashion as he lifted his arm off of Dusty sitting up a little and looking around the room in a semi comatose state. He looked over at the big double doors with the latch thrown on them and he could see the warm perennial rays of the morning sun emanating their way through the crack between the doors that had a calming and soothing effect on the two signifying all was well at least for now. And that they had survived the nights grave uncertainties un intruded by that horrid thing that indiscriminately lurked about the countryside. Maybe it was due part in part to a combination of sheer dumb luck and the vast unlimited acreage afforded by a roaming countryside they could easily conceal themselves in. And that mere fact of that alone that kept that dreadful creature at bay and from just happening in on them once again for a night long deluge of relentless and unbridled terror. For in this particular instance the night was subsequently tranquil and unintruded, null and void of those ghastly God awful moans and creepy cackle like clucking in the distance signifying the incursion of grave and imminent doom.

Then Cameron lethargically rose to his feet and went over to fetch his duffle bag to retrieve their morning rations. He knew he wouldn't even be moderately successfully in cooking breakfast at least in the conventional sense, on that broken down eyesore of a wood burning stove he knew it was a futile prospect so therefore he wasn't even going to try. The most he could do with it was build a fire in it to warm the place if the temperatures really dipped to unbearable levels in the night but no doubt he'd have to gather the wood in the day for painfully obvious reasons. So instead he made a substitution of the next best thing. An assortment of about a dozen hardboiled eggs at the house and brought an ample supply of beef jerky and a very large thermos that kept coffee hot for days at a time. And there was also a loaf of some type of Greek bread that was stale, course and stiff in it's consistency like tearing apart cotton candy or fiberglass insulation for houses, and it had a funny sweet taste to it. He really didn't like it much and sometimes it came with raisons in it but he would eat it nonetheless as it would go good with this cold much to be desired rangy breakfast he prepared. And besides he was poor and beggars can't exactly be choosers and it was better than nothing. His distant aunt in New Hampshire had baked the bread and always made to much and always sent that out to him over the holiday's and he brought it along for consumption before it went totally hard and stale and had to be thrown out for the birds.

Dusty heard Cameron rustling about and groggily rose to a seated position there on the floor and jammed the knuckles of her balled up fists into her eye's while yawning and then stretching out her arms as she awoke from a deep exhausted sleep. She just sat there for a few moments flumped there on the floor. And in her mussed disheveled appearance turned to Cameron who glared at her over the brim of his bright orangish-red coffee stained mug with the iconic Marine Core bulldog logo on it. Cameron' did I wake you? She had her arms folded across her knees in a huddled position on the floor paused for a moment and uttered no…then she abruptly turned her head saying well yeah kinda I guess I heard you stirring around so I figured I might as well get up too. She sat there in a leering grin at him for a few moments oh it get's so cold in here at night…He just sat there warily anticipating yet another one of her discontenting digs about the quality of their lodgings or his packed lunches. Do you mean to tell me we slept right here on this dirty old floor all night with no blankets? "Cameron" we had mutual body heat to keep us warm…I guess we were so exhausted from the overwhelming stress and anxiety of this thing that we just collapsed and passed out right here on the floor. But your going to wish it still was once that's replaced with the searing heat of a midday sun high overhead starts reigning down mercilessly on us once we resume our hike…were gonna have to draw from as many waterbeds and streams as we can to keep from dehydrating and dropping dead from heat prostration. She continued to leer over at Cameron…is that breakfast? He took a gulp from his coffee mug lowered it while slurping and said yep…it is. What is it? Can I have some? Well let's see here, gee I dunno if it'll meet your exceedingly high standards of palatability I mean after all Mrs. Folgers didn't brew it and you might think it tastes like warm rusty water or paint thinner or something…and I wouldn't wanna put you through such an unpleasant experience again now would I? She just looked over at him grinning, aw c'mon now don't be such a sour Gus! I was just fun in and I'm sure that what you have there for us for breakfast this morning will surpass the taste thrill of one of those armpit sandwiches that were fetched out of a dirty old sweat sock on a hot summer day!!

Cameron became moderately incensed at her incessant comments belittling his perceived lack of culinary skills prompting his minimal level of amusement to wear a little thin. The constant ribbings he took on these little outings at his expense directed at his shortcomings in food preparedness and the quality thereof that cracks were beginning to appear in their friendship exposing what was fast becoming a raw and open a nerve. And with that last cutting remark he tersed…ya know if the grub I bring along out here on our little excursions doesn't meet with your satisfaction and your critically high standards of palatability you don't have to eat them anymore!…you are more than free to start packin' your own lunches!

Dusty' could see the hurt in his eye's and didn't want to aggravate the situation by further adding insult to injury by needlessly rubbing anymore salt in the wound. After all there was really no viable purpose to it anyway so she made appeasing, detracting statements to in attempts to placate his ensuing aggravation. Aw c'mon now take it easy I was just kidding I'm sure that what you have there for breakfast will amply suffice, pause…..what did you bring us for breakfast anyway? "Cameron" lowly murmured hard boiled eggs beef jerky and a loaf of my aunts Greek style bread and a thermos full of hot coffee…cream only. Dusty' what I didn't hear you? And then Cameron repeated the same sentence in a louder tone of voice. Oh that's wonderful it sounds great, can I have some? "Cameron" uttered in a sullen lull…yeah I guess so I mean, I made this stuff because I figured it wouldn't be feasible to try and cook meals on this old wood burning stove breakfast or otherwise, so I figured this would be the next best thing. Dusty' It's perfect!! You showed great thought and careful planning as well as concern in seeing to it we had the next best thing to bacon, eggs, toast or home fries it was very thoughtful. After breakfast the two did what little they could in the way of personal hygiene with a washcloth a bar of soap and an old wash basin filled with heated water Cameron found in an old cupboard, As the two proceeded up the flight of old wooden stairs to the outside

Cameron abruptly turned to Dusty firmly placing his open hand on her forearm as he reached in the old leather satchel for the thirty two. Better wait here until I check it out up top and see to if everything is clear first before you come up too…I just wanna make sure Mr. Fedders is not up there lying in wait to ingratiate us with another one of his fond warm heartfelt receptions pre-arranged for our benefit, heh, heh. Dusty' And here and I always thought that thing was strictly nocturnal, you know a creature of habit, one that only manifests it's vile nightmarish presence for the specialized benefit of those lucky chosen few at night. You mean he comes out in the day time too!?…Cameron turned to look at Dusty and hemmed, yeah he comes out in the day too goofus,…Dusty', Won't he just melt like my ex-land lady or the wicked witch of the west or dry up and blow away like Count Dracula or something if he's exposed to daylight? Cameron replied to her with laughing eyes while shaking his head back and forth saying You know I really think you watch to many of those corny old movies on television,…Dusty' oh no not at all… but I think it would probably slow him down drastically and he would experience a great deal more difficulty in carrying out his malignant exploits that's all. But we do have to consider that possibility as well before we proceed on ahead further. Now you stay here and wait while I check it out up there ok…then he turned to her and said…And don't you get any funny ideas like taking matters into your own hands in doing something rash or foolish now….We've come to far to have anything in the way of a monkey wrench thrown into the internal components of this carefully set out plan. You know a squad leader's first priority is in safeguarding his men prior to proceeding further on with military operations….You know, and before he could finish his sentence.

Dusty joined in with him in an old military adage…you know in the marines we used to have a saying, Dusty sarcastically chimed in and the two finished the sentence together. This really infuriated Cameron as he exclaimed yes!! in a very peeved manner at Dusty's utter contempt and lack of respect which seethed through in a moderate level of disdain moreover at their threatening and disparaging circumstances came through in a mocking level of distain, and total disregard for spree décor or the military's regimented and established structure resonated through once more in the disrespectful tone of her contemptuous sarcasm and this led to a yet another contentious debate on the subject. And then instead of going the rest of the way up the stairs to finish his topside security check he abruptly stopped placing his palm on the side of the wall steadying himself and turned to Dusty...Ya know I've had more than my fill of your smart-ass remarks I'd say about ten miles back to the tune of It's a long, long way to Tipperary that will undoubtedly more than hold me over for the remainder of this trip and then some, as well as your constant complaining making what we gotta do even harder than it already is, and for someone who not only lacks any discipline themselves doesn't have even so much as a modicum of respect for this country's former service members!! "As a disparaging result Dusty began to vent as a direct result of the mounting pressure and stress and intense fear of the looming uncertainty of the situation than, that of the random topic of discussion that was about to vehemently ensue like two rams locking horns in bitter and volatile contention. Is that so! Well for your information buster, I just happen to be a member of a military family myself an Army one as a matter of fact and I've heard all the stale repetitive rhetoric to death!

From the halls of Washburn Haven to Tripoli and back, sung to the same tired worn out old tune with very little if any variation! And to tell you the truth, I've had my fill for quite some time now in just having to constantly hear about it just about at every turn when I was growing up!! ....and needn't I remind you here sergeant!! that were not a company of infantry soldiers here!!, Cameron' I wasn't a sergeant I was a lance corporal..."Dusty" whaat...And like a little kid without a care in the world went on in his relaxed and blasé' explanation that just further infuriated Dusty to the point of unbridled rage. I never made sergeant but I was a squad leader and we got to wear an armband signifying that. Dusty' Oh Gawd!!...semantics your killing me with friggin' semantics!!...who cares!!...it's been about ten years ago or so since you got out now hasn't it!! so why don't you just put a proverbial cork in it and give it a rest!...and for that matter we're not a platoon!! and there's not even enough of us to make up a crummy squad! I hate to be the one to burst your bubble but you can just snap outta your self infused delusion lance corporal and start joining all the rest of us here in the real world! Cameron just sat there lowly looking down in a subdued and dejected manner like an admonished little boy who'd just had the total summation of all his self enthused expectations suddenly deflated like a prized carnival balloon he'd won at the county fair by one of his parents. Or in that he wasn't going to get any cotton candy or carnival toys this year because maybe they weren't going to be able to make it there after all. Dusty' we're just two mentally exhausted, nerve ravaged and thoroughly terrorized people who are just tired enough, and fed up enough and angry enough to form this pathetic inadequately fortified little posse' and go after that horrid thing on our own volition and hopefully catch it off guard and ambush it without being totally immersed in a dreadful sea of that horrid dark green slime ourselves in the process! And then inadvertently a contentious debate slowly began to unfold on the subject of the credibility of honor modern non-conventional warfare tactics held out that was initiated by Dusty moreover as an indirect result of the steady surge of pent up tension and resentment resulting from the looming threat of imminent danger that was always present and hung over like a black ominous storm cloud. But moreover as an involuntary pressure release valve stemming not only from the mounting animosity poised by the outward contrast clearly evident in their two conflicting personalities. But in such lame and blustering attempts to try and get under each others skin and provoke an angered reaction.

The overwhelming tension and stress was so thick one could've cut it with a knife as a tersely sniping argument began to steadily ensue. Then in their inward strained contention arising from the steady escalation of their grave circumstance the two pugnacious contenders began to pick up on just about anything they thought they could effectively use as a figurative bludgeoning weapon to wield against the other they could get their hands on in vehement attempts to pummel the other into submission. This was sparked by a flustered ferocious and panicked level of angst down there in that dirty dismal old workman's dugout in a pitted bout of verbal pugilism. "Her steadfast position moderately incensed Cameron as she began to purposely goad him in further attempts to get an incensed reaction from him. Knowing full well he was once directly indoctrinated into such as part of his military hazing as a heated and contentious debate inadvertently began to ensue on the subject. But you seem to keep overlooking one important factor in something like this that's never gonna change!. In extreme and desperate circumstances such as this you just can't plunge forth blindly ahead out in the open cloaked under some figurative shield of a Victorian age code of honor in the self deluded notion that the false sense of security it brings with it will be sufficient. And in the lofty hopes that it will be ample to your survival based on some corny, syrupy bygone notion of knighted nobility and expect to remain impervious to very real and formidable danger! Dusty tongue tied at this point just looked on at Cameron with a moderately chagrinned expression on her face as he spoke. Now I can't overemphasize this enough, the same rule of thumb applies here!!…

Nothing else is more befitting, now on a seek and destroy mission such as this one we're on is and incidentally is one I was trained for, first and for mostly we are gonna have to move about carefully and methodically laying as low as we can pretty much the whole time in staying outta sight as much as possible!!…That statement neither swayed or impressed Dusty at that point in her sullen unenthused expression on her face. You mean they trained you to face off and do battle with boogie monsters in the Marines?…No smart ass!!… but I think my relevant background more than qualifies me to assume command here.!!….Now were going to have to draft an effective and mutually acceptable course plan of action that we can both live with. Our best defense will be in a well orchestrated and carefully thought out plan of implementation to root out the enemy and ambush there's no other way!!…."Dusty" were not in a war here!!…Oh yes we are, I beg to differ that's exactly what this is a war!!…And were certainly not infantry soldiers either BUSTER!!… "Cameron" Your damn right we are!!…That's just exactly what you are out here and there's no way around it so you just get that through your pretty little head right now and for your information you've just been drafted!!…And I think from here on out you should concentrate al of your inward combative energies against that horrid thing instead of me!!.. Now we have to slowly proceed outwardly with due caution kinda' like plodding a careful path through a mine field or something, got it sis!!…and especially in this case only under the strict guise of heavy concealment especially when it comes to confounding the ill designs of that horrid putrefying thing!…And as a former soldier myself, I strongly feel that in this particular instance this is the best and most practical approach, you know that two legged freakish slimy chemical garbage dump is still out there lurking about somewhere you can best believe that!!…

Dusty just turned her head to one side rolled her eyes and lowly uttered ooh boy. Cameron' Why do you think were both out here dressed in only green and brown clothes for?!…It's not because I'm overly fond of the color scheme,…were kinda like partisan's in a boogerized resistance movement. Now were gonna have to lay in wait to try and catch this vile invincible pus filled metamorphosis off guard and totally by surprise and strike it before it has a chance to react against the overwhelming force that will be used against it minimizing very grave risks especially to yours truly…Because in this particular instance TESS!!…contrary to popular belief, above all else when all is said and done I still put a very high price on my own bacon!!…And on this little pleasure excursion I've so painstakingly arranged for our mutual benefit and enjoyment!… I'm afraid I'm gonna have to be the one to take the lead here, for one thing I'm well versed in the fine art of covert opts, and like it or not I happen to be the only one standing in the limelight as your one and only main line of defense!!…Now were gonna have to continuously hone our skills in the fine art of concealment and ambush!!.. Dusty' do I have to smear green and black grease paint all over my face in the pattern of tiger stripes too?…"Cameron" yeah if ya want too, …Now, in doing it your way we'll just put ourselves in the direct line of fire and we most assuredly won't stand a snowballs chance in hell of coming outta this alive!…and most likely we will be gruesomely expunged, no totally immersed and saturated in that vile sea of dark green boogers like all the others we've been reading and hearing about in the news, immortalized in a dark green Jell-O mold, Pollyanna!! And that's where I come in this is right up my alley. It just so happens that it's my area of specialization!…

And then Dusty's outmoded and conventionalist beliefs on the subject began to resurface further igniting a slow and steady strain of underlying contention between the two friends. Ok,..ok…maybe you've got me there!…But do you always gotta keep bringing up the fact you were a Marine all the damn time? You know lotsa people were Marines!!,...so what!!...You know that really was a long time ago wasn't it? And I think you would've or should've mellowed out or even forgotten it altogether by now shouldn't you of?...and for another, I'm just a firm believer that a man a real man doesn't have to hide his face behind green, brown or black striped grease paint for instance and continuously throughout the remainder of his life and make references to having belonged to such an exclusive organization presently as a past tense in some Especially a warring one that operates under such covert guise's and go's to such extreme lengths to conceal himself from an adversary such as wearing subdued, camouflaged clothes, or moves from within the dense foliage of bushes, trees or the thick jungle terrain that dense vegetation affords, and fires on his opposition with a heavy machine gun or a field piece and often times from great distances and sometimes not even knowing if it's occupied at all.…I mean I feel a man, a real man should face his opponent openly and directly, in any type of conflict be it a fistfight or a Governmentally orchestrated one such as a ground war you know, and would forego such extreme measures to continuously remain concealed on a battlefield, I mean the latter is sort of cowardly don't you think? Then she contentiously winced over at him in fervent hopes that she'd struck a nerve in him and was going to elicit some kind of incensed reaction.

Cameron just sat there with the corners of his mouth curled up smiling in a taunting rhetorical grin. Oh you mean like Hercules, Sir-lance-a-lot the lone ranger or Prince Valiant or something right? and then he leered over at her in a mockingly defiant glare...Then he figuratively put the ball back in her court in a taunting statement, That's a rather corny brand of antiquated Victorian age idealism don't you think there Annabelle? and somewhat laughable by today's standards? That statement humiliatingly incensed and put her off as she was suddenly stricken by a humbling numbing cold pulsating adrenalin rush in her chest and throat as she could feel herself overcome by an embarrassing feeling of humbling animosity towards Cameron welling up inside of her as she could see that he was now beginning to taunt her in a mockingly subtle way in lieu of her conflicting views forcefully relegating her into a compromising position were by she was figuratively subjugated as she despairingly went into a defense mode. And after a momentary pause he went on to further state, no just a cold, hardened object in an impersonal brand of modern nonconventional warfare that's all, and the same rule of thumb applies here in us going up against that horrid thing, it's very befitting in this grave instance don't you think?… There was a momentary pause and a worrisome glare as Dusty made no comment she was now at a momentary loss for words….Cameron' and for another thing your not regarded as a man or trained to fight as one anymore as in the past you are now methodically transformed into some kind of hardened mechanized device a tool if you will with no more feeling of significance than an inanimate object totally void of the milk of human kindness manly or otherwise. And an integral part of the initial grueling process of your indoctrination is psychologically being torn down, rebuilt and relegated to the same similarity of importance as a tool or a mechanical device. Relegated to the same classification as a tank a claymore mine or a field piece.

Figuratively speaking they rip out those warm red squishy innards and replace em' with government issued one's made of iron and steel. You know in basic they used to tell us be an individual and we'll be zipping your cold stiff ugly toothless face into a rubber bag to a long box with metal handles!! And the D.I's used to refer to us as warm bodies,… sometimes they'd bark, gimmee three warm bodies over here!!. "Dusty" winced and said oh how awful who in their right mind would want any part of something like that…Cameron' well, anyone who couldn't find a job, got kicked out of the house by their parents when they reached 18 or for all intents and purposes had literally nothing going for them at all in the way of viable or remotely lucrative prospects. Dusty' Boy the world sure can be a very sad and cruel place can't it….Cameron' unfortunately yes, it often times can, but furthermore the grey undertones modern conflict encompass's are very often steeped in radical left-wing extremist held views in often times conflicting religious, political or economic ideologies. What you were describing there before deary was some kind of knight in shinning armor mounted on a girded white steed from long ago medieval times poised for the joust, it's utterly preposterous, and something that jumps out at you from the stale parchment pages of an old Grime's fairy tale storybook there princess,…it's antiquated Victorian age notion of chivalrous conflict that has been long since passé' my dear, especially from a globally modern ideological standpoint, in it's political, religious and economically grim and uncertain times!… And if it were somehow possible to physically manifest it and put it on exhibit in the Smithsonian right now it would be sitting right there next to a suit of armor or the iron horse…It's only symbolism is linked to some lofty unrealistic nineteenth century Provincial style code of honor that no longer exists or holds credence anymore except in corny old story books. Dusty just stared at Cameron in a chagrinned expression of waning defiance…Then Cameron lowly paused for a moment looking down at first and then turning back up to look at Dusty, and through a constrained expression on his face suddenly tersed… so just what is it you trying to say here?, that we just should go after and confront that horrid awful thing directly head on then? And just face off with that mortally heinous walking two legged nightmare with no cover or concealment right there out in the open!?…

Dusty just glared at Cameron through a somewhat mortified grimaced expression as he spoke. And on his terms nonetheless oh he'd just love us for that!! Just us two hombres huh?…slowly moseying down center stage Dodge then stopping there to stand there face to face in a pitted stare down with that horrific two legged mutated freak in some honorable boogerized showdown that you for some unknown reason feel we should engage in to insure what!!…our honor!!…And whereby we are most surely going to be at a supreme disadvantage!? Dusty' Ok, ok I think you've more than hammered home your point, but do I have to constantly be made to pay for my beliefs on the subject in having you pummel me to such a degree as well? "Cameron" Oh you can't be serious beat you up!!….. Is that what you think I'm doing here, Oh for god sakes!!…for your information I'm saving your ass deary! And whether you know it or not, I'm your only last and only remaining hope of you coming out of this nightmare in one piece!!…And your insistent strategy proposing lofty story book idealism of us taking up some christened emblematic sparkling and twinkling sterling silver sword and shield in some delusional form of chivalry knighted camaraderie just isn't going to cut it here!!.... And in your misty aloof scenario of us mutually slaying the booger spewing dragon before the world together in some far fetched concept of manly honor, honey I can most assure you is that a showdown like that is in this particular arena of conflict is a luxury we just cannot afford!!...THAT HORRID THING WOULD LITERALLY REND US INTO LITTLE BITTY PIECES!!...And with that statement there was a momentary pause as Dusty just stared at Cameron in a glare of strained contention.....

Then in a wide eyed expression the corner of Cameron's mouth turned up and he exclaimed. So just like Duke Wayne or Gary Cooper you say we should just come right out in the open waving a bright red flashing neon sign saying look!!,...here we are Fedder's were man enough to stand our ground as we've taken on the full overall body armor of honorable engagement, we are now impervious and can withstand anything your ready to dish out!!...come and get us!! Then Dusty looked sullenly off to the side and uttered, well that's not what I exactly what I had in mind...And then his face winced up as he crassly stated with an aggravated look of disparagement on it tersed.... Well what did you exactly have in mind? I didn't mean that we literally had to stand with it off face to face either, why do you have to interpret everything that way it's really aggravating. Well what other way can you interpret something like that in the way you put it, but in literal terms!?...

Then he paused momentarily and abruptly looked up at Dusty and tersed. You know when it gets right down to it, this is not going to be some kind of Ali-Frazier or George Foreman fight that's going to be held under the bright lights in front of thousands of clamoring spectators in all the splendor and pageantry of some grand sports arena with Howard Cosell giving a blow by blow!!...and that thing isn't just gonna stand there looking pretty and posing for the cameras taunting us and reciting poetry either. Now it's obvious that your completely caught up in the spur of the moment falderal of your enthused and stubbornly held position on this particular subject that for some unknown reason that seems to be near and dear to your heart. And as unequivocally enthralled in all it's alluring and debatable aspects as you are,... you seemed to have left out one very important and crucial factor here. But I'm willing to overlook all that for the time being just so I can refresh your memory. We are going to have to covertly and elusively maneuver ourselves amidst what has become a dark nightmarish shadow-scape wholly undetected. And if that horrid thing sees us again we won't be so lucky to be positioned up on a wooden platform safely 10 or 15 feet above ground just outta the reach of that wonderful river of vile putrid green slime he's been so notorious for lavishing on those lucky chosen few much less outta his grasp either, it's gonna try to, No that putrid, invincible pus filled malfeasant conglomeration of walking garbage will kill us!!....

That statement startled Dusty so much that she flinched back in a gawking wide eyed facial expression that was coupled by a flushed white complexion on it as he just sat there in a sullen momentary pause before he suddenly exclaimed, and just how well do you think we'd fair in such an instance? For your information sis this is a' war and tactically, that's just how we should and are going to approach it!! A boogerized one and we are the counter insurgency unit that has been assigned here for a search and destroy mission, got it! so you had best square your ass away and get with the program!!...Dusty just gazed off to one side in a befuddled wide eyed gape and lowly muttered Yeah I guess not so good I suppose....Cameron' WHADDA YOU MEAN YOU GUESS!! Look there's no guess work here!! It doesn't exactly take a genius here to surmise that SIS!!...Dusty' but then again this isn't a man were up against now is it? It's some sort of invincible putrefied metamorphosis isn't it.... It might just as well be friggin fire spewing Godzilla for that matter eh? "Cameron" in a wide eyed expression just pursed his lips while nodding his head up and down fretfully replied. Or in this case a slime spewing Boogerization, And then to try to appease a by now moderately incensed Cameron and momentarily shift his focus of attention, diverting it away from the ongoing contention stemming from their pitted rivalry which had by now culminated into a by now thoroughly exhausted stalemate. Then she subtly initiated a conversation on a much lighter and more neutral leveled position on the subject. Dusty' Ya know as long as were on the subject, just who invented such a crude baser concept like that anyway?…Cameron' like what? Dusty' war…Was it some ignominious ape that was somehow graced with a freakish ability for the gift of gab in having some kind of power and influence over people!…I mean just who came up with the abstract concept of two organized forces opposing each other in a mortal type conflict scenario? Ya know from a wholly spiritually evolved standpoint of mind and body in total objectivity of thought and observation, it's really pure unadulterated lunacy isn't it? Sort of a cruel enigmatic slap in the face to the ultimate scape of humanity, in all it's Neanderthalic and barbaric context huh?… Cameron' well put, you could say that but historically it's origins date back to mid-evil type Barbarians or maybe it was the caveman I'm not really sure which. Early Scandinavian type peoples like the Jung-Horde or the Vikings that hailed from mountainous Nordic regions of the time that retained little more than a walnut sized brain, coupled with a very limited and narrow scope and a short fuse to begin with were definitely among the first though I think, And then in a cynical wide eyed gawk through pursed lips he tersed. Yeah they were the Pioneer's alright, the founding fathers who in their imminent and abiding wisdom and foresight bore the torch of such bright luminescent light serving as a beacon for all humanity laid the initial building blocks in the foundation in paving the way for other like minded self-serving lunatics to follow suit in a preliminary draft for ETERNALLY SCREWING UP THE WORLD!!…

Dusty's eye's suddenly squinched and her cheeks puffed up as her mouth crooked in abruptly expelling a couple of puffs of air through a cynical and jaded laugh. "Cameron" I'd say in and around the tenth century or so in what were primeval and brutal forms of combat wielding crudely fashioned clubs with spikes, and dull bludgeoning swords and other primitive instruments of death as their brutish armies clashed with each other out in open ground on foot or by horseback in what was a very crude and dark age of unenlightenment…barbaric, backward, gory, ignorant, archaic and animalistic or whatever else you wanna call it, it surely was that. And Neanderthalic and Apish as the concept of an end means of solving regional or geographically incepted disputes itself is, especially when unintelligent governing factors that operate on gravely limited and narrow scope come into play. Ya know

Dusty if it's any consolation to you at all I can tell you is that in modern times it's just become a recreational way of life almost an institution, for backward, ignorant and educationally malnourished countries that would have a cringing reaction or be greatly repelled at the prospect of being posed with any form of viable education or social enlightenment or advancement you know sorta' like count Dracula would a crucifix or a clove of garlic, or my ex-wife would if you'd even subtly hint to her at the remote prospect of her maybe getting a job or for that matter for her father to get a brain, a personality and to stop drinking like a fish. Backward third world or middle eastern countries who've been known to chronically engage in it's miserable and protracted and unresolved activity in regarding it with the same leisured measure of human importance as put-put golf or chuck-e-cheese would for you and me. They typically in the past retained ruthless and corrupt power lords who despicably plunder and extort their impoverished countries in an iron fist like constricting reign of stifling misery, horrendous terror and merciless exploitation of them. It unfortunately would seem to be the only language some stuck in a psychotic and unreceptive mindset completely devoid of any and all elements of rational logic or any basic elements of human compassion of whom staunchly embraced the baser notion that the biggest hairiest smelliest ape is the only one who has the sole and inalienable right to wield power and govern nations seem to understand.

Those of the like before they were finally overthrown opportunistically assumed power in dictatorial roles as brutal war mongers abolishing of any and all objects of civil-liberties fair and impartial electoral process's or freedom of speech, And global bad-men like Hitler, Edie Amine, Saddam-Husain, Yasser Arafat or Bonito Mussolini to name a few fell directly into that category, yet these choreographers of world misery in the long run served to be little more than heinous scourges on humanity,….All-in-all they were really little more than mentally deranged, raving lunatics who should've been recognized by the masses at the onset as being just that a flock of malcontented loony-birds not politically qualified, mentally competent or capable leaders, and rounded up by massive hordes of angry townspeople like in that old Frankenstein movie and placed in a locked wooden stockade in the middle of the towns square so any passersby could at will feel free to just lob rotten eggs or tomatoes in their faces. Or at least had the local rubber room squad herd em' up with a huge butterfly net and deposit each of them in their respective state crackerbox palaces or booby-hatches!!...in a padded cell with a white canvas jacket with one sleeve!! And who by political or economically despairing circumstances were by in most cases by nefariously ill means were opportunistically able to seize or assume a dictatorial role in duping the masses in plundering and exploiting distressed countries. Wretched and insidious scourges that felt more than obliging to deceptively beset their insidious toxic remedy upon lowly despairing and indigent countries. Only to plague and exert their stifling and oppressive reign over a substantial area of demographics. And for literally decades now far to many middle eastern cities follow suit remaining in a permanent state of ruin typified by bleak repetitive scenes depicting long processions of tanks and armored vehicles parading down the middle of them.

You know I remember as a kid my grandmother turning on the national news and seeing kids who are raised into this backward and ignorant mindset roaming through the bombed out rubble of their city streets shouldered with bandoleers of ammunition and carrying a varying array of small arms. Terrorists who are so brainwashed and mercenary literally think nothing of strapping themselves with improvised explosive devices and detonating them amidst a crowd of people, or just going into a mosque and opening fire at will or even blowing up entire buses full of children. It's apish and backward origin was something spawned right out of the dark ages or even before then. Dusty just looked on in awe as he spoke. Boy you really are well versed on a lot of this war history crap aren't you I must say I'm kinda' impressed. Cameron' why coming from you I take that as a compliment in the highest esteem thank you I'm really flattered,... objectively speaking it's a kind of human paradox with the exception of South-East Asia and the insurmountable governmental and socio-economic factors that came into play regarding the almost insurmountable obstacles posed to the bohemian style culture of the day and how they constantly faced it in their ongoing and vehement protests which often culminated in volatile clashes with police.

It would seem to be one of the great unsolved mysteries of the ages and still remains an unanswerable question today in that nobody ever all throughout history thought to, organize against, question or contest it, maybe they were just to sheepish to I dunno. You know from a wholly spiritual and self actualized standpoint of humanity in a purely objective analysis and considering it in it's abstract form, you know it really does constitute, complete unadulterated and systematic insanity unleashed!! let's try to find a better way to resolve conflict and not become just another enabling byproduct or comply with it. Maybe they should've just amassed in great numbers in a profound humanitarian based revolt against the small insidious percentage that instigated it, but instead chose not to rebel or resist in any way in just blindly complying with and following like a massive herd of sheep.

Consequently all to many wound up arduously participating in what in many cases were brutal trifling conflicts under some corrupt and self serving figurehead or other ruthless and corrupt power lord of aristocracy who gave little or no thought in instigating them. And all to often was over something petty or trifling that in the end was something that was somehow only going to benefit them personally, but nonetheless where by untold thousands inexplicably did their bidding under a tyrannical and stifling reign of what comprised in many cases just a small sect of mentally unbalanced, and moderately deranged loony tune governmental figureheads as they sat aloof and sequestered away from battlefield danger in some far removed castle or other safe haven. Yet they themselves were to cowardly to directly take part in or dirty their own hands with blood of something they themselves brought about, as thousands at their behest fruitlessly perished in what were in many cases turned out to be found-less and fruitless conflicts, A leading forthright example of this being that of one of the worlds biggest chicken shits of all time, Adolf Hitler who all throughout a world cataclysm he nefariously and illegitimately instigated himself in almost single-handedly corrupting a German government and military establishment. He sequestered his worthless deranged and psychopathic hide safely hidden beneath a heavily fortified concrete bunker far below ground just out of effective range of allied bombs until the very end while the civilian populace upstairs took their respective lumps. Until what it has evolved into presently a non-conventional conceptual application to warfare steeped in the grayish ill defined undertones of global uncertainty, conflicting political, socio-economic or religious ideologies ...And besides modern conflicts are no longer referred to as wars anymore there called police actions, Dusty' Police actions!?... Cameron' Yes at least from the global standpoint of this country having at one time engaged in or intervened in the affairs of foreign conflicts goes,... now in modern times their referred to as police actions.

Dusty' boy that's a very polished term for something of such grievous magnitude isn't it?!...A police action,...boy if that isn't sugar coating it!!...Cameron' yep,...every war beginning with world war one whereby some brutish Neanderthalic ape like dictator such as Nazi Germany had at the time or communist faction felt the overriding propensity to needlessly and without legitimate cause invade and overtake some peaceable nation ultimately prompting noble old faithful and reliable Uncle Sam to come through to the rescue in the grand capacity of world cop!!...Dusty just hemmed, well you can just put me down for the one who say's their wars ...Cameron' well anyhow as far as your earlier comments on the subject goes anyway, all I've got to say along those lines is that's what's called guerrilla warfare it's an oddball fruity term and it's moreover fundamentally based on opt psychology,... breaking down an oppositions will...and believe it or not it's the most cruel and brutal form of warfare ever incepted. And it's foresee ably the worst kind a man could ever possibly find himself ensnared in and it's one I was trained to engage in, as a bush fighter. And in the weeding out process of the Green Berets for instance they start out with about a hundred of your so called he-men and by the end of the initial training phase only about a handful of them are left to form a counter insurgency unit. I've seen grown men brought to tears by hardened female D.I's in formation upon reception. Now take the revolutionary war of the colonies for example; the British wore a brightly red colored uniform and we Americans wore a dark blue one. Dusty' yeah so? Well that's a prime example of your staunchly held position on the subject of manly honor isn't it? I mean like a bright flashing neon light, they even went forth in battle dawning a highly visible non-essential wig under a huge brightly colored and obtrusive military headdress of the period, that looked more like a nesting peacock than an integral part of an infantryman's uniformed standardized issue!! ….ha, ha, ha, ha, ha,…. his jovially mocking taunts hit a nerve in

Dusty and struck a moderately incensed expression on her waning countenance as he further went on in his verbal castigation and admonishment. I mean in the field today you wouldn't represent anything honorable or noble at all! In fact by today's modern warring standards hypothetically, in shamelessly sporting such a ridiculous and outlandish costume you'd be branded as some kind of half baked fruitcake Bozo the clown or a gooney bird of sorts!!…and once, a densely concealed sniper wearing dark green tiger stripes with a bush on his head dug in at three or four hundred meters off would manage to regain his composure enough to stop laughing they'd be fired upon as nothing more than a brightly highlighted target! And there's nothing honorable or noble at all about being dead…your just dead. Dusty just grimaced while shaking her head back and forth in a moderate level of distain I just think you'll stop short of nothing in just trying to prove yourself right that's all…No I'm just citing thee facts here honey and I don't really need to substantiate my position either,…It's a hard cruel world in that aspect and the facts my dear speak for themselves. Which kind of puts us at a disadvantage anyway doesn't it?

Dusty' whaddaya ya mean? "Cameron" Mr. Fedders…he's already black or green or something isn't he? Dusty lowly grinned…I mean it's bad enough that he's so elusive but he's also naturally camouflaged as well, right? I mean it's gonna be almost just as hard for us to find and ambush him as it will be for him to find us isn't it? Dusty' in a disheartened and lowly reply murmured yeah I suppose so…. Only he isn't going to be opening up on us with any type of firearms,…we've gotta watch out we don't wind up on the business end of that horrid awful putrid river of that horrid green sludge he has the nasty and vulgar habit of blindsiding everybody he comes in contact with!!.. Then she loudly exclaimed Oh god when is this shitty nightmare ever gonna end!?…Cameron' Yes it will, eventually but only if you follow the carefully outlined strategy I've laid out for both of us without giving me any more guff over it, it will you've gotta start trusting me in that I know what I'm doing. Dusty' and you think all this covert guerrilla crap is really gonna help fortify us against that horrid putrid thing huh?…You bet your boots sis' cuz in this grave instance it's very befitting in the way that this situation calls for it ya know it'll most definitely give us the upper hand, yes that's exactly what I think!!… Can you think of a better way!?…And even though something as bizarre and freakish as this is isn't covered in the field manual under Marine Corps military preparedness training!!…What the hell else can we use as an model of example to follow and guide us?… now take the American civil war for instance these types of conventional attitudes in most instances implemented their rather antiquated tactical movements that are now completely ludicrous by today's strategic field standards in that they marched in open line formations completely devoid of any cover or concealment, right out there in the open serving no viable purpose other than to needlessly get scores of vitally integral military personnel obliterated. And why?…for honor?…C'mon now!! that's bullshit and you know it!! And in their obtuse mindsets they directly faced off with and charged at each other even from relatively close distances on dirt roads or in open clearings wearing their distinctive brightly colored uniforms clearly distinguishing themselves not only from the muddy subdued color schemes of nature such as brown tree trunks and branches or green leafy foliage and vegetation but only as courageous figures of onion!! markedly visible on the field of mortal conflict in the honorable, noble and conventional fashion, as you so put it real stand up type men…

"Dusty" with a chagrinned look on her face like an overly enthused kid who's over inflated prized carnival balloon was in the process of slowly having all the air let out of it, muttered yeah that's right that's just what I still believe alright…what's your point?…My point is,.. Ms. Old world honor and nobility the numbers here garner the day!…did you know that in this particular instance that in the battle of Gettysburg alone a total of approximately 58000 men on both sides perished in that particular battle as they both stood there facing each other out in the open at relatively close distances slugging it out with primal one shot black powdered ball muskets as you put it in an honorable and manly fashion of mortal conflict. Dusty' no I didn't know that either. Cameron' Well maybe you should've done a little homework on the subject, needless to say that at the time all they had was a crudely fashioned sluggish and primitive gun that took several minutes to recycle just to ready it to re-fire one lousy very sluggish and inaccurate shot! Oh I'm sorry I stand corrected I'm pretty sure the invention of a crude type of machine gun was incepted then called the Gatling-gun at around the same time as well, it was clip fed and was fired by a hand crank in the back or something, you know Dusty the invention that is largely responsible for the augmentation of world misery, two world wars and then two more theaters of Asiatic conflict. And during the course of mankind's inability to rationalize life or coexist not to mention scores of other political and geographical armed conflicts throughout the world since especially in middle eastern regions. But it wasn't implemented on a wide enough scale to have had any major significance then. Nonetheless it was a figure that directly paralleled the total amount of casualties suffered by the U.S. in it's involvement for the entire period of the distressed region of southeast Asia from 1958 to 1975 in a pitted protracted jungle war were by insidious bands of communist sympathizers whom descended from the north to converge on the south, roamed the countryside pillaging and terrorizing docile and non-threatening hard working villagers just trying to scratch out a meager existence from wet marshy rice fields!!

And in their insidious plight to overthrow a legitimate South Vietnamese government in place was through unlawful and brutal insurrection, and in all reality a political and demographic crime. Subsequently the U.S. was called upon forthright to give military and logistical aide to the distressed region. And whereby in most instances the two opposing sides were not directly facing each other on the battlefield and did so under the dense cover of a thick jungle canopy and camouflaged battle attire and typically from great distances in pitted firefights, mortar and rocket attacks. The dirt paths our guys took on jungle patrols were routed with makeshift land mines, concealed pongee stick pits and lethal spike tables that were trip activated. And the hills and underground tunnels were infested with hardened NVA regulars and communist guerillas. A faceless hit and run cowards war as you so vehemently put it…Dusty' Yeah that's just what I said alright…what's your point? The point here is that for one in a modern non-conventional type setting all we're really talking about is a combatants ability to conceal himself in the bush and hone in on an exposed target to dispatch it by any means necessary, the word honor really no longer factors into it anymore does it?. And in this day and age unless a soldier just desserts only in that instance I think he's deemed a coward.

Dusty just bit her lower lip and shook her head back and forth. Yet in your manly honorable and frontally exposed type of conflict just as many lives were lost in one strategically antiquated battle that lasted only over a period of several days than the U.S. incurred in it's seventeen years of involvement in the above mentioned were by modern weapons ground and air capable of mass destruction were implemented. Dusty' somewhat taken back mildly exclaimed ooh!!…Cameron' and as you put it, in any given instance men in a fight should stand there at close quarters directly facing each other slugging it out like real men…kinda stupid don't you think? Then a dumbfounded Dusty just looked down in a wide eyed expression in a moderately chagrinned reaction at just having been figuratively check-mated in the debate with a grimacing scowl on her face just rolled her eyes in a peeved backward fashion. And thus concludes Cameron's personal three step lesson installment of historical war strategy re-counts for the day…he then turned to one side and threw the latch pushing open the heavy double doors that sealed off the old mining areas workman's quarters to see if there were any uninvited guests leftover from the previous night prowling about the immediate vicinity.

Cameron just gazed out at the surrounding area and surveying it to see if that thing would make a surprise appearance again unannounced in having spent the night hidden somewhere in close proximity. And as he stood there on the top stair of the rickety old cellar doorway steps a nagging pang of uneasiness gnawed at the pit of his stomach as he panned out over the dreary setting and the shabbiness of the run down old abandoned mining area under the warm soft rays of the morning sun.

Dusty was right this place is creepy, it was drab and dismal and down right depressing even more so in the day than it was at night, but there was nothing that even remotely stood out of the ordinary but a twenty foot dirt and rock mound with ratty weeds and vines growing in, over and out of it and an old makeshift wooden sign with wooden spats, and a huge black ominous cawing crow resting on top of it bearing a skull and crossbones illustration at the base of it's boarded up entrance marked with a danger warning prompt scrawled in bold red letters to keep out! that was once an operational mine shaft. A long brick tunnel sat next to a set of dilapidated old box car tracks that was used for transporting loads of coal about fifty yards off vertically adjacent to it. There were also a couple of overturned coal cars with some of the wheels and wooden spats missing from a couple of the box carriers. The surrounding area was hilly rocky and permeated with snakes, lizards, big hairy spiders and ratty vegetation. Dusty' ya know, this place is downright depressing by day and creepy as hell at night what say you and I make tracks outta here before something bad really does happen huh?...Cameron' I'm with you on that note, and the two loaded up with their backpacks and bustled about to emerge from the entrance of the old abandoned underground workman's quarters as Cameron dropped the big heavy doors closed.....Phew!...it's a good thing this was here eh Dusty? it kept us safe overnight didn't it? Dusty' I think the only reason we were safe last night is because that thing is miles away from us and didn't know we were here. It's a creature of opportunity moreover than one who preys upon, seeks out or stalks out his victims he really doesn't have anything personal against anybody he's just putrefying predisposed to only one thing, killing. And if it did it would have showed up here at our doorstep ringing the doorbell of doom and bearing a found less grudge and doing his damnest to get in here just to ingratiate us with even more of his unwanted attention...heh, heh, heh. Cameron' maybe so, but you never know we may need this little motel six again sometime in the near future. I sure hope not she retorted breathing a long sigh, it's accommodations left a great deal to be desired in the way of basic amenities I mean you know? Cameron just grinned at the comment.

Then the two proceeded outwardly from the old abandoned mining area and unwittingly set out for their destination that morning covering several more miles of rugged desolate and unforgiving terrain sparsely wooded areas and open clearings while engaging in petty like minded debates and tripe conversation along the way. And just as they slowly began to approach the eerie desolate area of the long rocky gorge was located in, the air grew cold as evening dusk began to set in. The tired and worn down posse' duo paused momentarily from their languished sojourn across the open countryside to stand there for a moment surveying the rocky base of the steep ravine and Dusty was immediately stricken and overwhelmed in surmising just what was going to be physically required in undertaking it. It was a treacherous incline that was approximately one hundred yards wide and several miles long but was a piece of terrain they couldn't just circumvent and had no other choice but to have to engage and negotiate it in order to access the State facility the two girls were in. Dusty was the first to comment as she slowly reached up to lower one strap of her backpack dropping it to the ground with a pained look on her face and a disparaging look of contention blurted out, gees-o-wees I dunno if I'm up for this shit!! I'm no mountain man ya know!! And then she turned to Cameron and barked, What the hell do I look like Paul Bunyan or something!? good lord! Just look at that!! how we are gonna get way up there without literally half killing ourselves or maybe falling off in the process huh!? So I trust then that you brought all the essential gear, like fifty foot ropes and grappling hooks!?…Cameron' if you will just relax and calm down a minute and stop running off at the mouth, I'll tell ya! First of all were not going to enter it from this point it's to steep and treacherous and for that matter to far off the beaten path.

Dusty' well thank the dear lord above for small favors…you know if we were to run into Mr. Fedders now climbin' up this thing we wouldn't much have to worry about trying to do him in! This steep incline and jagged rocks would no doubt do the job for us eh. Cameron leered outward and smiled gleefully and said yeah I would thoroughly enjoy sitting there watching booger-face suddenly loose his footing while climbing up here in another one of his vile and despicable attempts to get at us here on this high elevated rise and then plummeting downward ass over tea kettle over the jagged rocks below only to come to rest at it's base with a broken neck…I'd laugh my ass off!! Dusty' yeah so anyway how are we gonna cross over this rock laden ravine without breaking our necks in the process huh flat or not? Cameron' well were going to have to bypass this location and proceed about three or so miles further on down the edge of the ravine traveling adjacent to it along sparse tree lines and thick bushy vegetation to a point mid-way where it tapers off and levels out some and then we can successfully get across with the exception of a running stream or two without to much trouble. Dusty' with a look of fused relief on her face smiled slightly and sighed oh yeah? Are there still piles of big rocks we still gotta trudge and stumble over? you know there's probably gonna be snakes too. Cameron' yeah I'm afraid so the rock bed is much more sparse but it's pretty much the same deal as this only it levels off a lot more and dips down a bit. If your not open to that prospect there is still one other option though… but I'm not sure you'll be up to it though…Dusty' looking on intently, yeah what's that? "Cameron well are you afraid of heights? Dusty' in a feigned timid reply, no not so much so I suppose. Well there's a decrepit old abandoned train trestle overgrown with ratty weeds and vines that extends and crosses over it, it's to deteriorated and rickety for a train to cross over anymore but it's safe enough for people to walk across it without falling through. If you don't have a problem with that, then that's the route we'll take aside from one other pitfall.

Dusty just winced and said in a constraining tone yeah what other pitfall do I have to circumvent on that this damn excursion of yours you drug me along on is routed with? Cameron clenching his chin pensively in his thumb and forefinger replied well…my advice here is just don't look down there's no safety railings and there's about forty or fifty feet drop to the ground below. There's also some pretty big spaces in between the ties as well but the unnerving panoramic view to the distant ground below is partially obscured by thick leafy vines and ratty vegetation that had grown and wrapped themselves around and in between them that sort of lent themselves as a safety net to one who crossed over it. And with a leer he gleefully relayed to Dusty of the stark panoramic view to the ground below,…as she looked back at him with a fretful and panicked expression. And through a wide eyed grin conveyed but don't worry my dear if you fall I'll be there to catch you. Dusty' in a inhibited and apprehensive reply in an worrisome demeanor muttered… that's not exactly very reassuring…

As the two kids set out that morning over the vast acreage of a raw sun ravaged and desolate landscape on their plight to somehow locate and bring an ignominious end to Mr. Fedders reign of boogerized terror. They were already half way there but still had the grueling task of negotiating miles more of some pretty rough and unforgiving terrain that would only prove out to be physically obstructing and cumbersome. As they arduously trudged along the base of the rock laden ravine were it sloped downward along the edge to reach an elevated peak where the old train trestle bridged the two neighboring jurisdictions. The other being a remote little town called Sandy Hook were divided by the dried up portion of the Sussex Madeline river the kids needed to cross in order to access the old state mental facility. It took several hours on foot for them to finally reach their destination as the ravines rocky base stretched for miles along sparse wooded areas trickling streams and deserted weigh stations once used for mining, the point of no return. The landscape was bleak barren and eerily depressing as it was punctuated by dilapidated old shacks, as the two kids warily trudged amid the searing heat of an oppressive midday sun high overhead. They were accompanied on their grueling and arduous trek by towering knotted trees huge rocks and sun bleached soil infested with snakes, lizards and big hairy spiders. The soil itself was completely stripped of any real life sustaining mineral or nutritional properties to sustain much of anything other than sparse ratty vegetation. And unlike the typical scenic landscape they were used to plodding the tone along the way was nothing more but dry, barren, bleak and isolated totally devoid of any and all warmth and basic amenities or hospitableness of terrain and it greatly unsettled the two especially Dusty. And the only birds they saw in the sky was the occasional chicken hawk or turkey buzzard ominously circling about in search of vulnerable prey. Dusty' while momentarily gazing upward towards the sky at the ominous site of mangy scavengers circling about high overhead, Ooh...I don't like the looks of that at all...Cameron' the looks of what? Those dirty mangy buzzards circling about they've been hungrily surveying us for the past half hour like were listed on the menu as the course,.. they're starting to give me the creeps ya know. Cameron just hemmed, scavengers, yeah, their strikingly similar to attorney's realtors or life insurance agents in that have a very acute sensory radar type receptors that are keenly attuned to distressed signals of vulnerability especially when it comes to scoping out the fresh scent of blood, they seize and consume everything sooner or later, and besides everything gives you the creeps...Do I give you the creeps too?....Don't answer that, you know you don't have to worry about those damn vultures unless of course your mortally wounded or dead and then in which case all your worries would be over anyway wouldn't they? So chill out,.. you can just kick back and relax here and enjoy the view... Dusty' boy that just put's my mind completely at ease.

Ya know that's what I've always loved about you is how you posses the gifted knack of just putting everything in such a positive and proper sarcastic perspective!!.... Cameron just glanced back at her with a look of morose anticipation on his face. Dusty' how receptive do you think the girls are going to be once we get there? I mean do you think they will be in any kind of shape to talk to us when we see them? Cameron' in a worried look of intensity on his face replied...gee that kind of thing is sorta hard to predict don't ya think? but especially in this case I sure hope so,... because if not were gonna be seriously screwed out of very vital information...And then in that case this we'll all have just been a colossal waste of our time and limited energy in us needlessly putting our asses on the line in having coming out here in the first place and making this trip for nothing. And in which case yours truly is not going to be a happy camper and we can just find ourselves right back where we started from at square one. No closer to finding the answer than when we started out this morning. Dusty'...Ooh I don't like the sound of that at all...Cameron' Believe you me sis' nether do I, but\what else can we do at this point? We have to pursue this course uncertain or not, it's our only hope of resolution in this unrelenting nightmare. Those two girls are the only other living souls besides ourselves that encountered that horrid thing and lived. You can just bet that they saw it too and I need to know just what they did after that poor head dude fired on it and his life was prematurely cut short. The authorities had to have started the interrogation process by now and attempted to exact some of the details of what happened to their little group on those old set of train tracks so they have to be somewhat coherent by now right?

Dusty' yeah I suppose so, but what if that rouse you concocted fails and the one girl Julie I think her name is says she doesn't recognize you much less know any Cameron Dillard and doesn't have any cousin from Connecticut or Massachusetts or whatever then what are you going to do there? huh smarty pants? That facility has to have very tight security it's not like a rest home or a standard hospital you know where visitors can pretty come and go as they please. And those girls were probably remanded under some kind of special priority watch and are sequestered from outside visitors. Well if such is the case I will simply tell whoever is at the front desk that I am a distant cousin she hasn't seen since she was three and that's why she doesn't remember me and I am here to get reacquainted on a concerned visit. They'll have to let us in!… Once I get in there with them and tell those two girls we saw that putrid thing to and had a run in with it in that old tobacco barn things will immediately begin to mesh and take off I'm sure of it. Then they will just be putty in my hands. Dusty' oh you really think so do you? Cameron' You bet I do I just have that effect on women. Dusty' Oh gawd!!, don't flatter yourself, and just what makes you think they'll tell you anything they haven't already divulged to authorities anyway? Then Cameron suddenly stopped and turned to Dusty placing his palmed hand over her upper arm momentarily halting her. Sure I do because at that point we'll have struck a mutual cord putting us all on common ground with each other that's why. Because at that mutual point of hallowed exaltation they will have no choice but to be a lot more receptive to someone else who also saw it, had a run in with it too and lived. Rather than someone who hasn't, especially a stiff figure of authority with ulterior motives and a vested interest dawning a white hospital gown or brandishing a badge and is just in there prodding them in a methodical and clinical fashion for detailed facts. Under such circumstances they probably just felt they were being held under the gun of scrutiny and intimidation and would be somewhat apprehensive in divulging any real facts. I mean the whole thing is so garish and surrealistic most people would think it was just some nut or crackpot making the whole thing up right. I'm thinking they were probably somewhat sheepish and evasive upon any type of questioning by any doctors, lawyers or Indian chiefs. And having said that he removed his hand from Dusty's upper arm turning to proceed on their walk along the base of the ravine

As the two went on a little further Dusty suddenly got her foot lodged in a hidden crevice between two rocks twisting her ankle and falling down with her foot caught the hollow of a hidden sink hole of this hot, dry, barren wasteland. She suddenly cried out in pain as she involuntarily whirled to the ground in a semi-contorted seated position. She sat there rocking back and forth wincing in pain as she leaned forward in fervid attempts to massage some of the pain from her twisted ankle. Cameron lagged just a few paces behind and immediately rushed over to her vicinity with the intent to lend her assistance when something that sounded like a maraca or a baby rattle abruptly sounded from an unseen position nearby. It just made a steady chink-a chink-chick like change jingling around in some ones pocket or somebody shaking a big bottle of pills. Yet as Cameron frantically looked about on the ground for it's source he couldn't see anything at first. Then he loudly barked, Dusty!! Don't move!! She immediately panicked and bawled what is it!... Cameron' JUST SHUT-UP never mind what it is you just do what I tell ya, and KEEP STILL. He didn't want to cause her further alarm as she'd start flailing about uncontrollably. They didn't see it at first but there was about a three and a half to four foot rattlesnake in a shallow pit area partially concealed by some rocks just about twelve or fifteen feet from where Dusty was downed. She just sat there bawling and slowly rocking back and forth and trying not to flail about. As she knew from watching enough westerns on television that if she did she'd surely get bitten.

Just then Cameron not taking his eye's off the snake very slowly without making any sudden jerky movements reached up to lower the strap of that big dark brown leather satchel and sliding his hand under the flap to retrieve one of the old loaded revolvers. He knew if he made any abrupt movements that snake would surely spring from it's coiled position to fly through the air open mouthed lunging at his neck. Dusty just sat there whimpering and bawling as Cameron slowly extended his arm and pointing the snub nose .32 in the snakes direction. The dreaded viper was coiled and preparing to strike vigorously chinking it's rattle in a monstrous intimidating attack mode with its fork tongue rapidly jutting in and out and it's icy piercing hypnotic eyes fixated on poor Dusty. The reptile was completely oblivious to the lethal force that was just about to be used against it. Then Cameron in a swift rapid succession capped off all five rounds at the vicious reptile exploding and tearing it's scaly body into pieces all over the ground.

As he lowered the his arm bluish gray smoke slowly billowed out from the end of the snub nosed barrel. Then with a wide smile on his face he turned his head and jokingly retorted in attempts to calm her down from her frenzied state and bring her around exclaimed hey!!...Dusty we'd better start gathering some kindling to build a fire, I think I just bagged tonight's supper!!...Snakes and big hairy spiders in this region were not an abundant or prevalent factor to be contended with, nor did they pose an overriding threat to hikers but nonetheless people still had to watch out for them in their travels. As their concealed burrows did sparsely punctuate desolate unsuspecting areas suddenly leaping out to surprise the occasional unwary excursionist who may have just happened upon them in plodding their way through this barren dried up wasteland.

Dusty' in a flustered state tersed if you think I'm ever gonna eat a snake your outta your ever-loving mind!! Cameron' haven't you ever heard that snake meat tastes a lot like chicken!...Dusty' I don't care if it tastes like fillet-min-yon the remnants of a rattle snake shall never pass over my lips!...*I'll eat a raw* cactus first, thistles and all!! And anyway I've heard it's a lot more like having a mouth full of cotton..

Just then Cameron came over to Dusty and knelt down beside her removing some of the large rocks from the little sink hole her foot and ankle was lodged in, in attempts to free it. I twisted my ankle I think I may have sprained it. I don't think I'm going to be able to walk on it I'm afraid I won't be much use from here on out. "Cameron" Oh god don't tell me that, now don't crap out on me now! Yes you will I'll make damn sure of that! You just lay still and let doctor Cameron do his miracle work!…were gonna have to make a liniment, I have an ace bandage here in my leather satchel for just such an emergency. Dusty' boy you've just thought of everything haven't you? Don't tell me you were a medic in the Marines too!! Cameron' mockingly grumbled no I wasn't a medic just the opposite, I was a trained combatant, remember?… but I just know you have to come amply prepared for this kind of crap when you negotiate rough unforgiving terrain such and this. One never knows what may happen. You have to anticipate any and all possible mishaps along the way. And while holding the injured booted foot in his hands stated now we have to get that boot off this leg in order to set the ankle.

Dusty winced and flinched back whining, no it's gonna hurt don't touch it! Dammit we have to!!… I can't just leave you downed out here in the middle of nowhere! now just bone up to the plate and bite the bullet!! And just let me do what I have-ta do here to get us movin' again, got it!!…Sometimes life is a little uncomfortable!… Ya know your just damn lucky that snake didn't bite ya sister boy you'd really have problems? "Dusty" you mean you couldn't work any first aide miracles on something like that? Well I know a little, I mean I know you have to immediately suck the venom out of the wound before it takes effect or something…I wouldn't just stand there and watch you die if that's what you mean…Now just sit tight and let me remove that boot lace first, and then it will just slide off painlessly unimpeded. After that Cameron bound her ankle as best he could with the bare essentials he had in his brown leather satchel in a crudely fashioned liniment in setting it. This enabled Dusty with minimal effort to somewhat stand upright and painlessly on it without it shifting around and causing further injury to her ankle thusly enabling her to slowly hobble around on it so they could continue on to their final destination, the jurisdiction of the old state mental hospital. He then proceeded to place a black partial zed metal and leather boot shaped cage

As he snapped closed each individual metal clasp that steadily harnessed the collapsible device securing it to the ace bandaged wrapped injured foot. The sole intent here being was so that the ace bandage wouldn't be in direct contact with bare ground. Then he threw Dusty's other boot in her backpack and the two proceeded onward along the base of the rock laden ravine. They didn't encounter anymore rattlesnakes big hairy spiders or other creatures of a treacherous nature along the way. Yet the one formidable threat that loomed on the horizon they really had to be on the wary lookout for was wild bores. They were reputed to grow as big as a volts wagon and they had a vicious and unpredictable temperament but they were rarity and sparse in numbers. And they were known to inhabit this region and to suddenly and without warning emerge out of nowhere in a highly charged volatile attack mode on unsuspecting travelers. There have been a number of reported instances whereby one has charged head on in broad siding a jeep or some other safari type of land roving vehicle totally demolishing it and sometimes killing the occupants inside. And Cameron really didn't have anything in his satchel with enough stopping power to bring one of those charging monsters down from an ensuing rampage other than a hollow point round from his .38. It's effectiveness would've been questionable at best unless maybe he was skillful enough to empty all nine shots into it's skull and then also had enough time to draw the .32. For good measure. But one really needed to have at least a 357 or a .44 to stand a chance against one of those rampaging beasts, but fortunately they didn't have to find out as none came.

Dusk began to set in a cool dreary autumn snap as the two kids warily approached the one end of the rocky cliff the old turn of the century train trestle was mounted to. It stretched about seventy five yards across the shallow gorge that accessed the Montcreef Sussex region where the old Mental hospital was. The air set a subtle tone of iridescence in the semi darkness of evening as Dusty nervously turned to Cameron while hoping against all hope and lowly murmuring is that it? The shallow gorge below was rock laden and punctuated with tall ratty weeds, and one could tell it had, had a river running through it a long time ago that had simply either dried up or had been dammed at some distant port of entrance. As the two stood there at the cliffs edge Dusty nervously turned to Cameron and murmured this is it huh…. this is what I have to cross with a bum ankle? I don't like the looks of it or those big wide gaping spaces in between the ties what if I fall or something?…Cameron' grinned wryly don't worry if you do you won't fall completely through, and if that happens there not wide enough for a human body to pass through and besides I'll be there to lend assistance should something happen…look just don't look down and try to only look at the ties you have to step across and you'll be fine. Trains don't go over this bridge anymore and I don't know why they haven't just torn it down or something it's really more of an eyesore than a legitimate historical landmark. But this I can tell ya, it's not gonna collapse if people walk across it,…you know at some point your just gonna have to trust me, ok…From the rock bed below you could hear the two muffled voices in busied conversations but from that vantage point one could not audibly make out what the two were saying as they lollygagged their way across the old train bridge. Yet at the structured base of the old bridge at the other end in a semi darkened area leaning up against a huge support beam with one leg arched and it's bumpy mutated clawed foot resting against it was that horrid thing. It stood there amidst the darkness insidiously concealed from sight, poised, with it's freakish wide, creepy bug eyed gaze transfixed in a wide Cheshire like cat grin that resembled the front grill of a late 1950's Buick as it stood there below hidden, foreboding and lowly festering in the shadows of it's evil and indiscriminate malignancy.

But just as the two got across and finally approached the base of the clearing through a gully, they just stood there on a rise just a few feet from a rickety old partially downed barbed wire fence attached to staggered weathered and dilapidated wooden posts sunk in the ground that stretched all along the rise on the edge of the field the old institution was in. There were also short stocky black knotted crab apple and blossom type trees that ran adjacently along side the old fence at about ten or fifteen yard intervals and the surrounding air resonated with the sweet pungent scent. The colossal and imposing sight of that massive stone and iron fortress in the clearing it sat in was ominous and it was just about seven hundred yards off from the edge of the rise. It seemed to insidiously peer out across the countryside in a morose stately imminence that boasted a dark unenlightened period of the mid 1800's. The two just stood there in the midst of that ratty field of high weeds, dragon flies, and little white off breed butterflies swirling about in ditzy indiscriminate flight looking back and forth at the institution and then at each other as if they were waiting for the other to offer up comment. It was massive one could tell even from a great distance. It was dismal and eerily surreal and the shadowy windowed and door hallowed portions of it's 19th century grandiose structure seemed to silently radiate grim and unsettling connotations that bespoke a stark and impending doom. "Dusty" looked out over the clearing,… it just gives me the creeps… Cameron' what gives you the creeps? That massive gloomy looking stone dungeon that's what! It's not a Dungeon goof, dungeons are basements in old castles and there below ground. Well it still gives me the creeps ya know…

Then Cameron abruptly jerked his head to one side while smoothing his bangs over so they were outta his eyes and loudly sighed, oh everything just gives you the creeps,…do I give you the creeps too? "Dusty"….well. Cameron' don't answer that, look it's just a great big dismal old building that's all and nothing more. Dusty' yeah well it's probably haunted or something it looks like it's about a hundred years old or so. A hundred and fifty more like, look this is part of the tasking we have to undertake on this fact finding mission so can you just put a lid on your spook talk just long enough for me to interrogate the girls,…huh? Then he said you know I've always been a firm believer that there's really no such things as ghosts or haunted places only haunted people. Dusty' abruptly stopped and turned to Cameron and tersed ok that's it!! Look if you don't believe in ghosts then just say so but do you gotta keep belittling me the way you do downgrading and poking fun at my beliefs all the time. Seriously, I've often heard that centuries old historical landmarks such as this and from credible sources nonetheless are notoriously reputed to harbor roaming specters from within. And then Dusty went on to fretfully state, I've even seen authenticated photographs of illuminated ectoplasmic fields shaped in human forms in the darkened rooms of old mansions and castles positioned on staircases and hallways in books taken from time activated and light sensitive cameras ya know. "Cameron" grinning from ear to ear, moaning and clanking their chains and all I'll bet huh?…then sarcastically he went on to say, look in the unlikely event that happens they will be more than welcome to just sit down and sup with us, they can partake in the sumptuous delight in the culinary expertise of my finely prepared dinner rations, they'll most assuredly make pleasant and interesting company and it will be a temporary reprieve from the monotony and aggravation of constantly seeking out and trying to locate Mr. Fedders. And it'll be a much welcomed and refreshing change of pace from this fun filled excursion were on. Hey, the moaning and groaning may very well be just a strong indicator they're just simply famished,…you know the level of expendable energy needed to roam halls, rattle chains, bellow and moan and groan while in the process of haunting a house and giving it's terrified guests the heebie-jeebies all night can work up one hell of an appetite!! And then he mercilessly cackled in her face. Dusty' chagrinned, you know the more you talk like that the more your going to start finding yourself treading in the direction of the evermore thinning ice our soon to be passé' friendship is beginning to take BUSTER.

As the two got within relative proximity of the old facility Dusty turned to Cameron and said what err' we gonna do about all this shit strapped to our backs huh? There's probably metal detectors we'll have to pass through at the main entrance, how err we gonna bypass one of those carrying guns? We'll just have ta toss em both in the bushes at a safe distance and outta sight from the guards and then we'll just retrieve em both when we get back out that's all, what other choice do we have? And as the two finally entered the facility they were both subsequently detained and asked to produce two forms of identification. From there they had to check in at the reception desk by a heavy set matronly woman in a cheap business type polyester dress that was a size or two to small sitting there banging out institutional forms on an old 60's typewriter with slightly greasy shoulder length dishwater blonde hair and a stone hard looking face defined with deep heavy lines. She presented a rough surly persona which put one off and made them feel ill at ease. Then when she caught the two kids out of the corner of her eye she immediately looked up and sternly asked who they were there to see. Cameron felt somewhat intimidated by the big woman's longshoreman type demeanor. But nonetheless he proceeded to dispense with the first order of business as he wistfully replied Julie Shafer and Crystal Parsons.

The big imposing woman gruffed oh, the two railroad tracks victims…who are you? Uh,… I'm her distant cousin from Connecticut that she hasn't seen for years and she probably doesn't even remember me. We haven't seen each other since we was kids. Anyway I read about this in the papers so I'm here with my girlfriend on a concerned visit. Then the big stern looking woman quizzically looked up at the kids paused from her typing and gruffed, she never told me anything about a cousin from the east then she paused momentarily staring at the kids and dubiously replied,…this made headlines in Connecticut papers? "Cameron" timidly replied,… yeah these bizarre occurrences are making national headlines…Then the stout woman stood up and gruffed well ok but this goes against my better judgment come this way…and then she ushered the two down towards the end of the hall to the two girls room 14 C on the left hand side of the hall. When the three got to the doorway entrance to the room the big receptionist turned to the two kids and said. "The two girls are in the same room together we felt it was a better idea than splitting them up and putting them in separate rooms alone". You know in that it would help loosen them up and bring them around more, in any case it would get em more relaxed and talkative somewhat. You know when we first got em they were in a grave state of catatonic shock they've put up a mental block which is not uncommon for traumatized subjects. Initially we had to sedate them both and induce a battery of psychotic drugs to help bring them around a little. And they also had to undergo extensive interactive therapy. I'd hate to speculate on what is was they actually saw out there but believe you me it had to have been something horrifically awful. That statement made Cameron inwardly shudder as he thought to himself, lady if you only knew but his guarded inner sense of reluctance prohibited him from offering up comment, how are they now? They are much more coherent and aware of their surroundings now. And they have become more relaxed and at ease and somewhat receptive to the idea of low interaction with people that's why we are allowing visitors at this point. We feel it will have a positive effect and make them open up even more and speed the road to recovery.

Then the big matronly woman said" you're her cousin huh,…well then you should know enough to go easy with her and treat her with kid gloves….No pushing, prodding, poking or cajoling for any reason understand?…If there's any sign of trouble or upset you'll be asked to leave understand?"

Then as Cameron and Dusty slowly entered the room they saw Julie solemnly sitting there in a wheelchair with a small blanket folded over her lap and Crystal was just sitting at the edge of her bed with a sullen gaze looking down at her hand while the overhead T.V. played on low volume as the two attempted to play cards. Then Cameron asked the receptionist to close the door part way stating that this was family and he wanted some privacy. Julie somewhat startled abruptly looked up at Cameron and was the first to speak. "Who are you, do I know you?" No you don't know us, I'm Cameron Dillon and this is my friend Dusty Moors. Then Julie lowly muttered, uh what do you want? And then Cameron whispered well I guess there's no easy way to say this but just to come right out and say it. We saw it too. And then Julie suddenly got a flushed startled look on her face and then nervously twitched at Cameron in a strained expression almost bursting into tears. And then in some contrived and lame attempt to divert and deceive him as to her total ignorance to what he was talking about muttered,….saw what? C'mon as if you didn't know,…you know damn well what I'm talking about sister!! that two legged boogerized freak that's what!! and I know for a fact you did too so let's cut the crap here and get down to brass tax, ok? And then Julies face began to wince as she began bawling and then Cameron went over to her hugging her against his shoulder whispering shhhhhhh,….everything's gonna be alright honey trust me but you have to calm down and open up and talk to me. And then the big surly receptionist burst into the room looked around and barked….what in Sam Hill is going on in here! She's all choked up!….ya know we haven't seen each other in years since we was kids, I'm one of the few remaining relatives she has left, and she's so overcome with emotion it moved her to tears just seeing me again. And the big woman looked down at Julie for a cue that there was no real trouble and that nothing was emotionally askew got a nod muttering it's ok and the woman left.

Julies reddish white flushed complexion looked imploringly at Cameron with tears streaming down her cheeks and bawled, what in God's holy name is it? "Cameron" I don't know some kind of chemical freak of nature I guess….but anyhow me and my friend Dusty here are on a mission to find it again and bring an end to it's vile and miserable existence!!…"Julie" I don't know if I can it's very hard for me to even bring myself to think about let alone talk about. I don't know where to begin we haven't said anything about this to anybody yet, the police, the doctors family, anybody it's so horrible, and then she cried our friend Todd was killed trying to defend us with a small handgun. Cameron unnervingly said yeah I know I read about it in the papers…look I don't want to scare you any more than you already are here, but gun fire isn't going to debilitate or destroy that horrid compilation of chemical malfeasance. Julie just looked up at him with an expression of abject terror. "Cameron" look honey you girls are safe just as long as you both remain in this stone fortress for awhile and give me and my friend here a chance to do what needs to be done. That's the main reason we're here and we haven't gone to the authorities in that it would only instigate floundered efforts and mass pandemonium. He has to be rooted out caught off guard and destroyed covertly and with more sound and effective measures than gun-fire. But for now I suppose I'm afraid your gonna have to open up and talk to us about what happened to you guys, that's the only way me and Dusty here are going to be able to find a potential weakness and eradicate this nightmare once and for all…look if it'll help to break the ice here, I'll go first in telling you what happened to us one stormy night as we took refuge from a raging electrical storm in an old abandoned mail-pouch barn. And how me my friend over there and her little brother did close quarter battle with it and how we managed to survive fair enough? And Julie made no comment as she looked back at Cameron in a fixed, entranced gaze.

Then Cameron went on to colorfully describe how the three of them wound up in the old barn when a nasty storm began brewing as the three of them where out in an open field by a massive downed tree when he was in the stilted process of giving his friend Dusty shooting lessons. He talked about how he spotted it's silhouetted figure against creepy flashes of lightning in the distance through a double door opening in the hayloft. And how after that he frantically ushered the other two up for safety reasons frantically pulling up the old wooden retractable ladder before that thing come upon the old barn prying away rotted portions of weather damaged boards in order to gain entrance. And how the just three sat up there for what seemed like an eternity in the dark quaking in terror in pitch blackness in hopes they wouldn't be found out as they listened to that monsters innocuous breaths and pounding thuds of it's clawed feet below as it indiscriminately searched the barn for yet another hapless victim.

Julie just sat there mesmerized as Cameron went on to further describe what led up to the discovery of their position by that thing and how they reigned down on it from above with a barrage of gunfire and a Molotov cocktail sending it reeling and shrieking on fire out of the barn. "Cameron" well that's our horrific story of our run in with Mr. Fedders and we haven't seen hide nor hair of him since, we thought maybe we'd meet up with him again on our way here and ingratiate him with our surprise bag of goodies, but no luck. "Julie" Mr. Fedders? "Cameron" Yeah that's our pet name for him you know he holds a warm special place in our hearts…Anyway me and Dusty here had to stay overnight in an old abandoned underground miners sleeping quarters for obvious safety reasons just so we could come out here and compare notes with you,…. you see we went to a lot of trouble for your benefit. I just hope our efforts won't be in vain. Julie totally captivated and moved replied you came all this way just to see me? that's not only very flattering but admirable and compelling. "Cameron" now what's your story? Then Julie suddenly got a disturbed stark wide eyed look of fearful apprehension at the prospect of having to mentally recount those harrowing events on the railroad tracks that fall evening with their late friend Todd. Tongue tied she fumbled for the words never in a million years did I ever think that...."Cameron" just go slow and tell us what you can, your safe here and nothing is gonna hurt you. I just need to know what you or your friend did to stop that thing and get away. I think that may be a link to some internal weakness it may have that's the key to it's vulnerability and then I can seek it out and destroy it.

Then Julie bawled...I hate guns, "Cameron" what? Todd tried to get me to learn how to use one but I just ridiculed him and gave him a hard time about it and refused to. And then she mentally flashed back to that horrific instance in her harried and traumatized mind and cried out, he got killed trying to defend us with one and then she hung her head down in her cupped hands and started to cry and whined oh it was so awful. Cameron looked over at Crystal who was just sitting there silently in a blank gaze and a look of bewildered fascination to the whole thing as he turned back to her and put a warm consoling hand on her shoulder and whispered there, there now honey we're here and your safe among your friends now and were not gonna let anything happen to you. Then he slowly moved in closer to her and whispered so what did you do then? And through a whining crying voice came the muffled and broken words a stun-gun, I had a stun-gun came through.

Cameron just turned to Dusty in an uncontrollable enthused wide eyed consuming glare at Dusty, just as though a great weight had suddenly been lifted from his shoulders as he was shed upon with a vibrant beam of enlightenment as though he was just on the verge of a major discovery, and it was a light- beam that was going to illuminate the whole town and it's surrounding regions.

CHAPTER FOURTEEN

The Final Showdown In Crabapple Orchard

THE VERY NEXT WEEK FOUND CAMERON JUST SITTING THERE ON HIS front porch one morning avidly listening to the staticky reception of am radio news for any further developments on the creature while fiddling with and playing with the antenna of an old seventies portable in attempts to get some degree of audibly unimpeded reception. He had warningly shifted the dial from the usual FM Hair band rock station he normally listened to, to faint buzzing AM news radio that only held talks on international affairs, or news broadcasts, played classical music or progressive jazz, the one all the old fogies listened to. He was wearing a pair of worn and faded cut off jeans and a shabby sleeveless white tank top leaning back on the two rear legs of a rickety old chair against one of the weathered old wooden porch support beams with peeling paint.

As he was sitting there awhile he suddenly felt a sharp pricking stab on the back of his lower neck close to his shoulder. He cried out in pain swatting at the area to kill whatever kind of flying pest had stung him and in the process stung the inner portion of his fingers as well, nonetheless killing a hornet that had landed on him. When he saw the crumpled body of the flying pest hit the porch deck while covering the bee sting with his hand he looked around and the up to see where it may have come from. Then he suddenly peered up at the edge of the old dilapidated roofs edge and right next to a support beam and bent corroded aluminum spouting was a crudely fashioned honeycombed hornets nest made of clay just hanging there. It was lopsided and fixed to the edge of the roof with a stem fashioned by the bees of and clay. There were a dozen or so hornets swarming around it and going in and out of the unevenly sized openings as Cameron's face had a stunned look of bewilderment on it at first and then was suddenly struck with a profound look of astonished enlightenment on it as he just sat there gazing upward.

He then immediately jumped to his feet and ran inside to call Dusty. The phone rang several times before she finally picked it up. Dusty? She hemmed and hawed yeah Cameron yeah what is it? Just what half baked scheme do you want me to pester me with now?....Just shut up and listen! I think I've finally stumbled onto something! "Dusty" sighingly replied oh yeah what? "Cameron" Well for your information Ms. Doubting Thomas just what it is that will definitely and without a doubt bring Mr. Boogers vile existence to an ignominious end that's what! I was just sitting there on my front porch and it suddenly hit me like a ton of bricks!!...Dusty in a startled excited reply exclaimed WHAT!! Just meet me on the far edge of the old crabapple orchard you know the one facing old Dittmire road and I'll fill you in on all the details when I get there ok!!

And there was a sudden click on the other end and the low buzzing hum of a dial tone…..He immediately ran down to his musty old basement amid the clutter of broken wooden crates, rusty old aluminum wash basins, cardboard boxes and other debris scattered about to retrieve a big roll of thick clothes line a few hundred feet long from a dirty old makeshift wooden shelf and a big clumsy old fisherman's net from a huge wooden barrel once used for catching lobster's and various other types of freshwater fish in that was about eight or nine feet in diameter a lighter and his satchel full of sparklers and roman candles. He then quickly made tracks to the location of the old apple grove. When he got there he found Dusty just leaning up against one of the knotted apple trees she obviously had time to think on the way over, and from the marked disparaging expression on her face she was pretty much fed up with the whole thing by now. The excited exuberant tone she displayed on the phone was now replaced with a chagrinned look on her face as if to say what has he concocted this time that I'm going to be drug into kicking and screaming? The morning air was heavy and muggy as it was very hot and humid and the loud audible chirps of locusts in the trees resounded throughout the countryside for miles. And the pungent scent of apple blossoms and downed crabapples rotting all over the ground permeated the air. As Cameron came up to the groves edge from the grassy meadow of grasshoppers, dragon flies and wildflowers that surrounded the long stretch of the apple orchard

Dusty barked ok genius what's this all about this time and what's all that rope crap your carrying and your satchel for? Ya know I think this is just another one of your wild goose chases and the goon squad outta come out here and just throw a butterfly net over you and finally get it over with once and for all and take you off to the state loony bin! Hey maybe you could even become roomies with your two compadres huh? Will you just knock it off for a moment!! We've gotta lot of work to do here before dusk sets in so were gonna have to move fast so just shut your mouth and do what I tell ya and we'll pull this thing off successfully without a hitch ok? "Dusty" ok, and again I repeat what's this all about? "Cameron" bees my dear sweet wonderful bees or in this case hornets. This crabapple orchard is just inundated with hives!! "Dusty" yeah so what! that's what you got me out here to tell me? That there's bees in the trees what-err we gonna do just sit out here and watch em pollinate and maybe get stung in the process? Ya know off the top of my head I can think of about a thousand and one other things I'd rather be doing on a Sunday morning like sitting at home picking the lint outta my belly button. I just think there's bats in your belfry Listen! Remember when Julie told us she immobilized the creature with a stun gun? "Dusty" yeah and again I say so what…What's your point?….."Cameron" point being is that the whole objective in having made that long trek out to the state hospital in the first place was to try and find a link to that two legged chemical mutants downfall right? "Dusty" folded her arms in a dubious intent gaze and lowly replied yeah that's right I suppose… "Cameron well when wasps and bees sting they release some type of neutralizing agent or poison if you will from there stinger into the victim, which in most cases has a very painful and paralyzing effect but in numerous and repeated stings has a deadly or fatal effect…you know sort of like natures little defense mechanism,… get it? Then Dusty paused for a moment and suddenly got an intent look on her face as a light slowly began to come on and she began earnestly listening to Cameron in an enthused and engrossed manner and said yeah…go on. Well what do you think would happen to a chemically based freakazoid stumble bum during the vile course of his putrid rush to judgment if he should happen to hastily bungle into such a trap activating it and setting in motion thousands of angry hornets massively grouping to came after him in total convergence and in a frenzied and enraged state? Volatility swarming around his trapped and suspended body several feet above ground caught in a large fisherman's net centrally linked, strung and attached to a number of tree branches with these hives just hanging from each one of them? Each one home to hundreds if not thousands of now angry bees who've just been violently provoked by having their homes abruptly shook and ripped from their fixed and suspended positions on these tree branches dislodging and destroying them as they plummet to the ground below while Mr. boogers flails about in a big clumsy old fisherman's net violently writhing around in it struggling to free himself huh? Then with a wide Cheshire cat like grin he delightfully posed the question to her, don't you think they'll want to come out and investigate the source?…Dusty, gleefully leered at Cameron while grinning from ear to ear and exclaimed ha-ha,… that's brilliant!!…Then bobbing up and down in an excited dance of exalted exuberance exclaimed did I say that's why you're in charge!!…ya know you have a mind like a steel trap!!… I just knew you'd come through!!….I want a ringside seat!! Then Cameron through an immense grin chimed yes, he's the bull and were gonna be the China closet…And then the two kid's quickly began laying the foundation by implementing a methodical step by step draft of Cameron's cruel but ingenious trap fuelled by reverberating rushes of adrenalin as both of their hands shook they nervously took out some of the items of makeshift wares from Cameron's old brown leather satchel. This was going to be their last and only hope it had to go off without a hitch as the device itself had to adhere to strict and avid attention to detail as there could be no mistakes or slip up's that could possibly render it faulty, in that factor alone would prove out to be disastrous....

They both gravely sensed deep within themselves, this was going to be their last hope of hopes and aside from maybe just electrocuting it,.... if this didn't work all was lost. Both the army and the marines wouldn't be able to save civilization from that invincible terror. As the two began setting the wheels in motion for that things ultimate undoing, it was undoubtedly going to be a frantic race against time and the searing heat of a midday sun high overhead. There could be very little if any conversation other than that relevant to setting the trap time was of the essence here. The two kid's had a lot to accomplish in the way of preparedness for Mr. Fedder's grand finale before dusk. "Cameron" we've gotta lot of work to do before the witching hour arrives so we have to move fast I want this net strung to as many tree branches with those hornet bombs hanging from them as possible, got it!! And we've got to be very careful in attaching this line so as not to disturb the nests one iota! Understand!! Dusty just gleefully leered at Cameron as her saving grace in that this up till now, totally unanswerable nightmare, but it was sure soon to be all over at the helm of his very capable hands, she enthusiastically replied got it, boss I hear and I obey!!

With that Cameron threw the huge net over his shoulder as it's immense size almost covered his form entirely and dragging it over to the center of the apple grove and tossing it down on the ground and began opening and spreading it out in the middle of the diseased orchard. Cameron' this is it, this is the spot for the magnanimous event!...wide eyed heartily exclaimed, "this is where it'll all go down"!!... And then he began tying long segments of the clothes line at measured intervals of the outer portion of the net. Boy that thing is huge isn't it? Dusty replied,...what's it for?...where'd you get? Cameron' as he began camouflaging it with sticks brush and other leafy compost, it was used for freshwater fishing you know like crabs and lobsters and such. It was just another item of leftover unwanted junk just sitting there in my basement from the previous tenant that's all. Dusty' How are you gonna get it to pick booger-face up off the ground and suspend him in the air and for that matter how are you gonna get him to step in it?...I mean if

we do by some miracle of faith somehow manage to lure him in here?…
AND if he does just by some miracle of faith happen by this way…Then
she suddenly gazed down with a bummed out expression on her face.
Cameron paused for a moment somewhat aggravated and replied, boy
you sure ask allot of unnecessary pain in the butt questions don't ya well
that's where all the careful planning I spoke of comes in"…If we set this
thing up right and don't screw something up in the works everything
should go off with clockwork precision, you just do what I tell ya hear!?…
Then he pulled out four moderately sized burlap sacks from his satchel
and two small hand held shovels with a rolled up length of rope heavier
than that of the clothes line and looked over at Dusty….What!! don't tell
me I gotta shovel dirt and rocks into two of those dirty smelly things…"

Cameron paused and glared over at her, well yah actually you
do!!…Look this is not a pick-nick were on and it's going to require some
heavy uncomfortable exertion in getting our hands dirty got it!!…Dusty
whined, dirt and rocks,… Cameron exclaimed yah dirt and rocks, so
quit yer bitchin and just get to it!!…we don't have any time to waste in
just standing around whining and complaining about it. It's what we
have no choice but to do, the morning is gonna be here before you know
it. And I'm afraid this is the only way were gonna be able to get Mr.
Congeniality hoisted up into the air in a state of suspended animation
for our mutual enjoyment for his ultimate date with destiny so keep that
in mind as our reward for a little heavy labor that's required here"!!…
Dusty' you mean I've gotta have to break my back filling two of these
smelly old sacks with seventy-five pounds of dirt and rocks?…boy this
really blows a big fat one you know what I mean!?….Cameron' well
I'm the one who's going to have to act as some ridiculous lame duck
decoy to lure prick face in here…ya know that doesn't exactly infuse
me with calm and complacency. Now I want you to take a length of
this clothes line over to a tree in a relatively straight proximity of this
clothes line sorta like a spider web and string it through the v-portion of
the trunk midway up and carefully tie it securely to one of the branches
with the biggest hive you can find on it, "got it"!…flip it over a higher
branch before you tie it to the lower one with the hive on it. You don't
have to pull it completely taut you as can leave just enough slack so

as not to disturb any of the bees and don't tangle it or wrap it around anything it's gotta be free to pull on the branch…ok? Move carefully and methodically and be sure not to shake the branches one iota. There not those infamous killer bees featured in those 1970's movies that seek out and attack people for no reason at all and migrate from North Africa or something,…Just don't make any sudden movements to draw attention to yourself, be inconspicuous!!… if you don't disturb them they won't bother you, got it!…Once we do that we can start filling the sacks ok.

They each took one of the lines over to a tree to begin setting the trap as Dusty got to a tree that had about three or four bee hives hanging from a number of outlying branches but one in particular was significantly larger than the others and was located about midway up and was in a perfect location on the outer portion of the tree facing the meadow. These knotted old trees were relatively short about twelve feet or so high so they didn't really have to climb up them to tie the rope to the lower branches. All they really had to do was to ball up the excess line and toss it over the intended section of branches and tie them on. When Dusty got to a tree she was a bundle of nerves and afraid of being stung. There were only a small number of bees swarming around each hive for the vast numbers were on the inside as Cameron said. You could hear the unnerving drone of hundreds if not thousands emanating from each one. She just stood there contemplating on what she had to do. Now what did Cameron say she thought to herself, if you don't disturb them they won't bother you. Then she bawled up the excess length of the clothes line and tossed it through the vportion of the trunk over a branch just above the target hive and the length unraveled to the ground below. All she had to do at this point was go around to the other side and pull it taut enough to fix it to the branch with the hive on it. The branch she had to attach it to was just a little out of reach for Dusty, she was a tall lanky girl about six feet in height but she was not going to be able to fasten the clothes line without standing on a rock or a tree stump or something. She looked around and saw several wooden crates and pallets with a few missing spats strewn about under trees and along the barbed wire fence left by seasonal farm workers they used for picking grapes apples or peaches with. There was even an old wooden carrier hitch that was used for hauling harvested fruit or vegetables in that was to be hooked to the back of one of their old pickup trucks. She then decided to drag a pallet over to the branch she had to tie the line on stack a crate on top of it to give her enough height to reach the designated branch. A small number of hornets swarmed around her in a circular fashion and then away from her but none attacked or stung her.

Her hands mildly shook with anxiety as she raised the length of the clothes line and tied it to the targeted branch as close to the location of the hive as she could. Then she slowly and carefully stepped down from the makeshift stepstool to repeat the same process on yet another branch. All in all about seven or eight lines were strung to segmented intervals on the outer portion of the old fisherman's net. The only thing left to be done now was to fill the sandbags with dirt and rocks and hoist them up from four of the taller trees at even points with the heavier rope that would be trip activated and would lift the netted creature from the ground and suspend him trapped in midair so the enraged bees would come after him and give him the works. After Dusty finished with her five branches she went over to where Cameron was. He was finishing up too when he asked how you makin' out with yours are we all taut with no snags? She said I'm done, how bout you? He was looking downward doing something with one of the lines and said I'm just about finished here I got six lines strung I think I have just about enough room for one more how bout you? "Dusty" No that's it for me I was only able to get five strung and from the looks of it I don't think we'll be able to string any more there's no room. Yer right it does look kinda like a giant spider web. "Cameron" Yeah and were gonna catch a big slimy fly…heh. I'm gonna string this last line and then we'll start filling the burlap sacks you know the fun part, and I just know how you can hardly wait to get started on that huh!!…Dusty just grimaced and uttered ugh. and Cameron went over to the last branch to tie on another line. Then he handed Dusty a burlap sack and a hand shovel and said don't just stand there gawking at me waiting for an invitation you know what you've gotta do so get shovelin. I want us to at least get two of these damn things filled before we break for chow so let's get to it. I want this trap set before dusk and he looked down at his watch and said it's already going on eleven o'clock now and if we continue to move along at this pace I think we'll just about make it before we have to take up our positions.

And Dusty said "positions, what positions"?…"Cameron" you as lookout and me as bait". Dusty then took her digging implements over to the edge of the grove where the ground piled up in a little mound just before the barbed wire fence where a shallow low lying gully like dip was located between the orchard and the old fence and ran the entire length of it. The soil was black and soft there with some rocks intermixed, unlike the harder more solidified ground was up by the trees. And she wasn't going to have to exert herself in expending a lot of energy in trying to repeatedly spear a small hand shovel into hardened and solidified earth in filling one of those old sacks. The air was permeated with the sweet scent of blossoms and rotting crab apples on all over the ground. And the loud resonating chirps of hundreds of locusts up in the surrounding trees steadily ushered in the hot humid heat that hung heavy from a midday sun. Dusty sauntered over to where it was semi-shaded sat down and with her right hand flailed her long flowing auburn hair to one side looked down lethargically opening the sack and slowly proceeded to start digging. Cameron looked over at her and barked "HEY OVER THERE SLOW POKE GET THE LEAD OUT!!….YOUR GONNA HAVE TO PICK UP THE PACE A LITTLE OR WE'LL NEVER GET THIS SHIT DONE BEFORE NIGHTFALL!!… WE DON'T WANNA GET CAUGHT OUT HERE WITH OUR PANTS DOWN YA KNOW!!…It took about an hour for each of them to fill their sacks with enough dirt and rocks to give them ample weight sufficient to be able to hoist and suspend a sizable slimeazoid. Cameron slowly walked over to the area of soft black soil where Dusty was sitting filling her bag. He was in the process of tying up his while looking down when he asked her, I'm finished with mine, how you makin out over here? I'm just about done with mine too can you carry it over there I can't seem to lift it being a weak and helpless female and all. "Cameron" Oh gees,… Dusty flailed her head to one side while tying up her bag asking, when's lunch?…I'm starved I haven't eaten anything all day and it's gotta be getting close to that time. And then she leered over at him and said, I'd even settle for one of your famous armpit baloney sandwiches right now.

You know the ones that landed you on the cover of cuisine magazine…
Oh boy,…shaking his head back and forth hemmed, there you go again,
you know your not going to spoil the moment here with another one of
your sniping cracks and your constant ingratitude concerning my food
preparedness skills. Nope I'm just to ecstatic in that I've finally found
a way to end Booger-faces miserable existence so I'm going to overlook
it. So honey this will be the last time you'll ever have to be forced to eat
one of them ok?….With that Dusty just looked a little sad at the prospect
that their comradery was about to come to an end. And after all it was
just part of the amusing aspect of their mutual bonding. Using such a
cynical and jaded form of humor to help alleviate some of the level of
ongoing tension and overwhelming stress from the grave uncertainty
of the present circumstances. Then she lowly stated how do you plan
to hoist these bags upward and secure them? And for that matter aren't
you going to have to implement some kind of trigger device to set the
wheels in motion? "Cameron" yes but I've got that all worked out. I'll
use this heavier rope here to suspend the bags you see how they all have
six one and a quarter inch eyelet holes with a metal ring in each one of
them? "Dusty" yeah" Well I'll just string this rope here through each
one of them and pull it tight and they'll be ready for hoisting. "Dusty"
yeah from where? These trees are kinda short and for that matter to far
apart aren't they?

Cameron looked up and surveilled the prospective trees. Yeah your
right that does pose as a problem doesn't it. He just stood there pensively
staring up at the trees for a moment when he got a wide eyed enthused
look on his face and said you wait here and break for lunch while I go
over in those woods for a few minutes got it! Aren't you gonna eat too?
Later I've got urgent business to attend to I'll be back in two shakes ok?…
"Dusty" what if booger face shows up while your gone whatta my gonna
do throw rotten crab apples at him? "Cameron" No and I don't think he
will it's to early in the day for that and anyway he's more of an evening
or night creature, ya know one of habit. Look if your that worried about
it the guns are in the satchel and their loaded ok? Dusty just paused
for a moment whirled a wide eyed expression in Cameron's direction
and sarcastically commented "sometimes I wonder if your head is,…

loaded I mean". Cameron abruptly stopped and replied through a crass aggravated grin commented ya know that's what I've always come to love so much about you is that sharp unceasing and cutting wit of yours at my expense. It just makes me wonder why on earth I ever drew down on a poor defenseless rattle snake. And through a wide eyed constrained expression on his face said now I'll be back but in the meantime have one of my slimy mouthwatering armpit sandwiches your always constantly raving about, oh and there's also some stale corn chips and flat as a pancake orange soda pop in there too so make yourself at home and eat up!!.

Then Cameron briskly made his way down the slight rise past the dilapidated barbed wire fence and through the ratty insect infested meadow with high weeds. He was escorted by swirling off breed white butterflies and tobacco spitting grasshoppers almost doing a jig like dance along the way until he momentarily disappeared into the darkened woods. Dusty just stood there shaking her head back and forth muttering to herself what 'a goofball, nutcase". Then she leaned back up against one of the old knotted trees holding the old brown leather satchel and slid down it's side to a seated position there in the shade against the tree. She unenthusiastically flipped open the lid and rifled through the other items pulling out two of the sandwiches. The cellophane made a plastic crackling noise as she examined the content. Ooh boy lucky me!!….I get my choice here of slimy sweltering barf out baloney or soggy peanut butter and jelly fresh from the humidor, just like mom used to mess up with just enough grape jam to totally soak through the bread slices. Umm,….umm,…good. If I wasn't so damn hungry I'd just blow chunks. Then she shot a look towards the woods and tersed to herself. You know as much razzing as he's taken over the years you'd think he'd look into more appropriate ways to prepare food so at least it's halfway eatable instead of wasting it in making this glorified garbage. Then looking down she uttered well it looks like it's gonna be good ol' pb&j. I don't know if I can gag down another one of those warm slimy bologna sandwiches. Then she slowly unwrapped the other sandwich and leaned her head back and chimed. As they say!….over the lips and through the gums look out stomach cuz here it comes!! Then while chewing she reached into the satchel again and pulled out a can of that cheapo off brand ten cans for a dollar soda pop and a bag of likewise stale corn chips. As she sat there eating lunch she saw Cameron slowly emerge from the woods carrying what appeared to be a small telephone pole or a tree trunk about a dozen or so feet in length. Then from a distance she noted it was a downed small tree with all the branches broke off because it was knotted. As Cameron crossed the meadow and got closer to the shallow gully to come up the rise to where Dusty was. She exclaimed what the hell are you doin' now and what's that for? It's for our trap there's another one like it just about the same size in there and I'm gonna have to go back for it.

This is what were gonna hoist the weighted bags of dirt and rocks up on. I was careful not to get one that was brittle or rotted. Now we just have to position em' parallel about the width of the net from each other up in those trees and just above it so when boogeration steps in the center of it he actives the trip line that will be strung to four steaks sunk deep in the ground with the rope going from them up to where these two tree trunks will be fixed with our weighted bags. Dusty just sat there with a dazzled expression on her face boy that really sounds awfully convoluted. Then she dubiously asked and just how do you propose getting one of those wooden poles up there high enough to thread one through a v portion of a tree branch strong enough to support the weight huh Einstein? Cameron just looked upward at the branch configuration towards the top of the knotted old trees. Then he gently bit a large portion of his lower lip, sort of holding it and hummed,… let's see here one of us is going to have to climb a tree as one eye rolled toward Dusty. Don't look at me!,…I was no tomboy and besides this little out door adventure you felt such an overriding need to drag me along on was your idea,…remember?…. You were a Marine you gotta be used to climbing up things like obstacles and such so that makes you the more qualified candidate here now doesn't it. Cameron sighingly replied, oh gees I guess so,… ya know your one of the biggest obstacles I've ever had to negotiate on a regular basis. Ok this is the deal I'm gonna climb up this tree with one end of this branch see. And then I'm going to slowly guide it into position so as to thread it through a v portioned branch structure up top. "Dusty" yeah and what do I gotta do? Then he looked around on the ground and murmured there's nothing around here we can use. I'll have to go back in the woods for one when I get the other. "Dusty" one what? Another long tree branch with a short V shape with the branches broken off at the end. For what? "Cameron" Look, your gonna be down on the ground below while I steadily thread mine through a V portion up top, get it? Then your gonna take the V portion of your end and steadily raise the other end up treading it trough that other tree over there at about the same height.

Then were gonna do the same thing about twelve feet parallel to this. Cameron looked down at his watch and moaned "oh gees we've gotta move!! it's almost two o'clock and we've still got those other two sand bags to fill before dusk were not gonna make it!" Now I'm goin' back into those woods for the other two tree branches see…..Then with a grievous worrisome expression on his face that greatly unnerved Dusty he barked. Look!!.. when I get back we've really got to hustle it up to wrap this whole thing up and no more bullshitting!…got it!!

If that thing shows up here we've got to be done and in position to spring this trap as it will most assuredly be our only line of defense, aside from us just running for our lives. With that Dusty's face constrained itself with a frantic worrisome expression on it suddenly got a sick queasy feeling in the pit of her stomach as a sudden rush of adrenaline surged from her chest up to her throat. Yes!…it was painfully drawing ever nearer to curtain call… it was just about show time and just the mere thought of facing off with that horrible night mare again gravely terrified Dusty to the very core of her being. As she fatefully recalled how they reigned down on it that stormy night with what otherwise should've been lethal force only to later on to her extreme horror find out it had freakishly survived only to go on to claim yet more innocent victims. She imploringly whined, when will you be back? "Cameron" Soon, scared? She just sullenly nodded her head up and down. I am too, I just don't show it but I am, I'm terrified of that monster all the time afraid he's gonna come out of nowhere. I just don't show it as much. Look one of us has to have a level head here and maintain somewhat of an even keel to be an effective countering agent and I guess that's me.

Now I'm only gonna be gone for about ten or fifteen minutes, Dusty just looked down in solemn despair as if she just lost her best friend. Cameron could see how terrified his friend was so to try and bring her out of it a little he put his arm around her shoulder gently hugging her and jokingly replied, look honey it's broad daylight! Two o'clock in the afternoon nonetheless fart face isn't scheduled to make his grand entrance for another three or four hours yet! And by that time we'll be ready to bestow upon him the star spangled reception with the rockets that spread glare he so richly deserves!! While grinning he said so relax and don't get your panties in a bunch…ok? And through a tense cloudy red and white flushed expression she managed a smile and started to laugh a little. Now I've gotta go back in those woods and fetch the rest of the items were gonna need, do you think you can hold down the fort while I'm gone? She slowly nodded hear head up and down signifying all systems go. Look if Fedder's shows up while I'm gone just use the most lethal weapon in our little makeshift arsenal. And Dusty muttered yeah what's that? "Cameron" just give him one of my sweaty armpit sandwiches with a bag of those stale six months old corn chips and that glorified battery acid labeled value time, arctic orange, ok?

Cameron strolled off the slight rise the apple grove was set upon and on down passed the shallow gully and through the ratty meadow once more to go back into the woods to retrieve the two small tree trunks. Dusty just stood there leaning up against one of the old trees when several moments went by she heard a loud pop and a snapping noise followed by what sounded like leaves rustling coming from the hollow of the darkened wooded area. Then she heard Cameron yell at the top of his lungs OH SHIT!! Followed by a steady stream of obscenities, Dusty got a wide eyed grinning expression on her face and started laughing when she yelled over, everything all right in there!! An audibly loud but muffled voice bellowed from the dark opening. No aside from tripping on a vine and falling on my ass I can't seem to be able to snap off these branches in the fork at the end of your tree branch so you can use it!! I'm gonna have to bring it over there and cut em' off at the ends with the teeth of my Rambo knife. Then she started laughing again while yelling over at him do you need any help!

Then in a loud muffled reply he yelled no I think I can manage from here on out. Then she saw Cameron slowly emerge from the darkened opening of the woods dragging the two long branches alongside him on the ground. The intense humidity that hung in the morning air seemed to dissipate giving way to a cooler crisper afternoon breezes as autumn approached. A bittersweet scent emanated from the scraggily vegetation in the meadow. Cameron slowly made his way as he trudged through the ratty insect infested field he was frequently dive bombed with a steady barrage of six legged pests that flew past his face as he vehemently swatted at the occasional grasshopper, dragon fly, mosquito or beetle while making his way back to the apple grove.

As Cameron made his way up the slight rise towards Dusty he reached into one of his pockets and pulled out a handkerchief to wipe the sweat from his brow. "Dusty" gonna make it there chief? Whew!… If the bees don't take care of funnel face the locusts will!! He tossed down both tree trunks onto the ground and immediately went over to retrieve the hunting knife out of the satchel. He pulled out the knife flipped open the blade to expose a long nine inch blade. Dusty looked at the dangerous ripple cut blade wide eyed and aghast good lord what's that for?!!…Cameron grinned as he held up his prized utility knife examining it's long deadly jagged tooth edge Ahhh,…this outta do it!…. For utility purposes as well as hunting and fishing, I use it mainly to gut and quarter deer small game and freshwater fish. "Dusty" Ohhh that's awful!! Why!? "Cameron" to furnish a good portion of meals my dear Pollyanna, surely not for the fun nor for that matter the taste of it. Were poor remember!? Maybe I can better enlighten you with Cameron's lesson of basic economic equation here. The cost of a bullet .25 cents, the cost of a sizable roast at the local grocery store $18.00 and finally the cost of a deer a rabbit or a fish from a nearby stream zero, equals a minimal grocery bill get it!?… Then he bent down to pick up the branch Dusty was to going to use in positioning the other ends of the makeshift beams that were to suspend and secure the weighted sandbags in a fixed position up top. Now then let's see here, this tree branch appears to be just a little to green to be able to snap off the elongated excess at the two extended ends.

Then he took the slender tree trunk in one hand while holding the knife in the other as he began sawing off the two extensions with the jagged toothy edge of the huge bowie type knife leaving about a five inch fork at the end. Then he handed it to Dusty saying now I'm going over to climb up that tree over there with my end. When I get about ten feet up it your gonna take the other end in the fork end of your branch and maneuver it into a sturdy v structure on the other side. Remember the most important aspect of our trap is that this is sturdy enough to support a substantial amount of flailing weight at least long enough to rock and roll those branches with the hives on em. Then he turned to her and grinned out one side of his face saying, you know I hadn't thought of this before but ya know once the bees converge on him it's not gonna matter at all if these tree trunks snap and he plummets to the ground. He's still gonna be toast!...Then he looked down at his watch again and exclaimed "oh my God it's already going on three o'clock it's going to start getting dark in a couple of hours were gonna be cutting it awfully close". We've still gotta fill two more bags yet and get these poles positioned up in those trees. We've gotta get movin!!...When Cameron reached the designated height to start positioning his long branch through, he slowly began guiding his end to a thick v portioned branch structure just above his head. Ok Dusty!, now start guiding your end. Then she took the long tree branch and held it towards the top somewhat close to the fork went over to the downed other end of the pole Cameron was holding. She picked up her end in the little fork at the end sort of clasping it extending it upward to the adjacent tree shimmying her hands down it as she slowly raised the other end slowly upward to a solid looking v structure at about the same height in that tree and sort of lobbing it into position. Then she lowered her little makeshift extension bar dropping the end on the ground and looked up at Cameron sitting there in the tree. Ok?...Cameron just beautiful!!

After the two repeated the same process on the other side they quickly began filling the other two burlap sacks with dirt and rocks. Time was of the essence here and they still had much to do before dusk. As that thing was reputed to materialize and attack during evening hours like those three poor unfortunate hair band rockers on the railroad tracks that fateful evening. It took almost an hour for the two to fill there sacks as it was steadily approaching four o'clock. Cameron thank God that's done, we've still gotta bout an hour or so before it gets dark. All we have left here is to tie these sacks with this rope at the ends hoist em up and fix the rope ends to these steaks I'm gonna sink in the ground. The steaks were heavy cleated and made of solid steel. Cameron looked around on the ground for a huge rock big enough to drive the steaks in the ground at four even paced positions a few feet away from and surrounding the big fishing net. He found a selection of good sized rocks laying around in the shallow gully and scattered throughout the edge of the meadow. Once the steaks were driven into their chosen positions Cameron pulled out a big huge ball of brown nylon rope from Dusty's back pack. I actually bought this item with my own money, I felt it was best if the rope was subdued and blended in with nature so's not to arouse any suspicion on the part of trench face. "Dusty" Oh that was clever thinking on your part, Ya know I can always count on soldier boy here to camouflage something in the steady course of events that may desperately need it!! "Cameron" was that another crack!? Oh no, no, I was merely commending you for having such keen and sound hindsight to cover all the necessary basis that's all! Cameron kind of turned his head inward and moaned I dunno it kind of sounded like another malicious dig to me, one never knows with you. Anyway on to the business at hand then he picked up one of the weighted bags and threaded the nylon rope through the metal eyelets and pulled it closed tied the excess in a couple of double knots and threw the excess over one of the poles threaded through the trees. Then he pulled the slack towards the tree and began hoisting up the sack. When the heavy sack was a few feet off the ground he turned toward Dusty and beamed her a stern callas look and tersed well, are you gonna just stand there and supervise or are you gonna gimmee a hand here!!...This damn thing is heavy! She thought to herself it would be outta turn at this point for her to offer up another cutting and caustic remark especially when they were fast approaching the home stretch and that putrid abomination was soon due to manifest it's vile form as the adrenalin rush fuel of nervous anticipation in both of them was brimming over to a fever pitch.

She then Lowy uttered "oh sorry, I wasn't thinking" as she went over and the two together began hoisting the bag up to the top along side the horizontally positioned suspension pole in the trees. Then Cameron took the taut end of the nylon rope and tied it onto one of the steaks sunk in the ground. They repeated this same process on the other three. In all it took about a half hour to forty five minutes to get that done as the onslaught of evening set in it was going on four o'clock. "Cameron" Now that, that's done there's only one more thing I have to do before we take our battle stations.

Dusty just stared at him silently, I have to string this trip line to those four sunken steaks about five or six inches off the ground so it's inconspicuous to Mr. Fedders view. At this point Cameron's complexion was flushed white as a ghost as, his hands began shaking and this unnerved Dusty. He probably has the screwed up vision of an insect like a fly or a spider or something but I feel we still have to exercise due caution anyway. At home I took the liberty of soaking the clothes line in dark green clothing dye just for this special occasion. Then he nervously commented as he secured the line to each steak all the way around the net, then with a worrisome contrived grin stated I've left no stone unturned and spared no expense. And in trying to somewhat make light of the imminent danger he stated" nothing is to good for our friend". Then he slowly and nervously rose up on his feet while mildly shaking and slapping the dirt off his hands and pants chimed,…"this is it the moment we've been waiting for, show time!!….. Now everything is in place, I just hope this thing il' work like it's suppose to. "Dusty" where am I gonna be"? Cameron just looked around and uttered now let's see here momentarily pausing. That's a good question, you've gotta be in the safest out of reach position I can put you in. How about up in a tree? "Dusty" you mean to tell me that if putrid thing sees me up in a tree it won't be able to just vomit a river of that vile green slime a few feet upward in my direction!! Cameron' hemmed,…yeah I guess your right. Then he looked around for other ideas, then as he looked toward the meadow he noted that the weeds and vegetation were almost five feet high or more in places. Then he beamed a smile at her while pointing towards the ratty field and firmly stated in there. Dusty' in the weeds!?

Sure!! Your dressed in green and brown colors and all aren't ya?, he'll never see you in there and more overly at dusk. And that'll freely allow me to act as a decoy without worrying about you and then I can then concentrate on luring him in to step in the net. There's bugs in there whatif I get eaten alive?!…Cameron' yeah maybe your right, well it's either that or possibly getting boogerized alive!! Look!…it's your only option here there's no dilapidated old structures we can run in and take cover out here so I'm afraid this is gonna the part where we or you, are gonna have to soldier!! I know it sucks but there's no other option. And besides I've come prepared for that too. Dusty just looked over at him as he went over to one of the supply packs to retrieve a can of insect repellent the kind campers use a lot and then he firmly instructed her to hold out her arms. As he sprayed her with the repellant over her entire body her face winced up as she began holding her nose, exclaiming oh that stuff smells awful!! It smells like the same crap my dad used on me for those camping and fishing trips we went on when I was a kid.

Cameron' now it's starting to get dark then he handed her a small flashlight fixed to a key chain. If you get scared there in the weeds in the dark just turn this thing on. Now get your ass in the grass private while I finishing getting things ready for Trench faces grand reception!…. Dusty just held her arms up crooked at the elbows as she steadily sauntered off the low rise and across the meadow about fifty yards off slowly dissipating into a thicketed patch of seven foot high weeds thus concealing herself from that thing. It made a low rustling noise when she went into it. Cameron yelled over to her, all set!…A lowly muffled reply resounded from the ratty patch of vegetation, yeah,…Ok I'm gonna take it from here, you just sit tight and keep a close watch on all the grand festivities and come out only when you can clearly see that things are all netted up ok!?…Dusty' Ok!….The sun was beginning to set giving off dreary sallow yellow rays amidst the cool crisp air of an approaching autumn evening. Then Cameron abruptly turned his head in the direction of the supply packs and the leather satchel laying on the ground over next to one of the apple trees. He could feel pulsating surges of adrenalin whooshing in his ears throat and chest and his legs quivered at the unsettling prospect that the trap might somehow malfunction leaving him and poor Dusty hung out to dry. He lowly muttered to himself time is running out it's gonna be dark soon, I'd better move my ass!!…As he picked up one of the back packs first unzipping it and pulling out some kind of big noise maker rowdy fans used at football games or inebriants on New Years. It was a moderate sized hand held horn with a big red rubber bulb at the end as a sounding implement. It's loud blustering and resonating shrill through an intense blast could be heard a mile or so away and would hopefully draw the vile attention of a certain beloved slimeazoid if he were just so happen to be in within a five mile radius of it's blast.

His hands shook as he reached into the brown leather satchel to retrieve a dozen or so roman candles and sparklers. Cameron was going to place a number of lit roman candles in outlying segmented points around the edges of the grove in lurid attempts to draw the attentions of that despicable creature in. a diversionary rouse to ultimately snare it in the old fishing net. Then he'd cut loose with the handheld horn as the candles would stay lit for a good long while like road repair work crews often do on the highway. Then once he heard or sighted the slimy goon approaching the orchard through the field he'd then light the staked sparklers positioned on the inner locations and he himself would yell and scream and make all sorts of commotion in attempts of provoking that horrid thing to give chase through and passed the snares of that insidious trap in desperate hopes of springing it and rescuing the adjoining towns and countryside. It was dusk and Cameron's short distance view was greatly diminished leaving him no other choice but to finish laying the final groundwork using his flashlight. He went around and stuck a number of carefully positioned roman candles at evenly staggered intervals outlying the edge of the old crabapple grove lighting each one along the way. Their incandescent light steadily shot upward giving off an eerie glow highlighting the location for miles drawing attention to it. And as Dusty looked on from her concealed position quaking in terror at the stark realization of that hideous and horrid thing could possibly manifest itself out here in the open at night making her shudder to the very core.

As Cameron lit the last candle he stood up and turned to the darkened field and countryside by this time he was just a bundle of quaking nerves as he held up the little horn to squeeze the little rubber air bulb in the back. It's piercing, unnerving blast resonated throughout the vast uninhabited landscape as he got a sickening feeling in his chest and the pit of his stomach at the terrifying realization at having just summoned that hideous thing from the darkened hallows and that he knew it would soon be manifesting it's blackened, gourd-ish charcoal grey form. And then Cameron turned about in various directions simultaneously aiming the little device in all directions emitting a loud shrieking trumpet like blast out over the darkened countryside several times. And then he lowered his arm and just stood there poised in the pitch blackness amidst a deafening silence fervidly listening in an anticipating mode of frightful intensity as surges of cold adrenaline rushes gushed over his sternum.. And then that faint ghastly moan that Cameron knew all to well suddenly pierced the night time silence bellowing in the distance in an eerily terrifying drone sending waves of indescribable mortal terror through the bodies of the two kids causing their blood to run whimpering but she knew enough by this time that if she made any loud outcry's it would surely giveaway her position and draw that things ill attention bringing it's vile, putrid designs down on her. At this point she was in such a terrified and frenzied state she was unable to function effectively enough to participate and assist in doing what had to be done to dispatch this blackened two legged nightmare from existence. But she somehow managed to compose herself enough to keep somewhat quiet and still as she sat there quaking and rocking back and forth on the ground lowly whimpering with tearful eyes squinting and grimacing in terror. And with both hands cupped over her mouth she completely relinquished all the responsibility of executing the last stage of it's cruel snares the two had methodically laid out just hours before with such precision for that hideous thing to blindly bungle into over to her friend to dispense with final business. The thing was pukishly drawn to the dimly glowing, luminescent light of the apple grove that the roman candles emitted. Cameron's ingenuity worked and it would seem that everything was going off according to plans. As the creature apparently drew closer that ghastly moan slowly intensified as it neared the far entrance of the grove and it's vilely twisted and contorted silhouette was terrifyingly apparent and struck a hideous and imposing visage as it steadily approached the mouth of the orchard. What stood there before Cameron at it's entrance was the wholly realized nightmarish composite of the horrifically abstract in full manifest. And that it had suddenly emerged from the far reaching depths of the sub-conscious mind. And in that it had somehow freakishly materialized itself in the raw and out in the open. The gnarled twisted abomination towered at the entrance of the apple grove with it's grotesque features subtly illuminated by the dull bluish incandescent glow of the moon and roman candles. The superficial warmth of it's bizarre body composite superseded the cold autumn chill in the air, resulting in scant swirls of steamy mist rising from it. It just stood there in a creepy blood curdling wide eyed gawk with the better portion of the whites of it's eye's exposed in a nerve shuddering evil and a famished leer at Cameron as if he were a meal it was about to gleefully consume. This was something dark and hidden from the world in that it had somehow managed to escape from the attic or basement of some dark, drafty and dismal oversized turn of the century house. It's hideous mouth jutted with uneven jagged and narrow elongated teeth with every other one broken off midway up, this made it closely resemble the gaudy design of a big 1950's sedan's front grill.

The surrealistic nightmarish visage was the total composite and embodiment of every vile and putrid abomination earthly conceivable and utterly symbolic of a sequestered and prolific evil. Cameron just stood there for a moment awe struck in utter disbelief at what his eyes had feasted on this was the boogie-man the real one. And just then a sudden sense of urgency came over him prompting him to light a couple of sparklers from one of his baggy cargo pockets of his BDU's he quickly began waving his arms about in a windmill fashion as hot white incandescent sparks shot in a steady stream from these things. Then he loudly taunted the monster,....come on you pukey pus filled son of a bitch here I am, come and get me!!... At first the thing just stood there momentarily in a frozen state just staring at Cameron in a macabre lurid gawk with that white eyed blank stare. Cameron was standing on the other side of the net just passed the trip line. C'mon trench face this is what you're here for come and get it I'm right here waiting!! And as the two sparkers he was holding suddenly fizzled out he quickly retrieved two more from one of his bulky oversized cargo pockets immediately lighting them with a little green plastic Bic. And just as he began whirling his arms about in a taunting fashion the creature suddenly lunged forward charging at Cameron making that loud creepy chant sounding almost like a turkey buzzard, Ballada,.. Ballada,..Ballada. He got a wide eyed expression on his face as he quickly stepped back while waving his arms about as he didn't want to be within firing range of that deadly wave of dark bluish green slime that would suddenly and without warning spew from that vile putrid cavern that was it's mouth in a copious gushing river. Cameron just continued to level a stream of jaded insults at the monster while backing up the whole way drawing him nearer to that fateful center area to the path of the trip line. C'mon you walking pus filled chemical garbage dump come and get me!! And just as the other two sparkers Cameron lit began fizzling out Mr. Congeniality haplessly bungled into the trip line.

There was a rustling sound of leaves and compost being flung about as the trap sprung swiftly taking the monsters legs right out from under him. Then the old fisher net clumsily enveloped the creature prompting the heavy burlap sacks to simultaneously plummet to the ground swiftly swooping him up trapping the grim mutated visage in the net several feet above the ground. The vile creature flailed about further entangling himself in the snares of the net and causing all those branches affixed with the bee hives to shake violently and dislodging a great many of them sending the crude oblong clay hives smashing to the ground. Cameron's eye's suddenly bugged out as he exclaimed, Oh my God now it's gonna get real hot!!…I better get the hell outta here!!…..He quickly turned while holding the flashlight in the tight grip of his right hand while saluting the monster and exclaimed Hasta-la-vista baby!!… He then made a mad dash for the wild flower meadow towards the large patch of high ratty weeds and vegetation where Dusty sat huddled in the center quaking in fear. As he ran he aimed his flashlight beam cutting a lighted path all the way through the dark field to meet back up with her again in the high underbrush of the gnarled ratty old clearing. And as he simultaneously pushed open the large tufts of high weeds aside and shinning the flashlight beam to illuminate the center of the enclosure to the dirt ground inside where Dusty was.

He just found her in a flustered state just sitting there in a huddled position on the dirt floor with her head and face jammed into her knees and her arms wrapped around her lower legs rocking slowly back and forth completely oblivious at first to his sudden presence lowly sobbing uncontrollably in fear. The surrounding air resonated with the frightfully intense high pitch droning of thousands of enraged bees in clustered hordes blustering about in a provoked, frenzied and enraged flight seeking retribution. Dusty?…you alright? When she heard Cameron's voice she stopped rocking, and slowly dropped her arms downward and looked up into the flashlight beam. Her facial complexion was flushed with tears streaming down her reddened cheeks, do you have to shine that damn thing directly in my face?….Cameron' oh sorry, Dusty' what the hells goin' on out there now? And what er you doin' back here so soon?…...It's all over…He's in it…Dusty just glared at him silently and intently. Cameron' stumblebum is in it,…you know in the trap it's only a matter of time now!…Dusty was in shock and it was going to take a few moments for her to regain her composure enough to grasp the long awaited momentous news for it to finally sink in. Her facial complexion was completely flushed a marbled reddish white suddenly got a bug eyed expression on it. Cameron' I think it's safe now except for maybe the bees, come look and see for yourself the whole area is lit up with roman candles. With the fervently awaited news of that latest development

Dusty hastily scrambled to her feet as Cameron assisted her up holding her elbow and forearm. The two then scurried from the dense concealment of the ratty underbrush and through the rise of high weeds and out into the open clearing. The two just stood there on the edge of the meadow in a state of awe on looking the bizarre outcome of what had just transpired and the freakish variables that had all come into play in the final scene. The inner portion of the ratty old grove was eerily illuminated with the faint powder blue incandescent glow of the moon as well as a number of lit and staggered roman candles sunk in the ground. You could see what appeared to be a dark silhouetted mass twisting and writhing about in the center accentuated by those tell tale blood curdling and high pitched screams they were all to familiar with in what looked to be from a distance a ridiculous and bizarre state of suspended animation.

That thing was ensnared in that big clumsy old net and hung out to dry as tens of thousands of angered bees had converged on it. After several moments the high pitched screams completely ceased and the center of the now motionless dark mass was an intense green glowing light flashing on and off. It was going on six o'clock in the morning and it was beginning to get light. The frantic endeavors entailing the kids desperate measures scrambling about to ensnare the creature had gone on for several hours before finally culminating in it meeting it's bizarre undoing. Large masses of the dark blobby substance which in actuality were thousands of bees immersed in that freakish green gook that had slowly separated from the old fisherman's net and was now slowly oozing downward in a number of gloppy piles. With the revolting appearance of glazed clumps of cinder enmeshed tar, they slowly and freakishly twisted and writhed about individually on the ground as thousands of encased bees were congealed in the soon to be solidified dark green material as they made any final and remaining last ditch efforts in their futile attempts to escape it …. The poison from thousands of bee stings had a debilitating and paralyzing effect on the rampaging monster, neutralizing and reversing the chemical composition of it's vile and freakish system in exacting a final and fatal retribution ironically turning it into the very substance it spewed onto it's poor hapless victims. Each pile of bee infested sludge had that slowly faint and diminishing incandescent green glow in the center, slowly blinking on and off until each one had finally ceased moving about and solidifying into a darkened rubberized mass. It was safe now, safe enough for the two kids to re-enter the apple grove and further examine the spoils of their arduous triumph. The monster had enveloped a good seventy to eighty percent of the enraged bees and hornets in it's putrid slime. The remaining few from the hives just wafted about in frantic and aimless flight. And as they both just stood there in the dull bluish-gray overcast light of yet another dawning day.

They took refuge in their anguished and exhausted triumph as they gazed down on the smoldering, fizzling remnants in a state of dazed bewilderment. Now ignominiously reduced to just a poor, pathetic smoldering monument to what had once stood as a towering, menacing vile abomination that held two adjoining towns and the outlying countryside in an unrelenting grip of night-stalking terror. Dusty just stood there looking downward at the fervid spoils of their anguished victory in solemn reflection, in a complete state of awe after weeks and months of diligent effort, planning and ingenuity it took that in the end finally paid off in laying waste to and bringing such a seemingly invincible abomination to its grave ends. And as she stood there with Cameron he slowly placed his big meaty arm around her shoulder as her head gently rested on his and lowly murmured it's over, it's finally over....Then she suddenly turned and looked up at him in a deep cow eyed tearful gaze and uttered," I have to admit I had my doubts about you all along, but in the end you really came through magnificently, you were just wonderful,...I owe my life to you'. Cameron just smiled and looked back at her grinning,...no we did wonderful,...I couldn't have done it without you and we owe our lives to each other.

And as the pair slowly strolled off the slight rise Cameron said "Ya know I think today is gonna be a great today...I think it'd be a great day to get married

ABOUT THE AUTHOR

I INITIALLY ASPIRED TO BE A PORTRAIT PAINTER BUT THERE DIDN'T SEEM to be a demand for that no matter how good you are. Then I went onto painting land and sea scapes and even had numerous works on online galleries and a couple down town ones here in Stroudsburg but that didn't pan out either. And after a couple of years she had to close and then had to have all the artists come and pick up all their works. So then I thought I'd put my creative powers to possibly a more lucrative venue writing, I have also published a children's book through covenant books entitled the Bubbloons that's listed online.

9 781957 220680